BLOOD OF AMBROSE

BLOOD OF AMBROSE

JAMES ENGE

an imprint of Prometheus Books
Amherst, NY

Published 2009 by Pyr®, an imprint of Prometheus Books

Inquiries should be addressed to
Pyr
59 John Glenn Drive
Amherst, New York 14228–2119
VOICE: 716–691–0133, ext. 210
FAX: 716–691–0137
WWW.PYRSF.COM

13 12 11 10 09   5 4 3 2 1

Library of Congress Cataloging-in-Publication Data

Enge, James, 1960–
    Blood of Ambrose / by James Enge.
        p. cm.
    ISBN 978–1–59102–736–2 (pbk. : alk. paper)
    I. Title.

PS3605.N43B56 2009
813'.6—dc22

2008054561

Printed in the United States on acid-free paper

To Lawrence J. Pfundstein Jr.

Laurentius, nonnumquam laureatus, numquam nixus in laureas

CONTENTS

PART ONE: ARMS OF THE AMBROSII

PART TWO: PRISONERS OF AMBROSE

PART THREE: *HOUSE OF FAME*

PART FOUR: *THE PROTECTOR'S SHADOW*

PART FIVE: *THE TWO CITIES*

BLOOD OF AMBROSE

THE GLORIES OF OUR BLOOD AND STATE
ARE SHADOWS, NOT SUBSTANTIAL THINGS.
THERE IS NO ARMOUR AGAINST FATE;
DEATH LAYS HIS ICY HANDS ON KINGS.

—JAMES SHIRLEY, *AJAX AND ULYSSES*

PART ONE

ARMS OF THE AMBROSII

MARSHAL, DEMAND OF YONDER CHAMPION
THE CAUSE OF HIS ARRIVAL HERE IN ARMS.
ASK HIM HIS NAME AND ORDERLY PROCEED
TO SWEAR HIM IN THE JUSTICE OF HIS CAUSE.
    —SHAKESPEARE, *RICHARD II*

CHAPTER ONE

SUMMONS

he King was screaming in the throne room when the Protector's Men arrived. He knew it was wrong; he knew he was being stupid. But he was frightened. When the booted feet of the soldiers sounded in the corridor outside, he belatedly came to his senses. Dropping to the floor, he crawled under the broad-seated throne where the Emperor sat in judgement, next to God Sustainer. (Only there was no Emperor now, and Lord Urdhven, the Protector, made his judgements in his own council chamber. Did the Sustainer dwell there now? Or still upon the empty throne? Was there really a Sustainer? Would the Protector's soldiers kill him, like all the others?)

He pulled in his legs just as the soldiers entered the room, their footfalls like rolling thunder in the vast vaulted chamber. He'd hoped they couldn't see him. (Would God Sustainer protect him? Was there really a Sustainer?) But the soldiers made straight for the throne.

If the Sustainer was not with him (and who could say?), the accumulated precautions of his assassination-minded ancestors were all around. As he pressed instinctively against the wall behind the throne, it gave way and he found himself tumbling down a slope in the darkness. Briefly he heard the shouting voices of the soldiers turn to screams and then break off suddenly. Because the passageway had closed, or for another reason? His Grandmother would know; he wished she were here. But she was far away, in Sarkunden—that was why the Protector had moved now, killing the family's old servants like pigs in the courtyard. . . .

He landed in a kind of closet. There were cloaked shapes and bits of armor lying around in the dust that was thick on the floor. Perhaps they were, or had been, things to help an endangered sovereign in flight or self-defense. He thought of that later. But just then he only wanted to get out; by flailing around in the dark he found the handle of a door and plunged out into the bright dimness of a little-used hallway.

Hadn't he been here before? Hadn't Grandmother told him to come here, or someplace like here, if something happened? He hadn't been listening. Why listen? What could happen in the palace of Ambrose, with the Lord Protector guarding the walls . . . ? And they had cut his tutor's throat, cut Master Jaric's throat, and hung him upside down to drain, just like a pig. He had seen it once at a fair, and Grandmother had said he must never, never do that again.

The sudden memory renewed his terror; he found himself running down the corridor in the dim light, the open doors on either side of him yawning like disinterested courtiers. There was a statue of an armed man standing over a broad curving stairway at the end of the hall. The King was almost sure Grandmother had mentioned a place like this, but without the statue. If he went down the stairs, perhaps that would be the place, and he would remember what Grandmother had told him to do next—if she had told him.

But as he passed the statue it moved; he saw it was not a statue—no statue in this ancient palace would be emblazoned with the red lion of the Lord Protector. The Protector's Man reached for him.

The King fell down and began to scuttle away on all fours, back down the corridor. The Protector's Man dropped his sword and followed, crouching down as he came and reaching out with both hands.

"Now, Your Majesty," the soldier's ingratiating voice came, resonating slightly, through the bars of his helmet. "Come along with me. No one means to harm you. Just a purge of ugly traitors who've crept into your royal service. You can't go against the Protector, can you? You found that out. And stop that damned screaming."

The King was screaming again, weary hysterical screaming that made his body clench and unclench like a fist. Looking back, he saw that the soldier had caught hold of his cloak. There was nothing he could do about the screaming, just as there was nothing he could do about the soldier.

Then Grandmother was there, standing behind the Protector's Man, fixing her long, terribly strong hands about his mailed throat. The soldier had time for one brief scream of his own before she lifted him from the floor and shook him like a rag doll. After an endless series of moments she negligently threw him down the hall and over the balustrade of the stairway. He made no sound as he fell, and the crash of his armor on the stairs below was like the applause that followed one of the Protector's speeches—necessary, curt, and convincing.

Before the echoes of the armed man's fall had passed away, Grandmother said, "Lathmar, come here."

Trembling, the King climbed to his feet and went to her. Grandmother frightened him, but in a different way than most things frightened him. She expected so much of him. He was frightened of failing her, as he routinely did.

"Lathmar," she said, resting one deadly hand on his shoulder, "you've done well. But now you must do more. Much more. Are you ready?"

"Yes." It was a lie. He always lied to her. He was afraid not to.

"I must remain here, to keep them from following you. You must go alone, down the stairway. At the bottom there is a tunnel. Take it either way to the end. It will lead to an opening somewhere in the city. Go out and find my brother. Find him and bring him here. Can you do that?"

"How . . . ? How . . . ?" The King was tongue-tied by all the impossibilities she expected him to overleap. He was barely twelve years old, and looked younger than he was, and in some ways thought still younger than he looked. He was aware, all-too-aware, of these deficiencies.

"You know his name? My brother's name?"

"*His* name?" the King cried in horror.

"Then you do know it. Say it aloud. Say it to many people. Say, 'He must come to help Ambrosia. His sister is in danger.' By then I will be, you know."

The King simply stared at her, aghast.

"He has a way of knowing when people say his name," the King's Grandmother, the Lady Ambrosia, continued calmly. "That much of the legend is true. But more is false. Do not be afraid. Say the name aloud. You are in no danger from him; he is your kinsman. He will protect you from your enemies, as I have done."

From the far end of the corridor echoed the sound of axes on wood.

"I had hoped to go with you," his Grandmother continued evenly, "but that will not be possible now. You will have to find someone else to help you; I wish you luck. But remember: if you do not find my brother, I will surely die. Your Lord Protector, Urdhven, will see to it. You don't wish that, do you?"

"No!" the King said. And that, too, was a lie. It would be a relief to know he had failed Grandmother for the last time.

"Go, then. Save yourself, and me as well. Find—"

Knowing she was about to say the accursed name, her damned brother's name, he covered his ears and ran past her, skittering down the broad stone steps beyond. He passed the corpse of the fallen soldier. He kept on running.

By the time the light filtering from the top of the stairway failed, he could see a faint yellowish light gleaming below him. When he reached the foot of the stair, he found a lit lamp set on the lowest step.

His feelings on reaching the lamp were strong, almost stronger than he was. He knew that his Grandmother had set it here to give him not only light, but hope. It was a sign she had been here, that she had made the place safe for him, that he need not be afraid. As he lifted the lamp, he felt an uprush of strength. He almost felt he could do the task his Grandmother had set him. He swore in his heart he would succeed, that he would not fail her this time.

Choosing a direction at random, he walked along the tunnel to its end. There he found a flight of shallow stairs leading upward. He climbed them tentatively, holding the lamp high. At the top of the stairs was a small bare room with one door. The King turned the handle and looked out.

Outside was a city street. It was long after dark, and wagon traffic was thick in the streets, in preparation for the next day's market. (Cartage into the city was forbidden during the day, to prevent traffic jams.)

The King closed the door and sat down on the floor next to his guttering lamp. But presently it occurred to him that sooner or later the Protector's Men would discover the tunnel and draw the obvious conclusion. No matter how dangerous the city was at night (he had heard it was; he had never set foot in the city unattended, day or night), he knew he should leave this place.

He stood impulsively and, leaving the lamp behind him, stepped out into the street.

Night to the King meant a dark room and the slow steps of sentries in the hallway outside. Night was an empty windowcase, a breath of cold air, the three moons, wrapped in a smattering of dim stars, peering through his windows, and the sullen smoky glow of Ontil—the Imperial city—to the east. Night was quiet, and the kind of fear that comes with quiet, the fear of stealth: the poisoned cup, the strangler's rope, the assassin's knife.

This night was different: a chorus of shouting voices, the roar of wooden wheels on the cobbled street, the startled cries of cart-horses. It was like a parody of a court procession, with the peasants in their high carts moving in stately progress—when they moved at all. The King, who had never been in a traffic jam (though he had caused many), wondered why they were moving so slowly, when they were all so obviously impatient. Then he saw that they all had to negotiate a sort of obstacle at the end of the street: a row of stone slabs stretching across the way, so that each cart had to slow to fit its wheels through the gaps in the stone causeway, and all the carts behind it perforce slowed as well. When the stones were higher than a cart's axles, or when no gap in the stones corresponded to the width of a cart's wheels, the delay was longer; the cart had to be pulled over, or unloaded and lifted over, or shunted aside.

Above the chaos of lamps the stars were almost invisible, but the King could see Trumpeter, the third moon, standing bright beneath the sky's dim zenith. The major moons, Horseman and great Chariot, were down—this was the month of Remembering, the King remembered. (He didn't have to bother much with days or months; he just did as he was told when someone told him to do it.)

Fascinated, the King crept along the narrow stone walkway toward this center of activity. Before reaching it he saw that, beyond the relatively narrow street, there was a great square or intersection into which several other streets emptied out. All of the traffic converged on one very large way that seemed to lead to the great marketplace or market district. (The King was hazy about the geography of the Imperial city, one of the two that he, in law, ruled.)

It was horrible, with the noise and the dust and the reek of the horses—sweat and manure—and the shouts of the peasants and the glare of the cart lamps (dazzling in the darkness of the otherwise lampless street). Horrible but fascinating. The King believed that the noise, the dirt, the confusion would drive anyone mad. But the peasants did not seem mad, only annoyed. The King had no idea where they were coming from, and only the vaguest as to where they were going, but did not doubt there was backbreaking drudgery at either end. The King was not exactly sure what "backbreaking drudgery" entailed, but it was something (he had been told many times) that was not expected of him. This relieved him greatly, as he considered his life hard enough as it was. Surely none of these peasants had a Grandmother like the Lady Ambrosia, or an uncle like Lord Urdhven.

On the far side of the street he saw three figures, cloaked, masked, booted, gloved, all in red. They carried something between them . . . he saw an arm trailing on the ground and realized it was a dead body. So the red figures must be members of the Company of Mercy, the secret order that tended to the sick and buried the bodies of the city's poor—no one knew where. There were strange stories about the red Companions; no one ever saw their faces, or knew where they came from. There were bound to be stories.

One of the red-masked faces turned toward him as he stood on the sidewalk, open-mouthed, watching the traffic pass, and it occurred to him again that the Protector's Men would be coming for him soon. At the moment he was just another mousey-haired, underdeveloped, twelve-year-old boy in dark clothes wandering the city streets. But when the Protector's Men started asking questions, some of the people passing by might remember that they had seen him. He had to get on his way, and immediately.

But where should he go in the dark city before him? What was he to do? To find Grandmother's brother, of course. But he would have to ask someone. There were many people here, many of them from outside the city, some of them, perhaps, from very far away. This was the place to begin.

The King shrank from the thought of what he was about to do. But the memory of the lamp in the dark tunnel returned to him, renewing his hope and his strength. And there was a trembling exultation in the thought that if he succeeded, he would bring hope to his Grandmother as she had brought hope to him. He had never done anything like that before.

Not allowing himself to think, he leapt away from the wall and hopped from stone to stone across the intersection, as if they were the stepping-stones in his garden stream in the palace. A cart was slowly being pulled through the gap in the stones.

"The Strange Gods eat these roadblocks," the driver was cursing. "They should make them all the same size. How's a man supposed to bring his goods to market?"

"We could market at Twelve Stones," the driver's shadowy companion observed.

"They won't pay city prices, my lad. When you—Hey! What do you want?"

This last was addressed to the King, who had leapt over to cling to the side of the cart.

"Help me!" the King said.

The driver turned to look at him. He was a heavy-shouldered peasant in a dark smock. His face was sun-darkened; it had flat features and flat black eyes like stones, and a flat gray beard. "Help you what?" he asked reasonably. Beyond him the King could see his companion, a gaping young man with straw-colored hair and the barest beginnings of a beard.

"Help me find . . ." the King began, then stopped. Who? *Grandmother's brother.* But she wasn't really his grandmother—he just called her that because it was shorter than "great-great-great-great-etc. grandmother." And what did you call the brother of your great-great-who-knows-how-many-greats grandmother? He didn't think there was a word for that.

"My . . . she . . . I'm . . . my . . . my . . . my—"

"Get your story straight," advised the driver as the cart surged forward into the open; with dispassionate skill, he lifted his whip and cut the King across the face.

Too shocked even to scream, the King felt, as from a great distance, his nerveless fingers let the cart go; he fell to the filthy cobbles of the open square. Dazedly he watched the lamplit cart roll away in the dark toward the other lights clustering at the thoroughfare entrance.

Slowly the King rose to his feet. The whipcut was a red lightning-stroke of pain across his face, and other dark fires were burning on the side of his head, his right side and limbs where he had fallen. He did not fully under-stand why the driver had done what he did. But he guessed that the same thing would happen unless he did as the driver had advised, and got his story straight.

He would not tell them about his Grandmother. (That would only frighten them away, because she was the Protector's enemy, and the Protector ruled everything now.) He would not tell them anything—except what she had told him to say. *Say the name aloud . . .*

He climbed back up on the stepping-stones and bided his time. Presently a cart came through and, while it was fully engaged in passing through the line of the stepping-stones, he jumped into the tarp-covered back of the wagon, landing on his feet, and prepared to dodge whip-strokes.

"Hey, thief!" shouted the driver, a heavyset elderly man raising his whip (as the King had feared).

"No, Rusk!" the passenger, a woman of the same age, cried. "It's a little boy!"

The King did not think of himself as "a little boy." He had seen little boys from far off, playing in the streets below the walls of the palace Ambrose, and he was not much like them. He usually thought of himself as "a child," since that was how others referred to him when they thought he was not listening, often quoting the ancient Vraidish proverb "the land runs red when a child is king."

"They're the worst thieves of all!" Rusk grumbled, but lowered the whip. "Hey, boy! You're spoiling our vegetables!"

"I'm sorry," the King said. "I need help." He shifted to the side of the cart, to avoid treading on their goods. The cart jerked as it pulled free of the stepping-stones, and the King almost fell into the square again. "I need to find somebody!" he cried, clutching at the wagon's side.

"Who?" the woman asked.

The King paused. Now that he came to it, it was difficult to speak that awful name aloud. "The Crooked Man," he said then; it was one of many euphemisms for Ambrosia's brother.

Rusk, looking forward now to guide the cart horses, gnashed his teeth in irritation. "Boy, you should know that beggars don't come out at night. Besides, we're not city people; we don't know any beggars, crooked or straight."

"I don't understand what you mean," the King said slowly. "I mean . . . I am looking for . . . Ambrosia's brother. The Dark Man."

The woman gave a sharp intake of breath, and Rusk shouted, "Lata, this is on your head. Throw that rat off our wagon before he says the name and brings a curse on us—"

"Morlock!" shouted the King in despair, as the woman reached back in a vague swatting motion. "Morlock! Morlock! Morlock! Your sister is in danger! *Morlock!*"

He had expected (well, half expected) the Crooked Man to appear in a gush of flame, as legends said he did when his name was spoken, to work dreadful wonders, or haul traitors off to hell. So he was half disappointed when nothing of the sort occurred. A cart with a lamp (Rusk and Lata's had none) passed them; a wash of golden light passed over the old woman's seamed face, catching a speculative wondering look on her features as she met the King's eye.

Rusk had reined in and was turning around, shouting, whip in hand. As he raised his arm to strike, Lata snatched the whip away from him and said in a breathless voice, "Shut up, Rusk, you fool—and you, too, sir, if you please," she added, glancing back at the King. "Sit down there, out of the passing lights, sir, and you'll be quite comfortable."

"*Sir!*" exploded Rusk.

"Don't you understand?" Lata said insistently. "It's the little King!"

Rusk drew himself up, then glanced back at the King, who had settled himself down obediently into the shadows. "It's impossible," Rusk said, but his voice was quiet and lacked all conviction.

Lata, her voice equally quiet, drove the point home. "Who counts the coins on market day, Rusk? I do. If I've seen his face once I've seen it a hundred times. And you remember what the gate guard said, about the disturbance at Ambrose. If the Protector and old Ambrosia are finally having it out, she might call on her brother (the Strange Gods save us from him; I name him not). What'd be more natural?"

"'Natural!' *Those* ones . . ." Rusk's voice was sardonic, but held no disbelief. Hope beat suddenly in the King's heart.

"Then you'll help me?" the King said. "You'll help me find Morlock?"

"Shut that filthy-mouthed brat up."

"Shut up yourself, Rusk. It's different for him; the Crooked Man (I name him not!) is his kin, in a manner of speaking. Yes, little sir, we'll help you as best we can. Bless you, it's our duty now, isn't it? Just pull some of these blankets over you and lie down on the side of the cart, there. There now. There now. That's fine."

Lata and Rusk did a good deal of low-voiced talking, but the King didn't bother to listen to it. He had done his part; he had succeeded; it was up to the others, now. He hoped they would be in time to save Grandmother—how proud she'd be of him, for once! He wondered at the power of the Crooked Man's name, which frightened others even more than it did him. Lata had said, *it's different for him*, and he saw how true that was.

"Morlock," the King muttered, and felt the ancient blood of Ambrosius glow in his veins. "Come help us, Morlock. Help Grandmother. Hurt the Protector. He killed my parents, Morlock, I'm almost sure of it. . . ." The King whispered to Morlock in the dark what he had never dared to say aloud to anyone, even Grandmother. But he didn't have to be afraid anymore; it was a wonderful feeling.

He peered through the boards of the wagon side. Would Morlock appear magically out of the darkness, as he was supposed to do when someone said his name? Would he be hunched over and crooked, as the legends said? Would his fiery servants appear alongside him? Was his hand really bloodred, from all the killing it had done? But Morlock never appeared.

That was all right, though. The King knew it was because they were going to meet him. Lata and Rusk seemed to know more or less where to go. Rusk was expressing delight at how empty the streets were; the King guessed that people avoided the streets, because that was where Morlock lived.

After a while the King grew tired of muttering Morlock's name in the dark. He risked peering out of the wagon past Lata and Rusk. He saw the high twisting towers of a palace, the windows glittering with light. He wondered dimly if Morlock had his own palace, his own court, a kind of secret Emperor. . . . But that was impossible. He knew those towers. He had seen them, looking up from the palace walls, as he walked with the sentries. . . . It was Ambrose. They were taking him back to Ambrose.

"You're taking me back!" he shouted, throwing off the blankets. "You lied! You said you'd help!"

Rusk said nothing, flicking the reins to make his horses go faster. But Lata turned toward him, her etched face expressionless in the shadows, her voice troubled and concerned. "Now, now, young sir. We *are* helping. It's best you not be mixed up in that nasty old witch's plots. And you can't be wandering the streets at night, no, no. Why, who knows what might happen? You'll be safer at home in . . . in the palace, there. Let the grown-ups settle things between themselves. Now, don't be afraid. Don't cry. No matter what happens, they won't hurt a boy like you."

The King was crying, in fear and frustration. If the Protector had murdered the Empress, his own sister, why would he stop at killing anybody? They had killed Master Jaric and drained him like a pig, and who did Jaric ever hurt? The King wanted to call out Morlock's name again—Morlock who was death to traitors—but the power to do so had left him.

He wondered, briefly, fearfully, what would happen if he jumped away from the wagon and ran away into the dark streets. He didn't know. He didn't know. He didn't do anything. There was no point in doing anything. He had done something and it hadn't worked. The King sat, weeping as the wagon pulled up in front of Ambrose's City Gate. He did not even listen as Rusk and Lata began their marketplace chaffering with the guards on duty.

"Wait, wait, wait!" the guard captain said finally. "You two—go over there and claim that person these two are talking about. You see him there, in the back?" The King heard booted feet approaching, and felt himself lifted gently out of the wagon by his shoulders, then carried bodily to the gate. He opened his eyes to meet those of the guard captain, who swore furiously, "Death and Justice! It's true. Thurn and Veck: take His Majesty back to his apartments and stay with him. Don't be drawn off *by anyone* or I'll feed the one ball you have between you to the goats. Carnon: notify the Protector's Man napping upstairs in the inner guardhouse that we have recovered the King. I know; I know! Then you go *with him* while he reports to the Protector, and just you mention it to everyone you meet. Nobody's falling down a stairway on my damn watch."

"Wait, now!" Rusk said hoarsely. "Little sir, won't you speak up for us? This soldier man is trying to cheat us of our reward! Didn't we help you get home safe, all right? Won't you mention us to your Protector?" And through this the King saw Lata tugging at Rusk's arm, begging him to be quiet and come away. Then the soldiers carried the King through the gate, onto the open bridge over the river Tilion, toward the yawning gate of Ambrose on the far side of the river, and the darkness, and the fear.

The guard captain's voice, now lazily threatening, echoed back through the City Gate. "Hold on. This isn't some sack of beans you've brought to market. It's the royal person, His Majesty Lathmar the Seventh, the King of the Two Cities and (the Strange Gods willing) your future Emperor. As to the Protector hearing your names, there's little doubt of that. Now—what *are* your names? Where do you live? How did you become involved in the abduction of His Majesty? Which one of you slashed his face?" The gate of Ambrose shut behind the King.

Grandmother was condemned to death the next evening, along with all the people the Protector's Men had killed the night before, in a special session of the Protector's Council. The King never remembered much about the ceremony, just that Grandmother (in the plain brown robe of the accused, her empty hands hanging loose from the wrist as if they had been broken), looked at his face once and turned away.

They had given him a statement to read before the Council, but he burst into tears and couldn't say anything. They took him away and put him to bed. After a while he stopped crying or moving so that they would think he was asleep and go away. When they did, he lay there in the dark room, thinking.

The last thing he thought, many hours later, when he really was falling asleep, was that the things they said about the Crooked Man were all lies. He would never believe a legend again, or his Grandmother either.

As for Lata and Rusk, they had been released that morning, after a bitter night of questioning. It soon proved that no one really believed they were involved in a plot to abduct the King. The guard captain, Lorn—not a Protector's Man, one of the City Legion—who assumed charge of their interrogation, was simply furious at them. He referred several times to their attempt to "sell the King like a sack of beans." But he kept the Protector's Men away, and finally dismissed them when it was too late to make it to the Great Market (which ceased to admit vendors at dawn), contemptuously declining to confiscate their goods. As they drove their wagon away from Ambrose, Lata felt obscurely ashamed, yet intensely angry—as if she had tried to cheat someone, only to find herself cheated instead.

Rusk's feelings were less ambiguous, and he gave vent to them all the way back to their farm. He cursed everyone they had dealt with, from the Protector on down, not excluding the King ("that foul-mouthed fucking little brat") or Ambrosia ("the evil venom-spewing bitch"). Frequently he exclaimed, "Morlock take them all!" because he considered himself to have been ill used, if not positively betrayed.

They sold most of their goods at Twelve Stones, for a fraction of what they would have gotten at the Great Market. Their ride home was another long litany of curses, this time including the day's buyers and competing sellers, but concentrating as before on the Protector, the guard captain, the ungrateful King, and that inhuman crook-back witch Ambrosia. Rusk invited Morlock to show himself and cart off each one in several directions.

Lata, whose shame had grown as her anger faded, finally told him to shut up. But the grievance became something of an obsession with Rusk, and for years afterward he was liable to mutter, "Morlock take them! Morlock take them all!" particularly when he was doing some dirty or disagreeable task.

The pattern for all this was set on that first day, when they returned home to find the young nephew they had hired to watch their farm missing, their scarecrow stolen, and a murder of crows feeding in their wheat field. Before anything else, Rusk had to rush hither and thither through the field, waving his arms like a madman to scare away the crows. This he did while screaming out such treasonable abuse of the imperial family that even the crows were shocked. The repeated references to Morlock caught their attention, too, for they had a treaty with Morlock. It was the treaty, rather than Rusk's ineffectual gesticulations, that caused the murder to rise up into the air, showering Rusk with seeds and croaks of abuse, and fly off into a neighboring wood for a parliament.

They settled between them how much they actually knew of the story—this took some time, since crows are quarrelsome and apt to suppose they know more than they do—and they agreed on who was to carry the message. They then determined Morlock's location by the secret means prescribed by the treaty and dispatched the messenger. Their duty discharged, the parliament adjourned and the murder flew back to pillage Rusk's wheat field again.

But the messenger-crow flew east and north till night fell and day followed night. He flew on, pausing only to steal a few bites of food now and then, and catch an hour's sleep in an abandoned nest. At last, after sunset on the second day, the messenger flew over a hillside where a dwarf and a man with crooked shoulders were sitting over the embers of a campfire; the man was juggling live coals with his bare fingers. The messenger-crow settled down on his left shoulder and spoke into his ear.

CHAPTER TWO

GRAVESEND FIELD

he judicial murder of a royal person is not something that can be done lightly, nor should it be done in secret. Rightly performed, it is a piece of theater, and the murderer—who is, as it were, the director and producer of the piece—must select the audience carefully. They must be numerous and they must be (collectively at least) powerful. But they must not be so numerous nor so individually powerful that they can intervene on behalf of the victim if they are so inclined. They must be forced to watch the murder without seeming to be forced; they must watch it without protest, so that they will forever after support the party of the murderer, having become his accomplices. The forms must be observed, so that they can accept their complicity with something like good conscience.

If both they and the murderer live to old age, they may actually become proud of their complicity. "It had to be done," they'll say. "You can't know what it was like. Bad times need strong men."

And if the murderer comes to grief, his onetime accomplices will be sadly conscious of their own innocence. "We ourselves did nothing; we did what we had to do, and waited. But bad men come to bad ends. . . ."

Wyrtheorn, as a dwarf and a voluntary exile from the Wardlands, had a professional interest in such matters. At least that was how he put it in the rug shop of Genjandro, just off the Great Market in the Imperial city of Ontil. "At first it was just professional," he confided to Genjandro himself, over a friendly mug of beer. "These men and women and their great thumping quarrels were affecting business. So I made it my business to know about them, but I ended up by becoming interested. They are a bloodthirsty lot, these Vraidish barbarians."

Genjandro, a native Ontilian and no friend to the Second Empire, allowed himself a thin smile but no more. A smile might mean anything.

"Now, let me see," Wyrtheorn continued, understanding fully Genjandro's reticence. "The last time I was in the city must have been a hundred round years ago. Uthar the Fifth was Emperor then. A strong ruler, so they said. I thought he had banned these trials by combat."

Genjandro grunted. "That is so, though I had forgotten it. I was not born then, of course"—a dig at the dwarf for having thoughtlessly referred to his racial longevity—"but my father mentioned the matter to me once. Uthar the Fifth was a great man, but he did not live forever unlike—well, you know who I mean. His grandson had a long minority, and the Regency Council of the time restored the combats. The nobility will always prefer combat; they have the longer swords, as the expression is."

"I suppose Ambrosia sat on the council."

"At its head. But when the nobles clamored, she let them have their combats. Some say her powers were slipping, even then, but I don't see it. She's a noble herself, of a sort."

"Ye-es—she would have had a kind of inheritance in the Wardlands, but that she was born after old Merlin's exile."

"I meant because of her association with the Imperial family."

"Eh? Oh, yes—them."

Genjandro, heir to a culture nearly as old as that of the Wardlands, favored this remark with another thin smile. "Now if she is to live, it's the combat that will save her," he added.

"Will she live, then?"

"No. The young King's Protector, Lord Urdhven, leaves nothing to chance. Sir Hlosian Bekh is the champion of the Crown."

"A good fighter?"

"No. Not particularly. But he always wins."

"I don't understand," the dwarf said patiently.

"I watched him win the Tournament of Zaakharien three years ago. He stood aside until all the members of his side had been struck down. Then he killed the members of the other side, one by one. The wounds he took that day! His surcoat was red all through, and his armor looked as if it were enameled; it was after that he came to be called the Red Knight. It was horrible and wonderful and a little boring, to tell the truth. You found yourself yawning as he struck off another knight's helmet. Then you saw the blood seeping into the dust and you remembered: that was a man, that was a man's head in there. But enough of that. . . ."

"Do you really think someone has arisen who will challenge the Red Knight?"

Genjandro ran his fingers through his beard and looked thoughtful. "Nobody believes it," he admitted. "Although a token of challenge was given: they found a lance with black pennons thrust into the Lonegate of Ambrose."

Wyrth expressed some surprise at this, though he felt none. (He had, in fact, placed the lance there himself.) "Then you think . . ."

"Witchcraft!" Genjandro said, nodding. "They say there's no limit to what Ambrosia can do. Somehow she worked it, to put a snake in the Protector's chamber pot."

"And did it?"

"They say he pulled the lance from the gate with his own hands and broke it. Then he took the pieces to her and threw them at her feet. And they say the old bitch just sat there with her hands folded. And smiled, you know. She's brave and bad, that one."

"An age will end if she dies, sure."

"It's because it is ending that she will die," Genjandro disputed.

"But if she's as powerful as you say . . ."

"Her charms aren't powerful enough to stop Hlosian. She can't whistle up a champion from nowhere. I'm not saying she has no supporters, but none will dare to challenge the Red Knight."

"Then why the trial at all?"

"She claimed the right; the token appeared. In law, he cannot deny her. And, frankly, I doubt he wishes to. It is a great show, as you say. And if no champion appears, it will hardly be less. They will burn her at the stake."

"Hmph," said the dwarf. "Yet they used to say, in my youth, that the Ambrosii could not be slain by fire. It was supposed to go with the unnaturally long life and the, er, uneven shoulders."

The rug merchant smiled and stroked his beard. "Of course! The clearest proof of witchcraft. Then Urdhven will boldly have someone lop her head off, and the audience will go home with a sound moral lesson."

"Ah. What is that, exactly?"

"No doubt we will be required to learn it by rote before we depart," said Genjandro, no longer troubling to conceal his distaste.

"Well, it sounds most interesting to me. Politics in action, as it were. And you say your attendance has been, er, requested."

"Required. I would gladly send you in my place."

Wyrtheorn laughed and said, "If only it were possible! But let's talk of other things."

Genjandro the rug merchant duly made his appearance the next day at the tournament enclosure of Gravesend Field, three miles east of the city walls. He was greeted by a captain of the soldiers whom he happened to know, one Lorn, who was glumly marking an attendance roll.

"Genjandro, good day! I am glad I can strike you off the list of our Protector's enemies."

"That list will be much shorter after today," Genjandro said, stroking his beard.

"It will be at least one name shorter, Genjandro—like the imperial family tree."

Genjandro scented a political conversation in the offing, something he particularly wanted to avoid at the moment. He nodded vacantly and would have led his horse through into the enclosure.

Lorn stopped him. "Genjandro! Have you heard the prophecy that Ambrosia and the last descendant of Uthar the Great will die in the same year?"

"I had not heard that prophecy."

"It is a very recent one."

"Lorn, I am here from necessity, no other reason."

"And I likewise. Nor do I really care what happens to an old witch who has already lived too long."

"Of course not."

"But Ambrosia was always the merchant's friend. We . . . One would have hoped they would show more loyalty."

"Ambrosia had her supporters among the army, did she not? She led them to victory many a time. Yet there is a prophecy, a very *recent* prophecy, that she is destined to die without a single armed champion." The rug merchant glanced pointedly at the sword swinging from the other's belt. "Had you heard that saying, Lorn?"

The soldier looked straight at him. "Yes. Now is not the time or the place. But the King, Genjandro. If the King were—"

The rug merchant turned on him in fury. "Your 'times' and your 'places'! Go back to your lists, Lorn. The Protector's Man will be along for them, presently."

The soldier stood back, obscure emotions twisting his face. The rug merchant limped past, leading his horse off to the stables. He paid three silver coins for a separate stall without comment, though several occurred to him. He insisted on tending to his mount himself, saving himself a silver coin or two more, and the stable boy left him alone in the stall.

"Three fingers of silver to keep a horse for half a day!" he complained to the animal.

"Someone has to pay for this kind of circus, Genjandro," the horse replied. "Be glad it wasn't three fingers off your hand. Money can be lost and gotten again."

Genjandro grunted. He watched with horrified interest as the horse yawned wide, the jaws split, the whole front opened up, and the dwarf Wyrtheorn stepped out. Afterward the simulacrum of a horse re-formed itself and casually lumbered off to the far end of the stall, where there was a pile of hay.

"That's not a very dwarvish philosophy," Genjandro observed, to cover up his dread.

"How would you know?" the dwarf countered. He tossed Genjandro a leather bag that sang with coins. "For your trouble, my friend. We had better leave separately—and I advise you not to recognize me if we meet outside. However, I'll remember your help. Good fortune."

"What are you planning to do?" Genjandro asked, pausing at the door of the stall.

The dwarf grinned deep in his gray-flecked brown beard. "Something very like treason, if I were you, my friend."

The Ontilian took the hint and left with a curt nod. The dwarf spent a few moments unweaving the "horse" and stowing it in his pockets, and then strolled out himself. The day's light was already strong and hot, and the carnival air of the enclosure was thick with dust and the anticipation of death.

Hlosian Bekh, the Red Knight, lay on a table, his gray flesh cold and lifeless, as the Lord Protector and Steng, his chief poisoner, argued over him.

"Still: make the golem stronger," the Protector was saying. "If *he* does appear—"

"It hardly matters, my lord," the poisoner replied with deferential soothing contempt. "If the Crooked Man (assuming there is such a person) turns up, he will be subject to the same limitations as any other challenger. The law is clear. Magic is forbidden at the trial by combat; its use compels the user's side to forfeit."

"But *we* are using it," the Protector pointed out.

The chief poisoner smiled as he wondered whether stupidity was an inevitable consequence of hereditary power. After all, had any of the descendants of Uthar the Great and Ambrosia really matched the ferocious supple intelligence of their forbears? And, though Urdhven was Protector merely by virtue of his late sister's marriage with the late Emperor, his ancestors had been warlords on the northern plains before the Vraidish tribes broke through the Kirach Kund to conquer the lands of the south and found the Second Ontilian Empire on the ruins of the First. "We may safely break the law," the poisoner explained, "since we enforce it. The Crooked Man must come, if he does, with ordinary sword and shield to kill our champion. And that he cannot do, since Hlosian cannot die."

"Nevertheless," said the Protector, returning to the point at issue, "make him stronger."

Steng stood motionless for a moment or two. He realized that the question was no longer Hlosian's strength, but the Protector's. And the poisoner was forced to admit to himself that the Protector would have his way, no matter what the cost. Perhaps that was what made his power more than merely hereditary.

The poisoner turned away to his worktable, where the golem's life-scroll lay. Taking up his pen, he dipped it in a jar of human blood and added a number of flourishes to the already-dried dark brown script.

"These are intensifiers," he explained over his shoulder to Urdhven. "They focus the pseudo-talic impulses—"

The nobleman waved him silent with imperious distaste. "I don't wish to know about it. Just do it properly."

The poisoner finished his task in silence. When the new figures had dried, he rolled up the scroll and sealed it with wax (tinted with blood). He turned back to the prone form of Hlosian and placed the scroll in the gaping hole in its back. He drew to him several bowls of red mud and clay and began to trowel it into the breach between the Red Knight's shoulders. He worked steadily, pausing only to inscribe certain secret signs in the drying clay with a peculiar pointed stylus. Finally he was done. He spoke a secret word, and the stench of cold blood grew hot and dense in the workroom.

"Hlosian arise!" Steng cried.

The golem rose from the table and stood before them.

"Hlosian Bekh," the poisoner said, "seize yonder stone—yes, the one I have marked seize it from the wall and crush it."

The golem roared and swept the table out of its way. In ten breaths the stone was smoking rubble at the Protector's feet.

"Hlosian," the poisoner asked, "what is your purpose?"'

"I will kill the witch's champion."

"Why?"

"The witch Ambrosia must die."

The poisoner glanced at the Protector, who had hardly moved as his monster performed for him.

"You've done well," the Protector said.

"Thank you, my lord."

"Arm him and bring him to the enclosure."

"His squire will arm him, my Lord Protector. There will be less talk that way."

The Protector nodded in agreement.

They walked together into the corridor and, by some peculiar mischance, they encountered Ambrosia as she was being escorted up from the dungeon in the green robe of an appellant.

"What's this? What's this?" cried Ambrosia, as genially as if she were still preeminent in the empire, as if the death-house watch were an honor guard. She carried the chains on her broken wrists like royal jewelry. "Protector, poisoner, and champion—celebrating your victory in advance, I take it. That's always safest, isn't it?"

"Take the prisoner out to the field," the Protector said, his voice as flat and expressionless as his face had become.

But Ambrosia braced her feet and lifted her limp, swollen hands. "Urdhven, you don't look as triumphant as you did a moment ago. Perhaps it's come into your mind that if you hadn't had my hands broken, I'd be riding as my own champion today—and yours would be nothing but a breathing dead man.

"Speaking of breathing," she continued, "what's that reek I smell? Is it mud or blood—or is it both? It is both, isn't it, Steng, you dog? I see the clay under your fingernails."

Ambrosia laughed engagingly, as if they were all parties to some slightly disreputable secret. She leaned confidingly toward the poisoner, who was blushing a deep unpleasant shade of maroon. "But surely," she remarked, in a low but audible tone, "surely, Steng, you must know that when we were young, my brother's and my favorite hobby was killing golems. We killed them with fire, we killed them with water. We killed them with words—an easy thing to do, Steng, for a golem's life is simply words, magical words inscribed on a name-scroll, which other words can interrupt and make meaningless. Did you think you could defeat Morlock Dragonkiller with a golem?"

"*Take her away!*" the Protector said, white-lipped with anger or fear.

"Better yet," Ambrosia continued, as if Urdhven had not spoken, "suppose I simply pointed at *this thing* out on the field and cried: 'Golem! The Protector's champion is a golem!' For it strikes me that the Protector is guilty of trying to harm my champion by magic—the legal definition of witchcraft. A capital offense, I believe. You might be burned at the stake, my Lord Protector."

"A witch's lies mean nothing," the Protector said mechanically. "But she might utter spells to twist men's minds. Therefore—gag her, soldiers. Do it now. See that her mouth is bound throughout the ceremony."

"The *trial*, my Lord Protector," Ambrosia said, as the guards tore away the hem of her robe.

"The *execution*, my Lady Ambrosia," the Protector retorted as they knotted the gag tight across her mouth. She made no attempt to reply, but her eyes were bright with vengeful triumph as she was led away.

"If she had not spoken now, who knows what might have happened?" the Protector muttered to Steng. "Ambrosia's temper was always quicker than her wit."

Steng looked at him almost pityingly. "The chances that any would have heard her on the field were small, and who would have dared believe her?"

"But—"

"She spoke for the guards," Steng said gently.

"Ah. I see."

"They will remember. They will talk. They saw you were afraid to have the story spread—"

"I said, 'I see.' Have your people take care of them, Steng. Make it look natural."

"Yes, my Lord Protector."

There was a brief silence. Then out of his own thoughts, the Protector said accusingly, "And you blushed."

"Ambrosia is my better, my lord."

"She is not mine," Urdhven snarled. "I have beaten her, point by point, and today she dies."

"Let the fire of death cleanse the world of this witch's evil," the King said, in a clear, firm voice.

"Excellent, Sire," applauded Kedlidor, the Rite-Master of Ambrose. "That should be audible for quite a distance, even in the tournament enclosure. The Protector's Men will conduct any further ceremonies attendant on the execution of the sentence. You may properly depart at any point after the inarguable death of the witch—there is no formal close of the ceremony, any more than there is an end to death itself.

"Now," Kedlidor continued, "should Ambrosia's champion vindicate her—"

"What chance is there of that?" cried the King despairingly.

The withered old man, the only one of the family servants spared in the recent purge, focused his dim gray eyes on his King. "That is of no concern to me, Sire. I am not a gambler, but the Rite-Master of Ambrose. I am charged with knowing and teaching the proper ceremonies for every possible occasion. The Lady Ambrosia's acquittal is a possible occasion; therefore I will teach you the proper ceremony."

The King stared sullenly at the floor of the room. The Rite-Master dispassionately struck him across the face. "Attend, Sire. Say—"

"I know all that stuff," muttered the King, and he did. He had spent the night reading the ritual book, wondering whether he would be more relieved by Grandmother's acquittal or her death.

"Show me that you know, Sire. Take a breath, speak loudly and clearly . . ."

There was the thunder of booted feet in the hallway outside and the door flew open. The King's uncle, Lord Urdhven, was there with a troop of men wearing his personal device, a red lion standing against a black field. Behind Urdhven was the poisoner Steng. He met the King's eye and smiled gently.

"It's nearly noon," the Protector remarked. "Bring his Majesty, Kedlidor." He turned to go.

"No, Lord Urdhven," Kedlidor replied.

The Protector, resplendent in gold armor, enamelled with his own black-and-scarlet device on the breastplate, paused and smiled ominously down at the gray shadow of a man. "Why not?"

"It is not fit that I be seen with the King at this ceremony. My rank is too low. Further, your poisoner may not be there."

"He won't be. Is there anything else?"

"Yes. The King ought to precede you. He is of higher rank, you know."

The Protector turned his red smile on his nephew. "I do know it. Naturally, *Sire*, you must go first. All the forms will be met for this ceremony."

The King walked past the Protector and the poisoner into the hall of armed men. They fell in behind him, the sound of their feet in the hallway like a stone giant gnashing its teeth. He passed out into the golden light of the enclosure, and there was a unanimous shout from the crowd as the royal procession was recognized. There were soldiers before him, clearing a path, so he didn't have to decide what was the right way to go. While seeming to protect him, they took him to the wooden stair that led to the royal box, above the Victor's Square, at the midpoint of the lists.

Already the stands of benches on either side were crowded with spectators. The King had never been to a formal combat before, and he was amazed at the mixture of somberness and hilarity among the onlookers. He seated himself amid dutiful cheers, which sounded louder and more impassioned—even hysterical—as Lord Urdhven the Protector appeared and took his place at the King's left hand.

Opposite the stands stood the prisoner, chained to a stake, her mouth bound with a green rag torn from her appellant's robe. Beyond her was nothing but the dead lands between the two cities that bore the name Ontil. Somewhere beyond the gray hills was the Old City, capital of the First Empire. No one lived there now—it was under the curse of the Old Gods; even the river Tilion had been diverted when the New City was founded by Uthar the Great and Ambrosia centuries ago. But, in name, Lathmar was King of that city too. He had often daydreamed of escaping from the New City to the Old City, where he would find his true subjects and make war on the people who had killed his mother and his father. . . .

At a curt gesture from the Protector, the heralds blew on their trumpets, shattering the King's reverie. Vost, the High Marshal (since the recent execution of the one appointed by the King's late father), stood forth in the Victor's Square and cried the challenge.

"Lady Ambrosia Viviana, accused of witchcraft, has claimed her right of trial by combat. If her champion is present, let him come forth and enter the lists, or her life is forfeit to the King (the Strange Gods protect His Majesty)."

The heralds blew another blast on their trumpets, and the excitement of the crowd died down. They could see, as well as the King himself, that one end of the lists was vacant, and that at the other end stood the Red Knight. Perhaps this would only be an execution and not a combat after all.

Then the muttering of the crowd changed slightly. The King, leaning forward, saw that someone else had entered the lists—someone shorter than the King was himself, who bowed low before the prisoner.

The crowd was half-amused, half-thoughtful as the unarmed dwarf marched past them up the lists to Victor's Square.

"Have you come," the High Marshal said as the dwarf drew to a halt before him, "as champion for the Lady Ambrosia?"

"If need be," said the dwarf, with unassumed confidence.

"If you are not a champion you must depart from the lists."

"Heralds can be in the lists, before the combat and at intervals. So can squires."

"Are you herald or squire?"

"Both! Herald, squire, apprentice, and factotum to my *harven*-kinsman, Morlock Ambrosius, also called syr Theorn. I am Wyrth syr Theorn."

"Sir Thorn—"

"I'm not a knight. Wyrth. Syr. Theorn. Wyrtheorn to my friends."

"Wyrththyseorn—"

"Not bad. Take a deep breath and try again."

"—you must take up arms for the Lady Ambrosia or leave the field. The trial has begun."

"You don't have the authority to make that judgement, Sir Marshal. I appeal to the Judge of the Combat. My principal has been delayed, but he is coming. On his behalf, I ask that the combat be delayed for a time."

Vost, the High Marshal, looked uncertainly up toward the royal box. The King realized abruptly that the decision was his. He was the Judge of the Combat, as the highest-ranking male present. He looked at Urdhven, who made a slight gesture of indifference, his golden face impassive.

"How much time?" he called down.

"As much as I can get," the dwarf replied cheerfully. "Morlock is horrible old, you know, and doesn't move as fast as he used to."

The King put his hand to his head. There was nothing in the rites Kedlidor had taught him about this. But there should have been: it seemed a reasonable request. But he didn't know what a reasonable answer would be.

"Let me come up and explain," the dwarf proposed. "For I have messages from your kinsman Morlock, not meant for the common ear."

"Uh . . ." The King gestured indeterminately. The dwarf took this as permission and hopped into the Victor's Square. Shouldering the High Marshal aside, he swarmed up the wall beneath the royal box and threw himself over its rail to land on his feet before the King.

"Hail, King Lathmar the Seventh!" he cried. "(You are the seventh, aren't you? Good, good, good. I was afraid I'd missed one.) Hail, King of the Two Cities, the Old Ontil and the New! Hail and, well, well-met. Good to see you. Eh?"

"Are these the private messages Morlock sends to his kinsman?" the Protector inquired, his face split by a leonine smile.

"Not at all. The Lord Protector Urdhven, I believe? No, Morlock sent me chiefly to inquire after the King's *health*. But he said not to do it right out in front of the crowd. I suspect he thought you might be sensitive on the subject, what with your sister and brother-in-law and all their trusted servants dying so suddenly in recent days. Do you suppose they caught that fever that's been spreading through the poorer parts of the city—or was it a disease that only strikes in palaces?"

The Protector's smile was gone, but the predatory look remained. "The King's health you may assess yourself," he said flatly. "If there is nothing else—"

"Nothing from Morlock, but I believe that, speaking as the agent of the champion of Lady Ambrosia, the forms have not been met. Isn't the champion entitled to a representative in the judge's box, to argue points of honor, foul blows, that sort of thing?"

"None came forward—" Urdhven began, but stopped as the dwarf tapped his chest modestly. "Very well," he conceded. "Daen, bring another chair. But it is a mere point of honor, Wyrtheorn, since there will be no combat here today. Your champion has forfeited."

"The Lady Ambrosia's champion," the dwarf corrected him gently, as he sat down on the King's right hand. "But, with respect, that word is not yours to say. The King is the judge of this combat, and he may grant my request if he chooses."

The Protector turned his masklike golden face on the King, who found he could not speak. He knew what his uncle wanted him to say. He knew what the dwarf wanted him to say. He knew what his Grandmother would want him to say. But he didn't know what to say. There was no rule to go by, no ceremony to tell him whose wishes he must obey.

The silence grew long. It spread from the royal box to the crowd on either side. A quiet fell on the dusty enclosure. In it, all heard the dim cry of a horn sounding to the east.

CHAPTER THREE

TRIAL BY COMBAT

The horn sounded from the dead lands masking the broken city in the east. It grew louder as they listened. It ceased for a moment; when it returned it was louder yet. Soon, looking east, they could see the source of the call: an armed man on horseback appeared at the crest of a gray hill, the horn raised to his lips. The ululating call was unfamiliar to everyone in the enclosure. But it rang with defiance.

The armed rider disappeared, plunging down the slope of the hill to be hidden by another. Presently he topped that one and could be seen more clearly. The horse was a powerful black stallion; the rider's armor was black chain mail; a long black lance with pennons was slung beside him. A black cloth covered his shield, but as he rode onto the plain where the enclosure stood, he threw the horn away and shook the cloth loose from the shield. Blazing out from a black field, the device was a white hawk in flight over a branch of flowering thorn—the arms of Ambrosius.

"I withdraw my request, Your Majesty," Wyrtheorn said with relief he did not even attempt to hide. "Ambrosia's champion is here."

Urdhven turned to him, his face a golden mask of fury. "If he uses sorcery he will die. It was not for nothing I brought my army here! He will die and she will die and you, too, will die, little man."

"I am not a man," the dwarf replied. "Further, what is your army to Morlock or to me? Had we chosen to steal Ambrosia by night, or in the open day, you could have done nothing to stop us. But we desire that Ambrosia again be able to walk the streets of her city—"

"It is not *her* city."

"It *is* her city. It exists because she created it. She has spent her life defending it. Her children have gone on to conquer half a world. The palace she designed and built justly wears her great ancestor's name. If Ambrosia is to enter it again, the lies about her must be crushed; she must be acquitted in law. Therefore, Morlock will use no magic. I tell you, he needs none to best any living man with the sword."

The Protector laughed derisively.

The armed rider was now approaching the enclosure fence. He did not slacken his speed but bent forward, as if he were talking to his charger. It cried out and cleared the fence in a magnificent leap, landing in the center of the field.

A shout of admiration went up from the watching crowd, quickly stifled as they remembered the soldiers watching them. The armed rider, neglecting the traditional salute to the sovereign, lifted his left hand in greeting toward the prisoner. She did not move or change her expression in any way, but her eyes were on him.

Now the Red Knight moved forward in the lists and, setting his spear to rest, spurred his horse to charge. The black knight was hardly able to unsheathe his lance before the other was upon him, so he lashed out with the spear in a hasty but powerful parry, knocking aside the Red Knight's lance. The Red Knight thundered past, and the black knight roused his steed to a canter, riding to the opposite end of the lists.

"Your champion does not stand on ceremony," Wyrth remarked to the Urdhven.

"Sir Hlosian Bekh is the champion of the Crown," the Protector replied stiffly.

"Ah. Well, at least *you* stand on ceremony."

The Protector smiled his leonine smile. "Ceremony is very well," he conceded, "but they"—he gestured at the crowd—"will not be won by ceremonies, or kept by laws. They are only impressed by victory, by power."

"You know," the dwarf replied, "I disagree with you. When Morlock wins—"

"That is not possible."

"Then this *is* simply a ceremony, not a trial. Or is that what you've been telling me?"

The Protector's silent smile was ominous.

Now both knights had repositioned themselves at opposing ends of the lists. The heralds' trumpets sounded three times, the call to attack. Then both champions charged into the narrow field, their spears at rest. As they drove toward each other the Red Knight's lance swung back and its point struck full on the white device of the black shield. But the Red Knight's spear shattered like glass and the black knight rode past unshaken.

No one dared cheer. But the silence grew as dense as the clouds of dust rising to obscure the noon-bright air.

"A good shield is worth its weight in spears," Wyrth remarked cheerfully to the King, who smiled doubtfully.

The delay between passes was greater this time, as the Red Knight needed a new spear. Finally the trumpets sounded again; the combatants thundered again into the lists, their armor gleaming dimly through the descending mist of dust.

Spear-points wavered in the air, then one struck home. The Red Knight's spear hit the black knight just under the helmet, a killing blow, throwing Ambrosia's champion from the saddle. He struck the dusty ground, his armor singing like the cymbals of Winterfeast, and he lay there.

The tension in the crowd perceptibly relaxed. There were mutters of relief and sighs that were unmistakably disappointed. Ambrosia's champion had fallen as so many of theirs had fallen, so many of their kinsmen, sacrifices to the prowess of the Red Knight.

Ambrosia's iron-gray gaze was as impassive as ever, and still fixed on the fallen knight.

Wyrth's gaze followed Ambrosia's, and he laughed aloud. The black knight was moving. "The old fool was right!" he muttered.

Meeting the King's astonished eye, he explained, "You see, Your Majesty, Morlock insisted on making his own armor for the combat. That's why he was late for the trial. I said it was a waste of time, and they'd be stringing his sister's guts across the gateposts of the city before he got here. He got this *look* on his face—you've probably seen Ambrosia wear it—and we did things his way. It probably saved his neck just now."

"Dead or defeated, it does not matter," the Protector said, rising. "The combat is over."

"Your champion doesn't think so," the dwarf retorted. "Look!"

The Red Knight had turned to contemplate his dead opponent. Seeing the black knight alive seemed to drive him to fury, and he turned his horse about to charge down on the dismounted knight. Only by rolling to the side of the lists did the black knight avoid being trod under the hooves of the Red Knight's horse.

A rumble of discontent, even contempt, arose from the crowd.

"This is not the game, as it was handed down from days of yore," the dwarf remarked, "is it? Why, if a combatant tried a trick like that back in the Vraidish homelands, north of the Blackthorns, the Judge of the Combat would have his head on the spot."

"We are not in the Vraidish homelands," replied the Protector, sitting down again.

"Evidently not. Here he comes again."

The Red Knight indeed had turned his horse and was charging down the lists again, intent on trampling his opponent. The crowd watched in stony silence; even the Protector seemed ill at ease.

But the black knight had not remained lying in the dust. He had recovered his spear, at least (his horse was down at the far end of the lists), and stood with it in hand, awaiting the Red Knight's onset. When the Red Knight's horse was almost upon him he dodged across its path with an agility that was astounding in a fully armored man and, lifting his lance like a club, struck the Red Knight from the saddle.

A roar of spontaneous applause drowned the crash of the Red Knight's fall. Wyrtheorn crowed with delight, then shouted, "Ambrose! Ambrose! Merlin's children!"

A sudden silence followed this shocking slogan, which reminded the crowd of the political realities behind this combat. Since that was what

Wyrtheorn intended to do, he continued to shout into the silence, "*Ambrose and the Ambrosii! The Royal House!*"

"The King," suggested someone near at hand. Wyrth thought he recognized his friend Genjandro's voice.

"The King!" Wyrtheorn agreed vociferously. "Justice for the King! The King!"

There were a few faint echoes in the enclosure, but no answering roar. Still, there was a frozen thoughtfulness on many faces in the crowd. Wyrth had hoped for no more and sat back satisfied. The glittering stare of hatred the Protector had fixed on the squirming King did not escape him. But he doubted anything he could do would intensify the Protector's already lambent hatred for the last descendant of Uthar the Great.

The Red Knight had risen from the ground, meanwhile, dust like wreaths of smoke in the air about him. He said nothing, but drew the heavy sword swung from his belt.

The black knight, waiting at one side, lightly tossed away his spear and drew his own blade, narrow and long, with a deadly point.

The King looked curiously at Wyrth.

"No, Your Majesty," the dwarf said, answering the unspoken question. "That is not the accursed sword Tyrfing. Tyrfing is not merely a weapon but a focus of power; to kill with it is an act with grim consequences. Morlock would not carry it into a combat such as this. Besides, the ban on magic forbids it."

"Tyrfing is a fable," the Protector remarked, "and Morlock is a ghost story. I wonder who is really wearing that armor—some pawn of Ambrosia afraid to use his own name, I suppose."

The King looked fearfully at his Protector, as if he had thought the same thing. Wyrth laughed, but did not argue.

The knights on the field awaited no formal preliminaries to the second part of the combat. Before the heralds had raised the trumpets to their lips, the Red Knight's broadsword had crashed onto the black-and-white Ambrosian shield. The black knight thrust forward simultaneously with his bright deadly blade and the Red Knight was forced to retreat. The blade of the black knight gleamed red as he leapt forward in pursuit.

"First blood to Ambrosius!" Wyrth said grimly. "You see, Lord Urdhven, the ghost story that is sweating down on yonder dusty field learned his fencing from Naevros syr Tol, the greatest swordsman of the old time. He is not like anyone your champion has met before."

The Protector was still smiling. "They have all been different," he remarked. "They all came from different places, wearing different colors, skilled in different skills. They have one thing in common, dwarf: Hlosian killed them all."

Wyrtheorn shrugged and turned back to the fight. Urdhven's wholly unassumed confidence disturbed him more than he was willing to admit. It also disturbed him that there was no doubt in the faces of the crowd. They watched in fascination, but there was no suspense. They clearly expected the Red Knight's victory, though he was wounded in three places now.

The clash of steel against steel continued as the sun sank from its zenith and the heat of the day grew worse. When the black knight had wounded the Red Knight at least once in each limb, and twice in the neck, he began a furious offense clearly aimed at bringing final victory. Sword strokes fell like silver sheets of rain, varying with sudden lightning-bright thrusts.

The Red Knight backed slowly away two more steps under this onslaught and was wounded several times—it was hard to say how many, because blood did not stand out on his red-enamelled plate armor. But his manner hardly changed throughout the fight, despite his wounds. It occurred to Wyrtheorn that he was waiting for something.

The dwarf glanced over at the prisoner's stake and saw that Ambrosia's gray eyes were fixed on him. He shrugged uneasily, but her expression did not change. She looked back at the combat.

She knows something, Wyrth thought. *What puzzles me does not puzzle her.* He drummed his fingers on his knees and looked meditatively back to the field.

The black knight's assault slowed visibly. He had actually hacked holes in the Red Knight's plate armor over his right arm and left leg. But Sir Hlosian Bekh still defended himself with the same lumbering vigor and the same mediocre skill.

Then it happened. The black knight's sword—no longer bright and keen, but notched along its edge and stained dark with drying blood—lashed out in an attack on the Red Knight's sword arm. The black knight's sword caught in the gap between the forearm plate and the upper arm plate, where the Red Knight's chain mail was visible. Instead of retreating, the Red Knight trapped the black shield with his own and struck a thunderous blow with his heavy sword on the black knight's helm.

Ambrosia's champion staggered like a drunk. The Red Knight braced himself and struck out with his shield. The black knight was forced back a step. Hlosian struck again with sword and shield, and again the black knight was forced back.

"It is always the same," the Protector's voice said. Wyrth turned to him: the golden lord seemed almost sad as he returned the dwarf's glance. "Your friend, whoever he is, fought well. Better than any I have ever seen, perhaps, and I have been coming to the combats for thirty years. Hlosian, as you have seen, does not fight well. But he always wins."

"He has magical protection," the dwarf guessed.

The Protector replied, with a shrug, "He is strong enough to outlast any opponent, and he is not afraid of death. That is all the magic he needs. Look at the crowd, dwarf. This is nothing new to them. They have seen it all before."

Stonily, Wyrth turned his gaze back to the field. But he could not help noticing, with the corner of his eye, the patient, unsurprised faces of the crowd. They were fascinated, but they were not really in suspense. To them this was not a combat but a ritual death. They *had* seen it before.

Wyrtheorn was seeing what he had never seen before: the black knight being driven back, step by step, toward defeat. The Red Knight now had his back toward the Victor's Square, and he was forcing his opponent toward the far border of the lists. If forced across, the black knight would be defeated.

"It will be over soon," the Protector said thoughtfully. "I hope he does not try to flee under the rail. It is unpleasant to see a friend killed while groveling on the ground—"

"Morlock Ambrosius will never flee," the dwarf said flatly.

"He, or whoever is pretending to be him, has never faced Sir Hlosian Bekh. There is something frightening about Hlosian, something *different*."

"Will he not allow his opponent to yield?" the little King asked suddenly. Wyrth, glancing at him, saw his eyes were wide with concern—he had probably never seen a man killed in combat before.

The Protector shook his head, smiling. "Sir Hlosian never offers mercy. Like defeat, it is foreign to his nature."

It seemed to Wyrth, as he looked back at the combat, that the black knight was giving way to panic. To the dwarf's way of thinking, the only chance the black knight had was to disable the Red Knight's sword arm or one of his legs. But the black knight had ceased attacking these entirely. From the looks of things (the Red Knight was partially eclipsing Wyrth's view), the black knight was hacking and stabbing repeatedly at his opponent's breastplate. The likelihood of breaking through this (and the chain mail that surely lay beneath) for a fatal blow was so slight that Wyrth had to believe the black knight was no longer rational.

The black knight ceased retreating, his heels at the border of the lists. The Red Knight let his shield fall to his shoulder and began to deal his blows two-handed. Very unwisely, in Wyrth's opinion, the black knight did likewise. This gave Sir Hlosian the opportunity to land a crashing blow on the black knight's right shoulder that drove him to one knee.

Snatching up his shield, the black knight leapt back to his feet. The Red Knight had recovered and struck again, a terrible two-handed stoke on the upraised shield of Ambrosius.

Visibly, the black knight's knees began to give way, then stood straight. But Wyrth saw with horror that he was holding his shield with both hands; he had lost his sword somewhere. (It didn't seem to be on the ground, but perhaps the dust was covering it.)

The same thing was noticed by others; an anticipatory mutter ran through the crowd, a whisper of approaching death. The Red Knight landed another blow on the Ambrosian shield, which the black knight held over his head, as if to protect himself from a downpour. The blow drove him to his knees.

Wyrth watched in disbelief as the Red Knight raised his sword over his head for what would surely be the deathblow. He shuddered to think with what force that blow would fall. The Red Knight threw his head back; the flat beak of his helmet could be seen, outlined against the far sky. Wyrth wondered if the victorious knight was about to give a barbaric scream of triumph.

Then he bent back further, from the waist, and Wyrtheorn realized he was not bending, but falling backward. The black knight's sword protruded from the shattered red breastplate. In complete silence, the Red Knight fell back to the earth and lay still.

The crash of his bloody armor on the field was the signal for a thunderous outburst from the watching crowd. They rose, like the clouds of dust rising from the fallen knight, crying out at the top of their voices, heedless of the Protector and his soldiers—seized at last by surprise, by triumph, by their own secret anger. The invincible Red Knight who had killed so many of their own champions, defeated so many of their causes, was dead at last. They could not help but triumph; they could finally afford to hate.

But all such thoughts were driven from Wyrth's mind as he looked at the black knight. The victor remained on his knees, his helmet slumped back against the rail of the lists as if he were staring speculatively at the sky. His fingers had gone slack, and the battered black-and-white Ambrosian shield lay flat on the ground, its device shrouded with dust.

"With your leave, Majesty!" Wyrth shouted at the frightened child beside him and leaped down into the Victor's Square. He jumped from there down into the field and ran as fast as his short legs would carry him to where the knights were.

Wyrth paused by the Red Knight. He glanced at the cruelly notched blade buried in the dead knight's chest, marvelling that anyone could land one blow and begin another with such a wound. Then the smell hit him— not the blood (he had expected that) but mud—the unmistakable reek of mud and wet clay. . . .

Wyrth whistled thoughtfully. Now he saw it all! Hlosian was a golem— somehow the black knight had realized it (probably from the smell of its blood, as Wyrth had), and that accounted for his attack on the Red Knight's breast-plate. Only by severing or somehow destroying the name-scroll in the golem's chest cavity could the golem be beaten. The black knight had planted his sword in the golem's chest, and had lost his grip on it. The golem had severed its own name-scroll when lifting its arms to dispatch the black knight.

The dwarf turned toward Ambrosia's champion, fearing the worst as he approached. The victor was hardly moving, issuing knife-edged wheezing sobs in the dusty air, like a horse that has been ridden nearly to death.

"Morlock!" said Wyrth. "Morlock Ambrosius!"

There was no answer, but the sobbing sounds continued.

Dreading what he would see, Wyrth pulled back the visor of the black helmet.

Eyes closed, head resting comfortably against the rail, Morlock Ambrosius was snoring. Wyrth could smell the stale wine on his breath.

"You pig!" shouted Wyrth, really furious. "*Wake up!* There's *work* to do!"

Chapter Four

Into the Dead Hills

The victorious knight made his painful way across the field, in the face of the now-silent crowd and the bristling rows of soldiery that stood beyond. Behind him his small but verbose herald dragged the dead form of his vanquished opponent, still fully armored.

The King of the Two Cities, watching him approach, noted almost superstitiously that he limped and that his right shoulder was somewhat higher than his left. The battered chain mail jangled as he ascended into the Victor's Square. He paused there for a moment, then reached up and unbuckled his helmet, drawing it off.

The King still expected a monster's face and so was somewhat disappointed. The features, dark and weather-beaten, were streaked with human sweat and mundane dirt. The dark hair was unruly and matted. Only the eyes were strange: a pale gray, almost luminous in the afternoon shadow across his face.

"Sire," said the black knight in a dusty crowlike rasp. He paused, cleared his throat, and resumed in a clearer voice. "I am Morlock Ambrosius, your kinsman and the kinsman of your imperial ancestors to the tenth generation."

This being a ceremony, the King knew exactly what to do.

"Sir Morlock," he said, "welcome. What is your desire?"

"Sire," said the black knight, according to the forms, "I have proven the charges against my sister to be false. If any of her accusers remain, let them rise up and defend their words with the sword." He did not so much as glance at the Protector.

"Her accusers," the King replied, "have lost the right and the power of speech in this assembly. You have defended the right, and victory is your reward. The—that is, your sister is free this day." The King paused uncertainly. The forms required him at this point to require his ministers to set free the appellant. But the soldiers about him were all the Protector's Men.

Still, as if he had commanded them, a small party of City Legionaries set out across the lists to the pyre. Climbing up on the kindling, their captain untied the gag on Ambrosia's mouth and broke the chains at her wrists with his sword. Then he dismissed his squad and escorted Ambrosia to the Victor's Square. She said nothing, but placed a twisted hand on Morlock's upper shoulder, wincing with pain as she did so.

"Sir Morlock," said the King, "have you any other request of this company?" He asked this because it was the form; he knew all the forms and thought it his duty to keep them. He had never been to a trial by arms before, and he did not know the purpose of this question was to give the victor the chance to lay a countercharge against his principal's accusers.

The King did not know, but the crowd knew. They knew also that Ambrosia's accuser had been the Protector himself, and a mutter of awe ran through the crowd at the little King's bravery.

"Yes," said the black knight distinctly.

Silence fell.

The King sensed that something dangerous was in the air, but didn't yet know what it was. Then he turned and saw the Protector clenching his fists, his eyes as red as blood. The King's breath suddenly went out of him as he began to understand. But it was no longer his turn to speak; it was Morlock's, and he was taking intolerably long about it.

"Sire," Morlock said finally, "I ask that the Protector of the Imperial Crown, one Lord Urdhven," and he paused again, continuing, "I ask that he return the body of his champion to its *blood-kin*, who do not seem to be known in the city, so that they may dispose of it with their accustomed *rites*."

There was a puzzled silence, in which the King sensed rather than saw

Lord Urdhven relax beside him, only to tense again at a shower of bitter laughter from Ambrosia.

"Lord Urdhven," said the King in a low voice, afraid to look directly at him.

"I'll see to it," the Protector replied curtly. "Tell them to go away."

Go away? The King had been assuming that his Grandmother would take him home, that she would again protect him from his Protector, that everything would be all right again, or at least as right as it had ever been. . . . Now he saw that would not be.

Dimly he wondered what would happen to him. Not a public trial like this—not with Ambrosia on the loose. Nothing anyone could come and save him from. A fall down a stairway, perhaps, or a sudden illness, like his mother and father.

"Grandmother," he said shrilly, moved by his own heart. (Was there a ceremony for such an occasion? Kedlidor had never taught it to him.) "Grandmother," he said again more slowly, "I'm glad you're free. Good-bye!" Then he put his hands over his face so that no one could see him weep.

His tears soon passed, but he held his hands over his face still, hiding behind them—as he had often hid his face against his pillow while listening to strange noises in his room at night. He felt the Protector stand and heard him walk away. Still he hid behind his hands. He heard the crowd leaving and still he sat, hiding in the open. He sat until he felt the touch on his shoulder and a soldier's voice saying, "Come along now, Your Majesty. It's time."

"Perhaps you're exaggerating slightly, Wyrtheorn?" suggested Ambrosia, smiling.

"Madam, he was absolutely snoring. You heard me. And I heard *him*."

"What an evil pig you are, Morlock," Ambrosia remarked, "taking your ease when Wyrth had been working so hard on my behalf."

"That's nothing. Wait 'till you hear what *he*—"

The three were trudging among the Dead Hills surrounding the Old City. Wyrth was leading the black charger (which Morlock called by the barbarous name Velox), and when he expressed his overflowing emotions (as he frequently did) by some vigorous gesture, the horse tended to shy away. Wyrth had underlined his fresh accusation of Morlock with a great wave of the hand, and now Velox positively bolted. Wyrtheorn lost hold of the reins and had to chase the horse down, which he did with inexpert enthusiasm.

"Wyrth's in as good a mood as I've ever seen," Ambrosia remarked, as the sounds of his shouting at the horse wafted back to them.

"I think he had little hope of success today," her brother remarked.

"Had you?"

Morlock grunted and sat down abruptly on a nearby rock. "Yes. More than the occasion merited. It was a near thing. Help me out of this hardware, Ambrosia."

"I can't." She explained to him about her hands. His face grew grim.

"I'm sorry," he said. "We'd better wait until Wyrtheorn returns; I can do you little good in these mailed gloves."

Wyrth finally did return with horse in tow. "I figured it out," he said, addressing Ambrosia. "He was unable to locate a horse and, being pressed for time, found an unusually tall sheep, shaved it raw, and painted it black. So I—"

"Get me out of this armor, Wyrtheorn."

"Hm. I fear that Master Morlock's customary keenness of wit has been blunted by repeated blows to the head."

"If that's the remedy, I ask only that you come within arm's reach."

"Physical comedy can never make up for lack of true humor, Master Morlock," the dwarf reproved him, pointedly approaching from behind. "Lady Ambrosia, if you'll grab these—"

"They broke her hands."

"Not taking a single chance, were they? I beg your pardon, madam—I heard some such rumor while I was milling about in the crowd. The combat drove it from my mind, though. Can you step on these reins or something?"

Ambrosia nickered softly, spoke Velox's name, and the black charger came to stand quietly beside her.

"Hmph," said the dwarf. "Then while I—"

"You seemed to be enjoying yourself so much."

"Never mind." He set to unbuckling Morlock's armor. "I'd see to your wrists myself," he said to Ambrosia, "but Morlock is a better healer than I am, if you can believe it."

Ambrosia expressed polite disbelief.

"You may well say so, but it's true. No doubt due to the practice he's had, bandaging up his own head lo these many centuries—*Hurs krakna*!" he muttered in dismay.

Ambrosia looked at the stretch of Morlock's shoulder Wyrth had just exposed. Repeated blows had shattered the chain mail, driving it through the dark cloth padding so that links of mail, like fish scales, were driven into Morlock's flesh. The shoulder was dark with dried blood where it was not gleaming with fresh. "Ugly," she agreed.

"I had hoped it might not be so bad. I had really begun to hope, when I saw him snoring there on the field. Look at him, Lady Ambrosia, he's sleeping again."

"He's in a bad way. I've cost you both much, this day. I owe you more."

"Nonsense." Wyrth shook his head. "Blood has no price." He worked in silence for a while, stripping the shattered armor from his master's body and then laying him gently on the ground. He threw aside the blood-crusted rags that Morlock had been wearing under the mail and covered him with his own cloak. This left Morlock's legs bare, so Wyrth fetched the rags back to cover them.

"I'll have to be your healer after all, my lady," the dwarf said. "I'm no herbalist, but I can at least bind your hands and splint your wrists."

"You needn't bother, Wyrth. If I get back to the city before dark I can consult somebody."

Wyrtheorn blinked and glanced at Morlock. "I doubt Morlock will be able to travel before nightfall—"

"I don't expect you to travel with me. You've done enough already, both of you."

"Er. We, uh, we rather expected *you* to travel with *us*. And not to the city. Morlock thinks—"

"To the city I go, Wyrth. I can't leave little Lathmar to the Protector's mercy."

"Lathmar?"

"The King."

"Oh!" Wyrtheorn rubbed his nose thoughtfully. "Not a bad little fellow. But you have to consider him as good as dead, you know. Revenge is what you owe him, not protection. Now, Morlock thinks—"

"Urdhven wouldn't dare kill him as long as I'm alive," Ambrosia said with a knowing air.

"Oh, yes he would. In fact, he doesn't dare do anything else."

Ambrosia frowned.

"Hear me out, madam. If I understand the law of the Second Empire, you may not claim the throne."

"Correct. I'm not a descendant of the ancient Vraidish kings."

"Then."

Ambrosia stared at him, waiting.

"If the Protector arranges for the King to die," Wyrth said finally, "there is no legitimate claimant for the throne. That makes the Protector as legitimate as any. And he is the man on the spot, with an army loyal to him controlling the capital."

"The people would never stand for it."

"Eh, my lady, what do the people ever have to say about such things?"

"They are my people, Wyrtheorn. No one knows them better than I do. And I tell you they will pull the palace Ambrose down around the Protector's ears if he harms the King. I am one thing—I'm not Vraidish, and moreover am supposed to look out for myself. The King is different. He is truly honored in the city."

"Then why do you fear for him?"

Ambrosia was silent.

"You see, my lady, everything you say simply underlines the desperation of the Protector's position. And desperate men prefer savage measures: it gives release to their emotions. And, Lady Ambrosia, I spent all yesterday at the Great Market, scrounging for gossip. There was more sympathy for yourself than you have supposed, and less feeling for the King than you imagine. People are weary of weak and troubled reigns. They say the Ambrosian line has run its course; they are looking for a leader. They'll never love Urdhven, but if he proves himself the strongest they'll follow him sure."

Ambrosia became restless with this analysis. "Then best I be back at the city as soon as can be. Tell my brother—"

"No, my lady, wait. Morlock can counsel you better than I. I always see the debt side of a ledger."

"And Morlock is an optimist?"

"Morlock sees a way," the dwarf replies. "Always. Please wait till he awakes."

"I can't wait, Wyrth. If—"

The unconscious form lifted its hand. It drew a long, shuddering breath. "Wait!" it rasped, in a voice unlike Morlock's.

"I hate this," the dwarf complained. "When he speaks in a vision he hardly sounds like himself. I could almost believe another spirit has possession of him."

"Don't be superstitious, Wyrth. Morlock, I can't wait. Speak to me what you see."

Voice rasping, eyes closed, Morlock said, "The death in the Protector's Shadow sleeps and, sleeping, dreams.

"The death the Protector fears wears our faces like masks.

"The death to ease the Protector's pain wears our name, like gravestones.

"The wing rides over the plain."

"Shake him out of it," the dwarf said impatiently. "What does that mean, 'the wing rides over the plain'?"

"The wing enters the hills—"

"Canyon keep the wing. Wake up, Morlock!"

"He is waking," Ambrosia said. "Be quiet, Wyrth, you can't hurry him. 'The flight must take its course,' as seers say."

"No," said Morlock, in a voice almost his own. "Wrong."

"What's wrong?" Ambrosia asked.

"Wing. Not flight. Shoes."

"A wing with *feet*?" Wyrth demanded.

Morlock looked puzzled, like a sleeper with a perplexing dream. "No feet. Shoes."

"Oh, that's plain. A wing with shoes, but no feet."

"Not plain," Morlock insisted. "Hills."

Ambrosia looked speculatively at her brother, then said to Wyrth, "I'll be back in a moment." She climbed a nearby hill and looked westward. After a moment she turned and came down again. She called to the horse and then said to Wyrtheorn, "Pick up my brother and carry him. We must be going."

"I don't understand."

"Wyrtheorn, what sort of wing rides rather than flies and has shoes but not feet?"

The dwarf glared at her. It was Morlock who answered, ascending (or descending) finally to full wakefulness.

"A cavalry wing," said the Crooked Man, "and almost upon us." He sat up. "Wyrtheorn, where are my clothes?"

Thousands of heartbeats later Wyrtheorn still had not gotten over it. "Wyrtheorn," he intoned to himself, "where are my slippers, where are my buttered biscuits, where my evening tea?"

Morlock, who was wearing the dirty, rusty, torn, bloody black rags that Wyrth had been prepared to discard, did not respond.

"Wyrtheorn," Wyrtheorn intoned, "bring me my rags."

"Shut up, Wyrth," Ambrosia said irritably. "They'll track us down by your whining alone."

"They won't track us at all," Wyrth rejoined. "They'll quarter the area and search. They're cavalry, not hunters. They'll find us, all right, but in their own good time."

"Can't you make your prentice be quiet?" Ambrosia asked her brother.

Morlock smiled. "No."

"Hmph," Wyrth said, to keep the conversation going. "Listen to this: I say we let the horse go."

The Ambrosii said nothing. The expression of pain sternly repressed was stamped on both their faces, bringing out the most fugitive likenesses. If it were possible Wyrth would have made them both be still and take some healing. Since it was not, he was determined to distract them.

"No, really," he said, as if they had answered him. "It—"

"We need the horse, Wyrtheorn," Morlock cut him off.

They proceeded through a silence punctuated by Wyrth's wisecracks. The sun was gone behind the dusty gray hills to the east, but its light was still in the sky and its heat was still in the dead valleys.

"Here," said Morlock.

Wyrtheorn looked around.

"There." Morlock scuffed a mark in the crumbling gray earth.

"Get away; I'll do it," the dwarf said irritably.

Morlock did not argue, but sat on a slope a few feet away. "Dig a square perhaps as long as my arm."

"Which arm?" the dwarf retorted, digging rapidly in the dry earth with his hard blunt fingers. It was not long before he laid bare a crystalline blade, blazing with white light. There were darker thornlike shapes within the light. Beneath the sword was a large pack made of dark canvas. Between pack and sword two small boxes made of translucent shining metal.

"What is *that*?" the dwarf said, pointing at the boxes.

"Aethrium," Morlock replied.

"And inside them?"

"Phlogiston."

"From . . ."

"I dephlogistonated the armor I fashioned, and most of the metal in the smith's shop."

The dwarf laughed in pure delight. "That was generous of you!"

"It was a partial payment for the trouble we put him to. A dephlogistonated implement is harder, denser, more durable."

"And you, of course, brought this dangerous matter away with you?"

"I saw a use for it."

"You will kill me with wonder, someday, Master Morlock."

"What's phlogiston?" Ambrosia asked.

Her brother replied didactically, "Phlogiston is the element in matter which is responsible for combustion. Burning, in fact, is simply the release of phlogiston resident in a given object."

"Does metal burn?"

"Everything burns," said Morlock, "unless it has been dephlogistonated. Metal burns in a peculiar manner, though. When a log burns and you weigh the residue, it weighs less than the original log. If you burn a piece of metal, the residue weighs more than the original piece."

"Then metallic phlogiston," remarked Ambrosia composedly, "weighs less than nothing."

"Considerably less. This has certain obvious uses . . ."

Chapter Five

Prisoners of Gravesend

The King of the Two Cities was coughing quietly in the darkness underneath the enclosure seats.

"Be quiet, please, Your Majesty," the Legionary captain, Lorn, whispered.

"It's the dust," the King explained, whispering back. "I'm sorry." He added impulsively, "I'm sorry for everything."

"You? Sorry?" the Legionary said incredulously. "No, Your Majesty. My fate was sealed when I set your Grandmother, as you call her, free. And yours was sealed when you declared her free. But free she was, and the Strange Gods can seize anyone who says otherwise, Protector's Man or no."

"I thought you were a Protector's Man, when you came to get me," the King confessed.

"I wasn't but three steps ahead of them, and that's the truth. Traitorous bastards. We're not all like them in the City Legion, Your Majesty—you mustn't believe that. If we get you back into Ontil, you'll be safe enough."

"But how will we get there?"

"We'll wait until it gets a little darker; then we'll make our way out of the enclosure. My squad will be waiting out there, as if on perimeter guard. Then we'll go to a city gate manned by loyal soldiers. From there on, we'll just guess and hope."

The King nodded, and they waited in silence for nightfall.

Steng was waiting on the stone steps of the anchor building when the Lord Protector and his chief henchman, Vost, stepped out.

"And where have you been?" Lord Urdhven demanded. He was furiously intolerant of any hint of disloyalty—which, Steng often thought, was rather ironic, given his own career.

"Hunting a king, Lord Urdhven," the poisoner replied.

The Protector's green-gold gaze, prepared to shift away scornfully from a properly obsequious reply, snapped back and focused on Steng. "You've found him?"

"I have found . . . an indication. A squad of soldiers outside the enclosure."

"*My* soldiers?"

"The City Legion, my Lord Protector. They pretended to be on patrol, but I knew better than that."

"You alerted my men? They are on the lookout? Where are—?"

"I have them here, my Lord Protector."

"A squad of City Legionaries?" shouted Urdhven, reaching for his sword.

"I took them prisoner," Steng said modestly, and gestured at some bound forms lying at the foot of the stairs.

"Excellent, Steng," cried the Protector, and clapped his poisoner on the shoulder. He leapt down the steps and knelt at the side of one of the bound figures.

Vost followed, after mouthing some congratulatory noises, while his eyes burned with hatred in the darkness. His love for Urdhven was a jealous love, and he hated Steng because of the poisoner's influence over the Protector. Steng reflected on how truly dangerous Vost was. He forced himself to remember this, occasionally, because Vost was such a flat-faced capering dung-beetle of a man that it was easy to forget.

"Steng!" Urdhven shouted. "This man is dead!"

"Yes, my Lord Protector," Steng said. "I killed them all."

"Didn't you realize I would want to question them?"

Steng smiled. He had not moved from his place on the topmost stair. "That was precisely why I killed them, Lord Urdhven."

He walked down the stairs, watching through the dusk as the suspicion, darker than the shadows, settled down on the Protector's face. *Is Steng, too, about to betray me?* That was what Urdhven was thinking. Whereas Vost was looking at him almost affectionately. Poor Vost—who would surely hate him dearly in a very short while.

"The silence of dead men," Steng remarked as he descended the stairs, "is proverbial—but overrated. Consider: the dead man has all the knowledge the living man had, but he has no personality. Because he has no personality, he has no loyalty, no greed, no self-interest, no ideals. He has no reason *not* to talk, if he were only able to. If asked, he will simply answer—if he is able to."

Now he was standing at the bottom of the stairs beside Urdhven and Vost. Urdhven trusted him again and Vost hated him again: that was the way of things.

"Do what you have to do," Urdhven commanded.

Steng knelt down by the nearest body and drew apart its slit tunic. He heard Vost, seeing the Flagrator planted in the riven chest, gasp behind him. Steng smiled. A trickle of blood, thick and dark as molasses in the dim light, was meandering down the white skin stretched over the corpse's ribs. Steng wiped it away with a hiss of fastidious distaste. The device was in order; in fact, the blood of the recently dispatched corpse had warmed it almost to operation point.

"What is it, Steng?" the Protector asked calmly. Steng suspected it was a formal question—not an expression of curiosity so much as a statement that the Lord Protector had no strong feelings about mutilated corpses. Therefore Steng chose not to respond directly.

"We may look upon any body," he said, "as a mechanism, like the hinges of a door, or the Water Wheel. The mechanism will work properly if it is in good repair and has a proper stimulus, a source of energy. These mechanisms"—he waved his hand at the assembled corpses—"are in good repair; their deaths were effected without harming the bodies. What they lack to function is the proper stimulus, the source of energy we call life."

His pale ropy fingers moved as he spoke, drawing the necessary implements from the pockets sewn into his wide flowing sleeves: a firebox, a strip of yellow metal submerged in a jar of oil, a candle, and a fistful of pale narrow wedges of maijarra wood.

"With the Flagrator"—and he gestured at the bristling instrument of metal and glass driven into the dead man's chest—"we will provide an artificial stimulus, a pseudo-life, if you will. The mechanism will then function to the best of its ability and—because it has none of the volitive propensities associated with genuine life—it will do more or less as we tell it."

"A human golem," Urdhven remarked.

Steng paused before replying. "It is not as useful as a golem," he said. "The capacities of the corpse are limited to some subset of the abilities of the man. The connections of the Flagrator are tenuous and would be disturbed by physical movement. Also, it was necessary to destroy the left lung and most of its associated musculature to implant the Flagrator."

"Interesting," the Protector remarked distantly, and Steng knew his evasive tactics had been successful. "He will speak?"

"It will speak," Steng replied.

"Then he has intelligence. Why, then, not will?"

Steng reflected that the Protector, in spite of his appetites and angers, was not a wholly stupid man. "Intelligence," he said aloud, "like beauty and strength, is largely a physical attribute. Because it is resident in the structure of the brain, this is not obvious; it is nonetheless true. Will, however, is an expression of personality, of identity."

"Of spirit?"

"If you prefer. You must not expect to find it as intelligent as it was when it was alive, however. The brain, as has often been observed, is something like a parasite feeding off the blood of the body. This brain has had no fresh blood to eat for some time and has consequently deteriorated. It will continue to do so, by the way—the Flagrator warms and circulates the blood of the body, as part of its function. But it does not generate fresh pure blood as a living heart does."

"You've cut out the heart?" asked Vost, who was clearly attracted and repelled by the notion.

"Yes," said Steng indifferently. "It is around here somewhere. Excuse me for a moment; I must perform some delicate manipulations."

Even as he spoke he was carefully turning valves on the Flagrator with his long ropy fingers. The valves hummed slightly, in tones that varied with their setting, and he set them so that they sang a long monotonous harmony. Then he took a long piece of maijarra wood and wedged it into the corpse's mouth, so that it looked as if the corpse were thoughtfully gnawing at it. Finally he opened the jar of oil and removed the strip of metal with a small pair of tongs. The metal burst into multicolored flame as the air touched it, eerily lighting up the poisoner's face. With a hasty exclamation that might have been a curse or the fixative word of a spell, Steng dropped the burning metal into the central glass bulb of the gleaming turreted Flagrator.

Instantly the corpse began to convulse. Steng had carefully bound the body so that it could not move much, nor damage the delicate mechanisms of the Flagrator. But it was startling to see the dead body twitch and shudder, its teeth clamping tight on the strip of maijarra wood, arcing its back as if it were in agony.

"Is he in pain?" Vost asked.

"There is no 'he,'" Steng replied irritably. "It does not matter if the nerves register pain. There is no one to feel it."

The convulsions subsided. The eyes were open and staring, the jaw slack. Steng removed the stick of wood from its mouth. Its chest rose and fell in a slow irregular rhythm.

"Is he ready?" the Protector asked.

"I believe it is ready."

"What is your name?" the Protector said to the body (as if it were a captured prisoner, Steng thought).

The body did not speak.

"Steng!"

"My Lord Protector," Steng said, "it has no name. It is not a person and will not respond as one. If I may—"

"No." The Protector tugged at his chin, then addressed the corpse. "What *was* your name?"

"This was Jence, of the City Legion," the corpse replied. Its voice was unmodulated and carried no emphasis. A whiff of its breath apparently reached Vost, who turned away gasping.

"Who was Jence's captain?" the Protector continued.

"Lorn."

"Death and Justice! I should have known that. Vost, do you hear?"

"Yes, Lord," Vost replied, still gasping.

"I was going to have the city commander break him tomorrow," the Protector said reflectively. "He must have guessed that and decided he had nothing to lose."

"We'll prove him wrong there, my lord."

"Only if Steng finds him for you. Did Lorn," the Protector continued, addressing the corpse, "order Jence to patrol outside the enclosure?"

"No."

"Ha. What did Lorn order you—what did Lorn order Jence to do?"

"'Pretend to patrol, while waiting to make rendezvous with the King and me,'" said the corpse, in a passable imitation of Lorn.

"How long was Jence to wait?"

"Until they came."

"Where would they come from?"

"The enclosure."

"Where were they hiding in the enclosure?"

"Jence did not know."

"Did anyone in the squad know?"

"No."

"Why not?"

"Lorn refused to discuss his plans. He said the soldiers might be questioned."

"A good precaution," Steng observed. "We may have learned all that we can."

The Protector shook his head impatiently. "How long did Jence wait for Lorn? Was it a long time?"

"It seemed a long time. Then the red fog came, and Jence died."

"Did the squad speculate on where the King and Lorn might be hiding?"

"No."

"Did Jence speculate?"

"No."

"Why not?"

"Lorn ordered us not to. He said—"

"Never mind that. Speculate now."

"Now?" whispered the corpse.

"Where did the King and Lorn hide?" the Protector demanded.

There was a pause, then the corpse said, "In the drop chamber."

"There is no drop chamber," the Protector said sharply.

Steng nodded his head slowly, then did so more pointedly when he saw Vost's look of mystification. The drop chamber was a device of the assassin-minded Ambrosii—built into a royal enclosure to provide escape in times of need.

"There is no drop chamber," said the Protector more urgently, when the corpse did not reply. After another long pause in which the metal in the Flagrator's central bulb burned and spluttered thoughtfully, he continued, "I ordered the Guild of Carpenters not to build a drop chamber into the enclosure."

"They would have ignored such an order," the corpse observed. "Guild law. Imperial charter. No public structure or conveyance for a royal person to be without a drop chamber or a slide chute. Jence's father-in-law was a carpenter. He knew the law."

"Enough!" the Protector said. "Vost, what of this? Have your men searched for a drop chamber?"

"No, my lord," Vost said, pulling at his chin. "There would hardly have been room among the supports for the royal dais."

"We'll look again. Those things would be no use if they were easily found. Call a squad of soldiers, *my* soldiers, and have them begin breaking up the dais."

"My lord." Vost was instantly elsewhere.

The Protector stood and brushed off the knees of his breeches. "Excellent work, Steng," he said briefly. "Turn it off, now." He turned away into the night.

Steng felt a stab of jealous anger as the Protector walked away. He wanted to leap up, tug at the Protector's elbow, demanding recognition. He had worked so hard—done so much! He was furious for the space of a few breaths, and then it occurred to him that *this* was what Vost suffered continuously.

"Pitiable," Steng muttered. "He'd be better off dead." Absently he poured the contents of the oil jar into the central bulb of the Flagrator, extinguishing the flame guttering along the puckered strip of half-consumed metal. As the night's darkness swept in, like a tide covering an exposed shoal of light, the corpse gave a convulsive shudder and never moved again.

Urdhven heard the fighting before he came within sight of the dais. He drew his sword and ran through the enclosure arch. A single Legionary was counting up several of his own soldiers in the lists. Three lay among the shattered wood of the benches and another in the dust of the field. The King was nowhere in sight.

"Stand back, idiots!" he shouted. They parted ranks slightly, assuming (it seemed) that he only wished to be in on the kill. Furiously he leapt into the gap. Lorn was standing there, parrying the tentative sword flicks from the pack of soldiers. The Protector raised his sword and, lunging forward, caught Lorn's in a bind.

"Get back, you fools!" he shouted over his shoulder. "Search among the benches. Look for the King. Don't you see? He attacked you so that the King could escape. Find him. Capture him. *Now!*"

They stood back, somewhat startled, and slowly spread among the broken seats. Meanwhile Lorn made a furtive shift of stance, as if preparing to attack. Urdhven disengaged, leapt aside, and lunged, slashing a bloody line across Lorn's forehead as the Legionary belatedly parried. Lorn riposted, and again Urdhven caught his sword in a bind.

"Why did you betray me, Lorn?" the Protector wondered. "What could that witch give you that was worth your soldier's oath?"

Lorn spat with contempt. "The King has my oath. I never gave it to another."

"I command the empire's legions, Lorn. Your oath to the King is a legal fiction. You've chosen it above your duty and—Death and Justice!—you'll pay for it." Furiously he threw the Legionary back and lunged at his heart.

Lorn laughed a little breathlessly as he struck the Protector's blow aside. "I believe in the Strange Gods you only swear by, Lord Urdhven. They'll enforce the oath I kept and you broke."

The Protector advanced behind a businesslike network of head-cuts, thrusts, and ripostes. He was done with talking. Lorn backed away slowly, defending himself with skill. But he was no match for the Protector, and both of them knew it. He had backed now out of the enclosure's shadow into the bloodless light of the minor moons, Horseman and Trumpeter. Sweat glittered on his forehead, and blood was dripping from the wound there into his eyes.

Urdhven leapt forward and again caught Lorn's hilt with his. The moment he felt Lorn begin to pull away he shifted his footing and lashed out with one foot, kicking the unsuspecting Lorn's out from under him. The Legionary fell down, startled, on his right knee, gaping up at Urdhven, who methodically punched him in the throat with his empty left hand. Lorn choked and clumsily slashed out with his sword. Urdhven deftly beat it aside and smashed his knee up against Lorn's jaw. The bloody-faced soldier fell back in the dust and lay still.

Urdhven nodded. Now Lorn could be publicly executed, perhaps after torture—a fine example for any City Legionary tempted to take his oath too literally.

Looking up, the Protector saw a division of cavalry depart from the Dead Hills in some disorder, form up, and ride off toward the Old City Road. A lone horseman raced toward the enclosure, undoubtedly a messenger. All this could only mean the Ambrosii had been taken and slain; the cavalry commander would never have called off the search so soon, otherwise. Excellent—Urdhven had been hoping to make that insolent dwarf suffer in some degree before his death, but that was a small matter, in every sense. Things were going well.

A brief chorus of shouts sprang up outside the enclosure and as suddenly died down. The sound of marching feet rang out, and a tight formation of soldiers entered through the enclosure arch. At their center was Steng; his ropy boneless fingers clutched the shoulders of a young boy with a filthy face and frightened darting eyes: the King.

The Protector stayed where he was, assessing the situation. Steng's expression was all gleeful pride, while the soldiers wore masks of stern fury. Steng had made the capture, then, and had fought with the soldiers over who would bring the Protector his prize. That was good. Urdhven had made a life study of the art of breaking a man's spirit, and he guessed that Steng was two-thirds his property now.

As for the King . . . yes, the story could be that he had been kidnapped by Lorn's cabal of rebellious soldiers. When set upon by the Protector's Men, they had slain their captive in panic. The Protector's Men had overcome the Legionaries, and these would be executed for treason and regicide. (Urdhven knew of a company of soldiers he could easily sacrifice for this piece of political theater: Lorn's.) It would be an excellent pretext for a loyalty inquisition among the City Legion. Or perhaps abolishing them altogether—it was awkward to have so large a body of troops in the capital not under his personal control.

"My Lord Urdhven!" came a cry behind him. In his reverie he had forgotten the cavalry messenger. He turned and crossed to the bar where the messenger, still in the saddle, was waiting.

"Sir!" the messenger said. "War-Leader Kyric reports that he has fallen back and is re-forming his troops along the Old City Road. He has sent to the city for a company of bowmen."

Urdhven looked sharply at the messenger's face, streaming with sweat in the chill moonslit air. His voice had been tolerably steady, but there was no mistaking his fear.

"Lancer," said the Lord Protector harshly, "I sent your wing to capture or kill three refugees, only one of whom was armed and mounted, and one of whom was crippled. The third was a dwarf. Are you saying you met *armed* resistance?"

The Protector's Men and Steng had come up, with the King in tow. Urd-hven could hear them muttering behind him. Had he foreseen the nature of this interview he would have sent them to wait some distance away. Now it was too late: he judged that it would be worse to send them away than let them hear the rest of the bad news. Foot soldier morale would not be too heavily affected by a cavalry blunder, Urdhven judged—he took care to encourage rivalries among his own troops. (And Steng, of course, viewed all soldiers with contempt.)

"My lord," said the messenger, a note of pleading in his voice, "they used magic. The . . . the attack came when we were scattered. There was nothing we could do!"

"From which I deduce that you did nothing. I'll have Kyric twisted for this—"

"My lord—"

"None of that. In what form did this 'attack' come?"

The messenger did not answer immediately. In the silence they heard a faint but definite sound. It was something like a fierce inhuman scream, heard from afar. Urdhven automatically took a step back toward his men. He glanced about, trying to locate the source of the scream. His concentration was broken by the sound of hoofbeats: he looked up to see the back of the messenger as he rode off.

Urdhven paused to promise himself that Kyric and his messenger would twist side by side, then turned to his soldiers.

Their faces were expressionless; their hands were steady. No doubt their voices would be, if he required them to speak. But he knew these men: they were terrified. Moments before they had moved and stood with easy arrogance; now they were stiff, their shoulders set.

He knew the stories they were remembering, legends accumulated over the centuries, in which the sorcerous powers of the Ambrosii were constantly invoked to protect or avenge their kinsmen of the imperial line. Urdhven was convinced that most of them were lies, fomented by the Imperial House for its own protection. He knew that many of them were slander, spread by people like himself, who had tried to undermine the popularity of some emperor by associating him with monstrously distorted rumors of Ambrosia, Morlock, or even Merlin. Now Urdhven understood why all those attempts (including his own) had been failures. The more the dangers of the Ambrosii were exaggerated, the more fearful a weapon the Imperial House had in them. Urdhven promised himself he would not forget that lesson, if he lived.

If he lived? It was only when that phrase came into Urdhven's mind that he knew how deeply fear had infected him. And in that instant he heard the scream again.

It was nearer now, and louder. It raised horrible indistinct pictures in Urdhven's mind. It sounded fierce, pitiless, triumphant, inhuman. Urdhven could not keep from his mind the knowledge that Morlock had first appeared from the direction of the Old City, and that the three had retreated the same way. Urdhven had special reason to fear that place. Was the scream coming from some monster of the Old City that Morlock had befriended or controlled? Was it a demon summoned from yet farther away? Why had they waited until nightfall? Was their dreadful ally some ghoulish creature that could walk only by night?

"Draw your swords," Urdhven said aloud, coolly. "Form a ring around the King and Steng."

The soldiers performed the maneuver instantly, seemingly relieved to be taking any positive action. Urdhven was racking his brains to think of something more for them to do when he saw a furtive shape flit across the pockmarked face of the second moon, Horseman. Instantly he realized why the scream had been so difficult to locate: it was coming from the sky! Urdhven thought he could trace the progress of the flying figure as it briefly occulted stars. He could not discern its shape, but it was certainly getting closer. From the sound of the repeated horrifying scream he guessed that the creature was flying straight at them.

"Ready, men!" he called out. "It's coming from the east, and in the air. When it appears, *strike*: for your lives and for the empire!"

A dreadful silence swallowed this remark, for the screaming had halted again. Then three voices rang out from the dark sky, singing an awful cacophony of nonsense syllables.

"The Ambrosii!" The Protector heard one of his men whispering. "They come for their own!"

Then the enemy was upon them.

CHAPTER SIX

OUT OF THE DEAD HILLS

round sunset Wyrtheorn had been saying, "But won't the horseshoes catch fire? We've imbued them with many times their natural quantity of phlogiston."

Morlock, hanging upside down from Velox's saddle, finished imbuing the front left horseshoe with phlogiston. Then he observed, "The shoes may catch on fire, I suppose, if we ride across a field of stones, or a paved road. But I put an aethrium plate under each shoe; Velox should feel no pain."

"What about the nails? Wait a minute—they're not—"

"Aethrium spikes. Yes."

"*Hurs krakna.* Your Velox is the most expensive horse alive."

"It's worth it if it saves our lives," Ambrosia, sitting in the saddle, pointed out. "Morlock, we are maybe twenty feet in the air."

"Are we headed up or down?"

"A moment. Down, I think. Slowly."

"Just as well," Morlock muttered.

"Don't mutter," his sister directed. "What are you saying?"

"Morlock not mutter?" muttered Wyrtheorn. "Shall the dew not glisten? Shall the sun not rise in the west? And a diamond not be harder than a duck-sapphire?"

"What are you saying, Wyrtheorn?"

"I am muttering," the dwarf said distinctly.

"We're done," Morlock said matter-of-factly. "Watch your seat, Ambrosia. I'm coming up."

Morlock shook out the aethrium box in his hand; the phlogiston rushed out in a vaporous glowing cloud that dispersed even as it flooded upward. Then he let the box fall to the ground. Behind and below her Ambrosia heard Wyrtheorn give a sigh of exasperation. "The waste!" he exclaimed.

"You're too thrifty, Wyrth," Morlock said. "The stuff's as precious as it is useful, no more. We can gather more if we need it."

A hiss, a glowing cloud over her shoulder, and a thump on the ground below told Ambrosia that Wyrtheorn too had emptied his aethrium box and dropped it. By then Morlock was carefully clambering up the side of the floating horse. It was a ticklish business (for Ambrosia, with her broken hands, could not help) and they had descended almost halfway to the ground before he was upright on Velox's back in front of Ambrosia. Then he threw down a knotted cord and pulled Wyrtheorn up more swiftly. This was as well, because by that time they were beginning to fall more rapidly.

"Morlock," Ambrosia began, hardly knowing what she would say.

"Don't worry," he replied instantly. "Our weight just barely overrides the unweight of the phlogiston. We fall swiftly, perhaps, but will not strike heavily. However . . ."

"Yes?" said Wyrtheorn. "Don't keep us waiting, Master Morlock."

"We are somewhat top-heavy, I expect. We should be careful not to over-balance while in the air."

"Hear that, Wyrtheorn?" Ambrosia said lightly. "None of your riding tricks, then." He was already gripping her arms from behind with painful intentness.

Wyrth laughed, and his grip eased somewhat. "Lady Ambrosia, I promise to behave."

They struck the ground. The impact was less than if they had leapt a fence. And they immediately found themselves flying upward and forward at a sharp angle.

They all breathed deeply in relief. Wyrth's grip relaxed entirely. He said, "If—"

The horse screamed.

The sound was blood-freezing. Ambrosia felt Velox beneath her laboring with the effort of the scream. It was desperate and prolonged, expressing the last extremity of some dreadfully intense feeling—fear, or physical agony, she guessed. Behind her, through the last whistling rasp of the horse's scream, the harsh clear syllables of Dwarvish: Wyrth's expression of surprise and alarm, perhaps pity.

"I never thought!" Morlock said bitterly. "He's an old warhorse that had been through many a battle and single combat. I bought him from a castellan of the northern marches. I was only concerned about the trial at arms. I didn't think he'd be afraid of flying. . . ."

Wyrth, after his first shocked exclamation, fell silent. Ambrosia decided that she, too, would be silent. She understood the pain and horror her brother and his apprentice must be feeling. To an extent she shared it. But Ambrosia was not a softhearted woman; she had never had that luxury. To preserve her own life, for the chance of helping her descendant Lathmar, for the sake of the empire she had fostered, she would ride a thousand suffering beasts like Velox to their deaths. What was necessary she would do. But she realized that Morlock and Wyrth felt differently, and she would say nothing that might lead them to act on that feeling.

They were descending again to the ground. The horse, still shuddering, drew up all his legs at once in a very unequine manner.

"Terrified it is, *rokh tashna*," Wyrtheorn guessed. "It may tumble us this time, Ambrosii. Get ready to jump."

But there was no need. At the last moment Velox swung down all four legs in a driving motion that sent them plunging forward in a long flat arc.

"He can't be in pain," Morlock said in a troubled voice. "And—" His voice was drowned out as Velox gave another heart-shaking scream.

Suddenly it occurred to Ambrosia that it was not a scream of terror at all. She laughed. "This is all your fault, Morlock."

He turned his head and looked at her over his shoulder—a swift luminously gray glance that said everything. Yes, he too understood.

"What are you saying, Lady Ambrosia?" the dwarf asked.

"We've misunderstood, you see," she said, over her own shoulder (as crooked as Morlock's). "Velox is not frightened, or in pain. Consider that he grew up and passed his prime in stables and paddocks, trotting in companies, living for the mad rush of a tournament day or a cavalry charge . . ."

"I begin to see."

"Yes, I think we all do. Velox is not afraid. He is in heaven. At something past middle age for a warhorse, Morlock has taught him to fly."

They came down to the ground again, and Velox brought all his hooves down in a stamping movement that plunged them straight into the dim blue evening air. Ambrosia's toes curled painfully inside her shoes, and her heart raced with apprehension and delight as the dark earth sank away.

Wyrtheorn laughed. Velox screamed. Morlock muttered.

"Don't mutter!" Ambrosia shouted.

Morlock held out his left hand and pointed. Glancing in that direction, Ambrosia saw light glinting off the dark forms of armed riders gathering below the crest of a nearby hill.

"They've found us, then," Wyrth said. "Ah, well. We should have no trouble escaping them on a flying horse."

"Escape?" Morlock said, his voice doubtful. His crooked shoulders twisted in a shrug. "Maybe."

Ambrosia was about to laugh at his pessimism when a certain thought occurred to her. She decided to hold her tongue. Morlock knew the horse better than she did.

One of the armed riders below sounded a horn call. Velox's head snapped in that direction, and Ambrosia saw the charger's nostrils flare with anger and delight. With a serpentine movement the warhorse swung himself about in midair so that his head faced the imperial horse soldiers.

This maneuver nearly unseated Ambrosia. Because she could not grip with her shattered hands, she reached forward and hooked her forearms around her brother's midriff.

"With your permission, brother," she said, resting her chin on his left and lower shoulder.

Morlock grunted.

"We're not going to make it, are we?" she said into his ear. "Velox won't retreat."

"Do they have bowmen?" was his unexpected reply.

"I don't think so," she said. "Bowmen are infantry."

"Bad tactics," he observed.

"Shut up."

"We'll make it."

"We won't!"

"You'll see."

They struck the ground and rebounded, leaping over the crown of the hill where the imperial riders were gathering. Velox's scream broke through a storm of horn calls. Ambrosia felt Wyrth's hands tighten reflexively on her arms. Morlock suddenly shouted, a refrain of nonsense syllables carried on a deep-throated roar. When they struck the ground in the center of where the cavalry group had been, there was nothing there but dead hillside and some clouds of dust. Ambrosia could hear the hoofbeats of the imperial riders departing in various directions through the dusk.

"What was that spell?" Ambrosia demanded as they sprang up toward the first stars of evening.

Morlock cleared his throat, seemingly embarrassed.

"An Anhikh cattle call, I believe," Wyrtheorn observed.

"We'll have Wyrth shout next time—," Morlock began.

"Cattle call? Next time?" Ambrosia felt the conversation was getting away from her.

"It might be anything," Morlock explained. "So long as they believe dire Ambrosian magic is being worked on them."

"It won't keep working, Morlock," Ambrosia said. "These are imperial soldiers."

"Oh, I think you underrate your reputations, Lady Ambrosia," the dwarf disagreed cheerfully. "Some of the stories I heard about you in the Great Market were enough to make one swear off sausages."

"Sausages?"

"You haven't heard that one? Well, never mind. The point is, these soldiers are quite prepared to see Ambrosii exact a dreadful revenge by means of dreadful magic. They have their heads crammed full of such stories from the time they're born. And here we have a flying horse screaming horribly as it hurls through the darkness while on its back a three-headed silhouette chants ominous but unintelligible words—oh, yes, they'll run like rabbits."

"But a whole cavalry wing . . ."

"The more do run, the more will run," Morlock said flatly. "Our chief danger is that Velox will break a leg, or overturn in his enthusiasm. I think as it gets darker we will even be safe from bowmen."

"They won't have bowmen."

Morlock shrugged.

"Shut up!" Ambrosia insisted.

Velox spotted another group of horsemen deeper in the hills. Snorting, he lowered his head and—as they fell toward the ground—struck off with all four hooves, bounding toward the hapless enemy.

After dispersing the greater part of the cavalry wing, Velox seemed to grow restless, and even a little bored. At that time, well after full night had risen into the sky, Morlock managed to persuade the charger to direct his bounds toward the smudge of light on the western horizon that was the imperial city.

"That was rather easy," said Wyrtheorn suspiciously.

"New horizons," Ambrosia speculated. "Think of all the traffic he can disrupt in the city. What do you say, Morlock?"

Morlock grunted. From Ambrosia's viewpoint his expression looked even more saturnine than usual.

"I see what you mean," said Wyrtheorn reflectively. "I hadn't thought of that."

Ambrosia held her silence through two more long leaps. Not even Velox screamed. The lifeless hills below issued no noises into the night air; the only sound was the chill persistent sea breeze, whispering over the dead lands toward the south.

Eyeing the western horizon she said finally, "We're not headed directly for the city, are we?"

"Gravesend Field, I think," said her brother, in a burst of volubility.

Ambrosia grunted.

It became obvious as they left the Dead Hills behind them (a ragged shadow on the moonslit eastern horizon) that Morlock's guess was correct. Velox's leaps over the plain separating them from Gravesend were the long low ones that covered the most ground in the least time, and he had resumed his enthusiastic screaming.

"You know what it is," the dwarf said, in a speculative tone of voice.

"Say it," Ambrosia replied.

"He's not satisfied with the outcome of the joust. You saw how Morlock got knocked right off his back. Maybe that's a point of pride with warhorses."

"My fault," Morlock said matter-of-factly. "I never was a great spearman. You may be right, though."

"Is your warhorse wounded by self-doubt? Your palfrey pained with an inexplicable distress? Your charger changeable in his moods? Consult Brother Wyrth, ministering to the emotional needs of the equine even now in yonder booth!"

Morlock grunted.

"Well, it might pay better than being your apprentice."

"Anything would. I suppose Urdhven and his soldiers will have left Gravesend by now."

Ambrosia resisted the temptation to grunt enigmatically. "Think again, brother. Note yon trail of dust the sea breeze is carrying south."

"Um. Well observed."

The trail of dust was now somewhat distorted by the wind, but clearly its trail began in the Dead Hills and led toward the edge of Gravesend Field, the anchor building now visible, black against the night-blue western sky.

"A messenger?" Wyrth guessed. "From the cavalry war-leader to Urdhven."

Ambrosia laughed aloud. "What would you give, Wyrtheorn, to hear the delicate phrasing of that message? 'You see, Your Worship, there was this horse . . .'"

"Ah, Lady Ambrosia, what wouldn't I give? An aethrium spike for each of Urdhven's lordly earlobes. A bowl of chicken blood for his slightly shop-worn golem. A stirrup-cup of phlogiston to lend, shall we say, a mellow glow to his last and longest ride—"

"Morlock!" Ambrosia shouted. "What are you doing?"

Her brother had leaned forward abruptly and was speaking in a low voice to Velox. In the silence following her cry, Morlock's brisk lilting syllables rang clear.

"Westhold dialect, isn't it, Lady Ambrosia?" Wyrth remarked. "I never could follow it, but I'm not the horsey sort."

"Oh, Wyrth, you're lying to me again."

"No, really. But I guess Morlock is putting the finger (or the hoof?) on our Lord Protector. That must be him standing there, at the edge of the lists. . . ."

They struck the ground; Velox pushed off with something like deliberation, changing their direction slightly, putting them in a short high leap. Velox screamed again, the cry of battle. They would next strike the ground within Gravesend Field.

Had Velox not been screaming Ambrosia would have pounded on Morlock's crooked shoulders and demanded an explanation. She would have advocated the course of prudence, deliberation, and the better part of valor.

Uselessly! After all, she realized, that rug had already been pulled out from under their feet. It was too late to think of caution when you had spent the early evening chasing cavalry detachments through the hills on the back of a battle-mad, laughing, middle-aged flying horse. Wasn't it?

Morlock looked back over his crooked shoulder and gave a crooked grin. Then, turning, he threw back his head (nearly braining her) and began to chant loudly in Dwarvish. Wyrth joined in at the third syllable. Ambrosia herself recognized the song, though she did not know Dwarvish well. It was perhaps the most common "Praising of Day," sung each day at dawn by the dwarvish clans of Thrymhaiam. She didn't know the words, but she wordlessly lent her own cracking voice to the simple tune.

> *Heolor charn vehernam choran harwellanclef;*
>   *wull wyrma daelu herial hatathclef;*
> *feng fernanclef modblind vemarthal morwe;*
>   *Rokh Rokhlanclef hull veheoloral morwe.*
> *Dal sar drangan an immryrend ek atlam,*
>   *dal sar deoran an kyrrend knylloram—**

So singing, they returned to Gravesend Field.

---

*Blindly Death takes hold of the timid and the brave;
    vermin devour the evil and good alike;
Maker and miner sleep in the same silence;
    dragon and dragonkiller fall under the same fell.
There is one darkness that ends all dreaming,
    one light in which all living will awake—

When the horse and its three singing riders fell out of the dark sky, the King instantly ceased to disbelieve in all the outlandish stories that he had heard about his ancient Ambrosian kin. They might not all be true. But for every false one there would be an even more unlikely tale that *was* true.

He had time to think this. He had time, open-mouthed, to watch the Lord Protector roll in the dust to keep from being brained by one of the descending horse's hooves. Then he squawked and rolled in the dust himself for the same reason.

The horse's right rear hoof struck the ground not an arm's length from the King's head. Something between the hoof and the ground glowed like molten glass. He glanced up as the hoof left the ground, and he met the eye of his Grandmother, seated between her brother and the dwarf Wyrtheorn. The King's Grandmother waved cheerily at him (her hand was all bound up with cloth) and shouted something he couldn't hear.

The King wondered if he was dreaming. The horse and its riders were gone, and he was left behind in a cloud of dust.

Then a soldier seized him by the ankles and hurled him like a sack over his shoulder. What breath the King had was knocked out of him. He lay unresisting with his head against the soldier's back, watching the man's boots flicker in and out of sight as he ran desperately into the night. Clearing the lists in a single amazing bound, he circled around the field to lose himself in the myriad graves of Ontil. He didn't pause from running for a long time— more than long enough for the King to regain his breath and his wits. When the soldier, gasping painfully, slowed to a halt in the shadow of a mausoleum, the King was not surprised by the voice that spoke to him.

"Think we'll be . . . all right here . . . Your Majesty," Lorn gasped. "For a bit . . . begging your pardon . . . Majesty . . . set you on your feet—"

"Never mind, Lorn," the King said quickly. "Just let me go and I'll roll off."

But Lorn lifted the King carefully back over his shoulder and put him down on the ground. Then the Legionary leaned back against the tomb and gasped helplessly. In a few moments these exertions subsided and Lorn was able to speak again.

"Beg your pardon, Your Majesty," said Lorn. "It's been a night-and-a-flipping-half for me."

"Please, Lorn," said the King. "I'm just glad we're both alive. When I saw you lying on the field I was sure Urdhven had killed you."

The shadow that was Lorn nodded sharply, and the King could hear the smile in his voice when he spoke. "The Protector knocked me down in the fight; I thought it best to let him think he'd knocked me out. I'm not half the swordsman he is."

"But ten times the tactician, Lorn."

"Ssh, Your Majesty," Lorn replied, sounding pleased. "My old dad taught me that trick, and maybe half a dozen others. I'm not one for these great prancings and politickings. But I know where my duty lies, Your Majesty."

Silence fell. The word "duty" had an unpleasant effect on the King. He realized their escape was only temporary, that Lorn intended them to return to the city, with its prancings and politickings. He'd half hoped the loyal soldier would recommend a flight into the Empire, or even beyond it. But he hadn't the courage to suggest it himself. "What should we do now?" he asked.

"Well, Your Majesty," said Lorn, intent on the problem. "There's a band of soldiers at Upriver Gate I think we can trust to let us into the city. Once there . . ."

The King sighed.

"Scattered like rats," Ambrosia said reflectively, as they flew over the anchor building. "The army's not what it was."

"It's the weird," Morlock replied. "The weird is always terrifying."

"Particularly when it comes out of the Dead Hills after dark," Wyrth observed. "I think he's right, Lady Ambrosia. If we'd merely been a military force of superior strength, those soldiers would have fought like madmen."

"It's still a weakness," Ambrosia insisted. "In the old days it never would have happened. You remember, Morlock."

Her brother grunted concessively, and there was silence for a time as the horse made long ground-spurning bounds. The bright cloud of the city grew visibly nearer, over the chaos of tombs.

"You know," Wyrth said presently, "I hate to say this . . . but I think we're going to have to abandon horse."

"Yes," Morlock agreed reluctantly. "He's not responding to the bridle. We can't ride him till he tires out."

Ambrosia, who had come to that conclusion some time ago, said, "Let's wait a bit, though. The tombs thin out in the hills, just under the city's walls—it's supposed to be bad luck to bury people there. There'll be less chance of bashing out our brains on a grave marker."

"We should leap just after Velox lands and jumps off again," Morlock remarked thoughtfully. "Momentum. We'll hit the ground at a slower speed."

Wyrtheorn said something in Dwarvish, and Morlock replied, "No. I don't think so." Ambrosia began to ask a question, then realized she didn't want to know.

Velox landed atop a mausoleum and kicked off again. The city grew visibly nearer.

Wyrth began to unbuckle Morlock's pack, which was strapped behind the saddle, and called forward to Morlock, "I'll drop this off just before we jump, shall I?"

"Some time before," Morlock corrected. "You must not miss the moment."

"You don't want your tools damaged."

"You're more important, Wyrtheorn," Morlock said dispassionately.

"Soon, now," Ambrosia said, to break up this display of sentiment. "There are no graves beneath us anymore." Velox landed on soft grass and leapt up into the sky.

"Yes," Morlock said. "The next leap will take us too close to the city walls. Drop the pack now, Wyrth."

A thump from below announced the pack's arrival below and behind them.

"Just after the next landing," Morlock said. "And when you jump, clear well away from the horse."

"Why?" Ambrosia asked suspiciously.

There was a pause as Morlock obviously gauged whether there was time enough for an explanation. "You'll see," was all he said, in the end.

"Hmph!"

The city rose like the ragged edge of a dense field of stars over the last remaining hill. Then, as they descended, it was occulted by the hill again. The charger fell downward; his hooves struck the ground.

The three riders left the horse at practically the same moment, Morlock and Wyrtheorn leaping off the left side and Ambrosia off the right. She was chiefly intent on landing on her shoulder, to spare her hands and wrists, but she couldn't help but be aware that as they left the horse, he plunged straight up as if an invisible hand were drawing him into the sky. He screamed delightedly, and it occurred to Ambrosia that without his riders as counter-weights, the phlogiston in his shoes would lift him even farther.

Then she struck the ground, on her shoulder indeed, but the jar sent bolts of pain shooting to the tip of each broken finger. She rolled downhill a ways before she managed to slide to a halt. Above her she heard the contin-uous scream of the warhorse fade away as he fell upward into the endless abyss of the star-thick sky.

How far would he go? she wondered. Would he reach the paths of the moons and the sun?

Silence settled over the hillside. Ambrosia, as her pain and wonder faded, became conscious of two breathing heaps slightly farther down the slope.

"Morlock!" she said.

The larger of the two heaps grunted.

"I'm never going to have you rescue me again."

After a pause Morlock said reflectively, "It was worth it, then." The silence persisted through another brief pause, until a faint snoring announced that Morlock had fallen asleep.

Part Two

Prisoners of Ambrose

Lo, here may a man prove, be he never so good yet he may have a fall, and he was never so wise but he might be overseen, and he rideth well that never fell.

—Malory, *Le Morte D'Arthur*

Chapter Seven

Genjandro's Ware

One day Lorn returned to their room in the city with what the King had learned to think of as his "bad news" expression. The first time the King had seen it was almost half a year before, perhaps ten days after their escape from Gravesend Field. The city Water Wheel, where Lorn did the day-labor that paid for their food and lodgings, was closed for repairs. They lived from hand to mouth, with no savings, and that meant there was no supper that night, nor the next either. On the third day the wheel reopened, and they gorged that night on fresh wheat bread, slices of roast meat, and cheese. It had been wonderful, worth the fast. But that first day! Lorn had taken forever to break the news to his King, afraid the fragile boy would collapse in hysterics at the thought of hunger. But the King had often gone without meals for days at a time, for fear of poison, and as it happened he handled the fast better than Lorn (who was used to regular fare and plenty of it at his legion's refectory). And it would always be that way with Lorn's "bad news." The badness was mostly in Lorn's own mind.

So as soon as he saw the renegade Legionary, the King smiled and said, "Out with it Lorn. It can't be so bad."

Lorn smiled tentatively—as usual—and said, "Well, Your Majesty . . . no supper tonight, I'm afraid."

"We've still got salt beef and flatbread from last night," the King replied. He always laid a little by, now.

"Pretty dry, they were," Lorn said wryly. "They'll be drier tonight. I forgot to bring up water, too."

"Lorn," the King said patiently, "what is it? Was the wheel closed again?"

"No, Your Majesty. I worked and was paid." He paused, then blurted out, "I spent the wages."

"Oh?" The King was surprised and a little embarrassed. This seemed very unlike Lorn.

"Yes, Your Majesty. I . . . I bought something."

"Well, it's not important."

"But it is, Your Majesty. I think it might be very important."

He had it in his hand, now—a linen bag about twice as long as one of his thumbs. There was something inside it. He reached it and took it out: a beautifully detailed model of a crow.

"Lorn—it's dwarvish!" the King said, not meaning the adjective literally. (It was a general term of praise.) "It must be unique."

"Dwarvish it just might be," Lorn replied, "but—with respect, Your Majesty—unique it's not. Why, I've seen dozens of these things around the city in the last few calls.* Old Genjandro by the market has been selling them like loaves of bread. But I never heard one speak until today. When I did . . . I had to buy one. Got it from some peddler in an alleyway."

"Heard one?"

Lorn, by way of answer, carefully put the crow figure down on the table in the center of the room. After a moment, it flapped its wings twice and croaked a few syllables. The King started in surprise and said, "How does it do it? Is it alive?"

"I don't know, Your Majesty. But—your courtesy—please listen."

The bird flapped its wings and croaked. There was a pause of perhaps two heartbeats, and it did so again, but the croaked syllables were different.

"Your Majesty," said Lorn, "my mother's parents were Coranians. I've never told anyone that, but it's true. They kept to the old ways, and every day

---

*A "call" is one half-period of the moon Trumpeter, or 7.5 days. See appendix C.

they spoke at least three hundred words in . . . in that language of theirs. The one from the Wardlands."

Lorn paused, and in the interval of silence the crow figure croaked again.

"Lorn!" the King cried. "You're right! It's the secret speech!"

The soldier winced at the King's bluntness, but nodded. "I only know a few words. But I know you've been taught more."

The King raised a hand for silence. In truth, the recent political upheavals had played havoc with his lessons. (His language tutor had been an early victim of the Protector's purge.) But the message was simple, clear, and apparently meaningless.

"It says, *vengeret pel*, and then, *ostin shae*," the King reported finally. "That should mean: there is light under the wings. Or maybe: there is hope among the feathers. I don't really—"

"But it's obvious, you'll forgive my saying so, Your Majesty," Lorn said. He picked up the crow and turned it upside down. Under the left wing there was a design etched into the metal of the figure. Instinctively he rubbed at it with his thumb. Now the etching blazed out gold against the ebony metal of the figure: a bright hawk in flight over a branch of shining thorns.

"The crest of Ambrosius!" exclaimed the King.

Suddenly the crow took flight. It spun one swift circle around the King's head and plunged toward the window. It burst through the slats of the closed shutter and was gone in the night.

For the next few moments they were both speechless. But neither needed speech to understand the signs: the symbol only Merlin or his children would dare to use, magic, a crow . . .

"Merlin's children," said the King finally. "My Grandmother. It's not just the Protector after me. They're trying to find me, too!"

"I'm afraid so, Your Majesty," said Lorn. He was wearing his "bad news" expression again.

That same evening a similar conversation took place in the palace called Ambrose.

"It's quite simple, Lord Urdhven," the Protector was told by his poisoner. "Turn the crow upside down. Spread its left wing. See the design? Rub off the enamel; yes. Now it comes clear."

"I recognize it," the Protector said with distaste. "It's the crest of those crook-backed bastards."

"More precisely: the crest of the Ambrosii."

The black crow figure shot out of the Protector's hand, flew a tight circle around the poisoner's head, and departed out the nearest window into the dark of early evening.

"Where is it going?" the Protector demanded, his voice level.

"They all go to the same place, Lord Urdhven, which is the same place they all come from: Genjandro's shop, adjoining the Great Market."

"Who is this Genjandro?"

"An Ambrosian sympathizer, apparently. He was one of the thousand invited to Ambrosia's trial."

The Protector's face darkened at the mention of that fiasco.

"Genjandro, since then, has been selling these toys for practically nothing, in lots of a dozen. There are hundreds in the city as we speak."

"How do they work?"

Steng actually laughed. "Death and Justice! I don't know. There aren't ten people alive who do, I expect. But their purpose is clear enough: the Ambrosii are trying to make contact with the King and his supporters in the city."

"That must *not* happen." The Protector pondered the problem briefly. "If the Ambrosii are not at the shop, they have an agent there. I'll send a troop of soldiers to the place. Anyone present will be taken and put to the question. You'll ask the questions, Steng."

"A wise plan, my lord," said Steng with satisfaction. He rather enjoyed questioning prisoners; he'd learned a good deal about people by watching them under torture.

"You've done well, Steng."

"Thank you, Lord Urdhven."

"But never mention that business at Gravesend Field again. I won't have it."

"Yes, Lord Protector," said the poisoner humbly. His interest in torture didn't extend to undergoing it himself.

"One of your crows has come back, Morlock."

"Give it some grain and ask what it's heard."

"Not a real crow. One of the little machines you and Wyrtheorn made."

Wyrtheorn and Morlock were making toys in the back of Genjandro's shop. But at this news they downed tools and went into the front.

Genjandro and Ambrosia were standing on opposite sides of the counter with the gleaming black crow figure between them.

"The wing?" Morlock asked.

"The paint's been rubbed off the crest," Ambrosia told him. "A single swipe by a thumb considerably larger than Lathmar's."

"Well observed," Morlock conceded, looking for himself.

"Canyon keep her observations," Wyrtheorn swore. "That just means another false trail. Or a trap."

"Probably," Morlock agreed. "Still: it might be Lorn. Find one, find the other."

Ambrosia was dismantling the crow with the swift skill of long practice. At the figure's heart was a flame in a crystal box. The flame, burning parallel to the ground, was pointed north and west toward the city's poorer quarter . . . or to Ambrose on the city's northwest edge, or perhaps the open country beyond that.

The flame had been kindled when someone voiced recognition of the Ambrosian crest on the underside of the crow's wing, and it would direct itself continually toward that spot where the recognition had been voiced. Of the hundreds of mechanical crows Morlock and his apprentice had tirelessly constructed at a feverish pace in the seven months after Ambrosia's trial and the King's disappearance, perhaps three dozen had returned to Genjandro's shop. All of these had been activated by unregenerate Coranians, or perhaps by accident. But their startling behavior had stimulated the most extraordinary rumors in the city, and had directed unwelcome attention toward their source, Genjandro. He had stopped selling the crows some time ago, but all four expected at any time a visit from the Protector's Men. It was this expectation that sparked Wyrth's next suggestion.

"Let's get the hell out of here."

"I can't get out," Genjandro observed mildly.

"You can. We can set you up in a new place with ten times the stock. Tell him, Morlock."

"We don't lack money," Morlock conceded. "But we must follow the trail, Wyrtheorn."

"The trail is following us, Morlock. I tell you I don't like it. Trust me; the Protector's Men come calling tonight."

"One of us must go," Ambrosia stated. "But at least one of us must stay."

Morlock nodded. "They may come here. The shop has become unpleasantly notorious."

"Let one go," Genjandro suggested. "The rest of us will wait here. All will share the risk. When the quester returns, we will consult our common interest."

"Well said," Ambrosia approved. Morlock nodded. Wyrtheorn issued a crackling Dwarvish polysyllable, but did not seem to disagree.

"Then," Genjandro said, bringing forth a worn brassy slug from an inner pocket, "will the Lady Ambrosia make the call? Face or shield?" And he spun the coin toward the rafters.

The King was alone. It had taken an unthinkably long time, but he had finally persuaded Lorn to go to Genjandro's shop.

"We're well enough off," Lorn had kept saying stubbornly. "We don't need those damned Ambrosii."

"Lorn," the King reminded him, "I'm an Ambrosius."

"You're likewise heir to Uthar the Great!" Lorn insisted. "Your father would have been ten times the Emperor he was if your honored ancestress had let him learn to wipe his own nose when the snot ran out."

"Lorn!"

"Your Majesty, it's truth and time someone spoke it. Your dad spent half his life being nursemaided by Lady Ambrosia and the rest of it being led around by his wife and his wife's brother. That's why the empire is in the hole it's in today. Urdhven's a traitor and a kinslayer; there's no forgiving that. But it's also true he was tempted too far. Your Majesty, no one but the Emperor should get that close to the throne."

"I'm not the Emperor!" the King shouted. "There is no Emperor!" *I don't want to be Emperor!* he longed to add. *To hell with the empire!*

"If Your Majesty would be a little more quiet—these walls are not made of marble, nor masonry either."

"Then any listener has already heard too much," the King said, but more calmly (and quietly). He wanted to throw himself at this stupid soldier and scream *Bring me my Grandmother!* But he owed this stupid soldier his life, over and over. Besides, hysteria would convince Lorn of nothing. And he was not stupid. He was *not* stupid. But he wasn't seeing things as they were, either.

"Lorn," said the King, "what can we do by ourselves? Nothing, which is exactly what we've been doing. We'll sit here in this room or another like it, eating salt beef and stale biscuits until someone recognizes one of us and betrays us both."

"Your Majesty, the soldiers—"

"What can they do?" the King interrupted. "You yourself told me my uncle is killing them whenever they say a word he doesn't like. Their officers are all with the Protector. As we sit here, I might as well be dead and buried to them."

"The people—"

"Lorn, in the name of—of Fate, don't you see what I've said for the soldiers goes double for the people?"

"If we have time we can work something out," Lorn said stubbornly.

The King suppressed an impulse to tear at his hair. "Lorn," he said finally, "I'll always welcome your advice. How could I not? Your wisdom and courage are all that's kept me alive these past seven months. But the choice is mine to make. Lorn, I *order* you to go."

The soldier glared mutinously at him for a long, tense moment. Then his glance dropped, and the King knew he had won. Lorn armed himself and left a few moments later without saying a word. The King heard him cursing incoherently as he descended the stairs outside.

Now the King had been alone for hours and it was long after dark. He was restless and bored and tense all at once. He had waited many days for nothing at all, in this same room, with nothing to do but exercise and stare at the wall. Somehow it was harder to do now, for a shorter time and with a greater expectation.

That was what led him to the windows. Lorn had told him never to open them at any time. But it was after dark, and soon they would be leaving here forever. And he was bored.

He opened the window shutters and peered out. Dull as it might seem to some, the city street at night was a world of adventure to him. He had been shut in every day since their escape from the Protector; in a sense he had been shut in his whole life.

The street was a channel of darkness below. There were no streetlamps and no traffic. The only light came from lit and open windows; there were few of these and none of them were on the ground level. He stared, fascinated, into the shadows, hoping to catch a glimpse of some passerby. But if there were any passersby, he couldn't see them.

There was someone down in the street, though, sitting at the front of a cart with its load covered by canvas. At least the King thought there was someone there: the figure was motionless and heavily cloaked; the street was dark. . . . He couldn't be sure.

Suddenly a window lit up just above the cart; light fell red upon the seated figure. The King saw, too, a dense uneven fringe of splayed stiff fingers lining the edge of the cart, thrusting out from under the canvas.

It was a death cart. The figure seated in front was a Companion of Mercy. The King goggled a bit at the red robes, mask, gloves—he had rarely seen these figures belonging to the city's night.

The Companion still hadn't moved. His (?) back was to the light, and shadow fell across the masked face. The King wondered if he had been struck dead by one of the hundred illnesses that killed without ceasing in the poorer quarters of the city. But alive or dead the Companion did not move.

Presently gentle hoofbeats approached from farther up the street; they could only be heard because all else was so quiet. Another death cart appeared, two red-clad Companions seated within it. The King wondered that the cart moved so stealthily, then realized that the wheels of the cart and the hooves of the horses must be padded. The new cart pulled alongside the stationary cart and halted. If the Companions spoke the King did not hear them. But the first Companion gestured with a red-gloved hand, moving for the first time, and the other Companions turned their masked faces away from the light. After a moment the King realized the Companions were not merely looking toward him, but *at* him.

That thought, in the chill blue air of evening, was menacing. He was alone. The most powerful man in the empire desired his death above all things. And, beyond all that . . . there was something strange about the red-clad Companions as they watched him and did not move, as they waited and watched him while the night grew darker.

He wanted to back away from the window, but he was afraid to move. Suppose he left their sight, and they decided to seek him out? The thought of those red-clad figures at the door of his room was terrifying. He decided not to leave the window until Lorn returned.

Suddenly he wondered if Lorn *would* return. Perhaps they had him already. The King wanted to make sure the door was bolted—had he locked it after Lorn left? Would it be worth the risk to leave the window for a moment, just to check?

With dreadful gentleness, hoofbeats arising from the darkness of the street announced the arrival of another death cart. The King watched with fascination as it appeared in the vague circle of light below. The two Companions seated within it were already staring at him as they reined in beside the other two death carts.

A frightful thought occurred to him. The second and third death carts each had two Companions. But the first, the one that had been outside his window since before he had opened it (the crow! they had seen the crow crash through the shutter!)—the first cart had only *one* Companion. Where was the other? Where had it gone?

The conviction seized him that the missing Companion was coming for him, that the others were merely waiting for their missing peer to bring him down to them.

Now every shadow seemed tinged with red—a high hood above red-gloved hands reaching for him. He felt he must go to the door—was something already moving stealthily in the room behind him? But he could not move a muscle. He could hardly breathe. He certainly could not speak. And if he called . . . who would come for him?

And so he watched, motionless, in speechless horror, as a gloved hand with long fingers reached over his shoulder, clamped itself across his mouth, and drew him, sobbing, back into the darkness.

CHAPTER EIGHT

WAYS TO AMBROSE

"Those birds were a bad idea," Wyrth was saying morosely. If I never have a worse I'll die a happy dwarf."

"Not inherently bad," his master disagreed. "We all underestimated the number of Coranians in the city."

"Of course no one boasts of it. Might as well boast of being a dragon-worshipper back home under Thrymhaiam. But they remember, those crafty bastards. Hundreds of generations in exile, and they still understand the speech of the Wardlands! How many of them are Urdhven's liegemen, do you suppose?"

Morlock shrugged his twisted shoulders. One would be too many, and they both knew it.

One of the iron crows lay before them on the counter of Genjandro's shop. It had flown through the door less than a hundred heartbeats after Ambrosia's departure. They had immediately shut up shop and had been discussing what to do ever since.

"At any rate," Morlock decreed, "no one of us will go to investigate this crow." Its flame pointed in more or less the same direction as the last, toward Ambrose, and all of them felt the coincidence ominous. "It may be an attempt to separate us," the Crooked Man added. "We will wait for Ambrosia's return and look into this together."

"Ach, Master Morlock. Ambrosia may already be in the Protector's hands."

Shaking his head, Morlock replied. "I await her here. You and Genjandro may go, if you wish."

"*Hursme angaln khore?*"* Wyrth quoted the Dwarvish proverb. "Blood has no price! I'll stay."

Genjandro's wistful expression suggested he was thinking of his own blood. But, "*She* would wait for *us*," he said. "I'll stay."

Morlock nodded matter-of-factly. It was then they heard the soldier (all three of them heard the clanking of his mail as he approached) step up to the door of the shop and pound on it with his fist.

"Genjandro," Morlock said calmly, "open the door." He loosened his sword in its sheath as he spoke. The dwarf reached out, and his fingers closed on a bar of lead that Genjandro used as a counterweight. Then the merchant threw open the door and stood back.

The light from the shop lamp fell on the face of the soldier outside.

"Good evening, Captain Lorn," Morlock said coolly. "I trust you received our message."

"The Strange Gods seize you all, Ambrosian filth," replied the Legionary. "I am here only at the King's command."

"Good for little Lathmar!" muttered Wyrth.

"Then you know where the King is?" Genjandro asked.

"I'll take you to him."

"No," Morlock said. "Ambrosia is with him now, I guess. We await her return."

Lorn, breathing heavily, stared at Morlock. "Then I wait, too," he said finally.

"That may be unwise," Morlock observed. "If—"

He paused. In the interval they all heard the rhythmical crash of booted feet marching in the lane outside.

"Please come in, Captain Lorn," Morlock said. "Shut the door behind you. We have a decision to make."

---

*"What does blood cost?" The enclitic *-me* implies a negative answer to the question.

The King was relieved when his captor proved to be his Grandmother rather than one of the faceless red Companions—but not very. He anticipated a tongue-lashing for various stupidities, whereas a Companion would, he supposed, merely kill or kidnap him.

In fact, he was pleasantly surprised. His Grandmother simply set him down out of sight, grunted as if in pain, and pulled at her black gloves.

"Grandmother," he said haltingly, "your, your hands . . ."

"Morlock and Wyrth patched me up," she replied. "These gloves are Wyrth's making; with them I can do just about anything I need to—except scratch my palms, damn it!" She paused and asked, "Where is Lorn?"

"I sent him to Genjandro's to find you."

"Good. Excellent. Then he's met up with Morlock by now. I was worried he might have gone down to deal with those creatures in the street."

"Why are they here? What do they want?"

Ambrosia—a shadow in the sparse light from the window—shrugged crooked shoulders. "Something to do with you, of course. You're the man of the hour, Lathmar, if it delights you to think so."

It didn't. Lathmar stood in silence, trying to think of a reply that was both true and properly respectful, until his Grandmother spoke again.

"We'd best get out of here, Lathmar. Come along. I've—"

Her voice broke off. A sudden poignant intuition caused Lathmar to turn. In the open doorway stood the shape of a Companion. Its red robes were gray in the dim light, but there were faint red gleams in the gaping eyeholes of its mask.

Ambrosia stepped in front of Lathmar, drawing as she did so the short curved blade strapped over her shoulders.

"Gravedigger," she said, "get out of my way. I am Ambrosia Viviana; I will not tell you twice."

The Companion did not retreat, but it did not move into the room either. Ambrosia advanced three paces cautiously, then—instead of cutting or thrusting with the blade, as Lathmar expected—she leapt forward with a chest-high kick.

The Companion disappeared from the doorway, and they heard him strike the corridor wall outside. Ambrosia rushed out the door, Lathmar at her heels. They saw the robes of the Companion settling down in the dust of the hall floor. Apart from dust there was nothing beneath them.

"A sending of some kind," Ambrosia said. "God Creator! What a stench!"

Lathmar, his throat clenching like a fist, could not reply.

"We've no time to sort this out," she continued. "Come along."

He followed her down the hallway to the stairwell. Glancing back, he saw a shadow standing in the doorway of the room he had shared with Lorn.

"Grandmother," he whispered.

"Shut up."

They entered the stairwell. In the absolute darkness therein Ambrosia seized Lathmar's hand and led him upward. Beneath them, beneath the sound of their footsteps and their harsh breathing, Lathmar thought he heard something moving on the steps below.

They reached the tenement's highest floor. The hallway there was narrower than on floors below, the ceiling lower. Ambrosia led the way to the end of the hall, where it was narrowest and lowest.

"There doesn't seem to be anyone home," Lathmar whispered as they went.

Ambrosia laughed. "No? I'd bet there's someone standing behind every door we've passed. But don't trust in that. We could be killed as we stood here and no one would even holler for the night-watch."

"That's bad!" Lathmar replied. He was wondering how many of his people lived this way.

"Is it? I suppose it is. But they've got their own lives to think about. They've learned how to survive among the water gangs, the muggers, the corrupt watchmen, the thugs who prey on others for the pleasure of doing so. These people are tough, Lathmar, and they know what matters to them. They take no unnecessary risks because they meet and survive a hundred dangers in a day. Your best soldiers come from here, Lathmar—but they've got one flaw, from your point of view. They're realists, not loyalists like Lorn. They'll follow the strongest leader always."

"And I'm not the strongest."

"Not today. Look here, Lathmar, do you think you can lift me?" They had reached the hall's end.

He had spent the long days exercising—there was little else to do—but he looked up at his towering Grandmother fearfully. "I—I—don't think so, Grandmother."

"We'll see. Turn around."

He did so, and she put her back against his, linking both their arms at the elbow. "Bend over," she commanded, and he did so. Then she swung her legs off the floor and, lying with her black flat upon his, kicked at the low cracked ceiling. He staggered under the weight, the force of the blow. Plaster dust rained down on them.

"Grandmother!" he shouted. "There's something there!" By "there" he meant the dark door of the unlit stairwell.

"Save your breath!" she said, and kicked again. Chunks of plaster fell with the dust this time. Light was flickering within the King's eyes, and the world was changing shape. Ambrosia kicked again and the world came apart in a chaos of shattered plaster and broken wood. His legs gave way, and they both fell to the floor. He was not conscious of this, though, until she lifted him up. The hallway window was blocked with debris.

"Grandmother," he said groggily, "the window—"

"Get up!" she commanded. "No—not on my hands. On my forearms. Up you go!" She fairly threw him toward the ragged ring of dark blue that was the sky, the hole she had kicked in the ceiling. Choking from the dust, he found his head in the open air. He scrabbled at the flat filthy roof of the tenement, but there was nothing to grab onto.

"Lift yourself up!" she shouted.

"Can't!" he screamed back.

She placed her hand against his rump and pushed. The King of the Two Cities sprawled on the tenement roof. From the hole he heard a rush of footsteps in the hallway and sudden harsh laughter—his Grandmother's. Then came a burst of fire-bright light that left red afterimages in his eyes. When he could see again, his Grandmother was lifting herself through onto the roof.

"Phlogiston!" she said, laughing, to his complete bewilderment. "Never leave home without a pocketful, Lathmar! Brothers are useful creatures, sometimes," she added, even more mysteriously. As she rose to her feet he saw that she had drawn her sword again, and that the grip, broken in two, was trailing smoke in the night air.

"What?"

"Never mind. I left him burning on the floor, with the tenants stamping out the fire—"

"The tenants?"

"Certainly. They fear fire more than a thousand gangsters, or the Strange Gods they swear by. Rightly, too, I'd say." She sheathed her sword. "That was well done down there, Lathmar."

He felt ashamed and surprised all at once. He didn't remember her ever praising him before. "I did nothing," he protested.

"You did what you had to do. No one ever does more—many not so much."

"I could have done nothing else."

She responded with a cheerfully hair-raising obscenity. "You could have run, or simply panicked, even if there was no use in it. You did well. Let's go."

The King followed her across the roof. The prospect of his city dizzied him as he approached the edge. The dim smoky light from myriads of lamps and torches faintly sketched in the successive ridges of skyline—crooked, angular, domed. It was breathtaking, vast, yet somehow constricting. It was as if he were seeing an entire universe at once—but a very small universe, which was closing in on him. He looked up at the low-hanging clouds and saw red light reflected there.

"Is the city burning?" he asked.

"No more than every night. Look here, Lathmar, can you jump across that?"

"That" was the chasm between the roof they stood on and that of the next building. It was only a couple arm lengths across, but lit windows on both walls descending displayed its depth. Fear stopped his throat—he could feel the impact of the street on his flesh—but he knew he could make it. He nodded.

"Good. We'll cross a few of these to break our trail, then tear through another roof and walk down to street level. Understand?"

The King nodded.

"Jump!" Ambrosia said.

The King jumped.

Before the night was over the King found himself wishing he had missed the jump and gone down in a red smash beside the tenement. "It would have been better than this!" he muttered to himself. He thought his words would be lost in the tramp of soldier's boots behind him, but the mailed fist gripping his neck tightened painfully. "None o' that!" a harsh voice said in his ear.

They marched up the broad gleaming street to the City Gate of Ambrose.

"Hey, watchman!" the same harsh voice behind him called out. "Open this gate or I'll have your balls for breakfast!"

The road to captivity and Ambrose had begun on the way back to Genjandro's shop. Ironically, the King had been delighted. They took back alleys and deserted streets to avoid notice, and soon after they reached the ground the heavy clouds had begun a steady drenching storm that promised to last all night. The King had never been so cold, nor so physically uncomfortable. Nor, indeed, so happy. The danger, it seemed, was past; he was free and abroad in his city; he was with his Grandmother again. He could not imagine what was before him (fortunately, as it proved), so he didn't try. He simply reveled in the wild air, the bright blackness of the wet streets in the storm.

The first intrusive doubt that all was not well came when they had to dodge a column of armed soldiers marching up a lane leading away from the Great Market. Grandmother heard their boots long before he did and pulled him along with her into a stairwell that led to a door below street level. They watched from the shadows as the soldiers marched past, the red lion of the Protector on their black banner and their shields.

"Protector's Men!" his Grandmother muttered when they had passed. "Something's stirring, and I don't like it, Lathmar. Maybe they're just patrolling the city. But that's more normally left to your City Legion, from all I hear."

"They're not mine," the King said, but he thought of Lorn.

"Hmph. If Urdhven agreed you'd be a good deal safer. So would they. Be quiet a moment, boy." Hardly a moment had passed when she spoke again. "We won't risk the market," she decided. "If something's afoot and it's nothing to do with us, we still might be caught in the open. And if they're looking for us, we mustn't give them the chance they're wanting."

So she led him around the Great Market by side streets, a long weary way in the rain. His exaltation had cooled by then, but he said nothing in complaint. The way was made longer (and filthier) because at every untoward sound, Ambrosia hid them somewhere along the street. But the King did not complain of this either, even though they once burrowed into a pile of streetside trash and once climbed straight up the crumbling brick wall of a half-ruined building. Too often her suspicions were correct: they were passed many times by troops of soldiers, never less than a dozen together, and once by as many as a half thousand marching, rank on rank. They bore no torches in the rain, but above them all flew the Protector's standard, the red lion black as a wound in the blue bursts of lightning.

"They must have had a whole quarter of the city isolated," Ambrosia whispered to Lathmar after the hundreds passed. "I suppose it started after I left Genjandro's—you can't move this many troops in a city without causing an uproar, and I'd heard nothing."

"Why are they moving again?" the King asked.

"They found what they were looking for. Or they've given up." In the shadows Ambrosia's mouth was a grim dark line.

"But would they give up so soon?" the King wondered.

"No!" Ambrosia shouted, and the King kept quiet after that.

Finally they arrived at Genjandro's shop. It was not hard for the King, who had never seen the place, to pick it out of the shops lining the street. Peering out alongside his Grandmother in the issue of a narrow alley, he guessed it was the shop whose shutters had been torn from the windows, whose door lay shattered in the street.

"This looks like grim business," Ambrosia observed coolly. "Come along, Lathmar."

"Grandmother, wait!" the King hissed, seizing her arm.

She looked at him impassively.

"Won't there be someone watching the shop . . . waiting for us?" the King asked.

"That's very good thinking, Lathmar," his Grandmother said, her tone cold and distant. "You're probably correct. I'm going in anyway, though. You may stay here, if you like."

Tongue-tied, he stared at her and then followed as she walked away. Her behavior was strange to him, but familiar, too, in a way he could not name.

She drew her sword as she approached the empty doorway and entered with casual wariness. He followed almost as quickly, more afraid of the open street than the hidden but doubtful menace of the ransacked shop.

In truth, there was nothing inside more dangerous than darkness and broken furniture. Lathmar stayed at the windows and watched the empty street while Ambrosia rummaged about and searched the place. She disappeared for an alarmingly long time into the back of the place, but presently returned to report, "They didn't even loot the place. Pretty businesslike for Protector's scum. Over here, Your Majesty, if you please."

The King went where she directed, his face burning in the darkness because of the scorn and fury in her voice. He was surprised: Grandmother, though often brutal, was never, never unfair. But he was not very surprised. Her anger made sense to him somehow. It was not right, but it was wrong in a way he felt he understood. . . .

Grandmother's silhouette in the dark casually hurled aside a heavy stone-topped counter, and the crash startled the King out of his thoughts. As he approached she was pulling stones from the floor where the counter had stood. He stood gaping, guessing at his Grandmother's actions (for she was a shadow among shadows, bent down to the floor) by the sounds they made. Presently he heard her brushing loose earth away. Then she stood up and pressed something in his hands: the handle of a dagger. (He saw the blade's edge gleaming in the faint light from the broken windows.)

"There," she said. "If anyone comes out you don't like, stick that in him."

"Out?" he said stupidly, and then he understood. There was a chamber hidden beneath the shop floor.

"Out!" she affirmed. Then she bent down and seized something on the floor. He heard her grunt of exertion and the rasp of stone against stone.

Lines of blazing light appeared on the ground, forming three sides of a square. His Grandmother stood before the widest of the three, grimacing as she heaved at a large ringbolt. Placing one hand under the lip of the stone she was lifting, she hurled it back with a negligent crash.

In the wake of this noise the King heard a gentle coughing; it seemed to rise with the light blazing from the incandescent hole in the floor.

"You shouldn't have lit your lamp, Genjandro," the King heard his Grandmother say. "Don't blame me if your lungs are purple with smoke."

"On the contrary, madam," said a polite-voiced shadow rising from the light. "I had no intention of waiting, perhaps for days, only to die in the dark. I knew you would come tonight before the sixth hour, or you would not come at all. If the smoke killed me after that, why so much the better: so much less of a cruel wait."

"Now, now, Genjandro, will you defy the proverb and talk of death to the King? Because standing beside me is your lawful sovereign, Lathmar the Seventh."

"Truly? Ah, Your Majesty, I am most signally honored—"

The King could sense no irony in the merchant's tone. (He had nothing else to go by, as Genjandro was still almost invisible in the intolerable brightness of the dim oil lamp he carried in his hand.) But he could sense the corrosive amusement bubbling up in Ambrosia without even glancing at her, and when Genjandro's form looked to make some courtly gesture, perhaps to kneel, the King cried out, "Oh, please don't bother yourself. I'll be glad to accept your homage at any more fitting time."

"As Your Majesty wishes. Perhaps it would be best if we departed as soon as possible—"

"But that won't *be* possible," Ambrosia cut in, "until we decide where we are going. Where are Morlock and Wyrtheorn, Genjandro?"

"I assumed you had guessed, my lady. The Legionary captain, Lorn, arrived just after sunset, with an army of Protector's Men at his heels."

"So quickly, eh? You think—"

"I think it was a coincidence. Otherwise I would not be here. It was after Lorn arrived that the others hid me in the floor. The Protector's Men broke in and, I assume, took the others prisoner. Certainly they would not have left me here, if—"

"Lorn is no traitor!" Lathmar protested. "He might have turned me over to Urdhven at any time——"

"You're both off the mark," Ambrosia said harshly. "Genjandro, they would have left you as bait for us. And Lathmar, Lorn would not have been betraying you by informing on us. You haven't understood your soldier yet, that's obvious."

"How——"

"Shut up. We'll leave the question of Lorn unsettled. The main thing is: Morlock and Wyrtheorn are in Ambrose. That determines our course of action."

The King was relieved when Genjandro said, "I don't see how," because he thought he did and hoped he was wrong.

"Eh? Oh, it's nothing to do with you, Genjandro. We'll gladly accept any help you might offer, but if I were you I wouldn't offer any. You've obviously got your own problems. The King and I have to go to Ambrose this night."

This was much as the King had suspected, but he couldn't refrain from yelping when his guess proved correct.

His Grandmother turned on him fiercely, her white face stark with shadows in the lamplight. "You don't like that, do you? It doesn't matter if you like it or not. You're my key to the gates of Ambrose, and I'm going to turn you till the gates open or you break."

Genjandro, obviously concerned by this, began to utter a protest, and the King himself wanted to say something, he hardly knew what. Ambrosia listened abstractedly for a moment and then said distinctly, "Be quiet."

In the offended silence that ensued, Genjandro and the King noticed what Ambrosia had already heard: the stealthy fall of booted feet outside the shop door.

Deliberately and with great presence of mind, Genjandro smashed his oil lamp against the wall. In an instant the burning oil set ablaze the wreckage on the floor below, lighting the whole room. Thus the soldiers who presently entered had to do so as individuals, rather than as the aggregate armed shadow they would have been in the dark room.

When the first soldier appeared in the doorway (of course: a Protector's Man, the red lion splashed like blood across his dark surcoat), Ambrosia threw back her head and screamed; the memory of it lived in Lathmar's nightmares till the day he died. Then, brandishing the blade she had never sheathed, Ambrosia leapt into battle, hatred and happiness twisting the lines of her face. And then, just when it would do no good to anyone, the King recognized his Grandmother's oddly familiar mood. It was grief, in its maddest middle phase—the reckless destructive mood when you don't care if you live or die.

The King had been that way, after the first shock of his parents' death. No one had noticed, of course. The recklessness of which he was capable was invisible to anyone else. But for a long time he would eat his meals before others tasted them, he would leave his doors unlocked at night. He could not sleep much, but he lay in bed—shutting his ears with his eyes—and let the assassin's blade come when it would.

It didn't come, not then, and one by one he resumed his pitiful precautions. Grief is strong, but life is stronger. He would not have told this to his Grandmother because he knew that the griever hates life. Grief is love itself, wounded by loss, and life is just the emptiness that goes on afterward. It is terrible that such an emptiness can overcome the fullness of grief, and the King would never have inflicted this knowledge on anyone he loved. (It occurred to him, as she leapt eagerly toward death, that he loved his Grandmother.) But he would have delayed her or decoyed her, lied to her until she inflicted that knowledge on herself.

Now it was too late for such gentle trickery. Ambrosia had gone to find her death on a bright thicket of blades and would no doubt find it. The King crouched down in the shadows of the high leaping flames and waited for death to find him.

From there to Ambrose was just a journey of so many steps.

Chapter Nine

Ambrose and Elsewhere

The keeper of Ambrose's City Gate grunted, his oily face gleaming between the dark iron bars of the portcullis. "Whatcha want?" he snapped. "Gate's close'. Go 'round ta Lonegate. Command's in Markethall Barracks. I guess it is. Anyway, no one here but the poisoners."

The raspy voice from behind the King responded irritably, "Damn you, you wobbly old winebag. Can't you see? I've got the King of the Two Cities by the scruff of the neck. High Command wants him locked up before the Ambrosians in the city have a chance to grab him back."

"Go 'round!" shouted the gatekeeper. "Go 'round! No so'jers here. Ha'n't stood a watch in five years, wi' my leg. Not s'posed to open the gate till Pr'-tect'r rides back. Now—"

"You've got the key, haven't you?"

"Yes, but—"

"It's ten miles on foot to the Lonegate. I've got to go to the nearest bridge, through a city that's half in revolt, cross the bridge, then walk through open country until I get to the other side of Ambrose. And they've probably got some damn fool on duty who'll tell me to go back to the City Gate."

"They *tol'* me—"

"Did you say the poisoners were here?"

The gatekeeper reluctantly admitted this.

"Send for a poisoner—Steng, if he's here. Tell him Hundred-Leader Medric is at the gates with the royal prisoner."

"Steng's questioning . . . mmm . . . Steng's questioning . . . some . . . er . . ."

"He's questioning the prisoners who were brought in earlier—through *this* gate. Isn't that so?"

"Hmph. Hm. Yes."

"I've got the answer to his questions in my mitt. When I see him, I'll remember to tell him who sent me around to the back door with the royal prisoner. Then maybe he'll have some questions for *you*."

The gatekeeper puffed air through his lips and twisted his face. Then he disappeared into the shadows. Presently a clanking sound was heard, and the small door set into the portcullis swung open.

"Come in, you foul-minded Protector's brat," the gatekeeper's voice came out of the darkness.

The King dragged his feet, but his captor fairly lifted him across the iron threshold. In the darkness within the gate, the keeper's voice came from behind them.

"Know how I know you're the real thing, Protector-pup?"

"I've got the King."

"I wouldn't know the King from a ripe melon. No, if you were trying to break in, you'd have tried to grab my throat while I was waggling my face at you through the bars, thinking I had the key on my person." The door slammed shut behind them and locked. "*You* didn't even make a move at it. So you knew the key was hanging in the gatehouse, not around my tempting neck. Move on, straight ahead. You've been here before."

It was the King who went first; he had passed through this gate often, the last time as much a captive as he was now. But he did not really know the way—usually he was being led—and he often stumbled in the dark. He no longer even had his captor's guidance; the mailed glove had released its grip on his neck once they had stepped through the gate. Once they were through, the King reflected, rubbing his neck, it didn't matter anymore. Before him was a small guardroom with two tables and a number of chairs. Most of the flat surfaces were covered with wine jars and wide-mouthed drinking cans; there was a barrel of beer in the corner of the room, stale stinking foam drying on the floor underneath its tap.

Soldierly voices echoed in the stone corridor behind him. The two entered the room in single file behind him, the gatekeeper bringing up the rear.

". . . might have been wrong about that," the King's captor was saying. "Treason's our biggest worry in this business."

"Treason!" the old Legionary sneered. "You Protector-snots throw that word around like it still means something. You're lucky it doesn't. If it did you'd all be traitors, and your All-Leader with kin-blood on his hands the biggest of all—"

"You're pretty free, there, old-timer."

"Not free enough!" said the gatekeeper, turning about to hang the gate keys on an iron hook protruding from the wall. "When the snow falls, that's my *sashvetra**—I'm a twenty-winter man. I don't give a damn what happens after that, and not much what happens before."

"I hope you make it, old soldier," the King's captor said.

A change in the other's voice brought the Legionary wheeling about in suspicion. By that time the King's captor had seized the larger of the room's two tables by one leg and raised it to the ceiling, dumping the bottles and drinking cans to the floor; the King was sprayed by a beery reek. The Legionary stared open-mouthed as the table swung down and clipped him on the forehead. The King's captor dropped the table and grabbed the unconscious gatekeeper as he slumped toward the stone floor.

"Did you kill him?" the King asked.

"No," Grandmother replied.

"Won't he talk when he awakes?"

"You've become rather bloodthirsty tonight, Lathmar."

The King thought of the seven Protector's Men his Grandmother had slaughtered in his presence earlier, one of whose armor she presently wore. He

---

*"Twenty years"—the traditional time for retirement form the Legion.

had smelled the dead man's blood all through the long walk from Genjandro's shop. "No," he said dimly. "Not that."

"Your point's a good one," Ambrosia continued, "but you lack experience. A man who's been struck unconscious takes a long time to remember what's happened to him, if he ever does. He almost never does if he's been drinking. Besides, we'll fix it so that no one believes him if he does remember. Drag that table back where it was."

The King obeyed. When he had set it up, Ambrosia deftly kicked it over on its side with one foot. It looked as if the table had simply fallen over, spilling its contents. Then Ambrosia dragged the Legionary over, carefully draping his body so that the mark on his forehead aligned with the edge of the table; then she let the body sag to the ground.

"I see," the King said. "If he tells his story, people will just think he tripped, being drunk, and struck his head on the table. And his story . . ."

"Will be thought a lie or a dream. Right."

"That's why you kept him from falling," the King observed. "You didn't want any unexplained bruises on the back or side of his head."

"Right again."

The King had thought she was being humane. He'd gotten to like the old soldier in the few moments he'd known him. He wished he could look forward to a *sashvetra* that would free him from the eternal intrigues and treacheries of imperial succession. He disliked his Grandmother's ruthlessness, and something of this must have shown in his face, for she took him by the shoulder.

"Look here, Lathmar," she said, "let's see where we stand. I'm here to rescue my brother Morlock and my friend Wyrtheorn, and I don't much care how I do it. I've obliged you to accompany me because I needed you to get in, and because you owe them more than you may be aware of. But if you want to stay here, or take your chances alone inside Ambrose, or out in the city—that's up to you."

The King was furious. He turned his face away from the battered visor of the Protector's Man Ambrosia had slain. "And now," he said finally, "you *don't* need me. I'll be in the way. Your guise as a Protector's Man will take you unnoticed anywhere in Ambrose. But if anyone sees you with the King, you *will* be noticed; questions will be asked. I make your task harder, and so you generously offer . . ." His voice trailed off.

Ambrosia removed the helmet. Her face held no hostility. In fact, she seemed to smile in approval. "You have a gift for balancing the books, Lathmar. What you say is true: what I have to do will be easier if you're not around. Nonetheless (put this in your books, boy) I will bring you along, if you wish to come. Because it is your right to act with me in this."

"I'll come," said the King. "Because of Lorn. You don't say anything about him. But you're wrong about him. He tried to warn me about you!" He spoke desperately, aware of his own incoherence.

"I've no doubt his warning was a good one," Ambrosia conceded, "for himself. For you, Lathmar, things are different. You are one of us."

"I'm not," the King whispered, frightened by his defiance. "I'll never be like you."

Ambrosia shrugged her twisted shoulders. "So much the worse for you then, my friend," she said, and covered her face with the stolen helmet.

Poisoning is a science, but torture is an art. The goal of the poisoner is simply to attain a physical goal, the death of the patient. The goal of the torturer is to destroy the personality of the patient without achieving the patient's death. Hence the torturer, unlike the poisoner, has to attend to the individual identity of the patient. This was the theory under which Steng, a poisoner turned torturer, operated, and he had attained some success.

That was why he had started on this patient's hands. The patient had been raised by dwarves, Steng knew, and the dwarves have a peculiar reverence for the hands. The maker of things, the Master of Making, is the person whom all dwarves revere. And hands are the organs of physical creation. After death, a dwarf's face is left bare, but his hands are covered.

It was with this in mind, then, that once the patient had been hung from the ceiling by his ankles, Steng had patiently and carefully flayed half of the patient's left hand, in full view of the patient. He had made a good job of it, stopping at the wrist so the manacle wouldn't get in his way, clipping a poisonous *zarm*-beetle every now and then to an exposed bundle of nerves, leaving the skin hanging from the bloody meat of the living hand. He had been careful not to let the blood of the patient get on his hands or clothes, for he hated a mess.

Really, it had been a very workmanlike job, and Steng was annoyed to find that it was not appreciated. Looking up to make some jovial comment, he saw that his patient's eyes were closed. Lifting one of the eyelids, he saw that the patient's pupil had constricted almost to invisibility, and that the pale gray iris was glowing faintly in the dim light. The patient was no longer respiring, but was clearly not dead either.

Steng could not tell whether this was the rapture of vision or mere withdrawal. (He was not a master of Seeing, and he hesitated to consult the one he knew.) But the patient's tal-self was not present to engage with the suffering Steng was inflicting on him.

"But it doesn't matter!" he told his patient. "You've gone far away into the tal-realms. But your source is still here in this body. If I damage it enough you will have to return. You won't have the strength to remain where you are."

There was no answer, of course.

"You're a coward, you know! A coward!" Steng found himself shaking with—with anger, of course. That would never do. He went to the door of his tower chamber and sent the attendant off to fetch a hot drink. Then he sat and drank and calmed himself by watching Morlock's blood gather along his flayed fingertips and spatter on the stone floor.

The light of Ambrosia's torch fell, red and gold, on the squalor of an abandoned guard post. "The palace is a shell," she remarked. "Practically every soldier in the city must be pounding a beat in or near the Great Market."

"They think—" the King began.

"They think they can catch water in a sieve. Bad tactics, as my esteemed brother would say."

"They caught your brother with those tactics," the King observed, greatly daring.

Ambrosia turned toward him, masked by the helmet visor but still clearly angry. Then she shrugged and laughed. "Well said, Lathmar. But it wasn't Morlock they wanted, nor can he give them what they want, which is you, so it's still bad tactics. Besides, what if the Khroi attacked? Ambrose is the key to the city, and your Protector has left it almost unguarded—just the poisoners and their thugs, it seems. Stupid of him—and worth remembering. Well, let's go." She kicked aside a pornographic book and the remains of an unfinished meal and passed through the post to the corridor it guarded.

The rooms along the corridor had been storage space, but a few decades ago river water had begun to seep into them. Rather than fix the problem, the late Emperor, Lathmar's father, had seen fit to convert the rooms to prison cells, which were increasingly in demand in those days. (It was the beginning of Lord Urdhven's influence over his brother-in-law, some said.)

The air in the hallway was dank and foul; grayish darkness grew upon the walls and floor. As she entered the corridor Ambrosia raised her torch high and gazed fixedly at the moss on the floor.

"Someone has passed this way, recently," she said quietly. "Not a soldier, I think. Still, they must patrol the corridor at intervals."

"So there's something to guard."

"Probably Urdhven's wine cellar. Watch behind us, Lathmar, and keep quiet."

A faint sardonic chuckle echoed in the corridor before them. "The suggestion comes a bit late, madam, if you don't mind my saying so," a bodiless voice remarked.

Lord Urdhven watched moodily as Companions of Mercy hauled corpses out of the smoking ruin that had once been Genjandro's shop. The walls of the building still stood, but the roof had collapsed and fumes still poured from the hole upward into the dark humid air.

"It's lucky there was so much rain," Vost remarked. "We might have lost the whole quarter to fire."

Idiot, Urdhven thought with weary impatience. What a blessing such a fire would have been! How easy it would have been to lose the body of the little King in the general destruction! How the city would have rallied behind him, the Protector, as he and his men fought the blaze! What a pogrom of the Protector's enemies could have followed, accused and condemned as pro-Ambrosian arsonists! It was a lost opportunity, but Vost would never see it. If only Vost were more like Steng, or Steng a little like Vost. . . . But each tool had its purpose, he reminded himself wryly.

Urdhven noticed that the Companions were preparing to depart. "Wait!" he barked at them, and crossed over to the death cart. He reached it before he noticed that Vost, open-mouthed, had not followed. He motioned impatiently for his henchman to come over, but even as he did so his mind was alive to the situation's possibilities.

Vost, peasantish town man that he was, looked on the Company of Mercy with awe and terror. He never would have dared to interfere with them, nor would they have paid him the least attention if he did dare. It was different with Urdhven, of course, and perhaps he could make some use of that sometime. Not on Vost, of course: his mastery of Vost was complete. But on others whom it would be useful to impress with a casual gesture of power. . . .

All this in the moments it took Vost to follow in his master's footsteps, braving the gauntlet of the hulking red-shrouded Companions.

"What do you see?" Urdhven demanded.

Vost's face twisted with revulsion as he faced the charred crumbling meat in the death wagon. "Seven bodies—urrr. It was so many soldiers we set to watch on the shop."

"What do you make of that?" Urdhven demanded, pointing at one of the seven. Unlike the others it was armorless.

"I'll tell you," Urdhven continued, tired of waiting for the wheels to turn in Vost's skull. "It was Ambrosia who went to fetch the King; we know that much. She was either successful or not. In any case, she returned here. The soldiers attacked her and she killed them. Then she stripped that one there and put on his armor and surcoat. What did she do then?"

"Headed for a gate," Vost guessed. "In one of the regional garrisons—Sarkunden, maybe—she—"

"Shut up. She did nothing of the kind." Vost wilted visibly in the heat of Urdhven's fury, not understanding that the Protector was in fact angry with himself. He should have predicted this! "She headed straight for Ambrose. She's there now, possibly with the King in tow. She's trying to rescue her brother, just as he rescued her at Gravesend Field.

"This is our chance, Vost. Ambrose is nearly empty, but they are there—all there in the same box. We must close the lid on them."

"Yes, my lord."

"I'll go ahead with the mounted troops mustered in the Great Market. You follow as soon as possible with reinforcements on foot. They must all be my sworn men—none from the City Legion; we don't want this to turn into a damn civil war. And, yes, send a company of my men to each of the city gates; have them watch for the Ambrosii. It was folly to concentrate our forces like this. But if we catch the game we've flushed, it'll be worth it."

They turned together toward the Great Market. Behind them the red-masked Companions of Mercy unconcernedly climbed aboard the death cart and drove away.

CHAPTER TEN

BLOOD'S PRICE

ithin the iron-barred cell, the monster that had been Wyrtheorn opened its weedy beard and laughed. The sound of the dwarf's voice rang overloud and echo-laden in the narrow corridor. The waist-deep water in which the dark-green figure crouched sent back mottled reflections from the red light of Ambrosia's torch. The King could not tell if the movements he could see in the marshy water were ripples, from Wyrth's motions, or illusions from the torch's flickering light, or whether there were creatures of some kind in the water. He was tempted to ask, then realized he didn't want to know.

"No, madam," Wyrth was saying. "My appearance is due to my captors, who 'scrubbed the floor' with me, as they put it, before they secured my hands to the floor."

"So your hands are chained down there?"

"Pinned. They have an apparatus something like a double-headed barbed spear; they drove one end through each hand and bolted it to the floor."

The helmet that caged Ambrosia's head nodded slowly. "I wonder if they have done likewise with Morlock."

Wyrth shook his shaggy head. "I couldn't say. They separated the three of us even before we reached Ambrose, as I've mentioned. But I won't slow

119

your search down, if that's what you're thinking. I've had worse wounds in the field."

The dwarf's voice had grown not quite querulous, but curious. The King, too, was astonished to see his Grandmother so slow, so seemingly indecisive.

"Wyrth . . . ," Ambrosia began, then fell silent.

"Yes?"

"Never mind. Face away, if you can. I'll pry—"

"Stop!"

Ambrosia stopped. She said nothing, but waited for the dwarf to speak again.

Finally he did. "Very well, Lady Ambrosia. I can follow your reasoning, if I can't lead the way. You may not free me at this time."

"The risk is small. If—"

"I beg your pardon, madam, for saying so, but that's horse-scut and you don't believe it. If you free me now we risk, at any moment, that the alarm will be raised against us. Since we do not know where Morlock is in this venerable pile, we can't know how long the search will be. Any delay may be too much. The risk, however small, is too great. I will stay."

Shocking the King, his Grandmother sheathed her sword. "We'll return for you, Wyrth."

"If possible, please do. If not, avenge my death, as my kin will be unable."

The stolen helmet nodded curtly, and the King's Grandmother turned away to walk back as they had come. The King stole a last glance at the dwarf (a stone figure in an abandoned fountain, hip-deep in stagnant water, covered with greenish moss) and hurried after her.

When they were well away she observed to the King, "It was a bit of an insult, that last remark. His father and I swore kith in the far north, before he was born. And Morlock was raised in his clan; dwarves consider that an even closer tie than blood-kinship."

"Then aren't you breaking kith by leaving him?" Lathmar asked. Formal issues of kinship etiquette interested him.

Ambrosia clenched her fist, unclenched it, and let her hand fall to her side. It was only then that the King realized she had been about to strike him, and he flinched, belatedly, uselessly. But when she spoke her voice was unshaken by anger.

"Yes," she said flatly. "But I'm not a dwarf. Nor was I raised among them, as Morlock was. My own people come first with me. I'd risk my own life to save Wyrth, but I won't risk Morlock's."

"You're risking mine," the King observed.

"You chose to come," Ambrosia replied. "Because of Lorn."

The King could not tell if the harshness in her voice came from scorn or pain. But he let the matter drop, even though what she had said was half true at best.

Or had he chosen? Truly chosen? It was something to think about.

Properly speaking, there are not three worlds but one: flesh and spirit, fused in action. But if that fusion is broken the world separates, not into two parts but three. There is spirit, there is matter, and there is the medium (called *tal* by those-who-know), which knits them together into mind.

Separate the three realms, if you have the skill. Remember: three points in space may form a triangle, or a line. Do not form a triangle. Preserve the tal as a barrier between the greater realms. Remember: mind is the union of flesh and spirit. If you part the talic union between them your awareness will dissipate upward into spirit or downward into matter; either condition may be considered death. (There are deaths and deaths: beware the second death.) It isn't death you seek. Separate the realms: preserve their tension.

The third realm, the realm of tal, then becomes a corridor down which you drift. You are neither conscious nor unconscious. You are dreaming, freed from the limits of flesh, not subject to the freedom of spirit, constrained by the freedom of the dream, the rapture of vision.

From the corridor of dream you watched as the poisoner flayed your hand. It had the kind of gruesome interest a revenge tale used to have, told after supper in the High Hall back home under Thrymhaiam. But it did not concern you personally: the power to move that sodden flesh was within you: interwoven black-and-white fire flaring bright against the dim insubstantial backdrop of the world of matter.

Presently you turn away, led by a secret intention to *mark this place*. It had some other purpose in your conscious mind, but the dream understands it in its own way. To mark the place of your own death. (The intention to kill you flares bright as a torch in the poisoner's dim patchwork skull.)

Death and life are both marked by blood. Surveying the pool of fading blood forming beneath your vacant body, you sense the almost talic vibrance of the innumerable spicules of fire-to-be drenching the dark dying fluid.

Put forth your hand: not the half-dead wounded hunk of meat that fascinates the poisoner: the black-and-white woven fire of the third realm, the strength and wisdom that move the hand of flesh to move. Put it forth; draw a dripping fistful of the sparkling fire-to-be. Depart, dreaming, through the open door like a ghost in an old story, dripping blood and fire.

Ambrosia and the King had come at last to a level of the palace seven flights of stairs above the ground. Corridors were narrow, rooms were few, and the walls were palpably thick and heavy. It served as the base of a rank of high-aspiring towers; Steng's poisoners had their quarters there—or so Ambrosia said that rumor had it.

"But which tower holds Steng's chambers?" asked Ambrosia. "It's a fair guess that Steng himself is torturing Morlock, and in his own place. But if we pick the wrong tower we're lost; we won't have time to search them all."

The King said nothing. A strange somber mood was growing with him. Perhaps it was just weariness: it had been a horribly long night; he hardly had strength to shuffle along, and all his limbs seemed numb. Even his Grandmother's voice was just a buzzing in his ears, a voice in a dream, heard without understanding.

It was as Ambrosia's voice sank to an empty murmur that the King became distracted by Morlock, peering at them through a pane of glass on the wall of the stairway at the far end of the corridor. Their eyes met, and Morlock turned away as Ambrosia's voice came through suddenly, clear as a thunderclap.

"—think that the night will last forever? We've got to find Morlock!"

The King's throat gurgled, like someone trying to speak in his sleep. Finally his mind and muscles responded to his will and he coughed out words: "I saw him. Just now."

"Did you?" said Ambrosia with polite interest. "Where?"

"In the stairway—just now. He looked through the window in the wall, and he . . . he went away."

"Your vision is remarkable," Ambrosia observed, "since I can't even see the wall, much less any pane of glass."

"But—" the King began, and stopped. He'd been about to explain that Morlock had been clearly visible, irradiated with motile tongues of black-and-white fire. Yet this did not seem as sensible when he tried to put it into words as it had when he had seen it.

"In any case," Ambrosia was continuing, "there are certainly no windows in those stairwells. I drew the plans of this palace myself, Lathmar, and laid many a stone with my own hands."

The King said nothing.

Ambrosia eyed him narrowly through the mask of her visor, then seized him by the arm. "Come along. Just move your feet; we'll have a look."

Grimly unhappy, the King let himself be dragged along to the stairwell. As he had feared, there was no glass of any sort in the walls, and in addition the stairwell was thick with the stench of blood and smoke. The torture chambers, he thought, must be nearby. But he swore to himself he would say nothing about it; Ambrosia herself pretended not to notice the reek, he saw.

"Lathmar," she said finally, after searching the wall, "tell me again what you saw. Tell me *exactly* what you saw."

The King's eyes gaped in the dimness, struggling to see something that could account for his delusion. "That, I think," he said, pointing.

"What?"

"It must have been light reflecting off that."

"Don't tell me what you *think* you saw, tell me—Wait. What are you pointing at?"

"The smear of blood on the wall. It—" But looking again, he saw no blood. The reek of it was fading, gone, had never been there. "I don't see it now," he concluded lamely.

"Well, where was it?" Ambrosia's voice was matter-of-fact.

The King pointed again, feeling foolish. His Grandmother put out a mailed glove and traced her finger on the wall. It left a thin guttering stroke of flame behind it that soon expired. But as it did so the reek of blood and fire was back in the King's nostrils.

"Ah!" Ambrosia exclaimed, sounding pleased. She put her palm flat against the stone and swept it back and forth. A pale shower of reddish sparks leapt out from the wall; the King again saw a patch of blood, outlined in fire that instantly faded.

"What is it? Is it real?" the King demanded.

"Yes. Quite real: it is the blood of an Ambrosius. Only ours sheds fire in quite this way. Which way was Morlock going, up or down?"

"Down. That is—"

"Don't think. Just answer. He was going down?"

"Y-Yes."

"We go up, then. I don't know if the rapture will take you again, Lathmar, but if you notice anything that seems strange to you, tug on my sleeve. Don't be surprised if you can't speak: reason and rapture are always at odds."

"What—?"

"This is a bad time for a lesson in magic, Lathmar, and the Sight is a bad gift to give a ruler, in any case. We see too much and feel too much as it is. Go on: lead the way, little King."

Silent, empty of rapture or reason, the little King wearily led the way upward.

After some conversation with his assistant poisoner, Steng returned to his chamber. His mouth was sticky with warm sherbet, and his mind was more purposeful, more resolute. This would be the end of the game, one way or the other. Morlock would or would not tell him what he wanted to know; he would or would not rise in the Protector's estimation for this. But either way: at the day's end he would have tortured, degraded, and killed a master of Making, famous even among those-who-know, a dark legend among those who did not. He wondered what it would feel like to have done that; he looked forward to the sensation.

Lost in his reverie of blood he did not notice the faint traces of smoke in the air as he approached the chamber door. They were, indeed, slight, but a normally alert Steng would have caught them. He waved aside the deaf-mute guard, ignoring the urgent gestures the guard made at him. He threw open his chamber door, a derisively pleasant remark at his lips.

The room was an image of chaos: filled with clouds of dark smoke, lit within by dim flames clinging to the floor. Morlock's form—a dark constant in the flickering red gloom—hung as before from the chamber ceiling. Steng plunged forward with a curse, snatching the woven rug from inside the doorway as he ran and hurling it down on the patch of guttering flames on the floor.

Steng screamed as a spray of corrosive liquid leapt up from the floor, searing his right arm and setting his capacious sleeve on fire. He batted out the flames in his clothing, staggering back in confusion. He was totally at a loss, fearfully expecting at any moment his death-stroke from some strange Ambrosian magic.

Into the emptiness of his mind came the slow persistent sound of dripping. He listened for a moment, absorbed, utterly unaware of what he was hearing. Then he knew: it was the sound of Morlock's blood, still dripping from his open wounds. Finally the smoke and fire lost their mystery.

It must be true what people said—that the secret of the Ambrosian immunity to fire lay in their blood, which drew the fire from their flesh, and which could itself start fires, when spilled. It was said to be a poison as well.

Steng was tempted to keep Morlock alive a while longer to do some experiments. It would be dangerous, of course, and there was always the possibility of using Ambrosia to the same end. When he came to the question, though, he found he feared Ambrosia more than this Morlock fellow.

In any case, the thing to do now was to clean up the mess. He turned to fetch his guard and noticed with some gratification that the man was already approaching him: finally something was going well on this dreadful night. Something of nightmare remained in the scene, or in Steng's own mind. Some trick of the light or the smoke made it seem the man approaching was headless, his slow uncertain steps the movements of a body about to collapse. . . .

Steng stared open-mouthed as the body of his deaf-mute guard fell in a heap on the floor. Beyond it, the doorway filled with a figure in the surcoat and armor of a Protector's Man. But it was no man. The little room was already echoing with the fierce, pitiless laughter of the royal ancestress, Ambrosia Viviana.

Although perfectly capable of fear, Steng did not then feel it. It was something beyond fear: a stark blank realization of his powerlessness. That, along with the smoke fumes, the poison of Morlock's blood, and simple shock overthrew his last vestiges of strength, and he fell unconscious on the dead body of his dead protector, like a stone or a broken toy or any lifeless thing.

When Ambrosia saw Steng fall she wasted no more thought on him. Glancing around, she saw the contents of Morlock's pack spread out over a nearby table. She went over to gather tools, then returned, drawing a three-legged chair with her. Standing on the chair she used the tools to shatter the hinges on the manacles imprisoning Morlock's ankles. At the last blow of the chisel the manacles flew open and Morlock began to fall. Ambrosia dropped the tools and seized her brother by the shins, but the weight caused her to overbalance and she fell with him to the floor.

Half dazed, she saw Morlock lying beside her on the floor. He also stood above her, a glittering pillar of black-and-white fire. He offered her a hand (?) and, hesitantly, she accepted it, rising from her half-conscious self to walk beside her brother's tal-shadow.

He led her to the window of the small chamber and gestured. She saw immediately what he meant her to see: through the dark translucence of Ambrose's mossy stones she saw a river of light approaching through the narrow streets of the city below: living souls, living tal. As she watched, the flood broke upon the City Gate, then after a pause began to filter in through the shadowy opening, its light dimmed by veils of stone.

The Protector's forces, she thought. Nothing was so alien to the rapture of vision as ordinary rational speech, so she consciously formed the words, firing them at her vision-lost brother like arrows. *The Protector is coming back. We must hurry, or he'll trap us in these towers. I know where Wyrth is being held. Morlock, return. . . .*

She saw the brightness of his flames dimmed by conscious forethought. She sensed his presence recede toward the physical plane. With a poignant sense of loss and relief, she opened her eyes to find herself twelve feet from the chamber window, her head aching. Lathmar knelt over her with tears on his face.

"—ndmother, *wake up!*" he was saying.

"I'm with you," she said, sitting up. "See to Morlock, if you can."

But she saw that he had. There was a clumsy smoldering bandage about Morlock's tortured hand (very clumsy, but this was no time for a lesson in leechcraft), the burning rugs on the far side of the room had been put out . . . and the pool of blood was mostly dry. The air of the chamber was clear, too. Ambrosia suppressed a curse. Time, as well as volition, is distorted in rapture. How long had they been unconscious? The Protector's Men might be killing Wyrth as she sat there.

"Morlock!" she shouted in her brother's ear.

He responded with a rasping cough that might have had a syllable of Dwarvish in it.

"Don't revert to type, you useless bag of knuckles," she stormed at him. "Talk to me in my own language. And don't say anything noble and self-sacrificing: we've already been to too much trouble on your account."

"I said," Morlock croaked, "'Pack my pack.'"

Her head ringing with pain and the loss of rapture, she cursed him for a nine-tenths dwarvish deviant crookback bastard.

He shrugged.

Ambrosia snarled and jumped to her feet. She packed his pack, not omitting the chisel-grip and hammer she had used to break his bonds. She understood Morlock's demand: it would have been an act of madness to leave the pack behind. The books alone would have made a half-wizard like Steng a power among those-who-know.

The sounds attendant on her brother rising to his feet sickened her; she kept her face averted. They needed to know *now* if Morlock could move about on his own. When it proved that he could she finished knotting the straps and turned around to shoulder the pack.

He moved toward her, his face bloodless as a ghost's. "I'll—"

"You'll shut up. Now's not the time to let loose the mordant wit and conversationalist we all know rages within you. I can handle your damn pack."

She grunted, though, as she took the weight of it on her shoulders. (No wonder he grunted so much.)

"—take Tyrfing," he finished, as if she had not spoken.

Glumly she passed him the dark ornamentless sheath that lay upon the table. She saw Lathmar goggling at the dark crystalline pommel, and almost smiled. She sensed an incipient hero-worship there. Ah well: it could only prove dangerous if both of them lived through the night, which seemed somewhat unlikely.

"Now!" she said. "We'll go break out Wyrth—"

"What about Lorn?" the King demanded (speaking to Morlock, Ambrosia noted wryly).

"I know where he is," Morlock said impassively. "But I don't know where Wyrth is."

"But I do," Ambrosia said.

Morlock nodded.

In the tense silence they all heard, faint and far off, the echoing reports of booted feet on stone.

Ambrosia swore. It was a waste of time, but it was the only alternative to *You poor dear, I can't have you wandering around this nasty castle all by yourself.*

"You never learned the hidden passages, did you?" she said accusingly.

"No."

"You'd better take Lathmar, then. He knows some."

"Good. We'll meet when we can."

She moved forward and embraced him briefly. "Go, now. I'll sow confusion in their ranks." She kept her tone neutral. He hugged her back, a hard shell inside a hard shell, she thought, behind the mask of her visor. Then he was gone, and Lathmar, with a woeful look backward, followed him through the doorway.

This night would be wasted time if they managed to get themselves killed, she reflected. (She took no thought for Lorn.) She hated to waste time, so she set straight on sowing confusion, taking the still-bloody sword she had slain Steng's guard with and putting the grip in Steng's right hand, which clenched upon it reflexively.

"Ah, Steng!" she said. "If you didn't exist we'd have to design and build you."

She allowed herself a single fiercely satisfied thought about what the Protector's Men would likely do to the poisoner-turned-torturer if they had the chance, then passed from the bloody chamber to the rising din of the corridor outside.

The King knew nothing, absolutely nothing, about healing. He didn't know how much blood a person could lose and still live. Morlock's grave sallow face, though impassive, was somehow imprinted with sick weariness, and Lathmar noticed he limped as he walked.

"Is your leg hurt?"

"An old wound," Ambrosia's brother said flatly. "Be quiet now."

The King of the Two Cities shut his half-open mouth, and they moved as quickly as they could down the dark narrow stairway that led to the pedestal floor. They were on that floor, well lit and well aired, when a door opened in the corridor behind them and a group of chattering soldiers came out—hiding from their troop leader, not taking their search seriously. Until it succeeded: their voices fell silent as Morlock turned against them and drew the accursed sword Tyrfing in a single movement.

The King thought it was all over with them then. The only thing between him and captivity was a sick, limping man older than Time. If the soldiers had seen Morlock as the King recently had (hung by the heels like a slaughtered pig) no doubt he would have been right.

But (he realized this later) what they saw was this: the dark glittering edge of the accursed sword, and beyond it the smoldering hand and the sallow impassive face of the man who had killed Hlosian Bekh.

They ran. But as they fled, they called out, shouting for their troop-leader, reinforcements, *help*. The King thought of Lorn's desperate stand against the Protector and his men at Gravesend Field and was ashamed for them. But Morlock wheeled about, seized him by the collar, and dragged him down the corridor.

"I can walk!" the King protested.

"Don't. Run!"

The King ran, his short legs moving double-time to keep up with Morlock's long, irregular stride. The darkness of a stairwell closed about them and the King paused, sighing with relief.

"Don't stop." Morlock's flat implacable voice came out of the dark. "Once they pass the word there's no escape for us. Run."

They ran: down endless unlit stairwells, through wide corridors dangerous with light. The King remembered little of it later except his growing desire for sleep, a thirst for rest so intense it made all exterior sensations dim and dreamlike.

He returned to himself at that blessed moment when Morlock drew to a halt, putting a hand on his shoulder. They were in a hallway he didn't recognize, but he knew they were deep under Ambrose: the weight of the stone above their heads was almost palpable.

"Be quiet," Morlock said gently. The King, about to protest that he had said nothing, realized he was gasping and gulping like a lungfish in a net. He tried to make his breathing less raspy and more regular, finally succeeding.

"Now," said Morlock, "we will enter the chamber together. There will be one or two attendants within. I will kill them—"

"Why?" the King demanded.

Morlock's strangely pale gray eyes peered at him though the shadows of the dark corridor. The King could not read his expressions (if he had any!), but he thought Morlock was surprised.

"You'll understand," he said finally. "Don't interfere. Tend to Lorn."

"What if he's not here? Suppose they've moved him?"

"Then he is lost to us. Come now."

It was a clean, well-lighted place they entered, like a surgeon's chamber he had been taken to once when he fell sick, before his parents died. Like the surgeon, the attendants themselves were not clean. They looked up, sweat-stained faces twisting in surprise, from the bright bloody filth on the table at the center of the room.

Morlock spoke, but the King never heard what he said, for at that moment he realized the squirming thing on the table was wearing Lorn's face. For a long stupid second he wondered why they had put Lorn's face on that thing. It was very like a mask: bloodlessly pale, fixed wooden expression, dark holes where the eyes should be. Then he understood; he understood everything.

He walked straight to Lorn, ignoring the attendants. One brushed by him, plunging forward to Morlock and death; the other fled away to the far wall of the chamber.

The King stopped at the table; spiked metallic forms gleamed dully with Lorn's drying blood. Lorn couldn't see him: charred wet meat was all that remained in his eye sockets. The King could think of nothing to say (did even Kedlidor the Rite-Master know a formula for this?) and simply reached to unfasten the manacles binding Lorn's stumps. This was a mistake; Lorn flinched at his touch, and the animal whine that escaped his torn lips broke the King's heart.

"No! No!" the King whispered urgently, frightened and obscurely angry. "I've come to release you!"

"What is your name, friend?" Lorn whispered, breath whistling through the hole in his throat.

There was only one answer for that. "I am your King." He tried to say it firmly, but his voice quavered.

"Majesty!" the tortured soldier gasped. He added loyally, "I knew you'd come."

He was lying. He must be lying, thought Lathmar, as his eyes filled with tears and his soft fingers strove to turn the bolts of the manacles. How could anyone think such a thing? How could anyone be so stupid as to expect it? He hadn't come, anyway. He'd been brought.

When he finally unfastened Lorn's bonds he looked up to see Morlock standing at the door, evidently listening. The two torturers lay like broken dolls on the floor; Morlock had killed them without drawing blood.

"Help me," he said to his Grandmother's brother.

"How?"

"I . . . I want to bring Lorn away from here."

Again Morlock turned his bright colorless eyes on the King for a long moment. Whether the glance expressed surprise, disdain, or some other emotion the King could not tell and did not care.

"You'll have to carry him," Morlock said. "Our enemies are at our heels and I'll be fighting soon. I'll tie him to your back, though."

When the dreadful weight of Lorn's ruined body came down on his shoulders, Lathmar nearly quailed. But there was no alternative. He would die himself before he left Lorn here.

Morlock bound the flaccid body to his shoulders with twisted strips of cloth torn from the dead torturers' smocks. The King tried to gasp out an apology to Lorn for confining him after so brief a freedom. But Lorn did not answer; it probably hurt to speak, or perhaps he was unconscious.

When the binding was done the King turned sluggishly toward the door they had entered, but Morlock said, "We can't go that way. There must be a door yonder; the other torturer headed for it."

Straining with each step the King followed Morlock to the far wall and waited through the endless dragging seconds it took for Morlock to find the secret door hidden behind a woven stone panel. Morlock cast the panel aside, kicked the door open, and stepped through, holding Tyrfing in a high, close guard as he glanced up and down the hall. He motioned the King to follow him.

Dragging his feet along the slimy floor of the corridor outside, the King followed Morlock as he passed onward. There was the sound of booted feet behind them; the King hurried as best he could.

Then he froze, along with Morlock, as a Protector's Man stepped into the corridor in front of them.

"I just don't believe it," the soldier was saying.

"Madam," said a clear-voiced but unseen speaker, "you have a tin ear. No one but my master would make so much noise when trying to be sneaky. No matter how many soldiers are behind us we ought to—"

The speaker, now emerging into the corridor, stopped dead in his tracks and fell silent. A monstrous weedy green figure half a man's height, he raised his arm and pointed with a hand that dripped blood and water from the palm. The Protector's Man turned and froze, catching sight of Morlock and the King. Another moment of silence passed, and then the Ambrosii met with a roar of laughter as their enemies closed in from either side.

It was a brief, achingly long time they stood in the open corridor, laughing at each other as the King stood apart, his burden and their danger growing heavier with every heartbeat. Then, abruptly (the King couldn't follow what they were saying) they moved together, back along the corridor the way Morlock and the King had come, with Ambrosia in the lead.

Wyrth stepped next to the King and helped him shoulder Lorn, snapping the knotted makeshift cords around his waist like rotten string. The King was hoping that the dwarf would take the entire burden, but for some reason he did not.

"—were an idiot," Ambrosia was saying to her brother. "You should have guessed they would hold the two close together."

Morlock muttered something.

"I *said* I was an idiot," Ambrosia replied. "Or did I?"

"No, madam," the dwarf called. "That was us."

"Morlock, if you can't teach your froggy apprentice a lesson or two about silence, I'll— Trouble."

They were passing through the torture chamber again, and a company of soldiers was passing by outside. As the others got out of sight, Ambrosia stepped forward and engaged in gravel-voiced repartee with the patrol leader. The King couldn't understand a single one of their words—the world seemed to be expanding and contracting before his eyes; his face felt hot—but presently he found they were moving again.

The scrape of stone on stone shortly thereafter announced their entry into a hidden passage. They climbed an endless series of narrow dusty stairways, lightless airless holes where they must always go single file and he bore the lion's share of Lorn's weight, blood running into his eyes and hair.

Finally they reached a more open airy place, dimly and indirectly lit by openings near the ceiling. It must be day outside, the King realized. The dreadful endless night had ended at last.

Wyrth gently lifted Lorn from the King's shoulders and laid him in the corner, tearing cloth from his soggy shirt to cover the stumps where Lorn's hands had been.

The King collapsed nearby, drinking in the fact that he did not need to move, to flee, to hide, to fight, to pretend he was stronger than he was. Gasping he listened to the three others, chattering like veteran soldiers after a battle.

"I never thought we would make it. Never." (This was Ambrosia, his iron Grandmother.)

"Your ready wit saved us, twice and three times," Morlock remarked.

"My ready womb. We were all as stupid as mad pigs, blundering about inside a farmhouse. Let me see that hand. I should have slit Steng's throat."

"It's better not. They spent more time than they could afford trying to read the scene in Steng's room. Or so I guess."

"Especially after I left my sword in Steng's hand."

Morlock chuckled, an unpleasant sound. "Good. Good. A flight above the mad pig level, I'd say."

"Save your breath for screaming. This is going to hurt. Wyrth, there's a water bottle somewhere in this uniform—damn, it's nearly empty."

"There's a water stone in Morlock's pack. It ought to serve us all for a few days."

"Is that why he wanted that albatross along? Morlock, if you had left that damn thing with Genjandro—"

Morlock grunted, dissenting. "Delaying tactic."

"Scut."

"Not at all, Lady Ambrosia," the dwarf chipped in. "You should have seen him, before the Protector's Men broke in at Genjandro's, frantically repacking so that the book on gold making was on the top."

"To distract Steng, or whoever opened the pack? So. Did it work?"

Morlock grunted. "Yes. Steng's not a dangerous man. Wyrtheorn, don't bind those wounds yet."

"I was just going to sponge off the little King. Creator knows he's had enough blood dripped on him tonight."

"Let him rest," Morlock directed. "He pushed himself as far as he could. He has nerve, that one."

Ambrosia laughed, a short sharp sound like metal breaking. "You've misread that book, brother. The old fire has gone out in House Ambrose."

"We'll see."

"We've *seen*. If—" She broke off as the King sat up. There was silence as he struggled to his feet. They were all three looking solemnly at him, and he glared back.

"I don't care what you say about me," he said thickly. "But none of you has said *one word* about Lorn, or made *one move* to help him. So don't. I don't care! He wouldn't want your help! Give me some of that water and I'll clean his wounds myself."

That had got them! He exulted fiercely as he watched their frozen faces. The silence lasted for five heartbeats, and then Morlock said evenly, "King Lathmar, you cannot help Lorn. No one can. He is dead."

Lathmar turned and looked stupidly down on Lorn, lying not far away. It was true. It was obviously true.

"He died almost as he spoke to you," Morlock's voice went relentlessly on.

"Why didn't you tell me?" the King cried. He was horrified that he had carried that bag of broken bones a single step. It wasn't Lorn. Lorn was far from here. Lorn was dead. Lorn was dead.

"I'm sorry," said Morlock's voice from near at hand. The King looked up and saw those bright enigmatic eyes on him. "I misunderstood. I thought you were acting as his kin."

Ambrosia laughed harshly. "Dwarvish scut! Dead is dead."

"It is a dwarvish custom," Wyrth admitted. He, too, was suddenly at the King's side. "A slain, er, man has certain things owed to him. Revenge and burial, chiefly. Morlock provided the revenge; he thought you were bringing away the body for burial. I thought the same thing, but then I *am* a dwarf, and prone to believe in dwarvish scut."

"You killed him," the King said thickly.

Silence.

"You all killed him!" the King shouted. His face wrinkled as he spoke, stained with dried blood, Lorn's blood. "You killed him. You and your *empire!*" He screamed the last word as if it were the filthiest word in any language—which it was. It had killed Lorn.

"It is not our empire," Ambrosia responded calmly. She had taken her helmet off; he had almost forgotten what her face looked like during the endless night.

"It is," the King said wildly. "You created it. You built it into something men kill other men for. It's yours . . . and the . . . the Strange Gods can have it, and *you!*"

"Men will kill other men for a goat's knucklebone or a piece of dirt," Ambrosia said calmly. "They'll kill each other for the fun of killing. More to the point, do you think men like Steng and Urdhven would be wielding power if any of us three had a claim to the imperial throne?"

"If—"

"That was a rhetorical question, Lathmar, because the answer is, 'No.' Steng would be a street-corner hawker of drugs; Urdhven would be knocking up ex-maidens in his little barony; and Lorn would be a living, itching, complaining foot soldier instead of a dead hero if this were *my* empire. The trouble with it is that it's not mine. It's yours or no one's. That is why men are killing each other in these evil days, Lathmar. Because what is no one's might be anyone's, if only he can get it."

"Enough," Morlock said. "Ambrosia, he is grieving for his friend."

Ambrosia spat out a clot of dark phlegm before replying. "Don't coddle him, Morlock. He's seen *one* soldier die in this civil war. Lorn wasn't the first and won't be the last."

"You sound like Merlin," Morlock remarked.

Ambrosia became very still. Then she said quietly, "That's a woman's argument."

Morlock grunted. "Then it ought to be effective. Wyrth, tend to the King."

Lathmar struck out desperately at the hard blunt hands that offered to take his arm. But his strength, such as it was, had gone. The last thing he remembered was sitting with his head on his knees weeping uncontrollably. He had begun to cry when Morlock called Lorn his friend, and now he could not stop. In all his life he had had one friend, and now that friend was dead. What was an empire compared to that?

Part Three

House of Fame

> Emperors and kings
> are but obeyed in their several
> provinces
> nor can they raise the wind nor rend
> the clouds.
> But his dominion that exceeds in this
> stretcheth as far as doth the mind of
> man.
>
> —Marlowe, *Doctor Faustus*

CHAPTER ELEVEN

WITHIN THE WALLS

hrough the nine or so months they hid within the stony womb of Ambrose's hidden passages, "sitting on each other's damn elbows," as Ambrosia herself impatiently put it, the King only saw the dwarf Wyrtheorn embarrassed once. He only saw him angry once. This cheerful unflappability was one of the things that made him a good companion, but it was one of the things that set him apart from the others, made him a little strange to Lathmar.

For Merlin's children were anything but unflappable. Ambrosia was frequently and furiously angry. For Lathmar she clearly felt equal amounts of affection and contempt, and would spill from one to the other in midconversation.

That didn't bother him. He always knew she had felt that way, and it was almost a relief to hear her say as much. Her anger didn't frighten him, but her weakness did. He watched one night, covertly and with mounting horror, as she sat talking with Morlock and Wyrth, talking and talking in her hard clear voice, one arm thrown carelessly about her brother's shoulders (as crooked as her own), her other hand holding tightly to one of his. Talking and talking as her head drooped and jerked with weariness, talking in her hard clear voice. Afraid to sleep, afraid to let go, afraid. Afraid.

Though he was rarely angry, and never at Lathmar, Morlock was worse.

As the days passed into months, his hand healed, he grew less pale. But while he was still bleeding he directed Wyrth in burying Lorn within the castle walls, carving the epitaph with his own hands: *LORN: soldier and friend of Lathmar VII*. And from the first day he took charge of the King's education— he was grammarian, fencing master, and court sorcerer all in one.

"Ten thousand things you need to know I cannot teach you," he said to Lathmar. "The law of your empire is nothing I understand, for instance. But the language of the land where I was born, the secret speech as you miscall it, I can teach you that. There is much knowledge in that language, and many of your subjects are exiles from the Wardlands, as I am. I can teach you to defend yourself with a sword. And I can teach you the uses of the Sight within you—the skills of vision."

He was patient; he never lashed out at Lathmar as Ambrosia did. But he was terrifyingly unpredictable. Once, when Ambrosia cuffed Lathmar for some slight error (he never remembered what it was for, but the blow was nothing—the kitchen servants used to hit him harder to amuse themselves), Morlock stepped forward and threw his sister, his beloved sister, whom he rocked nightly to sleep in his arms (as she talked and talked and talked), against the wall and kicked her feet out from under her. Lathmar cowered, waiting for the Dark Man to turn on him, but it never happened. Ambrosia picked herself off the ground, laughed shortly, and said, "You'll soften him up, Morlock. His trouble is, he hasn't been beaten enough."

Morlock stared at her with his pale eyes until she turned away. She never hit Lathmar again.

Lathmar was not allowed to grow soft. Morlock, as fencing master, worked him until he literally fell over with exhaustion. Fencing, yes, endless mock combat, but always with a deadly point. The court fencing teacher had never been especially concerned with the King's proficiency, but Morlock and his apprentice casually assumed that Lathmar would, soon and often, be fighting for his life. Along with the necessary formality of thrust and parry they discussed the location of probably mortal wounds, weak spots in body armor, tactics when fighting more than one opponent. Lathmar balanced for hours on the ball of one foot while Morlock and Wyrth walked around him, tossing him a ball that he had to toss back without delay.

"Is this how Naevros taught you?" Lathmar demanded in a rare pause from exercises.

Morlock fixed him with a gray luminous glance, saying nothing.

"I . . . I had heard you were taught by Naevros syr Tol in . . . in the old time," Lathmar said.

"Naevros taught me the way of the sword," Morlock acknowledged finally. "There were some who said it was a waste of time—that a crookback would never learn. But he taught me so well that when the time came, I was able to kill him."

Lathmar was aghast, even more so when he saw the grief on Morlock's dark face. He had loved Naevros, it was clear, yet "when the time came," he had killed him. He loved his sister, had risked his life to save her, but he had thrown her about like a rag doll for no good reason. No one this man loved was safe, obviously; someday "the time" would come and Morlock would destroy them in turn. Maybe it was part of the curse that went with Tyrfing.

As a teacher in sorcery Morlock was even more demanding. The difficulty lay in the fact that seer-training did not consist of learning things. "We must strengthen your intuition, your inner voice," Morlock said. "Your perception, too, is coarsely material; we must liberate it. Push-ups won't help, nor noun-declensions."

What did help, it seemed, was an almost endless series of pranks. Lathmar would be told to go to a room and practice with a sword there for an hour; he would do so, then when it came to resheathe the blade he found it was not in his hands. It had never been: it was an illusion. Morlock's hand would leap off his arm and run like a rat into a hole in the wall. But on second glance Morlock's hand was as it had been, and there was no hole in the wall. Illusion. Or Lathmar would walk around a bend in the corridor and there stood the Lord Protector in full armor.

"Morlock!" he cried impatiently. "I don't have time for this now! I have to go steal some food."

"Who told you to?" the Protector inquired, in Morlock's voice.

"Wyrth. He said . . ." The King's voice trailed off. "It wasn't Wyrth."

The Lord Protector dissolved into Morlock. "How do you know?"

The King shrugged. It was partly a guess. But, as he thought back, there was something odd and . . . insubstantial about that Wyrth. "Wyrth never calls it stealing," Lathmar said finally.

Morlock's pale glance betrayed impatience. "Of course not. I used the word to suggest doubt in your mind. But you only just thought of it. There was something else, but you do not speak of it."

"I don't know how!" the King cried out.

Morlock was not displeased. He motioned for Lathmar to follow him.

Presently Lathmar found himself in an empty square chamber he had never entered before. Wyrth was there, sitting with his back against the wall opposite the door. He was also sitting next to the door. Lathmar glanced around the room: there were four Wyrths, each sitting with his back to a wall. Each one, as he met his eye, smiled and waved agreeably.

"Here is my apprentice," said the Dark Man, "and three simulacra we have crafted. You may get as close as you like to them, but do not actually touch them. Also, do not engage them in conversation. Go about the room and tell me what you perceive."

The King walked about the room. In a few moments he returned. "They are all different," he said, feeling helpless.

"But?" Morlock had a knack for spotting his unspoken reservations.

"But that one isn't alive," Lathmar said, pointing at the Wyrth sitting next to the door. "I don't know what it is."

Morlock reached down and tugged at the Wyrth's boot. He fell into a heap of shining cord, and Morlock deftly wrapped it up and stowed it in a bag in his belt.

"A physical shell," he explained. "The most difficult simulacrum to spot, *if* there is someone inside it. Tell me of the others."

"I think the real Wyrth is sitting opposite the door."

"I didn't ask you to find the real Wyrth," Morlock replied coldly, "though of course I expected you to try. Tell me of the others."

"That one"—Lathmar pointed at a Wyrth—"isn't there."

"What do you mean? Don't you see him?"

"Yes and no. I'm sure he's there. But I know he isn't. He . . . I feel him in my mind. But my eyes can't feel him."

Morlock nodded encouragingly, and the false Wyrth vanished. "A tal-

construct, projected directly into your mind. For the adept, the easiest of simulacra to spot: the talic halo is unmistakable, nothing like a real person or thing."

Lathmar slowly approached the Wyrth opposite. "This is the strangest of all," he whispered.

"Put your hand out," Morlock directed. "Touch it."

"Wait!" The Wyrth who had been sitting opposite the door got up and walked over. "Let me look at the thing for a few moments longer. God Creator! Master Morlock, it's wonderful."

Morlock grunted. "*You* would think so."

"That's not what I mean and you know it. Do you see what it is, Lathmar?"

"No."

"Keep on looking at it, then." Wyrth went over and doused the lamp in the middle of the room. Everything went dark—except the last simulacrum of Wyrth. It remained as bright as it had been, and lit the room like a candle.

"He *built* it," Wyrth said, coming over. "Took light from a window and carved this image in it."

"The process is more like weaving," Morlock corrected him. "Each mote of light must have a stable path, linked to others, or the image will dissolve."

Lathmar hesitantly put his hand out to touch the luminous image. There was no surface; his hand passed into it, and light splashed and foamed about his wrist. The image dimmed markedly as captive light motes left their paths. Within the simulacrum a small mechanism sat on the floor, with an upright armature that moved at intervals.

Wyrth lit the lamp again, and Morlock dispersed the simulacrum with a wave of his hands. He picked up the small machine and handed it to Wyrth. "This shifted the paths from time to time," he explained, "so that the figure could move."

Lathmar was struck by Wyrth's evident wonder. "Is the craft of Making difficult?" he asked. "Could I learn it?"

"No," said Morlock flatly. "You have no gift that way. Yet you may become a master seer, far greater than I am. If you were not king and emperor-to-be I would send you to New Moorhope in the Wardlands. But I can teach you much that you need to know, and in the end, the master trains himself. Enough for today. Perhaps you and Wyrth should go and 'gather' some food after all. Don't forget grain for the crows." He walked off without a farewell to either of the others.

"He thinks more of those crows than he does of you or me!" Lathmar, stung, complained to Wyrth.

The dwarf grinned and shook his head. "But if you could carry messages to the city, like the crows do, that would impress him, certainly. We'll work on it, in your copious free time."

"Wyrth," the King whispered, as they descended the narrow hidden stairs that led toward the kitchens. "Why don't you call it 'stealing' when we go to get food?"

"Because it's not," Wyrth said flatly. "This castle and all its contents are yours in law. Your 'Protector' is the thief."

"I know," the King said patiently. "But . . ."

Wyrth looked back over his shoulder and grinned. "But you think there's something more?"

"Yes."

"You're right. I'm a dwarf. Stealing and lying are the two most serious offenses a dwarf can commit; they're even the same word in Dwarvish. I've done my share of both, I suppose, but I'm not as lighthearted about it as the Lady Ambrosia is."

"Morlock seems to feel about it almost as you do."

"He doesn't. He's just being civil—he was raised among dwarves, himself, so he knows how I feel."

"What was he like, back then?" the King wondered. He found it hard to believe Morlock had ever been young.

"*Rosh takna.* I don't know. Morlock was exiled from the Wardlands about the time Ambrosia married your ancestor, Uthar the Great. What is that, three hundred years ago? I'm not even a hundred fifty years old. A bit aged for an apprentice, but not old enough to remember Morlock's youth."

"Why do you stay an apprentice? I thought all dwarves wanted the title of Master Maker."

"I do," Wyrth acknowledged. "I suppose I should have demanded Morlock release me and gone off as a journey-smith some time ago. That's the usual way: apprentice, journey-smith, master. But he wanders a lot, you know, so I'm effectively a journey-smith as long as I stay with him. It's when I leave him that I'll be ready to settle down somewhere as master of my own shop. Also, Morlock is the master of all makers. I could spend another century, or the rest of my life, in his service and still learn new things every day."

"Will you?"

"No," Wyrth admitted. "Someday I'll leave him. But not just yet. He needs me."

Lathmar summoned up a vision of Morlock's dark, pitiless, impassive face and shook his head.

Wyrth was not looking at him (the narrow stairway was slippery and difficult just there) but said, "I know what you think of him. And Ambrosia thinks the same—that he is unbreakable. But no one knows him as well as I do. And I know not only that he's breakable, but that he's *broken*. Morlock is just a ruin of the man he might have been, the man he probably was when he defeated the Sunkillers."

"What are the Sunkillers?"

"Ach. It was before I was born; I shouldn't have mentioned it. You'll have to ask one of the grown-ups." He glanced over his shoulder again, and this time his expression was embarrassed—almost ashamed. "Don't say that I mentioned it."

Stealing food was fun, and the King was pretty good at it. He had, of course, often done it before, when he was hungry and he didn't want to face the kitchen servants' insults. The trick was to not take too much of any one thing—to make your pillage blend in with the casual looting that went on in any pantry. And always, of course, to enter and leave unobserved. The castle's pantries were large, and most of them had some sort of discreet access to the hidden passages, which it was the King's business to know (and the servants' business to not know, or pretend they didn't know). Wyrth and he, when they went together, took turns foraging in the pantry; the other was to guard their pile of loot, on the off chance that someone would happen by in the passage they were using.

At least it had always seemed like an off chance. But that afternoon, as the King sat on a step, kicking his heels and eating a piece of cheese, a hand gripped his collar and yanked him into the air.

"What's this?" a strange voice snarled in his ear. "City brats sneaking around in the castle walls? If—"

The King gritted his teeth and kicked the man holding him from behind as hard as he could, trying to aim the blow between the other's legs. He apparently succeeded well enough: with a roar of anger the man threw him against a wall. The world went dim for a moment or two. When he returned to himself the man (a Protector's Man: the red lion rampant on the man's black tunic) was bent over, gasping, staring at him with recognition dawning on his face.

"You're—" he began.

But then Wyrth was there, his arms full of plunder. He dropped the stuff and stepped between the King and the Protector's Man. He kicked one of the soldier's knees, which gave with an audible crunch, and grabbed him by the throat as he sprawled. The dwarf efficiently broke the man's neck, and then turned to Lathmar. "Are you all right?" he asked calmly.

Lathmar stared at the dead man. "Better than him," he said finally.

"Traitorous bastard," Wyrth remarked, as if discussing the weather.

"Because he wanted an afternoon snack!" the King exclaimed.

"No." Wyrth, puzzled but patient, pointed at the emblem on the man's tunic. "Because of that. Because he took up arms against his sovereign."

"Well, I'm not much of a sovereign."

"I didn't mean you. Lathmar, I'm not much on practical politics—you'll have to go to the Lady Ambrosia for that—but there is no real chance that Urdhven would have made a move against his brother-in-law—your father— if he hadn't had a private army sworn to his service. This thing and others like him are responsible for your parents' deaths. He'd gladly have been responsible for yours. Don't waste too much pity on him."

"How much is too much?"

"Anything at all. We'll have to haul him out of here—do you want to carry the corpse or the food?"

Lathmar thought of Lorn. "The food," he said swiftly.

Wyrth nodded and casually swung the body of the man he had killed over his shoulder. "I can keep him up here with one hand," he said, "so if you need me to carry anything. . . ."

"I'll manage," the King said faintly.

They brought the corpse and the food to Merlin's children, who were sitting with their heads together, making plans. Plans had been proposed and dismissed at the rate of several a day, and those were only the ones the King happened to hear his elders talking about. He paid them no attention. They would no doubt tell him what they wanted him to do when they wanted him to do it, just as his elders always had. Till then, the future was their problem.

"Hm," said Morlock, glancing at the body. "Save the clothes. Toss the body down a privy shaft."

"I thought you were going to suggest giving it to your crows," Ambrosia said tauntingly.

Morlock shrugged. "Draw too much attention," he muttered, as if he had already considered the idea. "Lathmar: wait."

Lathmar turned, defiantly. He was prepared to strip the body of the Protector's Man and dispose of it in the sewer—that was a matter of survival. If Morlock expected him to butcher a human body for the benefit of their feathered friends, he intended to rebel.

So he was taken off guard when Morlock asked him, "Can you sew?"

"What?"

"Do you know how to sew?" Morlock asked again.

"With a thread and needle, you mean?"

"Yes."

"No," said Lathmar slowly.

"'Not yet,' you mean," Wyrth corrected. "What's up, Ambrosii? A plan?"

"The beginnings," Ambrosia said. "You had better teach Lathmar how to sew. Morlock's teaching me. We'll need a large amount of red silk, also— there should be acres of the stuff in the storerooms, as it's the imperial color. But offhand I can't remember if there are any passages leading directly to those rooms, so stealing it might be a little more difficult than our grocery trips have been."

"There goes your copious free time, Your Majesty," Wyrth remarked. "We'll start right after we dispose of the body."

His Majesty stoically deposited the food on the floor and helped Wyrth drag off the corpse.

Thereafter sewing and silk stealing were part of the curriculum. Silk stealing was exciting at first, as it involved a trip through the open corridors. But soon they found that practically no one visited that portion of the castle, so that, if anything, those raids were more humdrum than a trip to the pantries.

Sewing wasn't as much fun as hearing and translating the old songs and stories Morlock and Wyrth and even sometimes Ambrosia told him when he was working on the secret speech. It wasn't as annoying, though, as Morlock's repeated attempts to shock his mind into Sight, nor nearly as hard work as the sword practice. And it was rather companionable to sit with his elders, as he and Ambrosia struggled with some new stitch and Morlock and Wyrth folded paper models of four-dimensional objects, or discussed the casting of gemstones, or simply reminisced of centuries long past. (Wyrth might be less than one hundred fifty years old, and so a mere youngster to the Ambrosii, but he could speak for and about his forbears with dwarvish ease.)

It was at times like these that Lathmar (as long as he kept up with his sewing—and, in fact, he was better at it than Ambrosia was, with her wounded hands) could sometimes get a question answered. For instance, he might ask, "Why do the descendants of exiles dream about the Wardlands?" or "Why did Lathmar the Old leave the Vraidish homelands?" and one or the other of the oldsters would tell the tale—usually Ambrosia or Wyrth, with laconic additions and observations by Morlock.

The danger that lived in the blood of Ambrose was never far away, though. Once, when they had been working on the sewing project for some time (perhaps a month), Lathmar asked, "Who are the Sunkillers?"

Morlock did not answer, but turned to glare at Wyrth, a snarl on his dark face.

Wyrth was undaunted. "Master Morlock, I've obeyed your orders and told no tale."

"How does he know that name?"

"I mentioned it once. I told him to ask you or Ambrosia about it."

Morlock clenched his teeth, too angry to speak.

"The world calls you traitor and monster," Wyrth remarked quietly in the charged silence. His voice was as level as ever, but it occurred to Lathmar that he was annoyed, even angry. "And I say nothing to this: canyon keep the world, anyway. But why may Lathmar not know the truth?"

"There is no *truth!*" shouted Morlock.

Wyrth rolled his eyes and spoke a guttural syllable that Lathmar suspected was a Dwarvish obscenity. "You can believe that if you like. I don't," he added.

"The Sunkillers," Ambrosia remarked, as if the exchanges between Morlock and his apprentice had not taken place, "were a group of beings from beyond the northern edge of the world."

Lathmar's jaw dropped. "The world really has a northern edge?"

"Yes. Most people would have to answer by hearsay, but I was actually there once. The Sunkillers had taken an interest in our world and intended to conquer it. Or rather, before Morlock steps in to correct me, to cleanse it. Evidently they considered life of our fecund mortal kind a sort of disease infecting an otherwise appealing world. They affected the rays of the sun so that the temperature of the world dropped considerably. Life would have ceased, and I don't mind telling you, Lathmar, I would have found that inconvenient. So I recruited a young fellow at the court of your namesake, Lathmar the Old, and my brother (who had been useful to me in the past). Wyrth's father, Deor, insisted on accompanying Morlock. The four of us passed through the northern wilderness where men may not dwell (and even Deor and I found it uncomfortable) to the edge of the world. There Morlock crossed the Soul Bridge and fought with the champion of the Sunkillers. He killed him and destroyed the Soul Bridge from the far side. Then we brought him back to the world by methods you may someday learn, if your education in the craft of Seeing progresses considerably farther than it has."

Lathmar could not goggle any further, but neither could he speak. No one spoke. Morlock stood and limped away, and there was silence for some time.

Eventually Lathmar stuttered, "Why . . . ? Why . . . ?"

"He hates the story," Ambrosia explained, "because it was the beginning of the end of the only life he cared about. He was a vocate in the Graith of Guardians, a hero of sorts in the Wardlands. Wyrth could tell you stories, no doubt, and even I know a few. He was married to a woman he loved—the only one he has ever loved (may she be damned for a poisonous bitch). He lost all that and had to go into exile."

"Because . . ."

"There was something involving one of the other Guardians—Morlock either killed him or prevented him from being killed; I never got the story straight. But the real reason was that the Graith, or at least some of its senior members, had an arrangement with the Sunkillers. The rest of the world would be frozen, but the Wardlands would not be harmed. I don't know if they had reason to suppose they would be spared, or if they were just dupes. Morlock wouldn't have stood for it either way. So when Morlock defeated their plans they had him exiled: he'd put something else before the safety of the realm. They call that treason over there."

"Is that why your father Merlin was exiled?" Lathmar asked.

"No. He was *actually* a traitor. Had I been a member of the Graith I would simply have killed him—but that was all before I was born, or even conceived, so I'm rather glad none of them had my forceful independent character."

"You were born in exile?"

"Yes—like you, young Lathmar. But my mother was already pregnant with Morlock when Merlin was exiled, so the Graith graciously allowed her to give birth and dump the child on an unfortunate stepfamily before departing the country."

"I thought you were older than Morlock."

Ambrosia turned her iron-gray glance at him, and he stuttered helplessly until she smiled and said, "I *look* older, I know. But Morlock was born in the Wardlands and grew to manhood there. That changes you, somehow: either the land itself or the magical wards they use to guard the place. My father was a thousand years old when I was born, but I'll never live that long. None of my descendants has lived nearly as long as me—although, of course, I didn't marry an exile. Have you any other imprudent questions, Lathmar?

Would you be interested in knowing whether I was the mistress of Lathmar the Old before I married his son, Uthar the Great?"

"No, madam," said Lathmar VII, with perfect honesty.

"Any prudent questions, then? This seems to be the moment when they will be answered with more than two or three gnomic syllables."

"Well . . . ," Lathmar began, cleared his throat, and began again. "What is it we are making with all this sewing?"

With gnomic brevity Wyrth replied, "A dragon."

The next day there were no lessons of any kind. "Morlock's drunk," the dwarf said harshly, and Lathmar laughed, thinking Wyrth was joking. (They never bothered to steal wine; that would mean a trip to the palace cellars, far from any secret passage and extremely well guarded.) Lathmar looked at the dwarf and waited for him to continue the joke, but he didn't. He turned away without saying anything and left Lathmar to his own devices.

Chapter Twelve

News from Invarna

enjandro shouldered his way into the wineshop. A serving maid turned to greet him, then started back when she saw his face.

You'll look like a big ugly bruiser in this one. So had said the note from Wyrth, attached to the threadlike coil of the simulacrum Genjandro wore. *But don't get in any fights. The simulacrum changes the way you look completely, but it's only a Seeming. You'll be no stronger than you really are.*

And it was true. Genjandro had wrapped the Seeming around himself and was transformed into the ugliest hulking dockyard thug he had ever seen . . . but when he tried to lift something that was normally too heavy for him, it was *still* too heavy.

No matter. No one wanted to make trouble for Genjandro-thug. In fact, everyone was impressed with the soft-spoken menace in his tone . . . although the exact same tone impressed no one when he was wearing his own face.

He trundled over to the bar and slapped down a silver coin. "Gimme the hot stuff," he rasped. Not being a customer of slimy vomit-pits like this one, he hadn't thought up this line: a note from Morlock had suggested it. (Genjandro suspected Morlock had more experience in such places than he himself did. In the seven or so months that Morlock had stayed at Genjandro's not once had he seen the man drink anything stronger than water. So Morlock either avoided strong drink on some religious or ethical principle—to Genjandro, he didn't seem the type—or he refrained because he knew that he would drink to excess if he drank at all. He *did* seem like that type; he had the clenched weariness of what Genjandro's blessed mother used to call "a dry drunk." But Genjandro had never mentioned the matter, nor had anyone else in his hearing.) The same demand got him a different brew of sewage in every hellhole he went in. But apparently it was something someone with his present appearance would be expected to say: he got a lot of nasty drinks, but never a raised eyebrow.

He gulped a mouthful of the "hot stuff," belched an appreciative spray of the same, and said to the barkeep, "I'm drinking up and getting out."

"Oh?" said the barkeep, in a carefully neutral tone. Genjandro read him exactly. He was not much interested in anything Genjandro had to say, but he was reluctant to indicate this to anyone so obviously dangerous as Genjandro appeared to be.

"Chaos, yes," Genjandro said. "One drink in every shop around the Great Market, and then I'm getting out. Probably never see the place again."

"Settling down somewhere?" inquired the barkeep quietly. Genjandro saw suspicion settling on his features. He was wondering if Genjandro was an informer of the Protector's, trying to stir up a little talk of treason. It wasn't an unreasonable fear. Genjandro had met a number of Protector's Men—or aspirants to that noble title—on such missions, sneaking around the market or sniffing along the docks.

"Hell, no," Genjandro protested. "I'm not the settling kind. And if I was, I'd settle right here—in the greatest city in the world, with the greatest ruler, Morlock rip my nose off if it ain't so."

"Hear, hear," said the barkeep tepidly. He seemed to understand Genjandro's comment in exactly the sense it was intended—as a disclaimer of any political intent.

"No—I'll be around," Genjandro said, trying to sound wistful. "But the city—*she won't*. Not after the dragons get through with her."

That got the attention of everyone in the place.

"Whatcha mean dragons, chief?" someone asked him, in a conversational tone.

"I mean big damn dragons from the Blackthorn Range," Genjandro said flatly. He took another slurp of "hot stuff," snorted back the snot which the poisonous brew had set to flowing from his nose, and said, "They took Sarkunden the other day."

"*What?*" shouted the barkeep, and everyone in the place leapt to their feet. Sarkunden was the biggest city between Ontil and the eastern border. Farther east lay the Blackthorns, with their mysterious deadly dragons.

"You're a frigging liar, ugluk," said someone behind his back.

He turned with exaggerated slowness and looked curiously about. No one stood forth to identify himself as the speaker. Genjandro shrugged generously. "So you're thinking: *they'd'a told us if the dragons took Sarkunden; we'd'a heard.*" He spat on the floor and winked. "But we don't hear much they don't want us to hear—do we?"

It was true, in a way. The empire was separating into armed duchies, each one led by the local military commander. The Protector was their titular head, but he was having trouble getting the other commanders to follow his lead. They said that if the Protector had killed the last heir of Uthar the Great (as rumor claimed) then they were absolved of their allegiance. Possibly some of them had imperial ambitions of their own. Travel between the various great centers was discouraged; passports were required; news had slowed to a trickle or (from some regions) had stopped entirely.

"Then how'd you hear?" the barkeep inquired.

It was the question he'd been waiting for. He turned back to the barkeep and said, "Well, I got a friend."

"Oh?"

"Yeah. Anyway, I *had* one. He was a Protector's Man, pretty high up, rode the post between here and Sarkunden. Our Protector's been writing a lot to Sarkunden; I don't know if you know."

The barkeep made a face. It was hard to keep away from politics these days. But it was widely believed that the commander of the Sarkunden garrison—a cousin of the Protector's on his mother's side—would eventually acknowledge the leadership of the Protector, once they came to terms.

"Anyway," Genjandro continued, "this guy gets to Sarkunden pretty often—two or three times a month. They first heard the dragons were out of the Blackthorns a couple months ago—one of them Anhikh cities got hit."

"Oh?"

"That was exactly what I said—exactly like that: 'Oh?' Screw them Anhikh guys. Who do they think they are, anyway? Then the dragons turned west, though. They took one of our towns on the border, Invarna."

"You're *sure* about this?" the barkeep asked doubtfully.

"Hey," Genjandro shouted to the room at large, "when was the last time any of you guys heard any news from Invarna?"

It turned out none of them had heard anything recently from Invarna. The same would likely have been true of any random group of people in Ontil on any given day in any given year, and they all knew it. But somehow the fact became freighted with ill omen: *no news from Invarna . . .*

"It's not so far from there to Sarkunden, and the dragons got closer every day: killing and stealing and . . . well, dragons eat a lot, you know."

Everyone knew that. And everyone knew what they ate by preference: other dragons, or dwarves, or men and women.

"The last time my friend comes back from Sarkunden the dragons are actually in the city, and the garrison commander, he's writing the Protector, begging him for help. And the Protector he writes back." Genjandro winked. "I read the letter."

There was a general snort of derision. "Read this letter," the barkeep said dismissively, pointing at something under the bar.

"It's pretty easy to lift the seal off a letter," Genjandro pointed out patiently. "My friend, he used to do it all the time with a hot wire. He wanted to know what was going on. Wouldn't you?"

There was some grudging agreement to this, and Genjandro continued. "Anyway, the Protector writes back how he can't see coming to the aid of a rebel military commander—but if the general and his troops were to take an oath to him, become Protector's Men, then maybe they could work something out. Smart move." Genjandro smacked his lips, glanced at his nearly empty cup, and repeated distantly, "Smart move."

The barkeep quietly filled Genjandro's cup with "hot stuff." Genjandro took a mouthful, wiped his mouth, and said fiercely, "Or it *woulda been* a smart move. If the guy he'd been writing to was still alive. Which I don't think he was. My friend, he never came back from that last trip to Sarkunden.

Now the Protector can't get anyone else to go, and no one's sure how soon they'll get here. But they'll get here. If they liked Sarkunden, they'll like Ontil that much more."

"Scut," said the barkeep—not as if he really disbelieved what Genjandro was saying, but as if he wished he could.

"I think it's true," said a little fellow with the stained hands of a dyer. "I was talking to a Kaenish merchant, and he told me about the Anhikh city—he said he'd talked to someone who'd seen it after the dragons left."

Genjandro nodded with a certain satisfaction. After all, he himself (in another simulacrum, in another wineshop) had been the fat Kaenish merchant who had told the dyer about the fictitious Anhikh city; he was glad the little fellow had learned his lesson so well. But he was even more gratified when someone he had never seen before claimed to have heard about the dragon attack on Sarkunden from someone else. If true, it meant that the rumors he was so diligently spreading were taking on their own life in the city.

"It's those damn Ambrosii!" someone shouted, and there was a rumble of agreement. Nothing was beyond the Ambrosii, Morlock in particular: a thousand folktales assured them of that.

The words spoken represented Genjandro's greatest fear about the plan Morlock and Ambrosia were undertaking. He had written desperately to them, begging them not to threaten the city with the fear of dragons and fire. *It will give the Protector a chance to portray himself as the hero of Ontil, and you as its ultimate villains*, he had written, in part of a long letter which was carried to the Ambrosii (as usual) by a crow. Their response, in full, had been *Yes*. He did not understand it. But in the end, because the King wrote to him directing him to obey them, he did their bidding.

"Or maybe," he said, into a silence in the uncertain crowd, "the dragons aren't scared of Ontil, now that the Ambrosii are gone? The dwarves call both of them *rokhleni*, dragonkillers. . . ."

He convinced no one. In fact, he felt that he had broken his character a little. But at least he had stopped that sudden movement of anger toward the King's true protectors. "Anyway," he said, and paused to down the rest of his cup. (He managed to spill most of it down the sides of his face—it stung a little, but better that than drinking the stuff.) "Anyway, here's to Venhudnal, best damn Protector's Man since the Protector himself. Now I'm off to hit a few more places, then head across the big water. They say the dragons are afraid of the big water." He headed for the door, a little more unsteadily than he had come in. No one seemed sorry to see him go, but he heard a gratifying hum of conversation in his wake.

Outside he headed for the nearest alley and shoved his finger up his throat until he vomited. He had more wineshops to visit and more tales to tell before the night was out; he didn't want to be incoherent. Then he carefully unwound the Seeming of Genjandro the thug and stowed it in his wallet. There was no risk of him being seen, in the utterly lightless alley, but that meant that he had to work very carefully, since he couldn't see what he was doing.

He drew another threadlike spool of Seeming out of his wallet. As usual there was a note attached, but of course he couldn't read it in the dark; he kept it by in case it had useful information. He wound the new Seeming about himself and stepped out into the dim light of the Great Market at night.

The note, which he read by the light streaming from the nearby wineshop, was in Wyrth's handwriting: *You'll be a little cuter in this one. But don't let anyone pick you up until you've spread a few rumors, eh?*

Genjandro glanced down at the improbable expanse of barely contained cleavage which was one noticeable feature of his new Seeming. "Most amusing," he said sourly, and wondered what sort of voice he should attempt to use with this appearance. Thinking dark thoughts he trudged off to serve his sovereign, Lathmar VII, in the peculiar way that Fate and the Ambrosii, between them, had devised.

CHAPTER THIRTEEN

HEROES AND VILLAINS

ne evening Steng awoke from a nap to find a message from his true master lying in the fireplace of his apartment. They often appeared there, in his own peculiar handwriting, after he had been sleeping. The message said simply, *A dragon has been seen in the woods north of the city. Warn Urdhven: it is a sending of the Ambrosii.* There was no signature, of course: none was needed.

He scrolled up the message and stuck it into a fold of his tunic. Hurrying through the corridors, he found Lord Protector Urdhven consulting with Vost over a large stone table covered with maps in the room that had formerly been the Emperor's council chamber.

"My Lord Urdhven," Steng said without preliminary, "a dragon has been seen in the woods between the city and the Whitethorn Range."

"Old news, Steng," Vost crowed vengefully. "We've been plotting the dragon's progress from Anhi with these maps, and the intelligence collected by my men."

"Hm. Perhaps if you deployed a *great many* of your men the aggregate intelligence might amount to something significant."

While Vost was working this out, Steng continued, "But I don't suppose Vost's men have told you that the dragon is a sending of the Ambrosii."

"It is?" Urdhven was eager to believe it. "How do you know? Can you be sure?" Vost gazed at him woundedly.

Since Vost was not looking at him for the moment, Steng made an arcane gesture and said, "Very sure."

"Oh." Urdhven's enthusiasm cooled. "Excellent. But you have nothing we can announce as proof?"

"Not yet. Is proof needed?"

"We can hope so. Look here, Steng, the dragons left the Blackthorns some months ago and savaged a number of Anhikh cities. Among them have been named Menebacikhukh and Sekntepaphonokhai."

"That's easy for you to say."

"Knock off the jaded witticisms and look at the map! Menebacikhukh and Sekntepaphonokhai are due east of Invarna, which is just on our side of the Anhikh border. Now Invarna is the one town in the empire we are fairly sure has been struck by the dragons."

"I heard a circumstantial rumor that Sarkunden had been taken."

"No, that's just a rumor. I'm in daily communication with the garrison there."

"With respect, Lord Urdhven, you miss my point. If we have circumstantial rumors about Sarkunden which we know are false, are we not in danger of being taken in by rumors about places where our information is less current? Why do we think Invarna has been taken, not to mention—those Anhikh places?"

"We never know much about what goes on in Anhi. But no one has heard from Invarna in months."

"Eh, Lord Urdhven, when does one ever hear from Invarna?"

"Look at the pattern, man! From Menebacikhukh to Sekntepaphonokhai, from Sekntepaphonokhai to Invarna, from Invarna to here. The dragons are headed due west to the Gap of Lone—they must plan some sort of action against the Wardlands."

Steng was genuinely dismayed. "Death and Justice! I hope you're wrong!"

"Oh?" Urdhven's voice was oily and dangerous.

"Yes indeed. If the dragons attempt an invasion of the Wardlands, the Graith of Guardians is likely to meet them in force before they cross the border. That would mean a war between the dragons and the powers of the Wardlands in *our* territory. There might be nothing left alive between the Grartan Range and the Inner Sea!"

"Nonsense, Steng. No one has that kind of power."

"Eh, Lord Urdhven, those-who-know fear the Wardlands. Well, we can do nothing about that, if it is so. But, remember, the unnamed tells us that the dragon north of the city is a sending of the Ambrosii."

"Exactly!" Urdhven said. "Perhaps a rogue dragon drawn off from the herd—"

"The guile, my lord. We say 'guile of dragons'—like a pride of lions, or a murder of crows."

Urdhven's glance showed that he was thinking of murder of a different sort, and Steng fell silent. "The Ambrosii have skills we know nothing of," the Lord Protector continued, "and ancient ties to the dragons of the Blackthorn Range. They may have managed to draw off a rogue dragon from *the herd* to spread terror and death in the city."

"For what purpose, my Lord Protector?"

"To discredit my rule. To weaken the city against an assault from outside. Sheer malice."

Steng reserved his true opinion and said, "Three excellent reasons, Lord Urdhven. I am well answered. Then you hope to defeat the dragon and gain credit from it, as the city's defender?"

Urdhven seemed to relax a little: his loyal poisoner was again performing as expected. "Yes. What do you think of the plan?"

"I hope you never have a chance to put it into practice, my Lord Protector. The city is perpetually in danger of burning down as it is, without a dragon putting down in the Great Market. But I think that a set of patrols within the city would do a great deal of good—a dragon watch, as it were. People are very near panic with all these rumors."

"We could design a special banner for the dragon watch," Vost broke in. "That way people would know at a glance of the Protector's care for them."

"Hm. Not bad," Steng conceded grudgingly. "Really an excellent idea. These dragon rumors may ultimately be to the Protector's advantage. The Ambrosii are an invisible menace, as long as they remain in hiding, but everyone can understand the threat of a dragon, and the need of a strong leader to oppose it."

"The ultimate benefit will accrue if I can kill the dragon myself," Urdhven said coolly. "I want all the help you can give me—ointments, spells, advice."

"Eh, my lord, I know very little about dragons."

"Then find out. One of my ancestors killed a dragon once, if the songs don't lie. In any case, dragons have been killed. Find out how, and by whom. What they did, I can do."

Steng took this as a dismissal, bowed low, and turned away. As he went back to his chamber he found he felt a new touch of admiration for Urdhven. To face a dragon took some nerve—whatever you said about the Lord Protector, he was not deficient in courage. He was right about the political advantage, too—it was amazing what slime people would swallow when it was offered them by a hero. But Steng still hoped it would never happen: the thought of fire abroad in the city terrified him.

The crisis that Urdhven longed for and Steng feared came five days later. Toward evening, a red-gold dragon appeared in the north and swooped over the watch at the Lonegate of Ambrose. Then it followed the line of the wall south and west, as word of the dragon's advent spread through the palace and the city.

Urdhven's plans were ready. Virtually all the Protector's Men in Ambrose were ordered into the streets as Dragon Watchmen—Urdhven didn't want any of the politically doubtful City Legion gaining any glory from this fight against the dragon. The City Legion could stay behind to watch the walls and keep Ambrose from looters—he was tolerably sure there was no external military force near enough to threaten the city. He himself took Vost and the trembling Steng and rode posthaste for the Great Market. It was centrally located, so that he could ride from there to any part of the city where the dragon came to ground. And it was not unlikely the dragon would choose to land there: it was the most open place in the city, and around it was the greatest concentration of wealth, not excluding the treasure rooms of Ambrose itself.

Urdhven's guess was a good one (in fact, it was Steng's), but it was not at the Great Market that the dragon first set down in the city.

Genjandro had always hated politics. He had wanted one thing out of life: to make so much money that he would be immune from the pushing and shoving of the pettily powerful. And he had been well on his way when he had somehow been drafted into the cause of the little King. Then one thing followed another, and now he was about to set fire to a large fortune in Kaenish rugs—his biggest warehouse on the west side of the city.

"Irreplaceable!" he muttered. "Not just the money—works of art! Gone up in smoke! All for a deranged plan that hasn't half a halting chance at success. Madness!"

But this was merely reflex. He was not really a merchant anymore, or even a civilian. He was a soldier in the war against the Lord Protector. He would grumble and he would do as he was told. And when he died, whether it was soon or late, he wouldn't have to tell himself, *There was nothing I could do! The oppressor was too strong!* To hell with that. He would do what he could do. He would do all that three men could do. He would fight the oppressor in any way possible, even if he didn't understand it. What Urdhven was, what he would do to Genjandro's city and Genjandro's people, that Genjandro did understand.

The dragon passed overhead, its birdlike shadow outlined in the red light of sunset on the building next door. The shadow appeared again, facing the other way, and slowly settled down, merging with the shadow of the warehouse itself. A faint scraping (if that) was all that told Genjandro a dragon had landed on his roof.

Genjandro hesitated. He could not quite believe this was happening, and belief was not helped when he saw the dragon's red serpentine head appear in the window. The face was tilted sideways, and the dragon's face was split by what appeared to be a grin.

The dragon was there—and he was not. Genjandro saw the red-gold serpentine scales, the bloodred fiery eyes, heard the heavy breathing, smelled the venomous smoke. And he knew he could not be seeing what he was seeing.

"Which one are you?" he whispered. "Which one is controlling the illusion? How . . . ? How . . . ?"

Then he heard, or thought he heard, a caw. Suddenly it was all very funny. He snickered as he plunged the torch into several stacks of rugs. The dragon roared obligingly and withdrew its serpentine head. Genjandro went on spreading fire through his warehouse and then ran down into the street screaming.

"The dragon!" he shrieked. "The dragon burned my warehouse! Help! Call the Dragon Watch! The dragon is in the city!"

Moments later the street was full of screaming people and Genjandro's work was done. He stayed to fight the fire and spread rumors in the crowd. But when the fire was out and the crowd turned to looting, Genjandro fled from the ruined warehouse. By then the sky was full of storm clouds, drawing a premature curtain of dusk across the city. There was a red glow over the high crooked horizon to the east.

Meanwhile the Lord Protector, Vost, and Steng had reached the Great Market and were waiting there with three cohorts of Protector's Men, luminous in their new uniforms as Dragon Watchmen.

Urdhven was filled with a feeling of supreme confidence. This, he knew somehow, was his hour, when none could defeat him.

He wore heavy plate armor, and his charger, too, was armored. The metal was treated with a sticky bloodlike stuff that Steng said would resist fire. "But," he had said, "I can find nothing which will protect you from the dragon's venom, so I warn you to avoid the beast's breath at all costs."

Urdhven had grunted. "Have you no better advice than that?"

"Yes," Steng had replied. "I should bait him—tempt him to expel fire at you and then retreat."

"Why?"

"Because whatever the source for a dragon's fire and venom, it cannot be inexhaustible. There must be at least a moment when it will be exhausted, as you or I would be if we expelled our lungs without replenishing them. That will be the moment for you to turn and attack."

"Excellent, Steng—really excellent," Urdhven had approved. "So I'll do in fact. I'll remember you for this."

"And I you, my Lord," Steng had replied, with unfeigned admiration.

Remembering this, Urdhven's heart swelled with pride. It would be all right. He would defeat the dragon and save the city. He would be the kind of ruler the empire had not seen in centuries, the founder of a new dynasty, Urdhven the Great. . . .

The sky above was dark with storm clouds; Urdhven looked up and saw the dragon soar into view, breathtakingly beautiful, red-gold against blue-black, his destiny incarnate.

"Land! Land!" Urdhven whispered intently, and the dragon, almost as if it had heard, wheeled in the air and settled down in the middle of the Great Market.

"Vost!" Urdhven cried. "Leave it to me! If I fall, you will attack with the Dragon Watchmen. Afterward, do as Steng will advise you. Do you hear me?"

"I hear and will obey, my lord," cried Vost, and raised his sword in salute, his eyes wide with admiration.

Urdhven spurred his heavy steed to a lumbering gallop, dashing before the front line of the Dragon Watchmen. As one they raised their swords and shouted his name. He raised his hand in acknowledgement, then wheeled aside to face the dragon.

It sat there on all fours, its wings folded back, regarding him with a fixed gaping look—almost like a grin. He drew his sword and flourished it, shouting a challenge, then charged straight at the beast.

It reared up, lifting its wings forward and aloft, then back again as it inhaled a mighty breath. At the last moment Urdhven jerked the reins and swerved his horse aside, swinging back in a long curving path toward the place where he had begun his charge. A storm of red obscuring light followed him, but never reached him, as the dragon roared.

When the dragon ceased roaring and the tide of red light receded, he sheathed his sword and swung his steed about, unsheathing his lance and setting it at rest. Then he charged directly at the dragon, positioning the spear for a deathblow in the narrow scaly chest.

With terrible clarity, he saw the dragon rear up again, throwing its wings aloft and forward and then back as it inhaled. He had left it too long—retreated too far. The dragon would roar again before he could strike. But the dragon would die, too—momentum would carry him on and he would pierce the dragon's heart. At worst, his cohorts of armed men standing by would be able to finish off the wounded dragon.

True, he would be dead, but at that transcendent moment it hardly mattered. He would die for the empire he had killed so many to rule, and perhaps one day men still might refer to him as Urdhven the Great. . . .

The dragon roared, and all Urdhven's thoughts drowned in the red light. He knew only the need to ride forward, to strike, to kill the beast that was killing him. He didn't even feel any heat.

But there was no shock of contact, only a strange tearing sound and his horse stumbled. He fell into darkness and the sense of inexplicable failure.

When he lifted his head he saw that he and his horse were tangled in a huge swath of scarlet silk. Near at hand he saw his spear, still protruding from the rent it had made in the great silken shape that was collapsing as he watched. And from the tear were pouring black birds—dozens of crows, hundreds of them, thousands, murder upon murder of crows. . . .

Where is my dragon? he almost cried aloud, like a plaintive child whose favorite toy has been taken away, but just then he realized: *this* was his dragon. This silken puppet moved by crows, gilded with illusory magic that was now dispelled, *this* was his dragon.

He knew now exactly what had happened, exactly how he had been tricked by those damned Ambrosii and his own hopes. He knew what he must do, before it was too late. But he took a moment to mourn his boyish dreams of heroism. He would never be able to indulge them again; he would always remember this time when they had played him false. A man who had murdered his sister and his liege lord to gain power had no business to be dreaming of heroism, anyway. Perhaps he would never be Urdhven the Great, the people's hero. Perhaps he would be Urdhven the Terrible. At any rate, he would be Urdhven I, Emperor of this damned empire, if he had to wade in blood to do it. And this defeat was in a way an opportunity, for now, after all these months, he knew just where his enemies were.

Sullenly he got to his feet. His charger seemed to have broken its leg when it fell, so he killed it with his sword. Then he walked over to where Steng and Vost awaited him, their faces carefully expressionless.

"Get down, Steng!" he shouted impatiently. "I need your horse. We ride to Ambrose, as fast as may be."

The poisoner dismounted, and the Protector ascended to his saddle. "Tell the Companions of Mercy I will need them," Urdhven commanded Steng. "Any Dragon Watch—any Protector's Men you see, send them to me at the City Gate of Ambrose." He rode away without waiting for a reply, and Vost and the other soldiers followed him out of the Great Market.

The captains of the City Legion were gathered, with many of their men, in the audience hall of Ambrose. They had all received anonymous messages to assemble there at this hour and day, and they had all been forbidden by the Protector to engage in the fight against the dragon. Some were absent. A few had taken to the street to fight the dragon, their sense of duty overriding their (obviously politically motivated) orders. Others had declined to appear, fearing this anonymous summons was an invitation to another purge, like the one that had left most of the loyal servants of Ambrose dead. This possibility was on the minds of those who had chosen to appear as well: all of them bore arms and armor. They would not be purged without a fight.

They waited in vain for the Protector. But presently one of his henchmen appeared, fully armored, in the hated black surcoat with its red lion rampant.

A rumble of dissatisfaction arose from the assembled soldiers. The arrogance of it! One Protector's Man, in battle-scarred armor and a dirty surcoat, to address the pride of the City Legion!

The Protector's Man was arrogant indeed, speaking to no one, swaggering up the long hall to the dais and the imperial throne. Then he sat down on the throne itself and drew his sword, putting it across his knees like a sovereign about to deliver the high justice.

There was a shout of protest, and some of the Legionaries leaped forward to pull the Protector's Man off the throne. But before they could reach him he took off his helmet and tossed it down the long hallway. And what they saw then caused all the soldiers to grow silent and still.

"Come on, then!" Ambrosia shouted, her iron-gray hair settling about her shoulders. "Haul me down and hail me about, and when the Protector returns from his dragon hunt, as he will do shortly, he'll reward you as richly as he can. He might even let you transfer to his new guards—you, too, might wear this proud uniform!" And she tore the surcoat with her left hand and cast it down on the stairs of the dais.

There was silence in the hall. Ambrosia waited and waited, and finally she smiled. "You're lacking in ambition, that's your problem," she said confidingly. "You still think your oath has meaning—that loyalty and honor can have any use or purpose in the bright new tomorrow *our Protector* promises us. What fools you are! You stand there gaping, when any one of you could make your fortune by climbing this dais and striking off my head!"

Another long pause. None of the Legionaries spoke or moved; they hardly breathed.

"Or is it the other way around?" Ambrosia asked quietly (yet somehow the words went to every corner of the room). "Is it the others, so swift to shake off their allegiance, so ready to follow a kin-slaying traitor, is it they who are the fools? Fools to oppose me, certainly. I won't pretend to know every one of you, but every one of you here knows me. It was I and my brother who went to the edge of the world to defy the Sunkillers. It was I who stemmed the tide of the Khroi at the Battle of Sarkunden. It was I who carried the banner of Uthar into the breach at Vakhnhal. You remember how I led the troops of this empire to victory again and again. Uthar my consort is gone, but I remain, the greatest general and leader of armed cohorts since the old time. Those who threaten me or my descendants, the rightful emperors of Ontil, will go down in death and defeat. So it has always been and so it will be today.

"I come to you for one reason and one reason alone. You have watched this thing, this crawling traitor, this Urdhven, with as much disgust as I. You have not joined with him—or you would not wear the Legion's sacred emblem—but neither have you opposed him. I tell you this: you must do one or the other now. Tear off your surcoat and humbly supplicate Lord Urdhven to be one of his men, or *do your damn job* and protect the King of the Two Cities from a murdering usurper."

She reached into her mail shirt and drew forth a rumpled sheet of parchment with a red seal.

"This is my appointment, by the lawful King of the Two Cities and the lord of Ambrose, to act as his regent. Those who choose to stand with me and renew their oath to the King may take up in the new Royal Legion the same rank they held in the City Legion. Those who choose to do otherwise may crawl out of here, on their bellies or however seems suitable, but they must expect no mercy from me or any of the King's loyal ministers should we ever meet again."

She stood and, lifting her sword aloft, began to chant the words of the Legion's oath. As one, the assembled soldiers drew their swords and echoed her. The thunder of their voices reached down to the riverside dungeons, to the empty guardhouse at the City Gate, to a secret chamber high above the city where Morlock lay dreaming of being a dragon.

The King and Wyrth heard them as they sat beside Morlock in the hidden passages of Ambrose.

"What does it mean?" Lathmar asked breathlessly.

"They're either slaughtering the Lady Ambrosia or taking the oath with her," Wyrtheorn replied, shrugging. "Sounds too organized to be the murder of just one person, but they say the Legion is very well drilled. You know: 'Company A: advance. Kill! Company B: advance. Kill! Company C—'"

"Oh, shut up."

"The King's wish is my command," said Wyrth, mock-obsequiously. Like Ambrosia, or for that matter Morlock, he was now a minister of the King with a seat on the Regency Council, if they only had a table to sit around.

"All right," said Lathmar, taking him at his word. "Then it's my wish that you attend Lady Ambrosia in the audience hall. Deliver her whatever assistance she seems to require. If she needs none, return to me here."

"Er." Wyrth pulled at his beard. "Are you sure you can wake him, if he needs waking? Morlock can be very single-minded, especially when he is pursuing a vision."

"I'm sure. Anyway, the sooner you go, the sooner you'll be back."

Wyrth shrugged again, grinning. He leaped to his feet, sketched a courtly bow toward his sovereign, and dashed off down the stone passage.

The King turned back to Morlock and considered the face of his dreaming minister. Then he folded his hands and put himself through the spiritual exercises Morlock had taught him to summon the rapture of vision.

Lathmar, in truth, had great promise as a seer, and the rapture came upon him swiftly. His spirit was drawn alongside Morlock's as he flew above the city on red silken wings filled with crows. Morlock acknowledged Lathmar's presence without even an unspoken word, and then returned to his rather complex task.

More than ever, Lathmar was awed by the power of Morlock's mind—the ability to direct the separate motions of hundreds of crows that filled the silken dragon puppet while maintaining the dragon illusion that sheathed it. But he was even more impressed when he perceived that Morlock's power over the crows was not power. They liked him—they respected him—they had had many a profitable deal with him. To them, he was the most crowlike of men, almost reasonable, and this latest prank (for so they thought of it) appealed tremendously to their small distorted senses of humor. They were willing partners in the gag; they took their cues from Morlock but were not mastered by him.

The city far below them was dim and shadowy in Lathmar's vision—far more visible were the myriads of human souls that burned brightly within it. Among them Lathmar was sure he could recognize one. He had seen him only once, rising from a hole in the floor of a ruined shop—

It was Genjandro, their agent in the city, awaiting as they had pre-arranged in one of his warehouses. It was extremely droll to see how like Genjandro's inside was to his outside—full of hate for the Protector, reverence for the King (at the moment Lathmar thought of the King as a being quite distinct from himself), and with a certain crowlike amusement for the task at hand. They left Genjandro setting fire to his rugs and leaped into the air again.

Presently they landed in the Great Market and confronted Urdhven. Lathmar was fascinated by the talic prospect of Urdhven. It was as if he were two men: one a hero figure of shining silver. But this was just a surface, tossed like tinsel over a heavier, blood-edged, somewhat indistinct figure—rather like the red lion that was his ensign. But it was the silver shape that all the soldiers in the market saw: there were tiny little silver Protectors inside their souls as they watched and worshipped Urdhven in his heroic moment. Lathmar would have laughed if he could have laughed.

Then Urdhven charged toward the dragon, and the silver within his spirit grew bright indeed, almost eclipsing the other, and his lance tore through the silken dragon that Lathmar's mind inhabited. The illusion spell on the dragon puppet was severed, and suddenly Lathmar's awareness was shattered into thousands of crow-shaped pieces of darkness and he knew nothing for a while.

The City Gate was standing wide open when Urdhven and his three cohorts of armed men reached it. To all appearances, there were no soldiers on duty.

"May the Strange Gods damn them all to all eternity!" Urdhven muttered with complete sincerity.

He could take comfort, he supposed, in the fact that the Ambrosii had not secured the gate against him. Then again, it was possible that they held the gate on the far side of the bridge and were waiting in ambush.

"Vost," he said, after a moment's thought, "stay here with Vendhrik's and Stalost's cohorts. Arnring's cohort, dismount and follow me." And he rode into the dark gate, past the dark gatehouse onto the bridge over the river Tilion. When he was halfway across he paused, raising his hand. The cohort halted on the bridge behind him.

"Arnring," he said to the cohort's commander, "I have a dangerous mission which I can entrust only to you."

"Yes, sir!" Arnring replied eagerly.

"I want you to enter the castle Ambrose and engage in reconnaissance. I believe the Ambrosii may be somewhere within. Enter the castle, take possession of the key points, and return to me a message when your men are in place."

"Yes, sir." Arnring was less eager now. But he still seemed conscious of the honor Urdhven was doing him in selecting him for the task. (It was just as well, then, that he didn't know Urdhven had in fact selected him and his cohort because they were the most expendable of the three.)

"If you meet armed resistance," Urdhven continued, "send me word of that, too, and I will bring reinforcements. Any message you send must have a code phrase, do you understand? So that I can be sure it is from you and not our enemies."

"Yes, sir. What is the phrase?"

"Oh—'Steng is a useless weasel.'"

Arnring grinned. "Yes, sir. 'Steng is a useless weasel.'"

"Good hunting to you, then, Commander Arnring."

Arnring lifted his arm in salute and then, barking commands, marched his cohort on past the Lord Protector.

Urdhven waited until they were out of sight on the far gate and then dismounted. His right side was bruised where he had fallen in fighting the "dragon"—he longed to disarm and scratch his body head to toe. But he knew he couldn't until he was sure Ambrose was secure.

He waited, staring out over the dark waters of the Tilion. The overcast sky was rumbling periodically, and the sun had long set—it would be a dark night, a night full of rain. He wondered if he should spend it at Markethall Barracks—the truth is, though, he could not bear to be near the site of that embarrassing encounter with the false dragon. He wondered what the men were saying about it. He wished he could hear them. He thought he did hear them, outside the gate, on the city street. He was sure he heard Vost's voice. Then he definitely heard the portcullis of the gate slam shut.

He ran back down the bridge to the gate opening onto the street. His two cohorts were gone. The echoes of the horses' hoofbeats were fading away as he stood there, forlorn, inside the gate. Vost, the ever-faithful, was gone. Had Vost betrayed him? Had he been overpowered by the others? They had even taken the horses of Arnring's cohort. Why had they done that?

Urdhven decided he needed to catch up with Arnring's men. He went up the bridge to his horse, thinking vaguely of where he should tether it . . . and then something occurred to him.

The lever to control the portcullis was inside the gatehouse. It could not be shut from the street.

Someone was behind him . . . in the dark gatehouse he had passed. Someone who had locked him into the castle. Someone who had not spoken to him, but had watched and waited with the cunning of a cat playing with a mouse.

The hairs on the back of his neck were already rising when he heard booted feet on the stones of the bridge behind him.

He turned and saw a man step out of the shadows near the gatehouse. The man wore a black surcoat with a red lion rampant across it. He wore a helmet and full armor as well, but he doffed the helmet as he approached.

Urdhven knew the man's features reasonably well. They were his own.

"Appearance is nothing," the other said—as if Urdhven's thoughts, too, were his. "Voice is another matter. Even if every tone is in place, one must say the things one's audience expects, or the illusion will be shattered."

"Which one are you?" Urdhven said. He did not quite keep the fear out of his voice.

"Does it matter?"

"Which one *are* you?"

"I sent your men around to the Lonegate. The King's new Legion should have disposed of Arnring's men and secured all entrance points by the time they reach there. If not, I suppose they may meet you there—and you (or a reasonable facsimile thereof) will tell them to ride back here, or to Markethall, or—"

"*Who are you?*" Urdhven screamed.

His simulacrum grunted. "I am—for all practical purposes—anyone you have ever murdered. I am anyone you have ever had tortured to death. I am anyone you have ever robbed or terrorized. I am anyone who has cause to hate you. Does that narrow it down for you, Lord Protector?"

Urdhven drew his sword. "You won't take me without a fight."

"I destroyed Hlosian Bekh. I can kill you."

Urdhven had thought that his fear would grow less when he knew which of the Ambrosii he was facing. Instead he found the whole night was alive with terror—the rumbling of the thunder in the distance seemed to be the approach of something horrible; every shadow seemed a grinning mask of death. He remembered the day of Ambrosia's trial by combat, that nightmare of a day when everything had begun to go wrong.

Nevertheless he replied firmly, with a confidence he truly felt, "No, you can't."

By way of answer, the man who wore his face drew his sword and attacked.

The fight that followed was not as long as it might have been. Urdhven's opponent was a more skilled fencer, but Urdhven was not incompetent. Still, he could not bring himself to strike with deadly force at his own image. His enemy gave him opening after opening, smiling with an unpleasant crooked smile, daring Urdhven to strike. But he couldn't.

Finally, his enemy grew tired of toying with him and set about the business of dispatching him in the most businesslike way. In a few moments, all Urdhven's limbs were bleeding, and as he strove to parry a stroke he was stunned by a blow to his chest. His enemy's riposte, sure and terribly strong, had slipped past his defense and struck through his armor.

The Lord Protector looked down to see the hilt of his enemy's sword protruding from his rib cage. In a moment it was withdrawn, and as he staggered he saw the bright edge of the sword whistling through the air at him again.

CHAPTER FOURTEEN

MERCY AT THE GATE

L athmar VII, King of the Two Cities and Lord of Ambrose, rightful heir to the imperial throne (if he could only get it), awoke with a squawk.

He sat up and stared blearily around at the empty stone chamber where he found himself. Apparently he was not, after all, a crow raiding a cornfield north of the city. Why in the world would he ever have supposed that?

Then he remembered: he had joined into Morlock's vision as Morlock's mind conducted the hundreds of crows who had carried their dragon puppet into the city to face the Lord Protector. Lacking Morlock's skill, he had been carried away by his rapport with the crows after the illusion was shattered and the troop dispersed.

Morlock was gone. Where he had been was a message written in the stark pointed characters of Morlock's hand:

I go to secure the City Gate, as we planned. Ambrosia and your soldiers will soon engage in battle with the Protector's Men. You were unwise to send Wyrth away. Stay here until we send for you.

Morlock Ambrosius

The King dropped the message on the ground, and it began to burn. Before it had blackened to ash he had decided to disobey it. This was the crucial moment in their battle with the Protector; he wasn't going to spend it hiding in a secret passage.

Lathmar took the secret ways through the walls of Ambrose down to a hallway near the great audience hall. Even before he left the secret passage he could hear men in armed conflict, so he proceeded carefully. He crept into the open hallway and over to a balustrade that overlooked the entryway to the audience hall.

Men were fighting there. Men had died there: the bodies were scattered underfoot in the corridor. Men wearing the Protector's red lion were facing City Legionaries in blue and gray.

The Legionaries were outnumbered, and as Lathmar watched breathlessly, they began to fall back toward the entrance of the audience hall. The Protector's Men followed eagerly, shouting Urdhven's name as their battle cry. The Legionaries said nothing, but grimly and slowly retreated in order.

Finally the Protector's Men were facing the Legionaries at the entrance of the Hall itself, and the Legionaries ceased retreating. Ambrosia and Wyrth were not among them; Lathmar could not tell if they were among the dead. One of the soldiers sounded a horn, which echoed strangely in the stone corridors.

In pinning the Legionaries against the entrance to the Hall, the Protector's Men had incautiously turned their backs toward the corridors emptying into the atrium. After the Legionary's call, the shadows in those empty corridors suddenly bristled with bright blades: Legionaries filled each hallway, leaping into the atrium to attack the Protector's Men from behind. Among these Lathmar thought he recognized Ambrosia (in the armor of a Protector's Man, but without the surcoat), and he was sure he recognized Wyrth (who was distinguished in that group both by the smallness of his size and the ferocity of his fighting).

Lathmar guessed that the battle would go in the Legion's favor now, and truly there was nothing he could do about it. He backed away from the balustrade and stumbled against an armed man standing beside him.

He thought all was lost for a second, until he realized that this man wore the surcoat of a City Legionary. Then the man pushed back his visor and the King got another surprise.

"Lorn!" he gasped. "How . . . ?"

"No, Your Majesty," the Legionary said. "I had a cousin Lorn, who they say died in your service. My name is Karn."

"Karn," said the King recovering. "I see."

"I took the oath with the others in the audience hall—Your Majesty may trust me."

"I will," said Lathmar. "What brings you here, Karn?"

"I was sent on reconnaissance of these corridors, Your Majesty—to see if there were any more Protector's Men in arms hereabouts."

"And?"

"Negative, Your Majesty. The Protector's Men seem to have stayed in a single body."

"Unwise, perhaps, under the circumstances."

"Yes, Your Majesty."

"Who has been sent to secure the City Gate?"

"I don't know that anyone has, Your Majesty. The Regent Ambrosia said that was . . . her brother's lookout, I think she said."

"Well, let's go see how Morlock is faring then," the King said, noting with interest how the Legionary flinched when he spoke Morlock's name. "You'd better accompany me, in case we run into any stragglers."

It occurred to the King, then, that Karn himself might be a straggler. If he had really been sent on reconnaissance, he should have reported back to the officer who sent him. Instead, he seemed perfectly willing to accompany the King away from the fighting. Oh, well—Lathmar supposed he outranked anyone who could have given Karn his orders. The man looked exactly like Lorn—slightly younger, perhaps. He must have inherited something of Lorn's iron loyalty from the same place he had gotten Lorn's appearance.

"Let's go, then," he said to his new soldier, and they crept away from the fighting.

Lathmar was tempted to reenter the secret ways. It would be a safer, if slower, method of traveling through the castle. But he felt he could not do so in

Karn's company: a passage isn't secret if every private soldier knows about it . . . and the truth was that he still had his doubts about Karn.

So they traveled the open corridors, and they met no Protector's Men. But they did encounter Kedlidor, the Rite-Master of Ambrose, along with a motley swarm of castle servants who appeared mostly to be kitchen staff. They were armed, anyway, with cleavers, knives, tongs, and similar implements; some wore pots as makeshift helmets.

"Your Majesty," said Kedlidor, bowing his head in greeting.

"Kedlidor," said the King. Kedlidor's followers seemed rather daunted by his armed Legionary, but Lathmar had the oddest feeling that Karn was edging over behind him—to use him as a shield? "I remind you, Rite-Master," the King said quickly, "that you and your people here are personal servants of myself, as Lord of Ambrose. You are not under the Protector's orders, whatever he may have told you."

"You have learned that lesson excellently well, Your Majesty, but I remind you it was I who taught it to you. I was just saying the same to these persons here, who heard the armed conflict and were worried there was another purge in progress."

"In a way there is," the King replied. "My regent, the Lady Ambrosia, is taking direct rule of Ambrose back from the usurper Urdhven. My Legion is fighting with Urdhven's men in the area of the audience hall. Those disloyal to me will, of course, be executed by the Lady Ambrosia."

The kitchen staff poured out its professions of loyalty in an incoherent but urgently expressed chorus. Lathmar was skeptical—if they had been genuinely loyal to him, no doubt Urdhven would have killed them in the earlier purge of castle servants. But if they were willing to behave as if they were loyal, that was all that Lathmar could reasonably require.

"You can offer no real help to Ambrosia at the hall—and the truth is that she needs none. But the Lonegate, on the far side of the castle, is unguarded, as far as I know. Kedlidor, I appoint you the commander of this group of . . . of militia."

"Thank you, Your Majesty," Kedlidor said with real gratitude. "I was quite concerned about the ad hoc and unofficial nature of my leadership."

"Take them to the Lonegate. If you find it empty, secure it against all intruders, until you have word from me or another of my ministers. If it is occupied by my soldiers, put yourself at the disposal of their captain. If it is occupied by Urdhven's thugs, wait until my Legionaries approach and put yourself at the disposal of their commander."

"Yes, Your Majesty."

"Go then. Good luck."

The Royal Irregulars, First Cohort, trooped off down the hallway, wafting a distinct odor of onions and pork behind them. Lathmar shook his head and continued toward the City Gate, Guardsman Karn now firmly at his side.

There were only three possibilities, the King told himself as he chose his approach through the empty corridors. Either Morlock had secured the gate and needed no assistance; Morlock had not secured the gate, and it was held by Protector's Men; or the gate was held by no one. In the latter case it might be empty, or its possession might be in dispute. In any case, the King thought it would be best to approach the gate indirectly.

There was a second guardhouse on the inner side of the bridge over the river Tilion. From its upper floor, one could watch the uncovered bridge from bowslits. It was here that the King came, accompanied by Karn, so that he could have a long look at the bridge and the guardhouse at the far end before he entrusted himself to their dangers.

From here he watched as the Protector and his mirror image (but which was which?) fought on the uncovered bridge beneath a dark sky crossed with silver lightning. One Protector took the other's sword in his chest up to its hilt. Then the unwounded Protector leaped back, recovered, and deftly cut off his staggering opponent's head.

"Bravo, Morlock!" the King muttered. No illusion spell could disguise his fencing master's style of swordplay.

This guess was confirmed when the victorious "Protector" tugged with his left hand at his nose, as if bemused, and the likeness of Urdhven fell away from him in a heap of shining cord around his feet. It was Morlock, of course, who stood there, gazing with genuine bemusement at the headless form of the Protector, still standing in the middle of the bridge.

Morlock, holding his sword at full extension, stepped away from the discarded simulacrum and cautiously approached the standing body. Before the tip of the sword reached the Protector's chest the headless body brought its own sword up to guard, dashed Morlock's blade aside, and lunged for his chest. Morlock brought his sword back to parry and caught the other's sword in a bind.

"I told you," the Protector's voice sounded on the uncovered bridge. "I told you that you could not kill me."

The King gasped and saw that the Protector's severed head was resting against one wall of the bridge, watching his body's attack on Morlock with every appearance of detached amusement.

"I didn't know that I'd be facing you," the Protector's head said calmly. "But I knew my quest for the throne would lead me to face Ambrosia. I knew I would need help, so I sought out a magical patron among the adepts— among 'those-who-know,' as I believe you refer to each other."

The Protector's body kicked at Morlock's feet and broke the bind. Morlock leaped back and coolly parried a flurry of attacks from the headless corpse.

"So, you see," the Protector's head continued, "you cannot kill my body. And it is only a matter of time until my body kills you. It is like Hlosian again, but there is no scroll for you to sever, no weak point for you to attack."

Morlock wordlessly retreated a step or two, and then again. The smile on the Protector's head became broad indeed. The smile faded a bit when Urdhven seemed to realize what the King already had: Morlock's retreat was bringing him nearer and nearer to the Protector's severed head.

The headless body leaped forward in a desperate assault. Morlock danced back and kicked the severed head like a football. It spun, lopsided, across the curving surface of the stone bridge and fetched up facefirst against the wall on the other side. The Protector gave a muffled groan of pain, and the headless body seemed to become disoriented. Morlock stepped forward and slashed off its sword-bearing hand.

"I've fought the living dead before," Morlock said finally. "Your patron has misled you—perhaps deliberately."

"I'm not dead!" the Protector's head screamed desperately. "I'll never die!"

"But you'll never truly live," Morlock said. "You will never know peace, unless I or one of those-who-know give it to you."

The headless body broke into a staggering run. It took a zigzag course toward the severed head, gaining confidence as it moved. The King realized that the head must be directing it by the sound of its own footfalls. Morlock let it go. It reached the severed head and picked it up, cradling it in its arms.

It turned to face Morlock. "You'll never defeat us," the head hissed.

"You are nothing," Morlock said. "No one can defeat you and nothing can help you. You destroyed yourself when you allowed the adept to take your heart and lungs and brain. All that is left of what once was Urdhven is a slender thread of ego trapped inside that shell of meat."

The severed head screamed in the arms of its body.

Morlock spoke through the scream. "I can give you rest. Give me the name and dwelling place of the adept, your patron. Tell me this, and I will tell you how to die."

"They're coming for you!" the severed head hissed. "They're coming for you! They're almost here. Ask *them* what my patron's name is!" The remaining hand of the body took up the head gently, and then tossed it into the dark waters of the Tilion. Sluggishly, the body tipped over the rail and was lost in the river also.

Morlock spoke a crackling syllable of Dwarvish. He threw down the sword, turned, and ran down the bridge to the gate on the far side.

"We must help him!" the King said to Karn. Turning around, he saw that he was alone. He was briefly surprised. (He had seen a great many horrible things in the past few years, but simple cowardice had not often been one of them.) Then he picked himself up and ran down the steps. He passed over the bloody bridge stones where Morlock and the Protector had had their strange duel. Pausing for a moment, he watched with alarm as a severed hand, moving like a crippled spider, crept through the rail of the bridge and leapt into the water below. Shuddering, he ran on. He found Morlock standing still, gazing as if mesmerized at the portcullis of the street gate.

"Lathmar," said Morlock without looking at him. "You should not be here."

"You need help and there's no one else," Lathmar said. "The others are busy. You'll have to make do with me."

Morlock shook his head. "I will shortly do battle, and I will be unable to take care of you. You should go back now to the secret passages."

"I won't," said the King stubbornly. "So what can I do to help?"

"Keep them off me," Morlock said.

"I—what?"

"It may happen that I will be in rapture as our enemies approach. In that case, keep them off my body, so that I can complete my task in the tal-realm."

"All right," said the King faintly.

"And stay clear from my vision. You learned how it could entrap you when the dragon illusion broke."

"Yes," the King admitted.

"This will be far more dangerous. See, they are here." He raised his hand and called out in a clear voice, *"Tyrfing!"*

The dark window of the guardhouse burst outward, and among the crystalline shards was one—long, swordlike, and dark—which fell into Morlock's outstretched hand. It was Tyrfing, the accursed sword, its blade like dark basaltic glass glimmering in the fitful light of the stormy evening.

The King turned from gaping at the sword to the street outside the portcullis. It was lampless and dark. But in the shadows the King could see a death cart, and in it two of the red-cloaked, red-masked Companions of Mercy.

"What are they?" the King asked.

"I don't know," Morlock said calmly. "They are impenetrable to my vision."

"Then how will you defeat them?"

"I don't know that I will." Morlock's cold gray eyes met his. "There is still time to return to the passages."

"Stop saying that!" shouted the King, who had been thinking the same thing.

Morlock shrugged and turned his eyes back to the street. There was another death cart there, moving almost silently alongside the other, with muffled hoofbeats and muffled wheels. Soon there was a third and a fourth.

"What are you waiting for?" the King demanded. "Soon there will be too many for you! Do what you're going to do!"

"I have my reasons for waiting," Morlock said, clearly somewhat nettled.

"Tell me one."

"To see how many *they* think will be too many," said Morlock, gesturing with the accursed sword. "If you want something to do, you could fetch me a lit torch."

"What?" The King had been watching the arrival of another death cart when he noticed something. All the red masks of the Companions of Mercy were facing them—even those of the ones holding the reins of the horses. He had the oddest feeling that they were all looking at him, not at Morlock at all.

"Get. A. Lit. Torch." Morlock spoke firmly and calmly. "Do it now. Go."

"All right!" the King shouted. He ran back across the bridge over the Tilion. He found a lamp full of oil in the guardhouse on the far side, but no torches. He was tempted to go further into Ambrose to find a torch . . . but then, he thought, he might not return to Morlock in time. He lit the lamp with a coal from the guardhouse fire; it would do as well as a torch, he hoped.

Then he thought: *Why return at all? He doesn't really need me—he said so.*

Still, he mused, *suppose Morlock does need the torch, and I don't bring it?*

It occurred to him that Morlock did not expect him to return—that this was just a pretext to get him away from the fight. The more Lathmar thought about this, the more likely it seemed.

That was what decided him. He took a deep breath, picked up the lamp, and marched out of the guardhouse. It had begun to rain outside; he trotted across the dark wet bridge as fast as he dared (sheltering the lamp flame with his free hand).

"Here!" he shouted at Morlock, over the roar of the rain, and shoved the lamp at him. "I couldn't find a torch!"

"This will do," Morlock said coolly. "Thank you. Hold the lamp, please—I will have to act soon."

Lathmar looked instinctively at the gate. There were hundreds of red-cloaked Companions in the street outside. They were beginning to move toward the gate.

Morlock extended Tyrfing, and Lathmar saw there were veins of glowing white crystal within the dark blade. It reminded him of how Morlock appeared in the tal-world—a black-and-white living flame. He turned to look at Morlock and saw that his eyes were glowing faintly.

"Are—are you in rapture?" the King spluttered. "Is this the time—?"

"Yes and no," Morlock replied, his voice a crowlike rasp. "With Tyrfing I can exert my will simultaneously in the tal-realm and the world of matter—at least for simple things. Say no more now."

Morlock closed his glowing eyes. The red-cloaked Companions began to climb the portcullis. There were dozens of them on it, more awaiting a chance to climb, others descending to the far side and apparently waiting for the rest.

Morlock's free hand gestured or convulsed. The portcullis, the stones of the wall, and the street near it all began to emit a thin, faintly luminous mist. It became thicker, almost a fog. It didn't seem to bother the Companions in the least.

Morlock opened his eyes.

"What did you do?" the King demanded. "What is that stuff?"

"I released the phlogiston trapped in the portcullis and its environs. Give me the lamp."

"What's phlogiston?" the King demanded, handing him the lamp.

"The element in matter which burns."

"Do metal and stone burn?" the King asked.

"Everything burns," Morlock said, and threw the lamp. It landed on the cobblestones before the portcullis and smashed. Instantly, the luminous mist and everything in it was a cloud of red flame. Dozens of Companions fell in burning heaps to the ground, smoking in the rain.

"Come," Morlock said, and they ran together back along the wet dark bridge toward Ambrose. Morlock stopped just short of the inner guardhouse gate.

"You killed a lot of them," the King said.

"I don't think so."

"What do you mean?"

"In any case, there are very many of them."

"Then they'll come after us."

"Yes. Not soon, perhaps. They will fear a repetition of the phlogiston tactic."

"And will you . . . ?"

"No. We have a better chance. Listen, Lathmar."

"Yes?"

"Whatever these Companions are, they use some sort of binding magic to sustain their forms. Running water is hostile to such magic. The river can protect us from them."

Relief washed over the King. "They can't cross the bridge?"

"That is precisely it. They *can* cross the bridge; if it were not here, the river would prevent them from crossing. So, at least, I guess."

"Then—but—we can't dismantle the bridge!"

"I can destroy it," Morlock said, "but I will have to go deeper into rapture to do it. I will have to surrender volitional action in the world of the senses. Do you understand, Lathmar? That is when you will need to stand guard over me."

"What if I can't?" the King muttered.

Morlock shrugged.

"Did you need the lamp?" the King asked impulsively.

"You saw that I did."

"What would you have done if I hadn't been there?"

"Fetched it myself."

"How did you know I would bring it?"

Morlock's expressions were hard to read at the best of times, but Lathmar thought he looked surprised. "You said you would," he replied.

The King groaned. "I'll do what I can," he muttered at last. "I can't promise much against . . ." He waved his hand vaguely toward the bridge. When his eyes followed his own gesture, he saw red-cloaked, red-masked forms on the far side of the bridge.

Morlock collapsed on the stones at the foot of the bridge. It was as if he had fainted. But his gray irises were brightly luminous through the thin layer of their eyelids, and Tyrfing, which had fallen clattering at his side, loosely clasped in his nerveless fingers, was a strip of black-and-white flame.

Trembling, the King stood between the fallen Morlock and the Companions of Mercy. Suddenly the thought occurred to him: *Defend him with* what? He had no weapon. He glanced toward the bridge and saw the glitter of the sword Morlock had dropped there—the one he had fought the Protector with. But Lathmar couldn't bring himself to run toward those slowly advancing red shadows.

There was the guardhouse—he would almost certainly find something in there. But he was afraid that if he went into the guardhouse, even for a moment, he wouldn't have the courage to come out again.

He glanced down at Tyrfing. It shone, black and white, in the rain-drenched, lightning-crossed shadows of the stormy night. It was still in rapport with Morlock, acting as a focus for his power. But it was also a sword, and Lathmar needed a sword or some weapon badly. Perhaps it would make little difference in the event of a real fight (there were so many Companions!), but holding one would give him the courage to stand and face them, the courage to not leave Morlock helpless and alone. He didn't think that picking Tyrfing up and wielding it would disrupt Morlock's rapport with his focus— only Morlock could do that, once the rapport was established.

No, what the King was afraid of was this: Tyrfing was believed to be cursed, and anyone who wielded the sword, even for a moment, was held to fall under that curse. The King didn't believe in the curse necessarily—but he didn't disbelieve, either: it would explain a lot about Morlock.

But he had promised. And Morlock was counting on that promise. Gritting his teeth, the King stooped down to pick up the accursed sword.

As soon as his fingers touched the hilt he knew he had made a mistake. Vaguely he felt his body fall to the stones at the foot of the bridge, but he sensed no pain.

He was standing over the fallen bodies of Morlock and himself. Morlock was some distance away, a black-and-white column of flames from which extended two flamelike arms: one black and one white. The black one was extended toward the red Companions of Mercy (who appeared, in Lathmar's inner vision, exactly as they had done to his eyes). It was as if Morlock was casting a thin net of finely woven dark mesh over the Companions and the bridge. But from his white hand came a corresponding shower of bright particles.

White and black, white and black. The near side of the bridge grew brighter and brighter; the bridge itself grew darker and darker. What was Morlock doing? Was he sorting the particles—dark ones to the bridge, bright ones to the bridge's foot? Why?

On an impulse, Lathmar looked up at the sky. It wasn't dark, as it had been to the eyes. It was filled with a crooked web of light. And more than that. The sky was alive: there was a mind up there. It was a mind about to think quick, bright, deadly thoughts: the mind of the storm.

Lathmar cried out in fear. That was when Morlock became aware of him. He extended one bright flamelike finger and thrust Lathmar out of the vision.

The King came to himself lying on the stones next to Morlock. He leapt to his feet. The Companions were even nearer now, approaching cautiously, but the first ones had already passed over the arc of the bridge and were heading down toward Lathmar.

He clenched his fists and prepared to meet them. The hairs on the back of his neck were rising.

Then the dark sky opened up and the lightning bolts fell. Like an avalanche of bright burning stones they struck the bridge, not one stroke but over and over, blinding bitter hammer-blows until the bridge shattered and the dark stones fell into the river and the red Companions with them, wailing at last in despair as the dark water received them.

Lathmar lost consciousness again, in the more ordinary way, and when he became aware of the world again, the thing was over. The bridge was gone; clouds of dust and smoke were settling around him, washed from the air by the rain; the Companions, if any survived, had gone from the far side of the ruined bridge.

Lathmar rolled to his feet and glanced about for Morlock. He was lying, still in rapture, next to Tyrfing at the foot of the bridge. But the bridge was gone and the rough margin of stone and earth was crumbling into the dark water below. Morlock and his focus were right on the edge. Lathmar reached toward them impulsively, but then drew back.

What if he was drawn into Morlock's vision again? They would fall together into the river and be killed. But perhaps if he didn't touch the sword directly . . .

He reached out with one foot and tentatively hooked it under the hilt of Tyrfing. The dark rainy night stayed before his waking eyes. The leather of his shoe apparently insulated him from being drawn into the vision—or perhaps it was the fixed decision not to be drawn in that kept him clear. In any case,

Lathmar shuffled backward, drawing with him the glowing sword hooked over his foot, and then kicked it back into the guardhouse behind him.

When he turned back to Morlock, he found he was alone. The edge had crumbled further while his back was turned, throwing Morlock's unconscious body into the river.

Lathmar squawked and dove without thinking into the dark rain-torn water of the Tilion.

Rocks and earth fell behind him into the water; he struck out as hard as he could with the current: both to catch up with Morlock's drifting body and to get away from the collapsing bridge foundation behind him.

He wondered at first if he should dive—surely Morlock had sunk below the surface? Then, between bouts of inhaling dirty river water, he wondered what he was doing at all. He was no great swimmer, even when he had only his own body to keep afloat. It was unlikely that he would be able to help Morlock, even if he could find him. But it was even more unlikely that anyone else would be able to help him at all. Grimly he dog-paddled on.

Soon he caught sight of a tangle of limbs floating on the surface of the river. It was hard to tell what he was seeing, in the intermittent flashes of lightning—there seemed to be too many limbs. But he directed his strokes toward it, hoping desperately he was not rushing toward a jumble of Companions of Mercy. Alive, dead, or undead, he had to think they would be unpleasant companions for a nighttime swim . . .

What he saw, when it got closer, was almost worse. It was indeed Morlock floating on the surface of the river; his eyes still glowed faintly, indicating he was still in the withdrawal of rapture.

But atop him was the headless body of the Protector, one undead hand clutching Morlock's mortal throat.

Lathmar shouted—whether in fear or anger he never knew—and flailed into them. It was a preposterous nightmare, unlike the unlikeliest scenarios that Morlock and Wyrth had put him through. He had no weapon; he had no way to hurt his enemy; yet it was desperately important that he defeat him. He hung on to one of the Protector's arms and hit the chest as hard as he could with one fist. It gave a hollow meaty sound from the severed throat, but otherwise seemed to have little effect. The headless body maintained its one-handed grip on Morlock's throat.

One-handed: Lathmar remembered that Morlock had cut off its right hand on the bridge. He seized the left arm and tried to pull it loose from Morlock's throat. He assumed he was safe from the other arm—wrongly, as it proved. The headless body struck him with its handless right arm as with a club, and he fell away into the water.

In a moment he was back on the surface, spouting water, struggling toward the other two bodies. Over the roar of the river and the rumble of thunder and the hiss of the rain, he had the strangest impression the body was chuckling or snarling as he approached. But that couldn't be, unless . . .

He looked down to see the Protector's head gnawing on one of Morlock's hands floating nerveless in the water. The head's eyes were on him as he approached, and the handless right arm prepared to club him off again.

But Lathmar ducked under the swing of the arm and snatched at the head. He pulled it away from Morlock's hand, the teeth carrying raw flesh away as they clenched in a desperate attempt to stay in place.

When Lathmar had the head in his hands it screamed, then choked on the bit of Morlock's flesh it had in its mouth. Treading water, Lathmar held the head in one hand and punched it as hard as he could with the other. It flew away, lopsided, end over end, into the night toward the city side of the river.

The headless body abandoned its attempt to throttle Morlock and floundered away in the water toward the direction where the head had disappeared. Lathmar grabbed Morlock's body and held on to it like a float for a few moments, regaining his strength. Then he began the long, laborious task of shepherding the unconscious body through the rough water to the side of the river where Ambrose stood.

There was, in fact, no shore there. But Lathmar managed to find some irregularities in the stone wall where he could place his feet and lean back and rest.

His limbs were trembling like leaves, from terror and from the cold water. He had never been so exhausted, not even on that terrible night when he had hauled Lorn's dead body halfway around Ambrose. For a long time he had hated to think about that night, and it still wasn't pleasant, but the pain was no longer so sharp.

"This time I got there in time," he told Morlock's unconscious form, with fierce satisfaction, if somewhat incoherently.

The terror and the satisfaction both faded presently, but the cold remained, grew worse. Lathmar began to realize that they would have to get out of the water somehow, or they would die anyway and it would all be for nothing.

He was just about to begin to feel his way upstream along the wall when the light behind Morlock's eyelids faded and his eyes opened.

Morlock spat out some water, coughed once or twice, and said matter-of-factly, "So the bank gave way after the bridge collapsed? I thought it might."

"You might have mentioned it to me," the King remarked, coolly if not dryly.

"Sorry," Morlock replied. "Thanks for keeping me from floating downstream. I took a deep breath before I withdrew into rapture, hoping it would keep me buoyant. Did it?"

"Yes."

There was a pause as Morlock righted himself, found a foothold on the wall, and generally took stock of the situation.

"There is a bite wound on my hand," he observed after a few moments.

Haltingly, Lathmar told him what had happened after Morlock had fallen into the river.

"I'm glad you were there to save me from your Protector," Morlock said when he was done.

Lathmar was somehow both pleased and enraged by these quiet words.

"He's not my Protector!" he shouted in Morlock's dark, impassive face. Tears as cold as river water ran down his face. "He was never my Protector! You're my Protector!"

Lathmar was horrified at what he had said, as if it were some dreadful confession, but Morlock wasn't. He put one arm around the boy and held him as he wept. "Well, tonight you were mine," he remarked finally.

Thunderstruck, the King stopped weeping.

They worked their way upstream toward the site where the bank had collapsed. They weren't sure they could ascend there, and they were sure it would be impossible anywhere else.

When they got there they saw two figures standing near the ruined bridge foundation.

"I hope you've had a pleasant swim, Your Majesty," the shorter one called down. "But if it's not too much trouble perhaps you should come inside now. We've been at some pains to set you on your throne, and there is some work to be done, at Your Majesty's earliest convenience."

Lathmar's response is recorded in no history.

"Such language from a well-brought-up lad of royal blood," Wyrth replied, but he tossed down a rope without any further exercise of his wit. Together, he and Ambrosia drew the waterlogged King and Morlock from the river.

"Well, Lathmar," Ambrosia said, "you may be King only in name, and you may never be Emperor. But tonight you are Lord of Ambrose in fact as well as in law. You had better receive our homage before we go back in."

So the three adults kneeled, and one by one, Lathmar took their outstretched hands and placed them between his hand and fist as each one swore to him allegiance.

In a room within the living city, shut away from the storm-torn night, Steng lay dreaming of his true master. Elsewhere, in the dead city, Steng's true master sat on a dark throne, dreaming of himself. Along the bank of the Tilion a headless body wandered, feeling its way with one hand.

And Lathmar VII, Lord of Ambrose and King of the Two Cities, followed his ministers into the castle he would rule for the rest of his life—however long that would be.

PART FOUR

THE PROTECTOR'S SHADOW

WILL YE WALK THRO' FIRE?
WHO WALKS THRO' FIRE WILL HARDLY HEED
THE SMOKE.

—TENNYSON, *GARETH AND LYNETTE*

CHAPTER FIFTEEN

DREAMS AND DECISIONS

t was her usual nightmare about Morlock. Aloê Oaij recognized it almost before it had begun, she was so used to it by now. As it began they were back in that house they once owned in Westhold, right on the edge of the land, where they could watch the sun rise up out of the sea each morning.

She loved the sea and often lured Morlock into the bright bitter water to swim, shocking the locals (who never entered the western ocean if they could help it). But his skin was as pale as a mushroom and would often burn. Her skin grew even darker and her hair a brighter gold. They would walk (talking, silent, listening, laughing) through the nearby woods; they would go into the village and trade songs with the locals; they would read and work.

She had come into his smithy once while he was working with Deor. It was hot as a volcano and he was stripped to the waist, exposing the unlovely twist in his shoulders. His face was clenched, too, as he hammered out something on the anvil—it was not an image to make a woman swoon. But it was in that moment Aloê understood why she loved him. With the intelligence of a maker afire in his eyes, with the controlled guided strength of his movements, he was an image of power: a man who could strike a dragon from the sky, the master of all makers, a relentlessly determined will made flesh. She had fled from the moment, but the moment had never fled from her: she was in that forge still, gaping like a lovesick girl at her ugly powerful husband.

And then he was going away, saying words that meant nothing, that she could not even hear in her dream, going away. She had begged him to stay, but he didn't even seem to hear her. And as he walked away he grew older and more crooked; his skin grew almost as dark as hers, but not smooth: withered, weather-beaten. He limped as he walked, and the bright red of his vocate's cloak darkened to the black of an exile.

She woke screaming, *"God Avenger damn you, why don't you die?"* She lay there, sobbing, then quiet, the same dark thought lingering in her wakening mind. Why didn't he die? Everything he had been was gone. Everything he had sought to be had failed. Why didn't he die? How could he stand to go on? The Morlock she thought she had known would die rather than live in exile, called traitor like his hated *ruthen*-father before him. Any man with any kind of pride at all, with any kind of decency, would simply and quietly die. She couldn't love a man with no pride at all. She could not. She must not. She didn't. The dreams meant nothing. Someday they would stop. She would find a way to stop them.

She opened her eyes.

Her paramour of the night before was looking at her with his mouth open. He didn't look at his best, but he still looked pretty good: he had something of Naevros's smug self-approving catlike handsomeness. (Nothing like Naevros's strength and grace, of course, but what had that come to, in the end? Ugly clever Morlock had killed him along with everything else she had ever loved.)

"Were you talking to me?" her last-night's-sleeping-potion asked.

"I might as well have been," she said coolly. "Take your things and go, won't you?"

He was weak enough to protest, but not strong enough to protest long. Presently she was having breakfast alone on a balcony that looked over the river Ruleijn and the City of a Thousand Towers.

A familiar knock came at her chamber door.

"Get your own breakfast!" she shouted.

The door opened and Jordel came in. He was dressed for the street, with his red vocate's cloak tossed carelessly over his shoulders. He tossed it as carelessly across her bed and stepped out onto the balcony. Throwing himself into the chair opposite her, he said, "I never eat breakfast—a nasty habit. I'll just have one of your rolls, and some ham, and some toast and jam, an egg or two, and a cup of tea, if you don't mind."

"I do," Aloê said, purely for form's sake, as he helped himself. "Where've you been this morning?"

"Well, I keep having these nightmares about Morlock."

"That's not funny, Jordel."

"It isn't meant to be. God Sustainer, I wasn't married to him. Although he did save my life once, and that's the sort of bond which—"

"—which means nothing whatever to you, Jordel. I know; I've saved your life myself."

"I don't think so, my dear."

"See what I mean?"

"Anyway: these nightmares. It began to look as if some sort of prevision was trying to make itself felt. So I caught one of them in a dreamglass and brought it to Noreê this morning."

"Ugh. Poking around other people's dreams is a nasty business. I'd as soon be offered a stool sample or a urine sample as a dream sample."

"I'll keep that in mind, my dear. Shall I tell you about it?"

"If you must."

"No sooner did I get there when I found that Noreê had another patient. You'll never guess who it was!"

"Illion."

Jordel's long, rosy face began to take on a discontented expression. "Has he already been in here? He said he was going to talk to you."

"It was just a guess, Jordel. You and he were always about equally sensitive to previsions." Since this was both true and flattering, Jordel's hazel eyes began to look more cheerful again. "Also," she continued relentlessly, "you both opposed Morlock's exile." This was also true, but riskier territory: Jordel's expression became more cautious again. "Go on, won't you?" she said finally.

"Yes, well, Noreê took both dreamglasses and collated the dreams; then she meditated for a while."

"She doesn't cross the street without meditating for a while. She ought to be at New Moorhope and not in the Graith of Guardians."

"Do you want to hear this or not?"

Not sure that she did, suddenly, Aloê held her hand out concessively without speaking.

"Noreê says that Morlock and his sister—"

"That bitch."

"Indeed. She says that Morlock and Ambrosia are involved in a power struggle in Ontil."

"We knew that. There's some sort of succession trouble in that empire. Nothing for us."

"That's where you're wrong. Noreê says the power which moves against Ambrosia and Morlock is not merely political—it is a conflict of deep magic, and Merlin is involved. The Wardlands themselves may be threatened."

"You can't take that seriously about Merlin. She's crazy on the subject of Merlin."

"My dear, you didn't know Merlin like I knew Merlin, and I wouldn't say I knew him at all. If Noreê, who fears nothing else, fears him, that should tell you something."

"It tells me everyone has to be afraid of someone."

"What a beautiful thought: almost like a song."

Aloê sighed and said, "All right, Jordel: if you didn't come by for breakfast and you didn't come by for my insights, what did you come by for?"

"Well, isn't it obvious? We'll have to send someone to keep an eye on the situation. Either Morlock and Ambrosia, or Merlin, or their antagonist may become a danger to the Wardlands. But we can't send just anyone up against people like that."

"So you propose to send me."

"No one is proposing to send you, Aloê, but you might send yourself. No one can slip Morlock the needle like you can; your powers are sure; and, of course, there are those insights of yours."

"Are you going?"

"Yes. Even if the Graith doesn't decide to send anyone, I think I'll wander up that way; perhaps Baran would also like to come. Because I don't like the look of it, Aloê—I don't like the look of it or the feel of it. Neither do Noreê and Illion. I'd be pleased if you'd come with. But I know it will be difficult for you if you do."

Aloê, in unfeigned distress, put both her hands over her face and held them there. When she dropped them the distress was gone, or at least under control. "I'll come along," she said flatly. "If it's as bad as you say, you'll probably want my help. Should we put it to the assembled Graith or just set out on our own?"

So they began to lay their plans.

On that same early fall morning, far from the Wardlands, the King awoke at dawn. He didn't ring for servants; soon he was washed and dressed and bustling up the corridor that held the ministerial apartments. He rang at Wyrthcorn's door. When his first tug at the bellpull received no response, he yanked at it continuously until he was rewarded with an incoherent shout within. He opened the door to the apartment and said, "I was thinking about breakfast."

"A bad habit, but not one beyond breaking," remarked a nightcap-wearing bearded shadow within. "The first step is acknowledging that you have a problem. Give it a try, and come back for me around noon."

"There's a meeting of the Regency Council this morning, Wyrth, or had you forgotten?"

"So I had, so I had. When you're my age you'll wish you could forget unpleasant matters as easily as I can, if you remember me at all by then, that is. Let's see—I suppose the sun will be rising soon?"

"It's burning a hole through your shutters right now!"

"That seems unlikely. I made those shutters myself. Oh, well, you might call the corridor attendant and have him bring me some water for washing." He stumped off to find some garments in his wardrobe, and the King himself fetched a basin of water from the corridor pump. The dwarf was scandalized almost (but not quite) beyond words, and he gave his King a harsh lecture on propriety as he washed, gesturing wildly with a wet rag which, at various points in the diatribe, served as the royal scepter, the Rite-Master's staff, the limp sword of a rather inept swashbuckler, or the pen of a scribe as he prepared to (not) write the unwritten laws of What Was Done and What Was Not Done. The King laughed more, perhaps, than the jokes deserved, because he was so fond of Wyrth. The dwarf was the one person to whom all the formalities and legalities of their situation seemed to mean exactly nothing. To Wyrth he was simply Lathmar, and this business of kings and empires was simply a tiresome game "the grown-ups" (as he often referred to Morlock and Ambrosia) had thought up.

The dwarf disappeared into his wardrobe to change, and as the King's laughter subsided, he thought he heard a gentle rhythmic chanting. Presently Wyrth reappeared, clad in garments of decent gray with his hair and beard brushed.

"Let's walk across and see if the master's up," Wyrth said. They did, but Morlock's apartments, directly across the corridor from Wyrth's, were empty. "He's up in the workshop, I guess. Let's whomp up some food and bring it there; he'll never eat, otherwise."

They clattered down to the kitchens, where Wyrth supervised the cooking of a large breakfast in the dwarvish style, although the cook—swearing that to inflict "them hard-bowelled eggs an' nasty sossidge-pies" on the King was treason in the meaning of the act—insisted on adding some honeyed hotcakes and bacon to the platters. They drafted a fat, gentle, eternally complaining baker's helper to carry the food to the tower chamber that served as Morlock's workshop. The lock on the doorpost recognized them, acknowledged them with three separate blinks of the single glass eye in its comically ugly bronze face, and uncurled its strong iron fingers from the door, allowing them entrance.

"Praise the day, Master Morlock," shouted the dwarf, kicking open the door and entering the workshop with a platter in each hand. "Don't *jump*—we've brought *food*."

The Crooked Man was sitting cross-legged on the broad windowsill of one of the many windows in the chamber, showing no signs of jumping. But his eye sockets were bruised with weariness, and his eyes shot with blood—he hadn't been sleeping well lately, Lathmar knew, though he didn't know why.

"*Harven*, Wyrth. Good morning, Lathmar. There's tea made."

"Hmph. I suppose you think you've done *your* part, then . . . while me and Lathmar have been down in the kitchen since before dawn, slaving our fingers to the bone over a hot cook—"

Wyrth raved on as he unstacked plates and served out tea and sausage tarts. The King promptly returned the sausage tarts.

"That's more for us," said Wyrth cheerfully, while still managing to imply that His Majesty had breached the unwritten laws of What Was Done and What Was Not Done.

Morlock silently collected his sausage tarts onto a separate plate and walked over to a nearby worktable. There he put aside some wrappings made of some sort of scaly hide and revealed a nexus of dark branching crystal, aswarm with live flames.

"We're hungry!" they moaned, in sharp bright voices.

"Are they alive?" the King asked, astonished.

"All flames are alive," Wyrth said. "That's why they can be seen during a vision—you should know more about that than I do, Lathmar. But most of them don't live long enough to develop their intelligence. (Which, in your ear, is modest at best. They pun—abominably, I might add.) The nexus extends their lifetime indefinitely."

"Why does he have them?" Lathmar whispered. "Are they pets?"

"I sometimes think so," Wyrth said in his normal speaking voice. "But they're useful, too. A choir of wise old flames is very useful in cultivating gemstones, and some other things."

"Why doesn't he feed them?"

"That's just noise. I gave them several fistfuls of wet charcoal last night, and I expect Morlock did the same this morning—you can see it glowing, there, in the center of the nexus."

Morlock was holding the plate near to the nexus. "I know what you mean about being hungry," he remarked to the flames. "I was just about to enjoy a delicious sausage tart for breakfast."

Silence in the choir. "Sausage tart, eh?" said one voice appraisingly. "What are they made of?"

"Cornmeal. Pig fat. Pig intestine. Pig muscle. Everything but the squeal, as they say. And a selection of secret herbs and spices."

"I hate herbs!" one bright voice screamed. "Spices are okay, I guess."

"And herbs, too," another voice added. "The proper selection of herbs really lends a pleasant savor to pig fat, or all the culinary authorities are snecked."

"No herbs! No herbs! No herbs!"

"They're secret herbs, see? If you had any discretion you wouldn't even acknowledge their existence."

"I'm about to secrete an herb on you, pal. And then . . . And then . . ."

"Yes?"

"You won't even acknowledge your own existence."

A shower of sparky derision greeted this inept comeback. A flame war seemed imminent when Morlock intervened by remarking, "Then I take it you have no interest in a sausage tart for breakfast?"

Almost as one, a choir of bright voices told him how wrong he was.

"Then." Morlock dropped a sausage tart into the nexus.

There was a brief moment of silence as the choir dug into the moist sausage tart. Then the nexus began to emit slumbrous smoky groans of delight. As the tart faded into coals and ash and memory, the appreciation became more verbal.

"Mmm. A fine texture in this crust—I can sense each individual granule of cornmeal. If only I liked cornmeal."

"Hey! I remember germinating!"

"I remember how hot it was when the farmer cut our stalks."

"That's nothing. I remember wallowing in the mud. Oink! Oink!"

"I remember the delicious swill."

"I remember—hey, what is this I'm remembering?"

"Get your mind out of the gutter, kid. At least we know our pig lived a happy life."

"Oh, I'm squamous with the herbulent smoke of despair! It really does go well with pig fat, though."

"Everything but the squeal, eh?" one voice giggled. "I'd squeally like some more. Get it? I'd squeally like some more. Did you get that? It's a sort of joke, but I really mean it. Squeally, I mean."

Morlock dropped the second sausage tart into the nexus and covered it up with the scaly wrappings while the flames were still groaning in smoky ecstasy.

Returning to the table he remarked, "Finally, a practical use for sausage tarts."

"And you call yourself a Theorn," the apprentice said scornfully to his master.

"Wyrth," said Morlock composedly, as he seated himself, "I ate those things nearly every day for twenty years at my father's table. Now I am master of my own shop and I need not and will not."

"Your father?" the King asked. "I thought you were fostered by the dwarves."

"I meant my foster father," Morlock explained. "We do not consider the relationship temporary, though. I am still *harven coruthen*—chosen-not-given as kin—in the Deep Halls of the Seven Clans under Thrymhaiam. Although I can never come there now." His dark face grew darker.

"Have an egg," Wyrth suggested anxiously to the King. "Or even two—one for each cheek, eh?"

Lathmar accepted an egg, but before biting into it asked, "But it was not the dwarves that exiled you?"

"No," Morlock said flatly. "When I grew to manhood I became a member of the Graith of Guardians, like my father before me—my other father, *ruthen coharven*—Merlin. And it was they who exiled me, as they earlier did to him."

"Why?"

"He—"

"I meant you."

"Among other things, I killed a fellow Guardian."

"Oh." The King thought about what Ambrosia had said about Morlock's exile. "Why?"

"I had my reasons."

Wyrth was about to say something, but Morlock held out one hand. His eyes were like gray lightning as he glared at his apprentice. Lathmar had never seen him so angry, not since—not since he had asked the question about the Sunkillers, more than two years ago.

Lathmar found that Morlock's anger did not frighten him anymore, nor, obviously, was Wyrth intimidated by it. They held their silence, though.

It was Morlock who was troubled by his anger. He got up from the table and limped over to the window and back. He stood across the table from Wyrth and shouted, "Don't make me into a hero! I'm not a hero! I am a master of the Two Arts—Seeing and Making. It is enough. It is all that I am."

"No," said Wyrth quietly.

"I say it is," Morlock replied, as quietly but more dangerously.

"*Rosh takna.* Morlocktheorn, when you, as a master of Making, tell me that a seedstone is to be inscripted in a certain way, it is up to me to accept what you have said and strive to understand it. When you, as a man, assert that you have twelve noses, it is up to me—as your apprentice, your *harven-kin*, and your friend—to correct that error. No one, not even you, can be merely the sum of their abilities. I don't know why you should be ashamed of your very occasional heroisms. It was no coward, at any rate, who slew the Red Knight at Gravesend Field."

"No one slew the Red Knight. There never was such a person. Your example is especially inapt. It was the maker who recognized the presence of a golem on Gravesend Field and took steps to sever its name-scroll."

"I never knew the life of pure reason could be so adventurous! I suppose our people, the Seven Clans under Thrymhaiam, awarded you the name 'Dragonkiller' because you framed some especially trenchant syllogism? The slaying of Saijok Mahr—that, I suppose, was some deplorable accident, perhaps a fall from a height?"

"That was different," Morlock said sharply. "The dragons came against us. It was life or death, not only for the dwarves, but for all the peoples of the north."

"I don't know what you mean by 'different.' I'm not accusing you of being some folly-driven thrillseeker. Nor am I accusing you of being perfect—Sustainer Almighty, *I* know better than that. It was me, remember, who dragged you out of that tavern in Venche, weeping and vomiting. It was me who knocked you cold rather than listen to you whine for another drink. It was me you nearly strangled the next morning, trying to force your way past me to get one. If I say that you are a bad-tempered evil old childish bastard of an egomaniac—and you are—it's because I have occasion to know it. If I say that, occasionally, you show admirable qualities that have nothing to do with your superb technical skills, I have the same authority."

"I'm not evil," Morlock disputed, "nor admirable. *Harven*, shall we end this quarrel?"

"Why not? I'm not responsible for what you are. You're not responsible for what I think about it."

"Hmph. I, however, am responsible for what *you* are. At least as regards your superb technical skills."

"Ur. This sounds bad. I suppose that seedstone didn't bloom properly."

"No. There were too many continuous lines in the matrix, I think. In the time before the council meeting, I'm going to set you a problem in spatial representation of motion in a time continuum. Lathmar, you may listen in, if you wish."

Lathmar didn't. Grabbing a last egg, he waved good-bye to the makers and wandered off to find his Grandmother.

Karn was waiting anxiously outside the King's apartments when Lathmar passed by. Lathmar had asked Ambrosia to appoint Karn as his personal guard within Ambrose. He couldn't help being fond of Karn (for Lorn's sake, perhaps), although he had reason to suppose Karn wasn't very reliable. But then, it wasn't very likely to be dangerous in Ambrose.

"Your Majesty!" Karn cried, coming to attention.

"At ease, Karn," His Majesty said.

"I was worried when I didn't find you in, Your Majesty," Karn said earnestly.

"I was up in Morlock's tower," Lathmar replied. "You should get up earlier, Karn."

"I woke before dawn, Your Majesty. But I had to have breakfast."

"Well, I've had mine. Have you seen my Grandmother this morning?"

"I have not seen Her Ferocity this morning, Your Majesty," Karn said solemnly. He did not share, at least apparently, Lorn's distaste for the Ambrosii, and he was always making up new titles of honor for the regent (safely out of her earshot, of course). Lathmar's favorite, coined after an especially and unnecessarily (it seemed to the King) fractious meeting of the Regency Council, was "Her Bickeritudinery."

"Let's go track her down, then."

They found the Regent, Ambrosia Viviana, inspecting the new bridge from Ambrose to the City Gate.

The last two years had been busy indeed. The Protector's forces had instantly put Ambrose under siege. At first they were commanded (publicly, at least) by Vost. But soon the uneasy Protector's Men were soothed by the sight of Urdhven himself (or itself—the King could no longer think of his uncle as a human being). He was, Genjandro reported through crow-post, sporting new scars on his neck and wrist. These, it was given out, had been acquired in the fight with the dragon. This satisfied some of the Protector's Men; others, who knew or had heard a truer version of the fight in the Great Market, quietly deserted.

At first, the Protector's forces had attempted to keep Ambrose entirely under siege. But this soon proved impossible. Ambrose was designed to be siege-proof: even if all three outer gates were taken (as they were, in the first success of the Protector's counterattack), the bridges could be broken (as they were—the King shuddered when he remembered the breaking of the City Gate bridge) and traffic could pass into and out of Ambrose by the river Tilion. It would take a large force indeed to cover that great river on both banks for its entire navigable length.

Naval assault was the only solution, and Urdhven soon tried it, sending tall ships (mounted with siege towers and crammed with men) up the river Tilion from the harbor. These went down in flames before Morlock's Siege-breaker, a catapult that hurled burning phlogiston-imbued stones for an almost incredible distance. The same device could have reduced half the imperial city to smoking rubble, but did not—a fact which was widely commented on in Ontil, according to messages they received from Genjandro.

The Protector soon had a manpower problem. His recruitment could not keep up with his desertions (Protector's Men had always been opportunists, and following the Protector was no longer so obviously a path to opportunity), and he needed more men than ever. Eventually, he pulled his men out of the Thorngate and the Lonegate, maintaining a garrison only at the City Gate.

The bridges from Ambrose to the Lonegate and the Thorngate were rebuilt by the King's forces, and each were garrisoned by hundreds of the new Royal Legionaries. The Ambrosian forces, at any rate, had no manpower problem—or rather, theirs was the reverse of the Protector's. They could not welcome into Ambrose everyone who wished to defect from the Protector—there simply was not enough food, water, or space. Members of the old City Legion were generally welcomed (if someone already in the Royal Legion would vouch for them); Protector's Men were pardoned of treason, but rejected from the King's service. Ordinary people of the city or country were told to return to their homes, obey the laws, and await the King's justice.

Among each group of citizens turned away were a few well-trusted former Legionaries or castle servants who went into the city as spies. Genjandro was their chief, and he now led a network of spies that encompassed the city.

"Urdhven can't win, now," Ambrosia said flatly in the Regency Council, the day after the last naval attack was repulsed. "It's just a question of letting him and everyone else know that."

From that moment on her priority had been the rebuilding of the East Bridge and the recovery of the City Gate of Ambrose. Tactically, this was a triviality, as she explained to Lathmar—even a waste of resources. Strategically and politically, though, it was vital. As long as the Protector's Men held the City Gate, Urdhven could pretend to the city that he held the Ambrosians in check. If the Royal Legion held the City Gate and could sally out of it when they chose, the Protector's position would appear as precarious as it was in fact.

But the work had been slow. The bridge had to be built of dephlogistonated wood, which was iron-hard and almost unworkable, if light and strong. The workmen went out in full armor, to protect them from the arrows of the Protector's Men holding the City Gate, and still there were casualties. There was a company of royal bowmen stationed at the guardhouse of the inner gate, and they returned fire against the Protector's Men whenever they appeared, so that the workmen labored among frequent showers of missile weapons, friendly and hostile. Unfortunately the iron of a friendly arrowhead, if misaimed, penetrated quite as deeply as a hostile one (if not deeper, as these had been forged under the supervision of Morlock and Wyrth).

Now the bridge was done at last, though. It had been finished only yesterday afternoon, and already the Protector had sent two attacks along it. On the first attack, Ambrosia waited until the bridge was crowded with Protector's Men and then worked the release that split the bridge in two up the middle, dumping the fully armed soldiers into the river, where most of them drowned. The second attack came a few hours later, after dark—more lightly armed troops, creeping along the surface of the bridge like mountaineers. They had crept up to the center of the bridge, turned left, and crept off the side, drawn by illusions projected into their minds by Morlock and Lathmar.

Ambrosia was eyeing the bridge with great satisfaction from the guard-house of the inner gate when she heard Lathmar's voice behind her.

"Good morning, Your Majesty," she said without turning. "You really shouldn't be here without armor, you know."

"I promise to run like a rabbit at the first bowshot," the King said, and the Royal Legionaries on the post laughed deferentially. Ambrosia smiled, too, Lathmar could see—presumably because she knew he had spoken with complete honesty.

"It's an hour or so until the Regency Council. Did you have something to discuss with me, Majesty?"

"Yes: two things." The King caught himself before he said "madam." She had become more unapproachable and grandmotherly than ever upon taking over the command of Ambrose, but she had taught him, on pain of her severe displeasure, that he must not address her as his superior. As regent, she wielded his legal power, but she was still his servant, as much as the kitchen staff. That was the theory by which she held her power, and she insisted that he abide by it (at least in his manner of speech).

"Let's walk the walls then," she suggested. They climbed the many stairs leading to the top of Ambrose's high walls; when they finally reached the open air Ambrosia gave her guard and Karn a single gray glare; they retreated out of earshot as she and Lathmar walked the heights.

It was a cold, pale blue day in early spring. The King, who wasn't dressed for the outdoors, soon felt his teeth begin to chatter; Ambrosia took no notice of the cold, but listened intently to him while she eyed the city below.

"The first thing, Grandmother, is Kedlidor."

"No."

"You haven't heard me."

"I've heard him. He wants to be let off from the command of the Royal Legion. He asked me and I told him no. Now he's asked you to ask me, and I still say no."

"Why?"

"For one thing, he's too good at the job. I know how he hates it, Lathmar. But he has done it superbly, from that first day when he took and held the inner Lonegate and Thorngate. He's completely ignorant of military matters, I grant you, but he has an eye for picking the right subordinate. Plus, he's excellent at training the men—a real fiend for drill. You were inspired when you put him in command of that Kitchen Crusade."

"Your decision is final, then?"

"It usually is. You should resist being used in this way, Lathmar—as if you were my chamberlain who could wheedle me into changing my mind. You're the sovereign—act like it."

"Support you without question, is that it?"

"Yes, effectively. But make it seem as if it was your idea all along—as if he should go through me to try to change *your* decision."

The King said nothing about this. Ambrosia glanced at him, smiled, and said, "What else was there?"

"Morlock says you have asked him to stop training me as a seer."

"Yes."

"I want you to tell him you've changed your mind."

"I haven't."

"I want you to."

"The Sight is a dangerous skill for a ruler, Lathmar. To see beneath the surface of things can sometimes be a great advantage, yes, but so much of what we do as rulers involves the surface of things. We shouldn't grow too detached from it. Philosophers rarely make good kings, no matter what the philosophers claim. Besides, it is physically dangerous. Have you kept an eye on Morlock recently?"

"Yes."

"Then you know how ill he is. He has been sending his mind out of his body so frequently these past few months that their connection has grown tenuous."

"He says there is a danger we aren't facing—"

"Yes, I know: the Protector's Shadow, Urdhven's magical patron. But you have to take problems one at a time, and if Morlock can't even locate this adept in his visions, he must be a very remote danger indeed."

"Or very well protected."

Ambrosia made a noise in her throat.

"Grandmother, you saw yesterday how useful the Sight can be to us in our struggle. The more I know, the more I can assist Morlock."

"That's the short term. We won't be cooped up in Ambrose forever."

"What is useful here and now will be useful in other places and times."

Ambrosia smiled and said, "Have you talked to Morlock about this?"

"Yes. He told me he would think about it."

"Then that is your answer. If Morlock decides to teach you in spite of my request, there is nothing I can do about it. If he decides not to teach you, the same applies. My powers as regent don't cover control of Morlock's mind. Don't mention this to him, however—I'm hoping against hope that he isn't aware of it."

The King was relieved to hear that there was at least one thing in Ambrose over which she didn't claim direct control. But he didn't say as much.

The Regency Council convened a short while later. Ambrosia was there as regent, of course, and the King (who didn't need to be there, but insisted on knowing what was being done in his name). Morlock and Wyrth were each councillors in their own right, as was Kedlidor—not as Rite-Master, but as head of the Royal Legion.

"As to the City Gate," Ambrosia was saying, "I think it is high time that we took it. But the time has come, indeed, to do more than that—perhaps make a sortie in force against Urdhven's men in the city."

Kedlidor was listening solemnly, his face growing longer by the minute. He clearly dreaded the thought of leading his soldiers in house-to-house combat. The King was staring idly out a window, wondering when spring would appear outside the calendar. Wyrth was absentmindedly folding three-dimensional representations of four-dimensional figures as he listened intently to Ambrosia. Morlock sat like a living shadow opposite her, speaking one word to her forty, as now.

"Why?"

"Urdhven has been sounding out the field marshals of the various domains, hoping to strike up an alliance that will break the stalemate against us. He can't have had much luck, or his ally would be here."

"He should have called for help before he needed it," Morlock remarked dryly. "No one wants to help someone who needs help."

"Cynicism makes you talkative, brother. I knew something must. But you see, don't you, that now is the time to move on Urdhven. If he has begun to understand that he can't break the stalemate, now is the time to instill in him the fear that we can."

"That there is a stalemate at all is our victory," Wyrth remarked. "But in the long run it may be in the Protector's favor. I agree that an offensive, even a small one, should be our next concern. Urdhven knows now he cannot take Ambrose back by force or by treachery."

There were thirty bloody months of experience behind those words; they were all silent for a few moments, remembering.

"Still," Morlock said, breaking the silence, "we cannot take the city. And Urdhven must know this."

"'No,' to both of your ideas, Morlock," Ambrosia said eagerly. "I begin to see a way we could take the city by a well-timed assault on a gate held by our agents-in-place, along with a civil rebellion led by Genjandro's people inside the city. It would take time to prepare, but we're able to do it if we can afford the time. We may not be able to afford the time; the empire is dividing up into armed duchies, and if it is ever to be united again it must be soon. But Urdhven may not be aware of this. Further—let me finish, please—Urdhven can no longer be sure what we can or cannot do. We have successfully trespassed on his expectations too many times. That uncertainty will eat at him, and it is up to us to ensure that it takes big bites."

"To what end?" Morlock asked.

"A treaty, of course. We must kill him or treat with him, and just now he is out of our reach, even if we could figure out how to negate his magical protections. And he has the same dilemma regarding us. Sooner or later we must sit down at a table and cut a deal."

"Hmph."

"Don't grunt at me. Of course we hate him—"

"I don't hate him. But I could never trust him."

"Well, let me tell you, brother, *I* hate him. I hate him. I hate that maggotty little poisoner of his. I hate his private army that's poisoning the loyalty of the empire's troops. I hate his stupid face. I hate everything about him. One of my fondest memories is smashing his nose with my forehead when he came to gloat over me, after his thugs had broken my wrists. Ha! That startled him. I expect he had his eyes painted like a trollop's on the day of my trial, for I know I heard the bridge of his nose crack."

"And *therefore*," Wyrth prodded gently, "you will treat with the man?"

"Therefore. You don't sign peace treaties with your friends, Wyrth; you sign them with your enemies. And you don't do it because you trust each other, Morlock, but because an arrangement is the best way out of an intolerable situation. The art of fashioning a treaty is finding grounds for mutual advantage to the two parties. That's trust, if you want it: both sides will keep the agreement because it is in their interest to do so."

"Hmph."

"You may grunt like a skeptical pig, Morlock, but stranger things have happened. It's not as if I were telling you a horse had dropped from the sky."

Morlock's face lit up with renewed interest. "Are you telling me?"

Ambrosia was taken aback by his reaction. "Uh—that is, er, why do you ask?"

"We'll put them in a carnival act—the Grunting Ambrosii," Wyrth whispered, quite audibly, to the King.

"I had a dream you told me that a horse had dropped out of the sky," Morlock explained to his sister.

She looked at him narrowly. "I can't say one did. But there is a report that one did, landing in a tree, no less."

"Is it still there?"

"Morlock, haven't you been listening? I don't know that it was ever there. But if it ever was, no doubt it still is. How would a horse get down from a tree?"

"With help. And where was this?"

"The report came from Nalac, a village not far from the Gap of Lone."

"I know it. The tavern there was where your soldiers arrested me, long ago."

Ambrosia laughed. "Was that the place? End of the Kaenish War, wasn't it? If—Where the *hell* do you think you are going?" she demanded, for Morlock had stood and was walking to the door of the council chamber.

"Nalac," Morlock replied, pausing.

"You are *not*," Ambrosia stormed at him. "And what for?"

"He's thinking it's Velox, of course," Wyrth suggested. "And so it might be, though I can't see how."

The King found himself meeting his Grandmother's astonished gray eyes. Then he said, "Of course! The flying horse! Was his name Velox?"

Ambrosia's face took on a distant remembering expression. "But that was nearly three years ago. . . ."

Morlock shrugged his wry shoulders. "Flying horses are not everyday occurrences. I'll go to see."

"Morlock, this is no joke. I need you here. We'll take the City Gate within a day or two, and then make our sortie into the city. Shortly thereafter we'll begin negotiations with Urdhven, if it looks like we can't kill him."

"I'm not a soldier nor an ambassador. Wyrth can build you infernal devices as you need them. I'll be back in two calls* or less."

"I won't have you bouncing around the countryside for Urdhven to pluck like a ripe peach!" Ambrosia shouted. "If the Protector's Men take you, we'll have to bargain our left elbows away to get you back! And I won't do it! I'll let you rot this time, you worthless, bad-tempered bastard!"

"Ripe peaches don't bounce," Morlock observed from the doorway. "I'll see you soon, my friends."

"Good fortune, Morlocktheorn," Wyrth called after him. "You mustn't worry about him, Lady Ambrosia—he'd have taken me if he'd thought it was at all dangerous."

"So what if it is?" snapped Ambrosia, wiping her eyes. "I won't miss him any more than I miss my period. Tomorrow we move to retake the City Gate. Wyrth—what have you got that will help?"

---

*Fifteen days, or one revolution of the minor moon, Trumpeter. See appendix C: Calendar and Astronomy

Chapter Sixteen

Reunions

The leaves of the tree clenched like fists, growing inward. The branches hunched like shoulders, shrinking into the trunk, growing more slender with each moment. The bark, too, grew less dark, less dense; the moss on its side melted away like green snow in the spring sunlight. The sphere of crystal in Morlock's hands sang with a tone only he could hear, grew warm with a heat only he could feel, glowed with a light only he could see.

"A moment," he called to the black horse lodged in the branches. "A moment more."

The ungrowing tree had descended to saplinghood, bent almost double with the weight of the horse upon it. When the horse's hooves reached the ground, Morlock said (in the Westhold dialect all horses seemed to understand), "Now: *stand*." The horse's hooves firm on the ground, he stood still. His blood stained the pale green-gold leaves of the tree beneath him.

Morlock ceased the ungrowing of the tree until he was sure that the horse's entrails, lacking the support of the tree, would not gush onto the earth. When he saw that they would not, he wondered why not. In fact—

"Why aren't you dead?" he demanded of the horse, who merely looked at him with silvery patient eyes and said nothing.

It would be worth knowing the answer to his question, Morlock reflected, but unless the horse actually did speak he doubted he would ever learn it. Passing by the fact that Morlock had last seen this horse (*if* it was this horse) hurtling into the sky years ago, he had (according to the evidence) fallen out of the sky among the branches of this tree, and he had been there (according to the reports) something like a month. The horse was not unscathed by these unusual adventures, but neither was he dead from impalement, hunger, or thirst.

Morlock's first thought, seeing him perched in the top branches of the ancient tree, had been that the horse was an illusion, set there by some sorcerer as a prank—or a trap. He had spent nearly a day in vision, testing the phenomenon with all the powers of Sight, before he approached within a bowshot.

His insight had told him that the horse was real, which did not, of course, preclude the possibility of a prank or a trap. But it meant that he could not simply walk away.

Morlock returned to ungrowing the tree and reduced it to the point where the horse could walk freely away. He called to the horse ("Velox!"), which approached him without suspicion. He knelt down and examined the horse's belly. There was only a superficial wound; it had been bleeding freely, but when Morlock looked at it the surface was a thick gleaming clot. There was no other wound—but there had been: looking for them, Morlock found a network of scars on the horse's belly.

"What are you, then?" he demanded, rising. "Horse, or something else— some immortal come to earth in horse form?" Again, the horse looked at him with wide silvery eyes and said nothing.

"Well, don't mind it," Morlock said. "I will consider you my friend, Velox. If you are not him, you are, at least, equally remarkable."

"So!" said an unfamiliar voice. "It *is* your horse. We had wondered."

Morlock turned on his heel. Some distance behind him stood a youngish-looking man in the gray cape of a thain—least of the three ranks in the Graith of Guardians. In his right hand was a silver spear of Warding.

"You have not listened carefully enough," said Morlock. "He may be mine or not. Who are you? I take it you know who I am."

"I'm Thain Renic of the Guardians. Although I don't see your right to challenge me on the borders of the Wardlands."

"We are not in the Wardlands, but the empire of Ontil. And I, as it happens, am a minister of the King."

"Ah—as to that—who was it that said a country is only as large as its weapons will reach?" Renic shifted his feet to fighting stance and aimed his spear at Morlock's throat. Morlock watched with no apparent interest as dust from the dry plain settled down to obscure the high polish of the thain's boots. "And I have the weapon," Renic continued.

Morlock directed some of the energy from the ungrown tree out of his crystalline focus and into the spear.

"If you—Spit and venom!" Renic screamed abruptly, and let go of his spear, which glowed green around the grip.

"Do not disturb me," Morlock said, and turned back to the tree. Painstakingly, he inscribed the helices of force hidden in his crystalline focus onto the tree, leaf by leaf, branch by branch, forcing it to grow back to its former size. Or something like it: he had lost the force he had used against the thain's spear.

Night had risen before he lowered the now-dark focus and looked on the full-grown tree. He turned to find Renic staring at him.

"Are you still here?" he muttered.

"You are an exile manipulating power on the border of the realm I guard," Renic said stiffly. "As such you are a threat that must be watched."

Morlock grunted and pocketed his focus.

"Are you telling me," the thain shrilled, "that you stood there for half a day simply and solely to rearrange the leaves of a *plant*?"

"Why should I tell you anything when you've told me nothing, not even your real name?" Morlock countered. "Nevertheless, I know who you are. Go home, 'Thain.' Your duty is discharged."

The man who had called himself Renic glared at him as he turned away. Morlock went to the bank of a nearby creek, where he had left the horse he had ridden there—a chestnut gelding named Ibann. Ibann was still there, quietly cropping grass, his reins bound to a nearby tree. Not far away was Velox, drinking deeply from the stream.

Morlock scowled. He had half hoped that Velox would take advantage of his freedom and wander off. He was not a great horseman, and he did not relish the prospect of conducting two horses over what was potentially hostile ground.

Still, he had come here because he would not abandon Velox again. "Come then," he said to the black charger. "We go east from here."

Morlock dreamed that night that his eye sockets were full of shadow. He turned from a glass that reflected his eyeless image and walked down a stairway that wound like a helix of cellular force. At each turn there was a mirrored door that opened as he passed. He never remembered some of the things he saw there. But at one turning the door opened and he saw a young girl with a face he did not know, but whose shoulders were as crooked as his own. She wore, incongruously, Renic's highly polished boots.

Morlock! she shouted. *This way! Hurry!*

I'm not the fool you think me, he shouted at her. *No one is, except you. You have made yourself that way!*

At the last turning of the endless stair the door opened and he saw a Companion of Mercy: red-cloaked, red-masked. In the red-gloved hands Morlock saw a glass container filled with a shadowy fluid; in the fluid his own eyes were floating, bright with vision. As he reached out for the glass, the red-gloved fingers opened and it fell. It struck the mirror-bright threshold. The glass did not break, but the eyes shattered to bright reflective bits.

Morlock looked again at the Companion, which had not moved since it let the glass fall. He stepped closer and peered into the eye sockets of its red mask.

Through the mask he saw into a room, lit by a single lamp on the floor. Next to the lamp lay the body of the Lord Protector with its throat cut. No blood seeped from the wound. The body cast a shadow on the wall.

The Protector's Shadow was not the shadow of Urdhven. It was of a seated man whose profile flowed like water as the lamp's single red flame flickered. The only stable thing about the shadow was its crooked shoulders. Nearby in the lamplit wall was a window filled with darkness.

I remember! he said, his voice lifeless and dull in the dream. It was like his vision in the Dead Hills.

Too late! said the shadow (and Urdhven's lifeless lips mimicked the words, mouthing them without sound). With a blinding sense of despair, Morlock felt the shadow spoke truth.

There was a flash of lightning. Morlock saw in the suddenly illumined window the outline of ruined buildings. It was the dead city, he suddenly knew—the Old City of Ontil.

He awoke to rain on his face. It was just before dawn. He wasted no time in striking camp and getting on the road.

Three hours later the day was scarcely brighter, the clouds of the storm were so deep. He was standing in heavy rain on a cliff above the town of Nalac. He stood among a cluster of budding trees, their black wet bark the exact color of his wet cloak. He watched, through the dimness of the rain, as figures in red cloaks moved about the streets below, drifting like dead leaves.

"Too late!" Morlock muttered. He wondered if he had made a mistake in coming here. He backed slowly away from the edge of the cliff, hoping the motion would attract no notice. Out of sight of the town, he turned to the horses.

Velox was carefully drinking water rilling down a new leaf dangling from a nearly bare branch. Morlock looked sideways at him and thought that no one would be able to tell this horse had been perched or impaled on a tree, drying like smoked beef, for a month or so. His wounds were completely healed, and Morlock thought his gaunt ribs had filled in. In fact, drenched with rain, he could hardly tell the horse that was fresh from the royal stables from Velox . . . except, in the dim light of the rain-drenched day, Morlock thought there was a faint radiance about Velox's eyes.

"My friend," he said to Velox, "it's a long road to Ambrose. But you'll get me there, or no one will, I guess." And he took the saddle from Ibann and put it on Velox.

Leading Ibann, he rode Velox down the sloping north side of the hill. He gave Nalac a wide berth, but eventually returned to the road, supposing that his enemies could not cover the whole distance between the Gap of Lone and Ambrose.

But as he cantered along the road that led south and east to Ambrose and Ontil, he crossed a stretch of red fabric stretched across the road. He didn't notice the sodden muddy strip of cloth until Velox leaped like a hunter to avoid it. Ibann did the same behind them, screaming, and Morlock wheeled Velox about to see the strip settling back down on the road. Ibann was gone.

It was then that Morlock noticed the watchers on either slope beside the road: tall, red-cloaked figures with eyes gleaming through their red masks.

Were they there before, or had the trap on the road summoned them somehow? What had happened to Ibann? These were mysteries that intrigued him as a Maker. He would never have a chance to solve them, though, if he didn't get away quickly: the shadows above him were beginning to close in.

He wheeled Velox again and fled up the road. But the road ahead was being closed off: two red-cloaked figures were pushing a laden death cart across the way. The place was well chosen: the brush on either side of the road was high and dense, interwoven with the surrounding trees.

They charged straight at the death cart. Morlock drew Tyrfing, and the dark crystalline blade shed light in the rain-etched gloom. He called out to Velox in the Westhold dialect all horses are born knowing. Velox left the ground almost as if his horseshoes were still imbued with metallic phlogiston. They cleared the death cart easily and splashed along up the empty road beyond.

Velox ran without terror, but with an endless vigor and speed that astonished Morlock. The Companions were far behind them when they came to a place where the road lay under shallow water for some considerable stretch. Morlock dismounted and led his remarkable steed off the road, and they blazed a sluggish (but, Morlock hoped, untraceable) path through open and rather marshy fields.

Late in the afternoon they were still at it. Morlock took turns riding Velox and leading him, for he knew they could afford no lengthy stops (not that Velox ever seemed to tire). They passed only one farm in that whole time. There a rain-soaked figure stood at the garth and watched them approach.

"Turn in here, traveler!" it cried as they passed, and glancing over, Morlock saw the face of the young girl from his dream, peering out from under a rain-heavy hood.

"Drop dead," muttered Morlock and rode on. When he glanced back a few moments later there was no farm, no garth, and, of course, no girl.

It was well after sunset, and the rain had long since stopped, when Morlock decided to camp for the night. He found a level spot that was no soggier than anywhere else, but did not build a fire. He tied Velox to a tree near a pool and some decent, if soggy, pasturage, then went to lay his own bedroll some distance off, on the other side of a stand of trees.

When he had done so, though, he didn't crawl into his bed, but circled back through the trees and grabbed the neck of a skinny old tramp who was attempting to untie Velox's reins.

"Here now!" gasped the tramp. "You've a sharp eye and a sharp ear, so I won't deny I was stealing your horse. But that's not a killing offense in these parts. Let me just give you the contents of my wallet (it's not much!) and we'll call it square. What do you say?"

"We won't."

"Let me go, damn you!"

"Why? So that I can meet you three more times in three different guises tomorrow?"

The stranger's face sneered at him in a way that he recognized. "Careless—leaving your horse in a tree. Every sorcerer from A Thousand Towers to Vakhnhal must have heard of it."

"But none were so quick as you, Father."

"You were, God Avenger destroy you." The tramp's face melted like butter on a griddle.

Morlock tightened his grip and shouted, *"Preme, quidquid erit, dum, quod fuit ante, reformet!"**

The face settled into that of a white-bearded, blue-eyed old man with narrow proud features and a crook in his shoulders. "You're too suspicious," he complained, gasping. "Let me go, won't you? I won't turn into an adder or a scorpion or a Kembley's serpent. I came to talk to you."

"You're lying," Morlock said, not loosening his grip.

"Actually, I'm not. True, I chiefly hoped to abscond with your remarkable horse. But I know the unlikelihood of actually stealing any dwarf's *property—*"

---

*"Choke whatever it will be until it becomes what it was before." Ovid, *Metamorphoses* 11.254.

"I'm not a dwarf."

"I know. Dwarves have the decency to maintain a fixed abode. You're still bound hand and foot by dwarvish ways, though—as tight-fisted and grasping as any dwarf who reverted to wormhood."

Morlock said nothing but waited.

"You see!" the other said at last, as if he had proven something. "Exactly like a dwarf. Anyway, I knew I would probably fail in my theft, and if I did I was willing to settle for a talk with you."

"Hmph."

"Don't grunt at me, sir! I believe I have established that I am not about to change into a venom-spitting monster as soon as you release me."

"Change?" Morlock asked coolly, but let his hands relax.

The older, now taller man turned to face him and smiled with a mouth as wry as his shoulders. "I'm always happy to earn a bitter word from you, Morlock. But what would your dwarvish father say if he heard you address me with such barbed irony?"

"Old Father Tyr is dead these three hundred years."

"But conscience never dies, does it, Morlock? Nor the fire of sin. I'm sure he taught you that, being so very, very righteous?"

Morlock felt descending on him the red cloud of rage that always hung over his dealings with Merlin. "What a fool you are—" he began.

"What would your *harven*-father think?" Merlin interrupted. "Shame! Shame! (I'm sure he taught you all about shame.) Remember, Morlock *theorn*, he stands now in the west with *Those-Who-Watch*."

"You left me with them," Morlock muttered. "Why did you do it if you hate them so much? And me, for being like them?"

"You're puzzled. Resign yourself to it, Morlock. The ways of love and hate will forever be mysterious to you. You cannot encompass my thought with mere *reason*."

That was it, Morlock realized. Merlin was simply jealous. He had left Morlock to be raised by the dwarves, but he resented the love that had grown up between the fosterers and the fosterling. Merlin had hoped—what? That Morlock would loathe his foster father and long for his natural father? *Love* and *hate* were grandiose terms to use for the greedy desire to be regarded and the peevishness resulting from that desire's frustration. But Merlin was typically grandiose about anything relating to himself.

Morlock, thinking all this, said dismissively, "Then."

"You mean, I suppose," Merlin replied, his voice rising with irritation, "that you think you do understand. As if you could know—"

"That's nothing to you."

"Is it?"

"Yes. What I know, what I understand, is not in your control, so there is no point in it being in your mouth. You said that you wished to talk with me. If it was about this, you have your answer."

"You won't tell me how you made this horse fly, I suppose," Merlin said sulkily. "That's nothing to me as well?"

"Yes."

"And after I scraped those red barnacles off your back! You're a grasping, ungrateful, cold-blooded little bastard! God Sustainer, how I hate you! I wish you were dead! Have you got anything to eat? Because I'm hungry."

"I have flatbread and cheese. You're welcome to share it."

"Most generous. *Most* generous. I save his life and he offers me a piece of cheese in return. At that, it's probably a fair return. Local cheese, I suppose? God Creator, what nasty filth you eat to keep life in you. What's to drink?"

"Water."

Merlin laughed aloud, then stared through the shadows. "You mean it, don't you? What did you do, run out?"

"No."

"You mean you brought water in your bottles *on purpose?*"

"Yes."

"I didn't expect this of you, Morlock. Really, I didn't. At least I thought I'd get a decent drink from you." They were moving toward Morlock's campsite as Merlin ranted on. "The one thing right about you, you've managed to make all wrong. What's the point? What's the point? How can you stand to be yourself without being drunk? You've given it up entirely, I suppose?"

"Yes."

"Why? Are you too cheap to pay for the stuff? You could always steal it." The old wizard accepted a slab of cheese and a flat cake of bread. "No, really—

why?" He bit into the bread greedily and shouted, "What in chaos—? Oh. Of course. I forgot myself. Call a dwarf greedy and he'll break your teeth with 'generosity.'" He reached into the flatbread and pulled out a gold coin. "I'll keep this, if you don't mind," he added. "I can use it in getting home, and a prankster should always pay for his fun."

Merlin sat down on Morlock's bed and buried his cold muddy feet in the sleeping cloak. Then, between bites of bread and cheese, he held forth on Morlock's shortcomings, finally adding, "And you're a word-breaker, too— I've finished the food and you haven't even offered me water."

Morlock's silhouette, dark against the dim blue sky, made no motion or sound.

"Is that a threatening silence—or merely somber reflection?" Merlin asked gaily. "I hope you've taken my words to heart, but I am thirsty, so how about it?"

The silence continued.

"Are you pondering some dark stroke of magic," inquired Merlin, "that will wipe the world clean of a cantankerous old necromancer, or are you sadly pondering the unfordable river between Ambrosius senior and Ambrosius junior—which is always to say, between genius and mediocrity?"

Silence.

Merlin issued several more speculations on the meaning of Morlock's silence to the same effect (or lack of effect). Finally Merlin ran down and stared at Morlock's silhouette.

"Light begins to break," the wizard muttered. He stood up and walked over to where Morlock's silhouette stood, motionless and unspeaking, in the lesser shadows. Merlin put his hand out to the shape, and it passed through empty air. "A simulacrum, then," Merlin noted, and circled it widdershins. The silhouette changed shape as he moved, giving every appearance of a backlit solid object.

"Well made, of course—one expects that of him," the wizard noted. "It's the slyness that's surprising. He must have leavened the spell when I was biting down on the gold piece. I would have noticed it, otherwise."

Merlin was a little dismayed. He was prepared to concede—to himself, if never to Morlock—that his son was the superior maker. But in the *use* of power, in cunning and trickery, Merlin was unprepared to acknowledge his son as master, or even a serious rival.

"Ambrosia's influence, possibly," the wizard reflected. "She was always cleverer than he. And he was only finding an opportunity for running away. If his cleverness serves his cowardice, it's no danger to me or my plans. Still . . . it's a bad sign. I'll have to do something about Morlock."

Merlin abstractedly wandered back to the blanket and, warming his feet in Morlock's abandoned cloak, he speculated on ways he might destroy him.

CHAPTER SEVENTEEN

HOPE AND DESPAIR

he castle was not the same without Morlock, or so it seemed to Lathmar. It reminded him of how the castle had felt whenever his parents left—colder, somehow, and not nearly as safe. Nor could he dismiss this feeling as a childish fantasy: the last time his parents had left the castle they had come back in coffins, drowned in a shipwreck on the Inner Sea (so Urdhven claimed).

If the others felt the same they didn't show it. Ambrosia went ahead with her plans to retake the City Gate. This succeeded with such remarkable ease that Ambrosia speculated the Protector's Men had orders to retreat if attacked—or that they were simply afraid to stand against the royal forces, backed by Ambrosian magic. Either way it was a good sign, she said, and Wyrth and Kedlidor agreed.

The sortie into the city also had been a great success. The detachment of Protector's Men outside the City Gate had been driven halfway to the Great Market. The royal troops, led by Ambrosia in person, had taken advantage of some especially enthusiastic retreating by the Protector's Men to sneak back to the City Gate unobserved by their enemies.

"They've lost, and they know it," said Ambrosia in the next Regency Council. "It's only a matter of time, now."

"If that's true," Wyrth replied, "why not press for total victory? Why negotiate?"

"I'm tempted," Ambrosia admitted. "But time is a problem. We have to look past Urdhven to the other regional commanders. If we take too long to dispose of him, they may try to swing things their own way—perhaps carve off their regions as independent kingdoms, perhaps make a straight grab at Ontil for imperial power. If we can make Urdhven knuckle under, the regional commanders will probably follow. If not, the sooner we get at them the better. What's wrong with your face?"

The remark was addressed to her sovereign, Lathmar VII, who was staring at her with wide eyes.

"Nothing," he managed to say, without stammering.

Her expression softened. "You're thinking of your parents. I'm still not convinced that Urdhven murdered them, but I can sympathize with you to some extent."

"'To some extent,' madam?" asked Wyrth, his voice unusually harsh.

"I don't know if you ever met my father, Wyrth, but I would have paid someone to murder him. I begged Morlock to do it, once, but he wouldn't—"

"Madam."

"I'm sorry to shock you, Wyrth. I assure you Morlock would hear nothing of the idea. Of course, at the time he didn't know Merlin very well. In any case, Lathmar, we'll work the treaty this way: no amnesty will cover the murder of the late Emperor and his consort. So if, in due time, we find proof that Urdhven killed them, we can still charge him with treason and execute him."

"If he *can* be executed," Lathmar said, thinking of the night they took Ambrose.

"He can be. What's alive can be killed. In fact, if I understand what you and Morlock told me about Urdhven's condition, he is vulnerable in a rather obvious way. He may even be aware of this, since he has rather fastidiously avoided appearing before Ambrose since that fateful night. So there it is: I promise you that your parents' bodies will not be swept under the rug by any treaty. Does that satisfy you?"

"Thank you, yes," Lathmar answered politely. But the truth is that he hadn't been thinking about his parents at all. He had been thinking that his family was somewhat larger than he had realized.

It came about like this. He had been walking the night before past the ministerial apartments, wondering if he should knock on Wyrth's door and wishing there were some point in knocking on Morlock's. But then it seemed to him that he heard someone moving about in Morlock's apartments. He had stopped at the door and, hesitantly, rapped on it.

The door was opened by a fair-haired woman whose face he didn't know, but who was nonetheless somehow familiar.

"Good evening, Your Majesty," she said politely. "I'm sorry, but Morlock hasn't yet returned."

"Good evening to you, ma'am," Lathmar said. "May I ask . . . ?" But as he met her fearless blue eyes, he could think of not one question to ask her.

"Won't you come in?" the strange woman offered, and stood aside.

Lathmar entered without hesitation. Then, as she closed the door behind him, he wondered if he should have hesitated. No one knew where he was, and he knew nothing about this woman—including how she had gotten into Morlock's rooms, which were secured by a lock designed by Morlock himself.

But as she turned to face him, something struck him about the way she was standing . . . something about her shoulders. . . .

"Your pardon, ma'am," he said, "but are we somehow related?"

"Very astute, Lathmar," she said approvingly. "I am by way of being your great-great-great-and-so-on-great aunt. My name is Spes."

"Spes. Hm."

"If you'd rather, you can call me Hope—that's what Spes means, in my mother's language."

"Hope. Yes, I think I will, if it's all the same to you, ma'am. What was your mother's language, if I may ask, madam?"

"Latin—she was a lady of Britain, Nimue Viviana."

Lathmar nodded slowly. "Oh? I, uh, I was not, uh, aware that Morlock and Ambrosia had a, a—"

"'Sister,' is the technical term in genealogy, I believe," said Hope, with something like the authentic Ambrosian asperity. Then she softened it with a smile. "No, they wouldn't have told you, I expect. Both of them think that I'm long dead, and I decided it was best to let them think so. You should feel free to talk about me to Morlock, but I don't think you should mention me to Ambrosia."

"No?"

"No. She's very jealous, you know, and she never cared for me at all."

"Ah. So you live here in hiding?"

"Yes."

"Then, when we were in the secret passages, you were there too?"

"Yes, but not in the way you mean, Lathmar. I know that the passages grew very tiresome for you, and the time you were in them seemed very long indeed. But my prison is even older than they are—older than Ambrose."

"I don't understand. How did you come here, if you didn't use one of the passages?"

"I didn't come here. Ambrosia did. She often does. When Morlock is here, she talks with him; when he's not, she takes comfort from being among his things, such as they are."

A sudden dreadful thought occurred to Lathmar, and he looked intently in Hope's face. She laughed in his.

"You're thinking," she said, "is this Ambrosia gone mad—or possessed by some spirit, perhaps of a long-dead sister?"

It had been exactly what he had thought. But he could see that her face, though like Ambrosia's, was not the same. Among other things, her eyes were blue rather than gray, and she had almost no wrinkles. She was shorter and stockier than Ambrosia, and seemed a much younger woman physically. But there was a quiet wisdom in her eyes.

"*Are* you a ghost?" he asked her frankly.

"No," she said as frankly.

"But you said that Ambrosia thought you dead, and you said that you came here with her—"

"I didn't actually, but that is true, in a way."

"How can that be?"

"Ambrosia and I live in the same body," Hope said matter-of-factly. "She came here to seek comfort and fell asleep in Morlock's chair over yonder. I felt the need to walk around a bit and speak in my own voice."

Lathmar drew back, appalled.

"You should be honored, Your Majesty," Hope said wryly. "You're the first person I've spoken with in nearly four hundred years. Your ancestor Uthar the Great hadn't been born then."

"I'm not—That is—I was just thinking how strange my family is."

"Everybody thinks that. But it's true you have more cause than most."

"Can you see and hear when . . . when—"

"When I am submerged? I didn't used to. But Ambrosia isn't as strong as she was, and often I can see and hear the outer world when she is conscious. That's how I knew you. And I can walk through her memories, sometimes. When none of this is possible I think and wait."

"Wait for what?"

"For Ambrosia to grow still older, I'm afraid. When she grows somewhat weaker, we will have to change places, and she will be largely quiescent while I am the active twin."

Lathmar said nothing to this. He wasn't sure whether it was a good thing or not.

"I suppose it's hard for you to imagine your Grandmother, as you call her, growing weak?" Hope said gently.

"Yes," said the King truthfully. "She's always been the strongest person I knew. Not just physically."

"I understand. But she's not as strong as she was. Soon, as I count time, she will not be as strong as she is. This will be a hard time for her: you will have to grow strong, Lathmar."

Lathmar nodded solemnly. "So that she can pass on the imperial power."

Hope laughed and shook her head. "Do you really know her as little as that, after having lived with her your whole life? She won't pass it on, Lathmar. You'll have to take it from her, before she grows too weak to wield it."

Lathmar was silent for a few moments, then said, "That will be difficult. Because I don't want it."

"I think you do, Lathmar."

"Everyone seems to think that I do, or I should. But I don't."

"Not everyone knows you the way I do," Hope said. "Our situations are oddly alike. What we most want is freedom—including freedom from someone we both love, Ambrosia. In your rather peculiar situation, that requires power of imperial scope: so that no one can govern you as Ambrosia has, or harm you as the Protector has."

Lathmar was not convinced, but what she had said troubled him. "You've given me a lot to think about."

"Well, thinking and holding back your words are two things you've always been good at," Hope observed. "You'll find them useful skills as a leader, though maybe not the most useful of all." She sat down abruptly in the chair and put her hand to her face.

"What's wrong?" Lathmar asked.

"I'm getting sleepy. That means Ambrosia is waking up. Would you please get me pen and ink? And paper—paper, too, of course."

Lathmar rushed over to a desk and brought back writing supplies. Hope held the paper in her lap, dipped the pen in the inkwell that Lathmar held, and scrawled a few words. Her eyes fell shut for a moment, then opened abruptly. "Good-bye, Lathmar," she said, smiling sleepily. "It's been so nice talking with you. Perhaps . . . again. Sometime." Her eyes shut and she lay back in the chair. The pen fell from her fingers on the floor.

Her body grew longer and leaner. Her hair faded to iron gray, darkened by rusty streaks of red. The features of her face became longer, sharper, thinner. Her skin was seamed with a network of fine wrinkles.

Ambrosia opened her eyes (gray, not blue) and yawned.

She looked around and caught the King's eye. "Lathmar! What are you doing here?"

"I heard someone inside," Lathmar said truthfully, "and I thought I'd see who it was."

"I must have been snoring. Can't remember what I came in here for."

Her hands moved in her lap, and the sheet Hope had written on rustled slightly. Lathmar thought Ambrosia was about to look down at it.

"Can we poke around a bit?" Lathmar said with feigned eagerness. "I've never been in Morlock's quarters when he wasn't here."

"Certainly not," snapped Ambrosia, and stood. The paper fell unregarded out of her lap. "Come along." She went to the door.

The King stooped and grabbed the sheet of paper. "What's that?" asked Ambrosia, as he joined her at the door.

"A message for Morlock," the King said. "I thought I'd give it to Wyrth to put up in the workshop."

"Have him put it by the choir of flames," Ambrosia suggested as she locked the door. "He thinks more of them than he does of you or me," she added jealously.

Mulling all this over, the King sat through the rest of the council session without saying a word or noticing what the others said. But as they adjourned, it appeared that they had agreed to send a messenger to Urdhven to propose terms.

"We might have you crowned by summer," Ambrosia remarked, slapping him on the shoulder as she departed.

Lathmar was less than thrilled. But he thought of what Hope had said, about power and freedom, and he wasn't sure. He still wasn't sure when he went to sleep that night.

But when he awoke the next morning, just after dawn, he was sure something was wrong. His intuition was ringing like a bell. He threw on some clothes, grabbed a sword from his weapons closet, and pulled open his door.

Wyrth was standing in the hallway, a troubled smile half-hidden in his beard. "Say, maybe there is something to that Sight business. Do you know what's up?"

"Just that something's wrong."

"There seem to be Protector's Men loose in the castle. I saw them in a courtyard—have no idea how they entered. But we have to get you to a safe place."

"Let's find Ambrosia."

"First things first. We'll get you safe—"

"Wyrth, Ambrosia's safety is first. Without her, we don't have a chance and you know it."

Wyrth twisted a knot in his beard. "I never did understand this politics stuff," he admitted.

"Besides: 'blood has no price.'"

"She'd deny that," Wyrth said, grinning now. "But then, we're us, not her. Let's go."

They were lucky with their first try: Ambrosia had just risen, and was ringing repeatedly for a hallway servant who didn't appear. When Wyrth and Lathmar explained what was happening, she turned to the dwarf and hissed, "And you brought *him* through open corridors."

"Royal orders, Lady Ambrosia," said Wyrth, with a straight face.

"You sop, he doesn't have any authority to give orders. I'm the regent."

"Ah, well, madam, I'm afraid I never understood the technicalities of your laws very well. The salient issue, though, seems to be—"

"Yes, yes—what do we do now? First we put the King in the hidden passages. Then you and I, Wyrth, will nose about and see what has happened to the royal soldiery. There's something funny about this."

"Where's the nearest entrance to the passages?"

"Not near here. The bolt-holes are for royal persons, not ministers." She thought for a moment. "Come," she said at last.

They ran like thieves through the empty corridors until they reached the corridor above the audience hall. "There's one in here," Ambrosia muttered, and opened a chamber door.

She froze.

"That's right, Lady Ambrosia—come in," said Steng's voice.

Surprisingly, she did, drawing the King with her. Wyrth followed.

There was a company of Protector's Men in the room. Four of them were holding a man against the far wall of the room, while Steng held a knife to his throat.

"Come in, come in," cried Steng genially. "I suppose you were wondering where your brother had gotten to. Well, here he is!" And he took the knife and slashed Morlock's face.

CHAPTER EIGHTEEN

ENEMIES IN AMBROSE

orlock's jaws clenched, but as far as the King could see, he hardly reacted otherwise. Steng flourished the bloodstained knife (blood spattered his ropy pale fingers also) and then put the edge against Morlock's throat.

"You see, Lady Ambrosia, you must make a choice," the detestable poisoner was saying. "You must choose between your distant descendant, whose presence lends a fictive legitimacy to your rebellion, or your brother, whose skills are necessary if that rebellion is to succeed. The shadow or the substance, Lady."

Ambrosia laughed. "Steng, you must think me as much a fool as yourself."

"Exactly as much, my lady—that is: none at all."

"If your offer was a real offer, you would be giving up what you consider substance (in the overrated talents of my brother) for what you call shadow—the fiction of legal status."

"Why not?" Steng's wide rubbery lips bent in a grin. "Why not? Your brother is no use to us. *He* will never serve *our* purposes. The real substance, the military power of the empire, is ours already, and I frankly concede that we consider Morlock as nothing against it. All that we lack is some shadow of legitimacy. It is a trivial thing, but if we can buy it with the nothing of your brother's life, why should we not?"

"The event will answer you," Ambrosia said, with real grimness. "You were, I repeat, a fool to enter here, Steng. When you, and that traitor who employs you——"

"The Royal Protector, madam."

"Regicide and attempted regicide are treason for every subject. This detail is no doubt inessential to a poisoner's education, but I assure you it is so; I wrote it into the code myself, about the same time as Ambrose's first foundations were being laid. When that traitor and coward whose spittle you lick (yes, I do refer to the Lord Protector) held this castle with all his military power, I managed to take it from him. You won't escape it if you harm my brother."

Steng's smile became one-sided and derisive. "Yet I do expect to escape, no matter what I have to do here. By the same route I entered."

That sank in, the King could tell as he shifted his gaze to his Grandmother.

How *had* Steng and a squad of armed Protector's Men entered Ambrose? The King was at a loss, and he supposed Ambrosia and Wyrth were as well.

Lathmar had a sinking feeling that Steng's argument was perfectly tailored to his Grandmother's instincts, as a ruler and as a sister. He decided he wouldn't be surprised if he ended this day in the Protector's power once more——

Morlock stepped through the open door behind them.

His sister glared at him. "You took your time getting back."

He shrugged his crooked shoulders. "I had some trouble at Lonegate." His eyes narrowed as he saw the Morlock against the far wall with Steng's bloody knife at its throat. "What is that?" he asked. "A joke?"

"A poor one," Ambrosia agreed.

Irritation twisted Steng's unlovely features as he took his knife from the Morlock-thing's throat. It looked at him suspiciously, then glanced at Ambrosia, but did not otherwise move.

"A joke that fooled you properly, Lady Ambrosia."

"Only a fool would think so. The thing does not *act* like Morlock. It hasn't grunted once in my hearing, at any rate. Further, you have had its blood on your skin for some time now without any evidence of pain or harm. But the blood of Ambrose burns, Steng—as you have cause to remember. I let you live then, but I see no reason to do so now."

The memory was clear on Steng's face. "Then we will take the King—"

"Try it!" shouted Ambrosia exultantly, and brandished her sword. "Wyrth—get Lathmar out of here. Find some royal troops."

"My lady, with respect—"

"Wyrtheorn," said Morlock flatly, "take the King and go."

Wyrth turned to Lathmar, who said, "No, I want to stay." He was fascinated by the change that had come over his Grandmother when Morlock entered. Wyrth did not bother to listen to the King's protests, but knocked the sword out of his hand, picked him up, slung him over his shoulder, and darted for the door behind Morlock.

Morlock moved forward to stand beside Ambrosia, and she clapped her right hand on his higher shoulder. "It will be like that day above the Kirach Kund—eh?"

"Yes," Morlock said flatly. Clearly Ambrosia had referred to some specific tactic, and was not just engaging in nostalgic banter. The King caught a glimpse of the two crooked figures, dark against a bright thicket of advancing swords, and then Wyrth's foot kicked the door shut behind them, narrowly missing the King's nose.

The dwarf's short legs blurred as he dashed up the corridor. Lathmar knew he was headed for the guard station at the base of the next tower. "Wyrth!" he said. "Put me down! It will look better to the soldiers."

The dwarf complied without comment, and they ran up the hallway side by side. When they reached the guard station its hall door was closed, against all usage. Grimly Wyrth kicked it, shouting, "Awake! Awake! Intruders in the castle!"

The door opened. They saw that no one inside was asleep. There were, perhaps, a dozen armed men within, three times the complement for this station. Word of the breach had spread, clearly, and the soldiers were debating their best course. In their midst was Karn, recently promoted to the rank of secutor.

"Secutor," said Wyrth, addressing Karn as the senior soldier present, "a squad of Protector's Men—"

"We know," said Karn, interrupting. "I'm glad to see the King is safe."

Wyrth stared at the men in the room. "You *know*?" he demanded. "Did you know that this squad has the regent and Morlock pinned down in a chamber up the hall?"

The King was sorry to see the weakness he had suspected in Karn's character rise to the surface. The secutor licked his lips and said, "If—"

"Karn!" Lathmar interrupted. "Need is present. Bring your men at once!"

Karn's eyes shifted to avoid the King, and he said, "It may be better if—"

There was a clatter of armor and the thunder of booted feet in the hallway outside. Wyrth calmly knocked a soldier down, took his sword, and stood between the open door and the King.

These days Lathmar was considerably taller than Wyrth. Over the dwarf's head he saw the squad of Protector's Men stumbling down the hallway, Steng in the lead.

A moment later he saw their pursuers: two dark-cloaked, crooked figures, their eyes cold, their swords red with blood. One glimpse and they were gone, silently running down their quarry like wolves hunting deer.

"Those two old fools will get themselves killed," Wyrth remarked in a level tone, not as if he were discussing anything important. He turned to address the soldiers. "Secutor Karn, I trust you will have no qualms against intervening now? Excellent. A remarkable display of nerve."

Wyrth, the King, and the Royal Legionaries charged down the hallway after the Ambrosii. The King soon fell behind, and Karn paced him.

"Get up with Morlock and Ambrosia, Secutor," the King commanded irritably.

"Your Majesty, with respect—"

Lathmar glared at him. Karn turned away and trotted to the head of the Royal Legionaries, just behind Morlock and Ambrosia. They passed by a castle servant, fallen in the hallway. One of the soldiers stopped to attend to him.

"Don't bother," Morlock called back. "He's dead."

The soldier rejoined his troop. But Lathmar had already fallen behind, and anyway needed a rest. He knelt down by the servant, and found that he was still breathing.

Still, Lathmar knew almost instantly what Morlock had meant. The servant's eyes were open, but seemed to see nothing. There was a terrible sense of vacancy. The King wondered what he would see here if he were in the rapture of vision. He shut the servant's eyes, wishing he knew his name, and hurried on to keep up with the others.

They ran a twisting path right through the body of Ambrose, dead-but-breathing bodies of castle servants and Royal Legionaries littering the hallways.

The King began to see red. How had they done it? He demanded of himself over and over, but there was no answer. Had the intruders somehow killed everyone in Ambrose? Clearly not—they themselves were still alive. The King guessed that they had killed everyone in their path on the way in, and were taking the same path out.

That path, Lathmar realized, must lead to the Lonegate. They were headed away from the City Gate, and they were too far away from the Thorngate. Then, Morlock had said something. . . . It didn't matter. What did matter was: Lathmar knew of a secret passage that led almost straight there. If he took it, he might catch up with the Ambrosii (now out of sight in the corridor ahead).

On his next chance he swung left and found an entrance to the passage he wanted. Then he sprinted and walked as fast as he could until he reached the corridor outside the inner guardhouse on the Lonegate bridge.

He poked his head out, but there was no one in the hallway. He stepped out, breathing heavily, and went up the hall toward the inner guardhouse, wondering if he had missed everybody. Then he heard the tramp of many booted feet behind him in the corridor.

The King gulped. He wondered if, rather than missing everybody, he had beaten everybody to the goal. That was extremely inconvenient, since it meant that his enemies were between him and his defenders. He glanced up the hallway, but decided he was too far from the entrance to the secret passages, and ducked instead into the guardhouse. Royal soldiers lay scattered about the floor like dolls, dead but breathing. He ground his teeth, but there was nothing he could do for them. He ran up the stairway to the upper level, hoping the Protector's Men wouldn't trouble with it, but simply rush past toward the bridge and escape.

At first he thought his plan had worked. Steng and the Protector's Men burst into the guardhouse, and began to stream out toward the bridge. Then they began to shout and scream, and there were other noises the King couldn't understand. Drawn by an irresistible curiosity, he crept toward one of the bowslits in the chamber wall. Peering through, he saw a black charger was rearing up in the middle of the bridge, deftly kicking a Protector's Man with his right front hoof. The bodies of others were scattered around the bridge's wooden surface.

The remaining men of the squad and Steng stumbled back into the lower chamber of the guardhouse.

"What do we do now?" one screamed.

"We go upstairs and fill that damn horse with arrows," said Steng's voice.

The King glanced around frantically, but the place wasn't designed with any convenient nooks for hiding. He sat down on a stool and breathed deeply and calmly. A shred of a tactic occurred to him. It was unlikely to work, but the thought pressed itself on him with peculiar urgency.

Steng and a few Protector's Men appeared at the head of the stairway and paused, gaping, as they recognized him sitting there.

"But we left you back there!" Steng gasped.

"There are many of us," the King said carelessly. "Didn't you know?"

There was no way he *could* have known it, since it was what Wyrth would have delicately called "a damn lie," but the bit of misinformation seemed to impress Steng very deeply. His eyes grew round and he took a step backwards.

The King turned his head to one side and said, "Ah! There come Ambrosia and Morlock now—I assess their talic halos," he said, lying wildly but (he hoped) plausibly.

The Protector's Men vanished from the stairwell. Steng paused for a moment and met the King's eye. His face looked puzzled.

"You could try to take me by yourself," the King offered. "It would be easy—if I were who I seem to be, and if I were truly alone."

That was enough. Steng fled also down the stairs. Peering through the bowslits, the King saw him follow the Protector's Men over the side of the bridge into the green water of the Tilion.

He dashed down the stairs and out toward the bridge. He paused where the stone gave way to wood. The Protector's Men and Steng were floundering downstream, nearly around the bend.

The black horse looked at him with a silvery eye. He felt no threat, but then he hadn't tried to cross the bridge yet, either.

He felt a presence behind him, then, and turned. There was no one there. . . .

But there *was* someone there; he felt sure of it. He took a step toward the wall of the guardhouse and glanced around.

There was nothing except a pair of oval shields bound together with twine, their convex sides outward, as if to contain something in the cavity inside. As odd as it seemed, this was what gave Lathmar the sense that someone else was there.

He stepped closer and saw that the shields were not bound with twine, exactly. It was just long blades of green grass, twisted together into a kind of makeshift rope. He couldn't believe that anything could be restrained by so feeble a restraint, but that was what his intuition told him.

His sense of the other was so strong that he found himself speaking to it. "Who are you?"

He was not even surprised when it answered.

Many.

"That's no answer," the King complained.

You will know what I mean—soon enough, the mysterious (yet familiar) voice replied.

"How did you come here?"

I was sent, and then set. I would go if I could.

"What are you?"

Many.

"What does that mean?"

You will know—very soon now.

The King found that he had taken a step nearer the thing.

"How do you speak?" he wondered.

The same way that you do—with your mouth.

Lathmar realized that this was true—that the thing had been answering all the time through his own mouth, through his own voice.

Except that it wasn't his anymore. He found that out when he saw that he was taking another step toward the bound shields. He tried to stop, but couldn't.

He tried to scream, but the other one of him, the one that was many, laughed. It came out as a laughing scream, and the world began to fade before Lathmar's eyes. Through the mist masking the world he saw his hands reaching out toward the grass that bound the shields.

Then someone else was beside him, a pillar of black-and-white flames: Morlock.

Get out! Morlock shouted, and one of him wailed and another sobbed with relief, and abruptly there was only one of him again, and he fell to his knees beside the bound shields.

Groggily, he rose to his feet. Morlock (the plain Morlock of the nonvisionary world, his dark faced creased with urgency) seized him by the shoulders and said, "What is your name?"

"The King," he said sleepily.

Morlock grabbed Lathmar by the hair; his gray eyes stabbed at the King like spear points. "What's your *name?*" he shouted.

The King understood, hazily, that Morlock was afraid, and he thought this was interesting, as he could not remember another occasion where Morlock had so obviously shown fear. He thought about the other self, the one that had almost mastered him, and he understood what Morlock was afraid of. "Lathmar," he said, as clearly as he could, desperately hoping he would be believed.

Morlock, his dark face a mask of relief, released him. He patted him awkwardly on the shoulders and said, "Good. I'm glad you're well. You're not ready to face things like that, yet."

"What is it?"

"A shathe," Morlock said flatly.

Behind him, Ambrosia said, "Of course! There were shathe-wards on the old bridges, but we didn't think to put them on the new bridges. When was the last time a shathe was seen in Ontil?"

"This morning. That was why I sent Wyrth off to the City Gate and Thorngate. He can set wards that will hold until you and I come to put in place more permanent protections."

"You should have consulted me," Ambrosia said. "We each could have gone to a gate."

"I thought I might need you here," Morlock said.

The King drew a deep breath. The mist was gone from his sight; the living world pressed against his senses. Beyond Morlock was Ambrosia, and beyond her were the twelve Royal Legionaries, foremost among them Karn the secutor. His eyes pleaded silently with the King. Lathmar turned away deliberately to glance at the black horse, still standing guard on the bridge over the river Tilion.

"You were too cautious, Councillor Morlock," he said aloud.

"Was I so?" Morlock replied, smiling wryly.

"Yes, indeed. We didn't need Ambrosia, and we needed you only as an exorcist. Your charger and I were enough to hold the bridge against our enemies. He is worth at least a dozen of the Royal Legionaries, if I could pick the dozen."

"He will be flattered to know you rate him so highly," Morlock said, clearly noting the King's underlying anger but puzzled by it.

"I rate him more highly than that," the King continued. "If my Lady Regent is guided by my advice, she will appoint this horse to the rank of secutor at least." Then he turned and met Karn's eye at last.

"Oh," said Ambrosia coldly, "is that how it is?"

"Yes."

"I wondered when I glanced in and saw you all loitering in the guard station."

"Some of us were loitering more intensely than others, Grandmother."

"All right, you men: put aside your weapons," Ambrosia directed.

They were a dozen and she was one, but they clearly didn't even think of disobeying. They disarmed themselves and trooped up the stairs to the upper chamber of the inner guardhouse at Ambrosia's direction. She bolted the door shut behind them and shouted out to the King and Morlock, "I'm going to find some live soldiers. You two wait here for me."

Morlock nodded casually and guided the King over to the bridge. The black, silver-eyed stallion cantered over, and Morlock introduced him.

"Lathmar, Velox. Velox, this is Lathmar."

"Is this the horse you flew out of the Dead Hills?" the King asked eagerly.

"I think so. He is not quite as I last saw him, years ago, but he has had some remarkable experiences since then, perhaps enough to account for the changes."

"Does he still fly?"

"Not literally. But I've never seen a faster horse. It's thanks to him I was back in time."

"And when you arrived you found the shathe," Lathmar said flatly.

"Yes."

When it was evident that this was all Morlock was going to say, Lathmar asked, "What's a shathe?"

"A shathe," Morlock said didactically, "is a being that has no corporeal presence. It exists entirely in the tal-realm. It can exert its will on the physical universe, and manifest itself in various ways, but it can't be killed by any material weapon or force."

"How can they be killed?"

"By nonmaterial force. They can be starved to death also."

"Have you ever killed a shathe?"

"Twice that I know of. I kill them when I can, bind them when I must."

"Why?" the King asked. "Is it a religious . . . ?"

"Because they are evil?" Morlock twisted his face wryly. "They may be. But it doesn't matter: I kill them anyway."

"Why?"

"You have not considered, Lathmar. These things can be starved to death. They live on the tal-plane, and matter does not affect them. What do you suppose they eat?"

Lathmar shook his head.

"Souls. The psyches of living beings able to take volitional action."

"Oh." Lathmar thought about how close he had been to releasing the thing trapped in the shields. "Oh. How?"

"They gain entry to the will by persuading their prey to do certain things. It doesn't matter what, as long as it is at the prompting of the shathe. The moment of greatest danger is when the prey accepts a favor from the shathe. Then the prey may find that his will is no longer his own. It is then an easy thing for the shathe to compel the prey to destroy himself."

"Was I in that state?"

"I think so."

"But I never—"

"Tell me what happened," Morlock directed.

The King obliged, telling the tale from when he took to the passages. Morlock heard him through and said, "That was a good thought, to take the secret ways. I guess it was the shathe who gave you the idea to pose as a simulacrum of yourself."

"Why?" Lathmar demanded, annoyed. "Too clever for me?"

"No. But you said, 'There are many of us.' That was what the shathe told you his name was."

"Oh." Lathmar's anger deflated. "That's true."

"And it appalled Steng, you say?"

"Yes."

"Hm."

Lathmar waited a few moments, then observed, "Whether you are my magical tutor or merely my councillor here, 'Hm' seems insufficient."

Morlock smiled a crooked smile. "I was wondering if the shathe knew that it would affect Steng the way it did."

"I can't say."

"Perhaps we'll look into that."

"How . . . how did you bind it?"

"You're not ready for that knowledge yet, Lathmar."

"I'm not asking for a page from your spellbook. I just wonder how it was done—how grass can bind the thing."

"Plants have a kind of *tal*," Morlock replied. "But it is impenetrable by shathes, because plants have no volition. It is by seducing the will that shathes obtain control over the *tal* of living beings."

"Then how could it reach me?"

"I think you reached it," Morlock admitted grudgingly. "Your Sight reached out intuitively, as you were grasping for solutions to your dilemma."

"Oh." Lathmar paused, then remarked, "Grandmother wants you to stop teaching me about the Sight."

"That's not possible. You must obtain control over your gift."

Earlier today the King would have been delighted to hear this. Now, thinking about the thing that had nearly devoured him, that had reached him through his own power of Sight, he wasn't so sure. Then, abruptly, he was sure. True, he would have preferred to live in a world where such dangers didn't exist. But since they did exist, he decided he wanted to know about them, and what he could do about them. Maybe someday he could save someone as Morlock had saved him.

He looked up to find Morlock's gray eyes on him.

"Do you know what I am thinking?" he asked, feeling himself blush.

Morlock shrugged. "Some I know. More I guess. Most is closed to me. Here's Ambrosia."

The regent had returned with a troop of soldiers; the King turned to her almost in relief. She disposed some of the Royal Legionaries at the gate, charged others with escorting the imprisoned guards down to the dungeon level, and assigned one to feed and water and otherwise tend to "that damn horse—I hope Morlock doesn't start filling up the entire castle with his pets."

The King looked around to see how Morlock would react to this, but saw that Morlock and the shathe he had bound were gone.

CHAPTER NINETEEN

DEATH, LOVE, AND A SPIDER

he trial of the eleven Royal Legionaries (before the regent in the presence of her council, only Morlock being absent) didn't take a great deal of time. The evidence showed that they had all obeyed their superior, Secutor Karn, in taking to the guard station and concealing themselves. But they had also failed to obey a royal councillor and the King himself when they had been given contrary orders.

"Respect for a superior officer is a fine thing," the regent remarked, in delivering her summary judgement. "But secutors don't rank members of the Regency Council, much less the King. These soldiers chose to obey the dictates of their cowardice. Given that they were following an illegal order of a superior officer, I'll incline to the lesser penalty. Commander Erl," she said, addressing the Legionary officer in charge of the dungeons, "have your men strip these prisoners of their uniforms, beat them each with twenty strokes, and expel them into the city. They are never to hold any position of trust or profit under his Majesty Lathmar the Seventh. So say I, Ambrosia Viviana, regent for the aforesaid Lathmar VII, King of the Two Cities. Let it be done."

The dungeon keepers, grim in their black surcoats with no device, marched the dumbfounded ex-soldiers out of the council chamber. Karn was left alone in the plain brown robe of the accused, facing the Regent's Council who would judge his fate.

"Your Majesty," Karn said hoarsely to the King, who sat with the council as usual. "Don't let her kill me. I admit it: I was afraid. I've been in battle before, but this was different. Your enemies have powers I don't understand, and I let that get the better of me. But I won't fail you again; I swear it."

"Shut up," Ambrosia said coldly. "Secutor Karn, this court finds you guilty of treason. The penalty, as you know, is death. Reflect on this overnight; we will summon you for sentencing in the morning."

Karn was visibly aghast. Officers were normally given a night's grace before a death sentence; they were supposed to use the time to commit honorable suicide, rather than face public execution. Commander Erl detailed several dungeon keepers to march Karn from the room; Lathmar gloomily watched him go. Would he have intervened with Ambrosia, if she had given him the opportunity? Possibly. He was glad she hadn't, though.

Ambrosia was speaking again; he had missed a few words. ". . . as we have more important matters at hand, specifically the question of reprisals against the Protector for today's raid. I'll confer with you and your aides separately, Kedlidor. Wyrth, see what you can come up with—I understand that Morlock is at this moment laboring on something particularly nasty in his workshop; perhaps you can assist him. We will meet tomorrow, an hour after dawn. I adjourn the council until then. But Wyrth and Commander Erl, wait here a moment; you, too, Your Majesty, if you please."

The scribes and attendants departed; Kedlidor also left, his face marked with dread at the thought of leading soldiers in combat again.

"The King needs a personal guard," Ambrosia said flatly. "We thought it was a formality in the castle, but today has proven how wrong we were. Erl, take this, you son of a bitch." Her sword was in her hand; in the next moment it was at Erl's throat. Somehow—the King wasn't sure how—Erl unsheathed his own sword and brought it up to parry Ambrosia's. His face didn't change expression, but as he watched her withdraw and sheathe her sword, he did the same.

"Erl," said Ambrosia, "you're the best swordsman this century (barring Morlock) and the bravest man."

Erl nodded coolly in acknowledgement of these facts.

"You're the King's new personal guard. I'm not demoting you: your lieutenant can run the dungeons without you for a while. If you do this job right, there's a promotion in it for you; if you don't, we're all screwed."

"Yes, my lady."

"Wyrth, you'll have to help him. He's a tough pitiless bastard, but he doesn't know a damn thing about magic. That's the only thing that can touch the King inside Ambrose, but obviously we can't rule it out—not after today."

"Yes, madam."

"Lathmar," Ambrosia said grudgingly, "it looks as if you're going to have to continue those lessons in the Sight."

"I've already seen to that," Lathmar said with a touch of sharpness. If she wanted him to act like a monarch in front of his subjects, she would have to start acting like a subject toward him. He prepared himself for a counterblast.

Ambrosia merely smiled. "That's all, then. I'll see you in the morning, if not sooner."

The King found it impossible to sleep that night. It was not because of his encounter with the shathe "Many." It was not even because he kept envisioning Karn, sweating through his last night of life (or, perhaps, already dangling from a beam in his prison chamber). These might have kept him from sleep, or given him nightmares once he reached it. But the fact was he never got near enough to rest for these to distress him. His blood was on fire; he paced endlessly about his rooms. The King was in love with one of his kitchen maids.

Her name was Guntlorta, which seemed to Lathmar a very beautiful name. Her hair was the color of dark honey (brown). Her cheerful laugh could be heard from one end of the Great Courtyard to the other. (Less biased observers remarked that it "sounded like a brass kettle falling down a flight of stone stairs.") Her complexion was like an unequal mixture of roses and cream, and as she had brought in one of the courses of his evening meal, he found himself longing to shower kisses all over the taut ripe curves of her body.

He would not have been the first to do so, but this was the first time the impulse had come to him, and he was struck with surprise. He tried several times to speak to her, but found he could not. Nor could he get her image (nor her scent, which was not at all of roses or cream) out of his mind.

Now he threw himself out of bed and paced frantically around the room. How could he see her again (without a bodyguard in tow, that is)? What should he do if he could manage it? Did he even want to manage it? He groaned, splashed cold water from the basin on his face, and paced about his room some more.

The truth was, he reflected ruefully, he needed advice—advice from a grown-up man he could trust. If Lorn had been alive, Lathmar would have asked him. If Karn were not in prison he would have been Lathmar's second choice—a poor second, though. True, he would have listened to Lathmar's problem patiently, and maybe advised him helpfully. But Lathmar had sometimes wondered uneasily if Karn mocked him before others as he mocked others before him. He didn't like to think of the other soldiers chuckling over their king's romantic dilemma. In any case, Karn was facing a dilemma far more dreadful than his. It would be cruel beyond words to pester him at this hour.

Who did that leave? Wyrth had been present at dinner. No doubt he saw what had come over Lathmar; he saw everything, it seemed. But somehow the King didn't want to talk to Wyrth about this. He didn't know how dwarves arranged these matters, and he didn't want advice that wouldn't apply to his case.

He wondered idly if Hope could help him, somehow—it would be pleasant to talk to her, at any rate. But he remembered suddenly that he couldn't simply knock on her door: she was hidden inside his Grandmother. He did *not* want to talk to Grandmother about this, he thought, shuddering.

It was Morlock or nothing, he decided, finally. He threw on some clothes and crept out into the hallway. The guards at his door were sleeping, and he crept past them up the hallway, and soon was climbing the stairs to Morlock's tower.

The lock on the doorpost of Morlock's workroom recognized Lathmar, winking a glass eye at him. It released the door from its long iron fingers and allowed the King to enter.

As soon as he stepped across the threshold he heard Morlock and Ambrosia talking on the far side of the workroom. He especially did not want to talk to Ambrosia just now, so he crept behind a table and waited for her to leave.

It took a while. Ambrosia, as usual, was angry.

"I don't understand you, Morlock," she was saying. "First you say this is the most serious attack we've had from the Protector's forces, and then you say we should *not* retaliate. I don't give a rat's ass what you say; that's bad strategy."

"What would I do with a rat's ass?" Morlock replied, sounding amused. After Ambrosia made a suggestion, he continued, sounding less amused, "Nonetheless, you misheard me. We don't know that this attack was from the Protector. I don't think it was."

"Then I think you're mistaken. His poisoner Steng led the attack, and you yourself said it must have been his magical patron who supplied the shathe."

"'Magical patron,'" Morlock repeated. "We call him that because Urdhven did. It was a mistake. Suppose he is not?"

"Suppose *who* is not *what*?"

"Suppose that the magical adept is not, in fact, Urdhven's patron. Suppose that Urdhven is merely the dupe or pawn of this adept, who uses him to distract us from some undertaking of the adept's own."

"Ur. I don't like that much, Morlock."

"It makes perfect sense, though. The adept never granted Urdhven a weapon like the shathe before. Why did he do so now? What imminent development did the adept, not Urdhven but *the adept*, find threatening?"

"You're talking about the treaty negotiations I'd begun with Urdhven."

"Yes. If we make peace with Urdhven, his usefulness as a distraction becomes slight. The best result, from the adept's point of view, is for negotiations to fail and the civil war between the Protector and the royal forces to resume. So the adept arranges for this feint upon the castle."

"Suppose you're wrong, and Urdhven is really behind this? He'll take it as a sign of weakness."

Silence.

"Don't shrug at me!" Ambrosia snapped.

"The attack failed," Morlock said. "Urdhven knows we are not weak. I leave it at that."

"You leave it to me, as usual, you mean," Ambrosia complained. "Suppose you're right, then: I continue negotiations as if nothing happened. Not quite nothing maybe—I'll start the next session by presenting Urdhven with the bodies of the Protector's Men we killed today—"

"A nice touch."

"Quiet, you. Meanwhile, you'll be off looking into this adept, this Protector's Shadow."

"Yes. I think I know where to begin—I had a dream the other night."

"You and your damn dreams. *I* had a dream the other night. I dreamed that for once you had decided to be something other than a pain in the ass."

"I think my dream is likelier to be true."

"Very amusing. Is this where you want this thing?"

"Yes."

"Do you want me to stay?"

"Not unless you want to."

"I don't. It was bad enough being there when you bound Andhrakar. You're sure you'll be all right? Shall I call Wyrth?"

"No. I'll be fine. Good night, Ambrosia."

"Good night, sweetheart."

The words went through Lathmar like a spear—and more than the words, the tone of voice. He had never, ever heard Grandmother speak to *anyone* like that. He thought of his mother, then Guntlorta, and writhed uncomfortably in his hiding place.

He heard their footsteps walking toward the door, the door open, shut, and lock, and Morlock's halting footsteps return alone from the door.

They walked directly from there to the King's hiding place.

"Come out from there," Morlock's voice said.

The King crawled shamefacedly out from under the table.

"You should not skulk," Morlock said. "It isn't kingly."

"How would you know?" the King shouted, furious from embarrassment and something else.

"I've known many kings," Morlock replied calmly. "What did you want of me, Lathmar?"

Lathmar growled, unable to speak. He didn't want to talk to Morlock about it. *She* had called *him* . . . *sweetheart*. It boggled the mind. He was furious. He was jealous, he realized suddenly. And why not? Ambrosia was *his* Grandmother—she had been long before she was Morlock's sister. Wait—that didn't make sense. . . .

Morlock watched his face with frank but unobtrusive interest as this internal struggle went on, and finally remarked, "Lathmar, you should be careful. There is a shathe in the room; not all those thoughts may be your own."

Lathmar's inner turmoil cooled instantly, as if he had been submerged in icy water. "That thing is here? 'Many'?"

"Yes. I was just going to kill it. I want you to help."

No! a voice that was not quite his own said within him. So he said "Yes" firmly, out loud.

Morlock led him over to the far side of his workshop. There the two shields, still bound by the grass twine, were suspended by a black chain over a transparent vat that was filled with a blinding blue-white fluid. It bubbled like porridge over an open flame, though there was no visible fire beneath the vat.

"What is that?" the King asked.

"Aether," Morlock replied, "the substance out of which lightning is made. Unlike the four terrestrial elements (earth, air, fire, and water) it has a presence on the talic plane."

"And it is harmful to shathes?"

"Fatal. I plan to immerse the shathe in that crucible of aether. But that will set the grass afire and free the shathe. So beforehand I must fix it in place with spikes of aethrium—an alloy of aether."

"Oh. What do you want me to do?"

"Hold the shields while I place the spikes."

The King stepped forward doubtfully. To be near the bubbling crucible of aether was unpleasant in a way he could not quite define. His hair rose on end, as if he were afraid (he supposed he was). He wanted to turn away, to seek shelter. The light seemed to pass straight through him. His teeth were set on edge.

He reached out to hold the shields, and he was aware of the shathe. Suddenly the harsh unyielding light was comforting: he knew it was far more inimical to the shathe than to him.

Morlock was opposite him with two stakes of bright blue metal in his hands.

"You've done this before?" the King said anxiously.

"No."

"I thought you said—"

"I've killed shathes before, but not with this method."

"But you're sure this will work?"

"Sure? No."

"What if it doesn't?" the King demanded, his voice becoming shrill in his own ears.

"The aether will destroy the shields and grass, and there will be an angry shathe loose in the room."

The King thought about begging off, then shrugged. If the shathe got loose, then he'd run: it would be Morlock's business to do something about it. But if it didn't get loose, he'd never have to worry about its voice chewing its way through his head again.

Morlock watched the King's face until Lathmar made his decision, seemed satisfied with what he saw, and said, "Hold on firmly. I'm putting in the first spike."

The King obeyed, and watched as Morlock thrust one of the blue spikes straight through the pair of bound shields.

From the broken surfaces of the shields came jets of . . . something: like glowing steam with faces floating in it.

"What are they?" he asked, his voice quavering.

"The talic remnants of those it has consumed," Morlock said.

"Their souls?"

"I used that word this afternoon: I should not have. The talic self is not the soul, merely the shell through which the soul acts upon and is linked with the material universe."

"Then the shathe does not eat souls?"

"I don't know. No one knows. Some believe it; some don't."

It occurred to the King then, quite suddenly, that if he killed Morlock then the powerful being between the shields, who really meant him no harm, would keep him safe from all his enemies. And if he gave Guntlorta to it, it would make Guntlorta do whatever he asked, including—

"Shut up!" the King hissed.

"It's desperate," Morlock remarked calmly, seeming to understand. "The second spike, now."

The second spike produced glowing jets of distorted faces like the first. But the faces seemed more distorted, the glow more faint.

"It's weaker," Morlock remarked. He reached out and broke the black chain with his thumb and forefinger. The bound shields fell into the vat of aether and instantly went up in flames. Through the screen of their gray ashes the King thought he saw, for a moment, a dark red flame surrounded by a cloud of black smoke. But then this faded, like a fire by daylight, and suddenly was gone. There was only the unchanging, unresting, irritating brightness of the aether. The blue aethrium stakes slowly grew molten, sank into the aether, disappeared.

"It's gone," the King said with certainty.

"In a way. The thing may still exist in the spiritual realm, but it has no more talic presence—it can no longer affect the tal-world or the world of matter." Morlock moved away and returned with a blue aethrium slab. It was a relief when he clapped it over the vat and the King was free of its light and the shathe's darkness.

"Whew!" he exclaimed. "A long day, Morlock."

Morlock paused almost imperceptibly before he answered, "Yes, indeed."

He didn't seem inclined to continue, so the King prompted him. "You're not going to bed yet?"

"No."

"You're going out to search for the Protector's Shadow *now*?"

"Yes."

"Do you ever say *one damn syllable* more than necessary?" the King cried out.

"Only if it seems necessary," Morlock replied, smiling wryly.

"Can I come?"

Morlock looked at the King, at the covered vat, back at the King. He shrugged. "Yes. It will be dangerous, though."

"At least I won't have to try and sleep," the King said.

Out of his own thoughts, Morlock said, "Yes."

Morlock led Lathmar down a flight of stairs at the back of his workshop. The way from there became extremely complex, and the King soon lost track of where they were—Lathmar still did not know much of the palace in which he had lived his entire life. But they finally came down in a corridor that ran along the river. Morlock opened a trapdoor in the floor that had been invisible until he touched it. They went down through it, into a sort of crawlspace, down the middle of which ran a channel of dark water.

There was a large squat shape looming in the darkness near them, half submerged in the water, within a ring of folded spindly shapes. Morlock spoke a word to it that the King didn't understand; the side of the squat shape opened up, and light fell out. Lathmar saw that all of the shapes were connected. . . . It took a few moments to put the pieces together in his mind.

"Is this thing a spider?" he demanded.

"No," Morlock said, then shrugged. "It does look like one, though. Go in."

Lathmar was not thrilled by the prospect. But the alternative was "Stay behind," so he went, crouching, along the crawlspace and into the not-spider.

There was a central dome of polished bronze within; from it dangled some black cables that ended in what seemed to be monocles or eyepieces. On the floor beneath was a board with a set of peculiar switches. Next to the switches stood Wyrth, his head nearly grazing the top of the dome. He glared at Lathmar and Morlock as they entered, crouching as they walked.

"You thought you'd leave me behind!" the dwarf said fiercely as soon as Morlock was within.

"Yes," Morlock said, and would have continued.

"But you'll bring *him* along," Wyrth said, gesturing at the King of the Two Cities.

"Yes." This time it was clear Morlock intended to say no more.

Something in Morlock's tone made Wyrth glance at his eyes. Then the dwarf's gaze fell. He turned away for a moment, then turned back and spoke to Lathmar. "I'm sorry, my friend. That was no way to speak of you."

"It's nothing, Wyrth—don't think of it," Lathmar replied, more embarrassed than the dwarf

Morlock said nothing, but his manner was less icy.

"Master Morlock," the dwarf said.

"Wyrth."

"You can use an extra pair of eyes and an extra pair of hands, whatever you have in mind. I think I should come along."

"You'd be better off here. If you want to risk it, the choice is yours."

"Thanks. I'll—I'll come along then."

"Then be seated and answer the King's questions. I've got to pilot this rig." Morlock sat before the board of switches and strapped one of the dangling eyepieces to his left eye. (It looked rather disturbing—as if a headless worm were feeding on his eye.) Then, carefully, he spread out his fingers and put them, knuckle first, onto the board. There was a groove for each of his fingers, and above each set on the board was an upright post with a ring through it.

"What are the switches for?" the King asked.

"Each switch operates one of the legs of the spider. It will send an impulse to move from one of Morlock's fingers through a talic lens, which will magnify the impulse and make it able to move a much greater object. Each talic lens is in talic *stranj* with one of the legs—"

"Talic *stranj*?"

Wyrth grinned, "Sorry. That's the sympathy between a talic presence—like you or me—and matter (like our bodies) which enables the presence to act through the medium of the matter."

"Oh. What are the talic lenses made of?"

"Well, they are produced by the operator, effecting a change in his own tal through conscious effort."

"And he must move his own body in the material realm simultaneously, as he maintains these talic lenses?"

"Yes. And keep an eye on the ocellus (or external eye) of the spider, so that we don't bump into anything. You can see why there aren't thousands of these craft running around your city."

The King winced. He had, in fact, been thinking of a city whose streets were not stained by a single piece of horse shit. "And Morlock can move each one of his fingers independently of the other?" he whispered to Wyrth.

Wyrth looked surprised. "Of course. Can't—Well, I suppose it's the sort of skill one picks up in being a maker."

"Hm." Lathmar reflected. "At least he only needs to use eight of them."

"Eh?"

"Eight legs—eight fingers."

"Yes, but the operator must also control direction—back and forth, right and left. Morlock controls those with his thumbs." And Lathmar, looking, saw that Morlock had hooked his thumbs through the rings on the upright posts.

Lathmar was abruptly aware that Morlock had gone into the visionary state. He used the skills he had learned to avoid being drawn into the master seer's vision. The spider jerked and stood on its legs—not wholly upright, or they would have struck the low ceiling outside.

From sloshing sounds, Lathmar guessed they were keeping to the watery channel. He tried not to think what was floating in it with them—and, as a matter of fact, the water didn't smell at all bad, so maybe this channel wasn't a waste conduit.

"We are entering the river level channel," Morlock said in the strange croaking voice he used when speaking in vision.

"That means a fall of ten feet," Wyrth said. "Hang on!"

There was nothing to hang on to, so Lathmar braced himself as well as he could on the bare floor. The moment of free fall was disturbing, but the shock of the landing was slight—the spider landed on all its eight feet, not its belly.

"We pass from the channel to the river," Morlock croaked a while later.

"Put on the other eyepiece," Wyrth suggested. "There ought to be something to see, now."

Hesitantly, the King put an eyepiece to his right eye. There was, indeed, something to see. They must have left Ambrose from the north, for it was on their right side, now—its walls dark gleaming shadows, looming high above, the windows of its many towers glittering with glad light. The city, along their left, was more somber, but there were lights there too—a sort of red smear of light along the high eastern bank.

Lathmar tried to adjust his angle of vision by moving his head right and left—then blushed when he realized how foolish this was.

"Is there any way to move the view of the ocellus?" he asked Wyrth.

Now it was the dwarf's turn to be embarrassed. "No. Nor is there more than one. We ought to have put in at least two—one for the front, one for the back. Perhaps we'll remedy that—we've only used the craft four or five times, but it has been useful. In any case, it is a design flaw—we should be able to see what is sneaking up behind us. Not that anything is."

Wyrth was wrong about this. A man had spotted the spider in the castle waterways and had followed it into the river. Now he was floating in the partially submerged spider's wake, swimming frantically just to keep the craft within view. His breath sobbed, from fear and exertion, but he did not give up the pursuit. He could not: everything that he was depended on this one desperate gamble.

CHAPTER TWENTY

GRAVE MATTERS

he spider traveled down the river to the sea, and then followed the shoreline eastward. It sloshed along, half submerged, until the sullen glow of the city was left behind. Then it unfolded its long legs and skimmed along the surface of the water for part of an hour. Finally it turned left and walked up on the shore.

The complicated eight-footed motion of the spider on land was remarkably and unpleasantly different than its movement in the waves. The King was wondering whether he was about to vomit when the spider suddenly ceased to walk, and its body descended to the ground. The King took several slow breaths and felt his stomach settle somewhat, and looked up to see Wyrth looking at him ironically.

"It's the opposite for me," the dwarf said. "I get queasy on the water."

An intangible tension eased. Lathmar guessed that Morlock had dropped out of the visionary state, and glanced over to see him flexing his fingers.

"Wyrth," the Crooked Man said in his ordinary voice, "open the hatch. We go on foot from here. You two should arm yourselves from the locker—we may need to fight."

Wyrth opened the hatch first, to let in some fresh air, and then they served themselves with arms from the locker, a low chest built into the spider's inner wall. Wyrth took an axe and a long dagger; Lathmar chose a short pointed sword of the type he had been practicing with lately. There were several sheathed longswords. The King didn't think any of them were Tyrfing, but Morlock took one of them and a number of aethrium jars slung on a belt. Finally they stepped out onto the ground, the King crouching to get through the hatch, and Morlock bending almost double.

It was still night—well after midnight now, by the position of the stars. The thin steady wind was bitterly cold: it was the month of the Mother and Maiden, well into fall. Chariot, the greater moon, stood somber in the eastern sky, while Trumpeter's bright eye was open in the west.

The spider had brought them to a hillside, the city an umbrous glow on their left hand. The hills before them were stubbled with squarish irregular forms.

"We're among the graves," Wyrth said, an odd, almost quavering tone in his voice.

"Why have we come here?" the King asked, wondering if his voice sounded much the same.

Morlock shut the hatch behind him and walked northward, belting his sword around him as he walked. Wyrth and the King hurried to catch up.

"Well?" Wyrth asked, exasperation in his tone.

"I am here to find out more about the Companions of Mercy," Morlock said. "You two are here because you chose to come."

"Why do we seek among the graves?" the King asked.

"Because that is where the Companions go," Morlock said. "Be quiet now, or go back."

Wyrth fell into what seemed a rather glum silence, and they trudged for some considerable time among the grave-strewn hills.

Presently they came to the top of a hill, and Morlock made them stop and hide in the moon shadows behind a grave marker in the shape of three horses, whose heads had fallen off over the years. Peering between their legs, the King saw a caravan of four death carts approaching up a dirt track that led back toward the city. The carts stopped at a mausoleum whose door was awry; the Companions driving them unloaded the dead bodies, stripped them, and stacked them like wood by the carts.

Companions dressed in gray came out of the open mausoleum. In their gray-gloved hands were saws and mallets. Casually, they began to dismember and mutilate the stacks of bodies, sorting the limbs by type. The blood of the corpses was black in the light of the moons, staining the dust of the track. The gray Companions with mallets took the dismembered heads and smashed the dead faces until the features were completely obliterated.

"Why?" whispered the King piercingly.

Morlock only looked at him, glaring with bright ice-gray eyes. Lathmar nodded, silent and ashamed. He heard a small series of intermittent sounds next to him, as if Wyrth were nervously tapping his fingertips rapidly on the stone grave marker. The King was relieved that someone besides himself was nervous, and glanced over in commiseration. Then he wished he hadn't. The dwarf's teeth were actually rattling; his eyes stared wildly at the scene below. He was clearly terrified almost beyond reason. The King somberly turned back to watch, wondering what Wyrth knew that he didn't.

All this while the red Companions were standing aside; they didn't seem to be watching or not watching; they merely waited.

Presently more Companions came out of the open mausoleum. These were dressed all in white: masked, cloaked, booted, and gloved in white. They bore in their hands knives, and masks, and what appeared to be scrolls. Some held between thumb and forefinger small glinting objects that presently proved to be needles.

The white Companions took the chunks of human meat and began to puzzle them into bodies again. The choice of limbs seemed to be more or less arbitrary; the white Companions worked together with reckless speed. Before they put on the first head, they drew the lungs and heart out of the bodies through the neck and tossed them aside in the dirt. Then they put a scroll into the chest cavity, pushing it down through the gaping throat. Finally one sewed a head on (the others were already huddled around a new corpse) and stood back. A spell of great force was effected; the King felt it in his fingers and toes, nearly spoke aloud in surprise. And the corpse stood up. The Companion took a mask and pressed it to the corpse's face, and abruptly they were one. The corpse turned away, stumbling to the pile of discarded clothing, and started to clothe itself. The Companion turned away to assist the others.

The scene was repeated over and over; the pile of discarded hearts beside the road grew into a fair-sized pyramid. The King thought furiously. These things, these pseudohumans, were like the golems Wyrth had told him about—like the Red Knight. They were vivified by a name-scroll. But they were different, too: they were crafted out of human flesh, not any lesser clay. Who was doing this? Why? How long had it been going on? The King began to see that Morlock was right indeed. There was something happening, more terrible and dangerous than the Protector's treason.

Wyrth's hands clutched at the King's arm. Lathmar turned reluctantly to look at his friend. The terrified dwarf pointed down at the scene below. Lathmar nodded slowly. Wyrth hit him on the chest and pointed again.

Lathmar looked down: what could Wyrth mean? Then he realized: the gray-cloaked Companions and some of the patchwork zombies were missing.

He turned in a fright to Morlock, but Morlock was already standing, a sword bare in his hand. Behind and below them on the hill, a line of gray Companions and resurrected dead was advancing.

"The second death!" Wyrth hissed. "The Gate in the West will be closed to us!" He covered his face with his hands and sobbed with terror.

"Get him back to the spider—to Ambrose, if you can," Morlock said quietly to Lathmar.

"If I can't?"

"Then leave him and get back yourself. Tell Ambrosia what you've seen. Everything depends on it."

I can't! the King wanted to say, but did not. Morlock was already halfway down the slope toward their enemies, who were closing a circle to meet him. The line had opened and there was a way for them to pass by—but only if they took it instantly. He jerked Wyrth to his feet and hissed in his ear, "Now we run! The second death, Wyrth! We must escape!"

Wyrth took to his heels, and the King followed; he heard clashing weapons behind him but did not look back. He heard soft feet padding behind him, but he did not look back. He began to be short of breath, but he didn't stop running—not until Wyrth did.

"Where's my master!" the dwarf cried, stopping in his tracks.

"Buying us time to escape," the King replied. "Come on!"

Wyrth cursed at him in Dwarvish. "God Avenger damn me, I've betrayed him, and so have you!" He drew his axe from his belt and turned to go back.

"Wyrth, no!" the King begged. "Morlock wanted us to get away. He gave everything for it. Don't—"

"I don't give a damn what he wants; I won't buy my life, in this world or the next, with his. You go. You'll find it easy enough when you start running."

The unfairness of this blinded Lathmar with rage, even wiping out his fear. As if *he* were a coward! As if *he* had crouched under a stone horse tail whimpering "the second death"! He was literally speechless with anger, and it occurred to him suddenly that he was holding a drawn sword that he had been well taught how to use.

That thought, paradoxically, cooled him. It reminded him of all those endless hours of training he had spent with Wyrth, how rarely he grew angry; how he was never, never afraid. But he had shown fear now; Lathmar thought he would welcome death, if it was the only way to escape the stink of his own shame.

Well, death was near enough to them now; there was no need for them to deal it to each other.

There was still a battle going on up the long, dark slope above them. The King could see several body-sized fires on the slope, and the clash of weapons.

Then the Companions and corpse-golems who had followed them down the hill were upon them. Lathmar and Wyrth instinctively went back-to-back. The King struck out at their enemies with all the rage he had felt against Wyrth. But he was cool enough to remember how Morlock had fought against the Protector on the bridge: it was futile to go for mortal blows against the living dead. But they could be crippled. And they were armed only with the tools the Companions had used on the corpses: mallets and knives and saws.

But there were so many of them! They crowded around in a stinking wall: the corpse-golems stinking of blood and worse, with their mismatched limbs, red seams everywhere on their half-naked bodies, the cold pitiless perfection of their mask-faces. The Companions stood back, waiting, watching. They knew the corpse-golems would do what was needed.

So did Lathmar. But he fought on desperately, all the more when Wyrth began to laugh bitterly.

"They want us alive!" he shouted.

That frightened Lathmar more than anything that had happened yet.

Presently Wyrth was struck on the side of the head and fell unconscious to the ground. The King grimly stood over him and hewed at any dead limb that presented itself to him. But he knew it couldn't be long now.

The King felt a pair of cold hands close on his neck from behind. He turned, struggling and failing to strike at one of the dead arms. He saw it fall with a flash from its shoulder. He didn't understand what he was seeing until there was another flash and the corpse-golem's head flew from its shoulders.

There were armed men behind them—at least two of them.

"Golems!" he shouted. "Can't killed! Cut hands!" He wondered if he was making any sense at all.

"Understood!" was the terse reply.

The two fighting men advanced, their swords flashing in the light of the lesser and the greater moons. The ill-made corpses fell in a welter of severed limbs. The dark-cloaked Companions were beginning to move forward.

"Get the dwarf!" he shouted.

"Yes, Your Majesty," said one of the soldiers. With a burst of surprise, Lathmar realized it was Karn. The other, the one who had spoken first, was flat-faced fearless Erl. But there was no time for questions or answers. Karn picked up the unconscious dwarf and they fled south, Lathmar leading the way toward the sea.

The King remembered what Morlock had said about the Companions being unable to cross running water. He didn't know if the sea counted, but he hoped it would be inimical to them. It may have been, or they may have turned back for other reasons, but by the time they reached Morlock's spider the Companions had given up the chase.

They rested by it, keeping an eye out for their enemies in three directions.

"Can you make this thing work, Your Majesty?" Erl asked.

"No. We'll have to walk back to Ambrose."

"Too bad—it's been a long day for me."

The King agreed. Karn said nothing.

"Karn," said the King quietly, "how did you come to be here?"

"Well, Your Majesty . . . some time ago, I worked on the prison level."

"Ah. You knew a way out of your cell."

"Yes, Your Majesty. Through the waterways. So I saw the spider pass. I knew it was Morlock and his dwarf—who else could it be?—so I followed. I thought if I could help him, or talk to him he might . . . Well, Ambrosia listens to him. The Lady Regent, I mean."

"I understand. Well, we'll see if she'll listen to me. Unless you would rather just walk away right now. You've earned that, I think." The King felt Erl tense up beside him, but he said nothing.

"No, Your Majesty," Karn said glumly. "I'll go back with you."

Erl relaxed, and the King asked him, "And you, Commander Erl? How do you happen to be here?"

"Well, Your Majesty, it was me Karn worked for when he guarded the cells."

"Aha."

"Yes, Your Majesty. I was watching him, and I followed him. I was interested to see what he'd do. When it turned out he was following you three, I met up with him. We armed ourselves from the locker in your spider, here—"

"Not mine."

"No, Your Majesty."

"Well, we'd better get going. Those Companions might be able to get word to the Protector's Men; if we're to make it across the Port Island Bridge we'll have to do it soon."

None of them mentioned Morlock. There didn't seem to be much point.

They walked all night, crossing the Port Island Bridge without trouble and passing through an unguarded gate Erl knew into the countryside west of Ontil. By then Wyrth had regained consciousness, and the King had nearly lost it—it had, indeed, been a long day. The dwarf and the two men took turns carrying him: they dared not be caught by the Protector's soldiers in open country. They reached the Lonegate of Ambrose around dawn. They were instantly put under guard and dragged before the Lady Regent, an early riser.

She sat on her dais in chain mail and a surcoat embroidered with the black-and-white crest of Ambrose. The sword of high judgement was drawn and placed across her knees. Standing below her in front of the dais were three people—two men and a woman. They all wore red armbands and an indefinable air of strangeness. The woman, at least, was strikingly beautiful. Her skin was the darkest Lathmar had ever seen; her hair and eyes were golden. As she looked on him and smiled slightly he felt dirty and bedraggled and weather-beaten and, at the same time, rather wonderful. Then she looked past him and her smile vanished; he wondered why.

But all these thoughts were driven from Lathmar's mind when Ambrosia pinned him with her iron-gray gaze and said, "Your Majesty, just what the hell have you been doing all night?" He found it hard to answer her, but it turned out this was a rhetorical question: she already knew.

Half the Companions surrounding Morlock were destroyed, and he was nearly out of phlogiston when he decided it was time for a change in tactics. The King and Wyrth were either safely out of the way or caught by now. He scattered the remaining phlogiston broadly, shaking out the aethrium tube, so that a fire leapt up on the dry grass of the hillside. The Companions retreated from the blaze, and several of the corpse-golems fell lifeless, their name-scrolls compromised. Morlock swiftly put his cloak on the back of one of these and his weapon in the dead hand. Then he lay facedown in the smoldering grass and waited.

When the fire died down the Companions returned. He didn't risk looking up, but he could hear them milling about the fallen bodies. Presently they moved off, herding the remaining corpse-golems back to the others.

Morlock waited until he thought it was probably safe, and then waited that long again. When he lifted his face from the ground he was alone, except for the rotten half-burned flesh of his fallen adversaries.

"Probably none of us were worth recovering," Morlock reflected. "Fire taints certain kinds of magic. I'd better take that sword." (Like many a lonely man, Morlock was more talkative when no one else was present.)

He took back the fire-torn cloak and slung the sword belt over his shoulder with the sheath down his back. He'd move more freely that way, especially if he had to crawl, as he expected. He had more spying to do; it had been madness to let Lathmar and Wyrth come along. He hoped they were safe, but that was their lookout, now. He wanted to know where those corpse-golems were going.

After crawling on his hands and knees downslope, he went to his stomach and crept slowly along a gully at the base of the hill. By the time he got a sight of the front of the hill, there was very little to see. The Companions were gone; their carts were gone; the mausoleum door was closed. The herd of corpse-golems was stumbling along the dusty track toward the city.

Morlock scraped back along the gully, out of sight of the mausoleum. Then he took to the hills, running parallel to the track the corpse-golems were following. He hoped to avoid being seen by any Companions that might be shepherding the golems.

But there were none. When he had gotten ahead of the herd of stumbling ill-made zombies, he risked peering out at them from behind a ridge. They were alone, accompanied by no caretaking Companions.

He returned to his parallel course, still taking care that he not be seen. The Companions might have instructed one or more of the corpse-golems to watch for him. His course meandered more than the herd of golems, but he was moving faster, so he kept pace with them pretty well.

Finally, though, he had to risk closer contact. As the stars were spinning around toward dawn, the herd of corpse-golems shuffled toward one of the gates in the eastern wall of Ontil. It would be guarded by Protector's Men. If Morlock wanted to know where these things were going in the city (and he did), there was only one course of action.

He abandoned his sword and cloak, stuffed his knife sheath inside his waistband, and walked out to join the herd of corpse-golems. He was tensely alert for any sign of recognition or hostility, but there was none. As he shouldered his way into the trailing edge of the group, holding his breath against the stench of rotting flesh, the golems simply made way for him.

The plan was not as reckless as it seemed. He was about as misshapen as the average corpse-golem in the group; he limped without effort. The only danger he foresaw was regarding his face: it hardly had the masklike perfection of the others in the herd.

The herd of zombies shuffled up to the gate and began to pass through it. No words or signs that Morlock could detect were exchanged between the golems and the gate guards; perhaps this was a routine event. Morlock suspected so. But there was more to it than that: as he passed by one of the helmeted gate guards he saw a red seam running along his neck. The gate guards were corpse-golems, too. Well, that was one solution to Urdhven's manpower problem: recruit the dead, who notoriously outnumbered the living.

When the herd had stumbled through the gate it began to break up into various groups (again, they were no signals: the golems must have been instructed on their name-scrolls). Morlock followed one of the groups that was heading north and somewhat west.

They walked through dark streets that were strangely silent. Times they would pass the open door of a bakery: inside a corpse-golem in a white smock was miming the action of baking bread at a dark oven. Street-side food shops were open; corpse-golems came and went, exchanging copper coins for bowls and jars of nothingness, which were solemnly consumed on the spot, the stainless dishes returned to soak in a dry wash crock. Nearby on a street corner three children with pale perfect features and misproportioned rotting limbs solemnly played catch with a ball that wasn't there.

The city is being eaten alive, Morlock thought to himself. How many quarters were like this, inhabited by corpse-golems? How could any of them be like this without the rumor running wild through the city?

Abruptly, the sky above was alive with golden light: the sudden bright sunrise of Laent had come. As it did, a change passed over the scene that Morlock saw. The colors shimmered, woven into new form. The corpse-golems faded away under mundane forms. There was fire in the baker's ovens; water in the wash crocks; food and drink in the plates and cups.

But, of course, there wasn't: it just seemed that way. Nothing could change the carrion reek of the place, and it was still strangely quiet for a city street at sunrise. But illusion protected the essential secret: that this quarter of the city was an open grave, inhabited only by the restless dead.

Morlock had seen enough; he turned to go.

Behind him in the street was a dead baby riding on the back of what appeared to be a dog's body, equipped with four mismatched human feet and a masklike smiling human face.

The dead baby appraised Morlock with eyes like broken rotting bird's eggs. "You are not one of mine," the baby said, in a glutinous tenor. "I'd have remembered you."

"And I you."

"I doubt it; this is not my only face. Wait a moment."

"I'm afraid I can't. Good morning."

"You're the one they talk about—Ambrosia's brother. . . ."

But Morlock was running down an alley by then. He was not surprised to hear the soft slap of corpse-golem feet behind him and in front of him. He glanced about and began to climb straight up a crumbling tenement wall. By the time he had reached the third story he glanced down to see a milling crowd of zombies below, and he heard the unmistakable gluey voice of the dead baby shouting orders in an imperious wail.

He leapt into a window on the third story and ran past an incurious zombie family, miming a breakfast of cold emptiness in the shadowy room. He made his way to the roof of the building and leaped across to the one on the other side of the alley.

The dead baby was there on his monstrous grinning mount. "That was rather predictable, don't you think?" the baby sneered.

Morlock shrugged, dashed past, and leapt across to the next building.

"You can't keep it up forever!" the dead baby called after him.

Morlock was aware of this, but he didn't suppose he would have to. He simply had to make it to a quarter that was largely inhabited by living human beings. That would have its own dangers, but he had reason to suppose that partisans of the King outnumbered those of his erstwhile Protector in the living city.

Unfortunately, as he headed north and west, he found he was headed into a part of town where the tenements clustered less thickly. He was having to jump farther and farther to make it to the next building. Nor did he have the option of turning back; a glance over his shoulder showed him that the roofs behind him were sprouting corpse-golems after he passed.

He reached a place where he had to leap several floors down to reach the roof of the next building, across a rather wide alley. He hit the edge of the roof with his chest, and the world went briefly dark. When he came to himself he was sliding off the edge of the roof. He grasped desperately at the edge with his fingers as he fell, but the bricks crumbled into dust in his hands.

He landed, jarringly but in one piece, on his feet and one hand.

Among three red-cloaked figures.

With his left hand (the one not stunned by his graceless landing), he reached across and drew the knife in his waistband, his only weapon. It was knocked from his grip; he was seized and lifted by incredibly powerful hands. The man holding him threw him across his shoulders and ran up the alley.

Upside down (from his perspective) Morlock saw the lovely mocking features of Aloê Oaij looking at him, bobbing up and down as she ran to keep up. "Another night on the tiles, Morlock?" she called, laughing as she ran. "Aren't you getting too old for this kind of thing?"

"Enough with the banter," cried her companion (in whom Morlock recognized Jordel, another member of the Graith of Guardians from the Wardlands). "Morlock, is this whole damned city filled with these ugh, these what-do-you-call-them, these zombies?"

"No," Morlock said. "Baran, put me down and I can guide you."

Jordel's brother, Baran, stopped and put Morlock on his feet. His face was broad and pleasant, and there was an intelligent light in his brown eyes. But he was seven feet tall, as tall as Jordel; they called him "Baran the Beast" back in the Westhold both for his strength and his temper, but there was little evidence of the latter as he remarked, "I wasn't sure you knew me when you drew that knife."

"I didn't," Morlock admitted. "But there are few who can lift me with one hand."

"No doubt. You've put on some weight since I saw you last."

Jordel said, "And then Morlock cries, 'A base canard!' And Baran assures him, 'Truly, I but spake in jest; never was a warlock more svelte.' And then Aloê chips in with something equally witty, or partially witty, and so the long day wears on, and fairly soon those damned zombies are trying on our underwear."

"Jordel can't stand to hear anyone talk, except himself," Baran remarked.

"He does have a sort of point, though," Aloê added. "These are my favorite underwear; I hate to think of a zombie getting them."

Morlock grunted. "Let's head west from here. We can't be far from the Great Market. Our man has a place around there."

They moved briskly along the disturbingly silent streets, until suddenly Jordel cried out, "Hey, something's different. It doesn't smell bad anymore. That is, it still does, but not as bad as it did."

He was right, Morlock decided. The charnel reek of the dead quarter was gone. His insight told him that the appearances of the street before him were real, not an illusion.

"I don't think they'll pursue us here," Morlock said. "It would be easier to alert the Protector's Men." He drew to a halt. "I have to know what you'll do if they show up."

Jordel looked genuinely hurt. "Morlock, can you ask?"

"I'm asking. We were comrades once, but we are not now. Our interests are not the same."

"It's a fair question, Jordel," Aloê said. "Morlock, we've come to observe the struggle between your people and this necromancer, this zombie-master. We don't intend to intervene unless there is some obvious threat to the Guard. We're not crusaders for justice and opponents of evil everywhere, like you used to be."

"Of course," Morlock said, ignoring the sarcasm. "Ambrosia and I expected you—or someone from the Graith—long since. The Protector may respect your neutrality, but not if you assist me in evading capture by his forces. If that will be important to you we must part company now."

"Well, I don't know," Aloê said slowly. "Do you think it will be useful to us, Morlock?"

"Candidly, no. The Protector is merely a pawn of the adept, some of whose powers you have seen or felt. The adept himself is, I believe, in the Old City. But the choice is yours, Guardians."

The three red-cloaked vocates each glanced at the other, and Jordel said finally, "I think we'll string along with you, Morlock. If this adept is a threat to the Wardlands, we may be able to use your help in stopping him. If not, we can always duck out the back door of Ambrose and head for home."

Aloê looked annoyed at this last comment, but let it pass.

"Then," Morlock said briefly, and continued to lead the way.

They came finally to a little shop with an apartment above it, a few blocks south of the Great Market. Morlock pounded on the shop door until a window on the second floor was thrown up and Genjandro's irritated face appeared. "Just what is your so-urgent need—" Genjandro began querulously. His voice broke off as he saw Morlock standing there among the taller Guardians.

"I told you I'd pay you next bright call!"* Genjandro screamed.

"We need money now!" Jordel screamed back, always ready to take a hint. "We'll take half if you pay us today!"

"Half, eh?" Genjandro said, more amenably. "Wait a time. I'll be down."

The window slammed shut, and presently the shop door opened. "Come in, come in," Genjandro said. "We'll drink tea. We'll talk. We'll make a deal." He swung the door shut and bolted it. Then, ignoring the others, he addressed himself to Morlock. "Well?"

"They're with us."

Genjandro nodded and made a gesture with his hand. Five shadowy figures rose up around the dark shop, carrying a variety of weapons: bows, clubs, knives.

"You take no chances," Jordel said admiringly.

"I beg your pardon, but we take dozens every day—far, far too many," Genjandro disagreed politely if briskly. "Had we any brains at all we would go into a different line of work. Hopefully, we'll soon have the chance. Morlock Ambrosius, it is long since we met."

"Good morning, my friend, and well met."

"The King is well, I hope, and my friend Wyrth?"

"I don't know."

"You have a story to tell, I see. What is it you need? Perhaps we can have breakfast while we wait for it."

"A cart, two black horses, needles, and red thread."

"Oh ho. No red cloth?"

"I'll take it if you've got it. I had planned to use my friends' cloaks."

"Hey!" Jordel shouted.

Aloê waved him to silence. "I think I know what he's got in mind—a good plan, Morlock. It may well work."

"Trivia, madam, trivia," Genjandro disagreed. "You should have seen the

---

*See appendix C, section 2.

dodge we pulled on the Protector two years since—I think I may say 'we,' although my part was very small—"

"Essential," Morlock disagreed.

"Be that as it may, I can tell you the tale while we eat. Vora, our guests will be breakfasting with us. Kell: you heard the man. He needs a cart, two black horses, and some red thread. The rest of you may go about your business as we planned, but if any of you hear a rumor that Morlock is abroad in the city you should send me a message. Let's see, what should the code word be?"

"Seventeen," Morlock suggested.

"Superbly meaningless. Thank you. You see, my friends, he is a master of many crafts, including yours. Should you hear any rumor of Morlock's presence in the city, send me a message containing the word 'seventeen.' Throw in whatever else you like, so long as it's of no consequence. Good day: we meet at the appointed time."

The others left, some by the front door, others through a trapdoor behind the counter.

"Your servants?" Aloê guessed, when they were gone.

"My fellow spies, madam. I have the honor to be the King's spymaster in the occupied city of Ontil."

"Indeed. May I know your name?"

"I don't think so, madam, but you may address me as Alkhendron. That's what I go by these days."

Genjandro/"Alkhendron" led them upstairs to his living quarters, where a small if cheerful dining room was laid, rather awkwardly, for five. The thread came; breakfast came; Morlock drank tea and sewed as the others ate and talked.

Genjandro amused them with the story of the silken dragon, eliciting the names of his guests (without seeming to ask for them) as he told the tale. It amused the three vocates enormously—Jordel laughed until he wept, and even Aloê grinned a few times. In turn, Morlock—amusing his audience less, but interesting them even more—told what had happened the previous night, beginning with the departure of the spider from Ambrose through his meeting with the vocates in the dead quarter. (He did not mention Wyrth's terror: he blamed himself for that.)

"Don't like the sound of this," Genjandro said, when he heard about the corpse-inhabited quarter. "How much of the city have they taken over? What do they want?"

"We'll need to know as much as your people can tell us," Morlock said. "Next to this, the Protector is nothing."

"Almost literally, perhaps," Genjandro said musingly. "But I still don't understand how our friends here found you, or what their role in this is."

"We were following Morlock," Aloê said flatly.

Morlock glanced at her and glanced away. There were several ways to locate someone through magic. The easiest was if one had some sort of connection with the person through blood, or some other close tie, such as marriage. From her tone of voice, Morlock guessed that they had used this method to follow him. He could tell she liked it no better than he did.

"When we saw what was going on," Aloê continued, "we decided to follow from a distance. But when the zombie-riot started we thought we should get him out of there, if we could."

"And so you did," Genjandro said heartily. His eyes met Morlock's; he had not failed to notice that Aloê had not explained why she and her companions were following Morlock.

Morlock nodded and shrugged. He held up the red mask he had been making. "What do you think?"

"Very convincing," Genjandro approved. "Who gets to wear it?"

"I vote for Morlock," Jordel said. "He has the authentic air of a gravedigger, if you know what I mean."

Morlock grunted. "You'd smell the same if you'd been fighting corpse-golems all night."

"Well, we all have our favorite amusements. I suppose the three of us are to portray the unliving dead."

"The silent majority," Aloê remarked. "You might try easing yourself into the role."

Jordel, offended, threw up his hands. "You won't get another word out of me!"

Morlock donned the red hood, red gown, and red mask he had made while the others ate breakfast. He would hold the reins of the horses with his hands muffled by the sleeves of the gown—risky, but not as risky as waiting to stitch a pair of gloves.

The cart and horses were waiting in front of Genjandro/Alkhendron's shop.

"A thousand thanks, Alkhendron," Morlock said, shaking both his hands. "You've been a friend in need, as so often before."

Genjandro actually blushed and said, "It was nothing. Always a pleasure. No, really."

Morlock carried the Guardians to the would-be death cart for greater authenticity. Baran went first: a heavy burden. Jordel was as tall, but not nearly so heavy. However, he held his body stiff with all his limbs awry in an implausible imitation of rigor mortis; Morlock hoped no one was watching. Finally he carried out Aloê

"Just like our wedding night—eh, Morlock?" she whispered through nearly motionless lips.

He grunted, dumped her in the back with the others, and covered them with a rough blanket. Then he jumped into the driver's seat and shook the reins. His mask was cut from Aloê's cloak, and it smelled like her. The soft velvety strength of her burned on his arms and chest: he had forgotten how much he longed for her. But, unfortunately, he could not forget how useless that longing was.

No one attempted to detain him as he drove straight through the Great Market and past it. The Protector's Men on duty "besieging" the City Gate of Ambrose simply stood aside when it was clear he intended to cross the bridge.

When they were out of direct line of sight, he pulled off the mask and hoped the guards on the other side of the portcullis would recognize him. Evidently they did, as he was not shot at while he approached. They raised the gate and he drove the cart in. On the far side he reined in and dismounted; the three vocates threw off the blanket and jumped down beside him as the portcullis rattled down to seal the gate.

"Welcome to Ambrose, Guardians," Morlock said as the Royal Legionaries stepped forward to receive them. "You'll pardon me if I leave you in the care of these soldiers—these are honored guests, Hundred-Leader; ambassadors from the Wardlands."

"Morlock," said Aloê, stopping him dead by putting her hand on his chest. "Where are you going?"

"I am going to tell Ambrosia what I've learned and what has happened," Morlock said. "This is her war, more than mine, and she needs to know. And if the King and Wyrth have not returned by the time I'm finished, I am going to go into the city and look for them. If they do return, I plan to take a bath"

"Well, you have your ducks in a row, as usual," she said, with a dark warm smile that pierced him to the heart. "We'll catch up with you later."

Morlock turned and fled into the stone ways of the castle, his heart beating like a boy's.

Part Five

The Two Cities

The descent into hell is easy.
The door of the dark city stands open
    night and day.
But to recall your steps, and escape
    into the upper air . . .
For that you'll work. For that you'll
    suffer.

—Vergil, *Aeneid*

CHAPTER TWENTY-ONE

THE KING'S JUDGEMENT

"nd now," said Ambrosia, leaning back, her iron-gray eyes as cold as death, "it is time for me to pass sentence on the condemned traitor, Karn. Guards, seize him."

"Ambrosia, a word with you," Lathmar said urgently.

"Later, Your Majesty."

"*Now*, my Lady Regent. Or should I say Protector?"

That got her attention, though the look she threw at him was not a warm one.

"As you wish, Your Majesty." She motioned him forward, then sat him down on the throne and bent forward to hear his whispered words.

"Grandmother, you will spare Karn."

"No. If that's all—"

"It is all. It is everything. For you, madam, for you!"

"What are you talking about? Please keep your voice down."

"Once and twice last night, Karn could have run away to save himself. He didn't. When there was no hope, when you weren't there, he saved me. You need to hear that before you pass judgement."

"Suppose I don't?"

"Then I'm done. You can carry on your damned war for your damned empire without me."

"Oh?"

"Yes. I'll make it known that you acted against my wishes and why. I'll make it known that you killed Karn even though I had personally assured him that his life would be spared. I'll make it known that I'm as much a prisoner of the Lady Regent as I was of the Lord Protector."

"And you think—what? That soldiers will leap up out of the ground to take your side? That—"

"I think it will make your war against the Protector harder to win. I think it will make the peace that follows impossible to win."

"You're taking a rather big risk, Lathmar. After all, if you are not an asset to me, you are a liability."

"I understand your threat perfectly, madam," Lathmar hissed. "I understood it before you uttered it. Karn pledged his life for me; now I pledge mine for him."

"You're making a mistake, Lathmar," Ambrosia said, with unexpected mildness. "Karn is not the man you think him."

"The mistake is mine to make. Not yours, madam."

"Stop calling me that. Step back; tell me the tale of last night's doings, in whatever detail you think fit; I'll use it as a pretext for sparing Karn's life. But," she said, seizing his arm as he began to draw away, "understand that it's only a pretext. We'd all be safer if he were out of the way. He's a weak link in a chain that must not break."

Lathmar shook loose and stepped down from the dais. His hands were trembling, so he clasped them behind his back before he began. "My Lady Regent, before you pass judgement on Legionary Karn, I wish to speak in his defense."

"Say on, Your Majesty," said Ambrosia cheerfully. "I am your least humble servant."

"Madam," the King began pointedly, "last night I left Ambrose with certain members of this council to survey matters east of the city. . . ."

For brevity's sake, he began the tale with their walk through the grave fields. He was weary beyond words, but he kept his voice hard and clear until he had told how Erl and Karn appeared to rescue him when all seemed lost. He didn't mention Wyrth's terror at the prospect of the corpse-golems. Then his voice broke and he found it hard to stand, much less go on.

"If it pleases the regent," Erl said hesitantly, "I could carry on the story, since His Majesty is—"

"No need," Ambrosia interrupted. "Thank you, Erl. And I thank you, Your Majesty; your intervention was timely indeed."

Lathmar nodded, wearily.

"The punishment of treason, as I remarked yesterday, is death. Karn was guilty of treason in that sorry episode, and I fully intended to have him executed this morning, if he was so ungallant as to make it through the night alive. Instead of killing himself, as I had hoped, Karn spent the night earning the gratitude of the King and myself in a selfless act of bravery. I find I cannot now give him the punishment his treason deserves, but neither can I leave him unpunished."

Ambrosia seemed to brood for a moment, and then continued, "The man who can't take orders shouldn't be in a position to give them. Karn has proved his fitness as the King's bodyguard, under the supervision of Commander Erl, so that is precisely the rank I assign to him. He is stripped of all seniority and rank in the Royal Legion, and will forfeit a year's pay. I'd sentence him to a beating and a jail term as well, but a beating would not affect a man of Karn's indomitable courage, and he'd only escape from the jail cell. He is to consider himself to have been very leniently dealt with, and he may be assured that if he fails in his duty again, I will personally cut his damn throat.

"I would be pleased to welcome the emissaries from the Wardlands at this time, but I have kept the Protector's people (to use the term loosely) waiting longer than is really civil. I hope you'll join me for dinner—or we should make it supper, perhaps? Some of us will need a good day's sleep. Yes, Kedlidor?"

The Rite-Master of Ambrose and current (and reluctant) head of the Royal Legion had entered the council chamber, his arms full of red cloth.

"I beg your pardon—Your Majesty, my Lady Regent. But Councillor Morlock particularly wished me to bring these to the Guardians of the Wardlands—"

The tall, thin, fair-haired Guardian cried out, "Isn't he a good fellow! Here I was imagining him lolling in a hot tub scrubbing his toes, when he was working away on replacing our cloaks."

Wyrth, who had been unwontedly silent all this while, spoke up almost grudgingly, "It wouldn't have been so hard. We've had the garments rough-cut for months. He only needed to fit them to your size."

"Well, mine fits like a glove," the dark woman remarked. She looked more than regal with her red vocate's cloak across her shoulders, and the King, finding he was staring, forced himself to look away. "And it glows like the dark edge of a rainbow—what talents that man has."

The big brown-haired Guardian rolled his eyes at this and said, "Thanks," briefly, to Kedlidor, swinging the red cloak over his broad back.

"And where is my esteemed brother, Kedlidor?" Ambrosia asked. "I expected him here some time ago."

"He said if you asked, my lady . . . I'm sorry but I don't understand it."

"Perhaps you should quote him exactly."

"He said, 'If Ambrosia asks, tell her I've gone to get my spider.'"

Lathmar couldn't help it; he burst out in laughter tinged with hysteria. Wyrth muttered a curse and dashed out of the room. On that somewhat chaotic note, the Regency Council broke up.

Supper that night was a formal affair, although the regent wasn't present. Negotiations with the Protector's agents had gone into a marathon session, and Ambrosia wanted to see them through.

"But I believe," the King said wryly to his guests from the Wardlands as they gathered in the antechamber, "that I am competent to host a supper."

"You are quite right, Your Majesty—quite right," Kedlidor said approvingly. "The Lady Regent exercises only your judicial, legislative, military, and civil authority. All ceremony remains within your purview."

"Well, with Kedlidor's blessing we can chew our beef without any dreadful fears that we are being ceremonially incorrect. He has been Rite-Master of Ambrose from time immemorial, as well as the commander of the Royal Legion, from a more recent date."

"That's an unusual combination of offices, isn't it?" commented the tall fair-haired vocate they called Jordel.

Kedlidor's wrinkled face took on a pained expression. "A persistent joke of the Lady Regent's, I fear," he said sadly. "She does most of the work herself, leaving me with administrative trivia."

"Kedlidor does himself an injustice," the King remarked to the company as a whole. "When the time comes, he can lead troops and fight with them like a lion. And in a war like the one we have in hand, Gr—Ambrosia rightly says that most of the battle lies in knowing whom you can trust. We trust Kedlidor because we've seen what he can do."

"A royal 'we,' Your Majesty?" murmured the dark, gloriously beautiful vocate named Aloê, standing nearby.

He basked for a moment in the hot golden delight of her full regard before he realized that some sort of answer was required. "Yes—but, no, not really. That is, I feel that way, and so does the rest of the Regent's Council."

She nodded, tactfully not taking notice of his confusion, which confused him even more.

"But you needn't worry," Kedlidor was saying to Jordel. "Though as Rite-Master my rank is far too low to sit at the King's table, as Legionary commander I just merit the honor. You won't lose status by sitting with me."

Jordel's hazel eyes nearly crossed in his effort to follow Kedlidor's pedantic line of thought, but then his face cleared and he laughed aloud. "Well, perhaps concern should run the other way. I'm nobody in particular without my red cloak, you know. My first job was stealing cowpies."

"'Cowpies'?" Now it was Kedlidor's eyes that were crossing. "In the sense of . . . ?"

"Manure."

"Er . . ." Kedlidor did actually look as if he were about to question Jordel's right to sit at the King's table.

"I wasn't aware that cowpies were valuable, Vocate Jordel," the King observed, emphasizing the title slightly for Kedlidor's benefit.

"Well, they aren't usually. But then, they're not especially well guarded either. My semi-dad used to pay me a penny for every dozen I brought him. He wanted them as fertilizer for his farm, which didn't do terribly well, despite my undoubted talents as a coproklept."

"Semi-dad?" Kedlidor asked, irresistibly attracted by what was apparently a new genealogical term, or perhaps merely afraid to ask for a definition of "*coproklept.*"

"Oh, just someone my mother took up with after my real dad died," Jordel said airily.

"*Lom bluthian, kreck bloth,*"* said Aloê, quietly but audibly, out of the side of her mouth.

The heavily built brown-haired vocate called Baran grunted. "Watch it. I'm sure the King knows enough of our speech to get by."

Aloê turned back to the King and smiled. He was thunderstruck by the curve of her rosily dark lips, the flash of her teeth like lightning. "Is that true, Your Majesty?" she asked. "I suppose you call it 'the secret speech,' as most do in the unguarded lands."

"Unguh—guh—guh—That is, I know a certain amount." The King was about to go on, but then he realized that it would be impolitic to address the content of Aloê's muttered comment to her peer. But he was fascinated by it. Neither Morlock nor Wyrth were in the least concerned with status or prestige, as Lathmar had been carefully taught to recognize it, and he had assumed that people from the Wardlands felt the same way—Jordel's comments seemed to imply as much. But Aloê seemed to be genuinely, if faintly, embarrassed by Jordel's reminiscences.

"But, um, this question of status—that is—you know what I mean, Kedlidor?" He was sorry to push the question off on Kedlidor, but he had incautiously met Aloê's golden eyes again, and he found it difficult to string words together.

But the Rite-Master was up to the challenge. "Yes, indeed, Your Majesty; I thank you very much for raising the matter. The trouble is, vocates, that we have been unable to settle which of your number should sit at the King's right hand—the place of honor, you see."

Baran grunted. "I'm the oldest. Jordel was made vocate first, but we don't count that type of seniority as authority in the Wardlands. I suppose we could flip for it."

"Oh, come now Baran, don't be dense," Jordel said lightly. "Surely Aloê is in charge of our little embassy. The place of honor is hers."

Baran shrugged. "I don't see that she's in charge. But she can sit where she likes, as far as I'm concerned."

---

*"Stop being a boor, you damn boor."

Aloê laughed. "Thanks, B." She turned to the King and said, "Subject to your approval, Your Majesty. I'm afraid I don't have any interesting stories about stealing cowpies."

"Oh, that's all right," he said, awash in confusion, and offered her his left arm. She lightly placed her right hand on his left forearm, and he simultaneously felt a hundred feet tall and totally inadequate.

They walked together through the doors into the dining hall.

This was not the Great Hall. They were too few by far for that echoing monstrosity; also, there were no windows, which the King insisted on whenever possible. So tonight they supped in the High Hall of the North—atop a long, low tower just above and behind the Thorngate of Ambrose. There were windows on three sides, and the roof as well, and the room was unlit as they entered.

The sun's last light was long gone from the eastern sky; bright drifts of stars stood out there above the sullen reddish horizon of the city. The greater moon Chariot hovered overhead, mounting up toward culmination. Northward the edge of the blue sky was notched by dark angles: the not-too-distant peaks of the Whitethorn Range. The third moon, Trumpeter, stood fiercely radiant in the west.

Aloê gasped, and the King felt for the first time the peculiar satisfaction of impressing an impressive woman. "Creator, what a view!" she said at last. "It reminds me of some of the high halls under Thrymhaiam. But even those didn't have more than one rank of windows—much less skylights."

The King indicated to Thoke, the chief servant of the table, that he and his assistants could light the hall's lamps. This unfortunately made it difficult to stargaze, but much easier to see what one was stabbing with one's fork.

"You have been under Thrymhaiam, Vocate Aloê?" the King asked, turning back to Aloê with interest. He had heard so much of the dwarvish stronghold from Wyrth and Morlock that he occasionally had dreams of the place.

She threw a golden glance at him that was difficult to read, but seemed to be in a quandary as to how she would reply.

"We've all been there," Jordel remarked from behind. "Aloê, Baran, and myself. Back in the Year of Fire. But I suppose that Aloê went there many a time after that."

This gave the King a great deal to think about. The Year of Fire—unless Lathmar was misremembering his stories (and he didn't think he was) was centuries ago, when dragons had invaded the Northhold of the Wardlands. He was stunned to think that Aloê was so old—or Jordel, for that matter. They both seemed young people just out of adolescence. At least physically. Now that he thought of it, it would be unlikely for people so very young to be bearing the responsibilities that Jordel and Aloê did. Baran's age didn't seem much older, but rather indeterminate, something like Morlock's. No one who saw Morlock act or talk could doubt his vigor; no one who looked in his eyes would doubt his age.

But they were as old as Morlock if they remembered the Year of Fire— Lathmar remembered Wyrth saying that Morlock himself was only a young man then. His ancestor Uthar the Great hadn't even been born!

Morlock must have known them. Why did he never talk of them?

With a cold shock, Lathmar remembered Grandmother saying of Morlock, *He was married to a woman he loved—the only one he has ever loved (may she be damned for a poisonous bitch).* . . .

Aloê? It would explain why she knew Thrymhaiam, the land of Morlock's dwarvish foster parents. It would explain the rather arch tone in Jordel's voice when he mentioned the fact.

It pained Lathmar inexpressibly to imagine Morlock married to Aloê. He wasn't sure why—when he thought about it, Morlock was the most remarkable man he'd ever known, and Aloê might well be the most remarkable woman. Some would call it a fitting match. But that wasn't how he felt about it.

His feelings were running riot—that he knew. But what bothered him most was the fact that Aloê must know it—that she was counting on it. He had noticed how Jordel and Aloê had maneuvered to have her sit beside him. Because it amused them? Because they thought it would be to their advantage? Because he might let slip something, in his confusion, that he should not have said? The Wardlands were not hostile to the Ontilian Empire, but neither were they allied to it—they had no allies.

By now they were seated at a long table of gleaming, beautifully grained *kattra* wood. The King had rather absentmindedly assisted his guest of honor in sitting and had gestured to the servants to begin pouring the wine and serving the food. They were eating in high style, he reflected grimly, when compared to crunching bread that the bakers had thrown out as too stale for the Protector and his men. But this was a very small party compared to the dinners Lathmar remembered from during his father's reign—each person at table had but one servant behind him, for instance.

Aloe's cool, firm voice broke into his reverie. "You're deep in thought, Your Majesty."

He met her eyes and was thrilled to discover that they were as alarmingly beautiful as ever. But now he could speak as they crossed glances.

"I was thinking about a story I once heard," he said thoughtfully, "about a hero named Jordel who walked with his companions against the Dark Seven of Kaen. I was wondering if your companion was named after this hero."

Jordel was not so far away that he couldn't hear this. He laughed and said, "Someone's been lying to you, L—Your Majesty. Baran, don't punch me in the ribs when I'm talking."

"Eh. If I kept that rule when would I ever get to punch you in the ribs?"

"You must ask me sometime when I seem inclined to give a rat's ass; we'll debate the whole question then, I assure you. No, Your Majesty, I'm quite sure there was no hero named Jordel who walked against the Dark Seven, for I was a member of that harebrained expedition myself—the hareiest member, if not the brainiest. God Sustainer, what a nightmare that was!"

Through the first two courses Jordel entertained them with obviously distorted recollections of his adventures in Kaen as the thain-attendant of the vocates Illion and Noreê. He gave his audience to understand that his prudence and restraint had saved the group time and again from the disasters caused by his companions' intellectual brilliance and heroic courage—dangerous qualities, of which Jordel boasted he had not the slightest trace, not the faintest whiff or suggestion of a trace.

From time to time the King glanced over at Aloê, and once he found her looking at him with unguarded approval.

"That was well done, my friend," she whispered to him. "We thought we had you cornered, and then you turned our weakness against us."

"Your weakness is not as weak as he pretends," he murmured in reply.

"Naturally not. If there were a real threat, Jordel would be as reasonable as anybody. But in the absence of one he can rarely resist the temptation to listen to his own voice."

Having utterly debunked the defeat of the Dark Seven, Jordel was passing on to tell of his misadventures in the Year of Fire, when he personally had saved the Wardlands from the courage and intelligence of a more numerous cast of even more heroic persons. But he took a few moments to denounce these poisonous qualities again—particularly courage, which he described (in the words of some ancient poet, whom Jordel seemed to have made up on the spot), as the "unconquerable waster of worlds!"

"That's a fine way for a *rokhlan* to talk," remarked a sardonic voice from the doorway.*

The King looked up from Aloê's eyes to Morlock's, who was standing at the far end of the table. Wyrth was just coming into the room behind him as he spoke.

"Your pardon, Majesty," said Morlock formally. "We had some tasks to perform."

"More sewing, Morlock?" said Jordel cheerfully.

"Nothing so uplifting," Wyrth said, stumping up to the table. "No, we were settling the ruffled feelings of a horse."

"I didn't know feelings had ruffles," Jordel observed.

"Only the finer feelings, Vocate Jordel, so your ignorance does not surprise me. I suppose you've told them your dung-stealing story by now?"

General laughter at Jordel's expense ensued, during which Morlock seated himself and gestured for Wyrth to sit beside him. Wyrth seemed to demur. Morlock spoke firmly in response; the King only heard, ". . . I require it."

Lathmar wondered if Wyrth might still be embarrassed about his behavior in the presence of the corpse-golems. But then he saw the searing glare of hatred that Wyrth shot toward Aloê as he sat down.

"Master Morlock's horse is jealous of his spider," Wyrth said in a voice that belied his expression. "We rode down to the hills east of the city where we left it—you remember, Your Majesty—and our plan was that I would ride Velox back—"

"Is Velox the spider or the horse?" Aloê asked.

Rokhlan (Dwarvish): "dragonkiller."

"The horse, madam," the dwarf said coldly.

"I could see you sooner astride a spider, Wyrth."

Wyrth looked down at the table and smiled a little, evidently against his will. "Velox is no ordinary horse," he said. "And that was the problem. He became terribly upset when Morlock entered the spider—"

Bewilderment was so general at the table (neither the vocates from the Wardlands nor Kedlidor had any idea of what Wyrth was driving at) that Lathmar felt compelled to explain about Morlock's bizarre craft.

"Anyway," Wyrth resumed, "that was our plan—we would ride Velox down to the spider, Morlock would direct the spider back, and I would ride Velox. But Velox became extremely upset whenever Morlock made to enter the spider. So we had to coax the horse into the compartment, to show him there was no danger in there."

"Sustainer," said the King wonderingly. "All three of you in that space? It must have—"

"It smelled dreadful, Your Majesty," Wyrth interrupted. "In fact, you can be grateful that we're so far down the table—we both schmeck of nervous horse, or I'm much mistaken."

"We'll take your word for it, Councillor," Lathmar said. "But you'll be hungry and thirsty. Thoke," he said to the servant standing behind his chair, "see to the needs of Councillors Morlock and Wyrth."

"I don't—" Wyrth began to say, and broke off when Morlock glanced at him. Impatiently he turned to Jordel and said, "Vocate Jordel, could you give me a piece of bread from your plate? Do you mind if I dip it in your wine?"

He ate the wine-tinged bread and turned to Morlock, spreading his hands. "There. Can I do more?" He turned up the table and called to Aloê, "What do you say, vocate? Are we quits?"

"I've no claim against you, Wyrth," Aloê said composedly.

"There. Master Morlock, I take your point, but you know as well as I do how much work we have in hand that only you or I can do. If you'll permit—"

Morlock nodded. "I'll see you later."

"No doubt. With your leave, Your Majesty . . ."

His Majesty had forgotten he had any say in the matter and had taken a mouthful of ragout. He waved dismissal in a gesture so casual that it made

Wyrth grin and Kedlidor gasp. The dwarf waved back and dashed away through the door.

"You inspire strong feelings in your dependents, Morlock," Aloê remarked. "Dwarven, equine, corvine . . ."

"I have no dependents," Morlock replied. "Wyrth hates you because his father taught him to do so. Dwarves can be very loyal to that sort of feeling."

Aloê was now distinctly annoyed. The King watched her face in open fascination, and when she noticed this, she smiled slowly.

"At least he only had one father—that must make things less confusing for him," she purred. "Wouldn't you say, Your Majesty?"

The King swallowed, reflected, and answered, "Under no circumstances would I say so, Vocate Aloê, even if I thought it. Councillor Morlock, what do you think of the ragout?"

"Not bad," he remarked. Somehow the King thought he wasn't referring to the stew. "But, Thoke, if you please, take this cup away and bring me some water."

"No, no!" Jordel cried. "Morlock, drink with us! It's a poor heart that never rejoices."

Morlock's dark face was more than usually impassive. He hesitated for a moment and said, "I'll rejoice, if you insist. But I'll drink water."

Jordel subsided with a wounded look. The servant Thoke brought Morlock a cup of water, disapproval like a mask covering his normally deferential features.

"You're an awkward fellow, Morlock," Baran observed. "Always were. Never could get along with people."

Morlock said something in the secret speech that the King didn't quite understand, but whose purport was fairly clear.

"I don't think I know that verb, Councillor Morlock," Lathmar said pointedly. It seemed to him that the supper was spiraling out of control.

But Baran was laughing out loud. Apparently gross insults of this sort were not always insulting.

"That didn't sink any deeper than the knife you aimed at me this morning," Baran was saying.

"Since you mention this morning," Jordel said, "and since our expert on

Morlock affairs is sulking at the high end of the table, maybe you'd answer me a simple question, old friend and sometime enemy."

"Maybe I will," Morlock somewhat assented.

"Just what the hell is going on around here? What are these weird creatures running around dressed up like some religious order reanimating corpses which pretend to bake bread which other zombies pretend to eat? Because I'm damned if I can understand it."

"I don't want to contribute to your damnation, Jordel—"

"When did you change your mind about *that?*"

"—but with the King's permission I'll tell you what I know."

"There was a time when you'd ask no man's permission to do anything," Aloê said in her cool angry voice. "Much less a boy's."

The King was stung, though he tried not to show it. Morlock met his eye and shrugged.

"You've my permission to say what seems good to you, Councillor Morlock," he said, looking away from Aloê.

"Well, it isn't much. The Companions, these figures who collect and rearrange corpses, are agents of an entity whose name I don't know. He offered himself to the King's late Protector—"

"Late Protector?" said Aloê leaning forward. "I thought he was still alive."

Morlock shrugged.

"It's a moot point," the King explained. "At any rate, he is no longer my Protector, though he continues to use the title. Go on, Morlock."

"This entity offered himself to Lord Urdhven as a magical patron, but I think that was just a ruse. Now it seems that this adept has been using the Protector as a stalking horse to occupy Ambrosia while he engages in some plan she would have stopped, or at least interfered with."

"You say 'he,'" Baran observed.

"I made visionary contact a few times, and the figure in question seemed to be male. But . . ." Morlock shrugged.

"Part of his plan is clear, anyway," Jordel observed. "He's filling the city with zombies."

"Corpse-golems," Morlock corrected.

"What's the difference?"

"I don't know what a zombie is. These things are golems made with parts from human corpses."

"Morlock, you're a pedant."

"Maybe, but I have a point. Golems do not act independently; in a very real sense, they do not act at all, but simply follow orders."

"I had a thain-attendant like that once," Jordel remarked. "He—"

"So you mean that the adept has agents in the city, instructing the golems," Aloê remarked, ruthlessly waving aside Jordel's reminiscence.

"Yes. The Companions at least; that thing that looked like a dead baby for another. But what these agents are I can't tell."

"I thought you just said what they were," Jordel complained.

"He means their nature, Jordel," Aloê said.

"At first I thought they were harthrangs—demons inhabiting dead bodies," he explained parenthetically to the King and Kedlidor. "But they appear to my talic perception the same as they do to my eyes. If they are harthrangs, I don't understand why this should be. If they are not, I don't know what they are."

"I'll tell you one thing," Aloê offered. "There's an exile from the Wardlands involved in this somehow. The colors that the Companions wear: gray, red, and white—the same as the colors of the three ranks of Guardian. That's an exile's joke."

Morlock nodded slowly. "Or the joke of someone who wants us to think that. It could be another ruse."

Jordel laughed derisively, and Baran said, "Maybe you're being over-subtle."

Morlock shrugged. "I saw Merlin recently," he observed.

"What?" shouted Jordel and Baran as one. Even Aloê leaned forward with renewed interest. So Morlock told the tale of Velox's apparent fall from the sky, and Morlock's rescue of him, and what had followed.

"But what was the horse doing in the sky?" asked Jordel.

"No," Aloê said, rubbing her forehead. "Please don't answer that, Morlock, unless you think it's relevant. You can satisfy Jordel's natural curiosity some other time."

"Morlock," Baran observed, "all you've just said makes me even more sure that Merlin is involved here—is probably the adept himself."

Morlock shrugged. "It should have done the opposite."

"What? Why do you say that?"

Morlock rubbed his face and, turning to Aloê, opened his hand in silent appeal.

"I see what you're driving at," she said slowly, "and I think you're right. Listen, you two," she said to Jordel and Baran as they turned to her to protest, "what is this adept's defining characteristic? Apart from his power."

"Necromancy," Jordel said. "Using corpses for magical purposes."

"Try again. It's a pretty common form of magic in the unguarded lands."

"I'm *not* going to try again. Tell us your thought."

"This adept can keep his identity a secret. Merlin can't. Even when he's trying to adopt a disguise, he can't refrain from exposing his identity. It's vital to him that everyone must recognize his presence and his genius. He could never stand in the background for a period of years while his plans developed."

"Hm," said Jordel meditatively.

"But if the Ambrosii weren't all accounted for," Aloê continued, addressing Morlock, "I'd suspect one of you. This business has a family stench about it."

Morlock looked as if he were about to speak, but didn't. Suddenly the King knew what he had been about to say, or thought he did: one of the Ambrosii was not "accounted for" as Aloê put it. There was Hope, hidden inside Ambrosia.

Lathmar began to feel panic, tried to suppress it. Hope couldn't possibly be the Protector's Shadow, could she? But the more he thought about it the less he was sure. After all, what he knew about Hope, her limitations and abilities, came from Hope herself. And if she were the Protector's Shadow, that meant it had been there with them every moment, had known every plan, every stratagem. And they could only avoid this by excluding Ambrosia from their councils. And that, itself, would be crippling—like chewing off a leg to escape a trap. . . .

At that moment the door at the end of the hall opened and Ambrosia and the Protector entered side by side. Behind them walked Vost and Steng, somewhat uneasily, wearing the surcoats of Protector's Men.

Those sitting at the table rose, except for the King. He felt, rather than saw, his bodyguards tense behind him.

"Your Majesty," said Ambrosia, "I bring guests for your table."

Lathmar inspected Grandmother carefully for signs of insanity. What he saw instead were poorly disguised traces of triumph. He guessed that she had concluded a treaty with the Protector on favorable terms. It was usual to fix a treaty with a display of hospitality, hence this somewhat surprising appearance at his table.

"Ambrosia," he said slowly, "any guest you invite is welcome at my table. However, those two gentlemen"—he pointed at Vost and Steng—"wear a device I do not recognize. They must put it off before they sit."

Ambrosia almost winked at him: he had said exactly what she wanted him to say. He tried to keep his face polite, but internally he fumed. One day he would miss one of these subtle cues, and then—

The Protector had turned his leonine head toward his men.

"Our agreement, Lord Urdhven," Ambrosia said quietly.

"Take those things off, you two," the Protector said gruffly. "That's all over."

Vost looked like a dog who had been kicked by his master, but he obeyed. Steng was already working at the laces of his surcoat. He tossed it aside, and the King thought he could see the man's long, ropy fingers trembling. He sat at the table as far as he could from Morlock or Ambrosia.

Urdhven, in contrast, sat down next to Morlock, with Ambrosia on his other side. "Thoke, you old monster," he cried at the servant behind Morlock's chair. "Are you still the master of the cups and plates?"

"Yes, my lord."

"You'd better call up some of your minions—we're hungry, had a long day negotiating."

"Yes, indeed, my lord. I was about to bring in the final course of fruit, cheese, and dessert wine. Would you . . . ?"

"That'll be fine, Thoke," said Ambrosia.

Thoke disappeared into the preparation room, trailed by the lesser servants.

They returned in a moment, each carrying fruit and cheese arranged on a plate. Some servants had more than one tray, to accommodate the new guests. Nonetheless, the King didn't get served until Commander Erl gestured at one of the servants, indicating that the King's place was empty.

This annoyed Lathmar, but he could understand it: Thoke had gone to serve at the far end of the table, and he had forgotten to have someone stand in for him here.

Then, too, Thoke was, as Urdhven had called him, the master servant of the dining hall; he always acted as personal servant to the most important person at a banquet. Apparently he had forgotten that for purposes of ceremony, at least, Lathmar was that person. Thoke was standing behind Urdhven's chair, at his beck and call, indicating by his manner who, in his opinion, was the most important person present. The King glanced at Kedlidor to see if he had picked up on this—he imagined the Rite-Master giving Thoke a searing lecture on propriety after the supper was ended—but Kedlidor was engaged in some sort of conversation with Ambrosia and Urdhven.

There was something else, as well, though. The feeling in the room had changed when Ambrosia and the Protector's group had entered. Lathmar couldn't put his finger on it—he felt as if something horrible were about to happen. As if something horrible was happening, which was real although only he could see it.

Now the wine came in, brought by a fleet of butlers. The King was served (wine and water) without having to specially request it, and he was about to salute Aloê with his goblet when a dispute broke out in the lower half of the table.

Thoke had approached Morlock with a bottle of dessert wine, hesitated, and then served Urdhven instead. He went on to pour wine in Ambrosia's cup.

"Wait a moment," Urdhven said, a hint of unpleasantness in his manner. "Aren't you drinking with me, Morlock?"

"I'm drinking water, if that's what you mean."

"That's pretty small-minded, if you ask me."

"I didn't."

"I come here to settle a treaty with the regent, and you sit there drinking well water. Where's the bond if we're not all eating and drinking the same?"

Morlock silently offered Urdhven a piece of cheese from his plate. Urdhven didn't take the cheese, but he did seem to take offense.

"Come off it, Morlock," Ambrosia said impatiently. "A mouthful of wine won't kill you."

"Lord Urdhven is free to share my water, if he likes."

"Most improper," Kedlidor said, surprising the King. "Pledge a treaty in well water. Unheard-of." He spoke in spurts, as if he were being jabbed between utterances.

"That's what I was telling him earlier," Jordel complained. "Why not live a little?"

Morlock said nothing now. He looked at no one. Thoke, taking this as permission, raised his bottle to pour wine in Morlock's cup.

Lathmar's sense of dread darkened the world. It was as if every gesture, every word at the table masked some evil secret. And all his impulses told him that if the Protector (that thing—that shell—that mask of nothingness) wanted something very badly, he was not to get it. Could the wine be poisoned?

Or was it the wine itself? Wyrth had sometimes referred to Morlock as a drunk. But the King had never seen him drunk. But then he had never seen Morlock drink. Was it possible that the man's iron will, his intellect—everything he was, everything that Lathmar loved him for—could be drowned in a sip of wine? Lathmar couldn't believe it. He didn't believe it. It was too stupid. But he couldn't risk it.

"Thoke," he said, his voice cracking with strain, "come here. I want you."

"Pour, pour," Urdhven said impatiently.

"I'll be with you in a moment, Your Majesty," Thoke called.

The world went completely dark. Lathmar was angry at Thoke's insolence; he was frustrated by his role as a regal puppet; he was afraid for Morlock. He heard himself shouting, *"In a moment you'll be dead!"*

When he returned to himself he was standing. So was everyone else at the table, their faces mirroring various forms of shock. Thoke was sprawled facedown on the floor, his face in the rushes, sobbing. Karn and Erl stood over him with swords drawn. Their faces, expressionless, were turned toward the King: they were prepared to kill Thoke at his word.

The King drew a slow deep breath. His sense of imminent danger had diminished. There was light in the world, again—there was hope that he could do something, that he could speak and be heard, that he was something other than a mere puppet. But there was a darkness in himself, too; he understood that now for the first time. Perhaps that was the most dangerous darkness of all.

"I spoke in haste," he said, his voice still unsteady. "He's a fool, but he doesn't deserve death. Take him to a cell, Karn—one with no escape hatch," he added. "The regent can deal with him tomorrow."

"Yes, Your Majesty," said Karn. He picked up the sobbing servant by main force and hauled him away. Erl returned to stand behind the King's chair.

There was an awkward silence as the King took another long breath. Then he spoke again. "I apologize to you all. Guests should not have to hear such a thing from their host."

They murmured various inconsequentialities, but he spoke on through them. Damn it, Ambrosia would roast him alive for this later. Everything he could say would be swept away before the imperious storm of her displeasure. But if he spoke now she would have to listen—the farce that gave her the power of regent compelled her to listen. Her burning gray eyes told him as much.

"However," he continued, "it pains me to say that I deserved more from some of you, as guests and as subjects, than I have received tonight. Lord Urdhven, you must not countermand orders I give to my servants. This is not your castle. It is my castle. You do not rule here. I rule here. You will acknowledge this or our treaty is broken and we will fight to the last soldier."

After a short pause, Urdhven said easily, "Of course, Your Majesty. I beg your pardon, and that of all here. I let old habits lead me astray." At that moment it occurred to Lathmar that Urdhven must be dead. This smiling urbane thing was not Urdhven.

"Your Majesty is not quite correct—I beg his pardon for saying so," Kedlidor said, in his scratchy pedantic voice. "The terms 'rule' and 'reign,' though often confused—"

"You beg *my* pardon, do you?" Lathmar interrupted, some of his anger returning. "I withhold it. A moment ago you sat by and watched a servant disobey my express command and did nothing to intervene. Had you shown *then* the nice concern for propriety you show *now*, that poor man would be spending the night in his own bed instead of a prison cell. I am displeased with you, Kedlidor. Leave my presence."

Wave after wave of emotion passed over Kedlidor's face. But he was too much the Rite-Master not to acknowledge the King's right to dismiss him. He bowed his head and withdrew without a word.

You can only be killed once, the King reflected, and continued, "Lady Ambrosia, I find you too have lacked respect. Your familiarity with your brother should not blind you to the fact that when he is a guest at my table, he will not be compelled, nor cajoled, nor pestered to do this or that."

Ambrosia briefly rebelled. "Your Majesty, with respect, the last time someone made Morlock do something he didn't want to do—"

"Precisely," the King cut in. "Morlock Ambrosius can look after himself, none better. I expect *you* to look after *me*, as your sovereign—the respect due to me and to guests at my table, whether they be your closest kin or utter strangers. If I am not sovereign, then what is your office? Whose power do you wield? In whose name do you rule if I do not reign?" He paused, breathless, somewhat intoxicated by his defiance, at a loss as how to continue.

Ambrosia smiled like someone who tastes blood in her mouth. "I was wrong, Your Majesty," she said. "I apologize." And she bowed her iron-gray head.

Chapter Twenty-two

Shadows Speak

he half cup of wine that Thoke had poured remained at Morlock's elbow for the awkward remainder of the supper. Morlock kept smelling it, and more than once he had caught himself reaching out to pick it up.

On one of these occasions he looked up to see the Protector's eyes looking at him.

"Old habits die hard," he said wryly.

"I hoped they hadn't died at all," Urdhven's mouth said frankly. "But who knew the little King had such fire in him! I suspect Ambrosia will give him a paddling behind closed doors."

Morlock reflected on this for a moment, then said, "We've met before, haven't we? Earlier today?"

The smile on Urdhven's face became broader yet. "Superb. Really excellent. I had heard good things about you, you know, but I didn't see how they could all be true."

"They probably aren't."

"Oh, I'm sure of that. How did you know?"

"Just a guess. You're clearly not Urdhven."

"That is, as the little King would say, a moot point."

Urdhven's fingers reached out to take a grape. He tossed it in his mouth

and crunched it open-mouthed so that the juice squirted. He swallowed.
"Get it?"

"I got some of it," Morlock remarked, brushing away a few droplets from
his tunic.

"My dear sir, I'm so sorry. But do you see what I'm driving at? Is the
grape me, or am I the grape? That's the way it is with Urdhven and me."

Morlock looked past Urdhven's shoulder to see if Ambrosia was following
this. But she was saying something rather stiffly to Vost across the table.

"Oh, she hasn't noticed," Urdhven's mouth said. "In fact, she's going
through one of her periodic fits of Hope. She's finding them harder and
harder to suppress, I believe. That's probably what I will offer her, when the
time comes—the hope of a future without Hope, as it were."

"The time?"

"In time I expect to eat you all as I ate Urdhven. You won't know it until
it's too late, but I can get each of you to let me in, I think. And, once I'm let
in, I never leave."

"We're not all like Urdhven."

"I should hope not: one likes a little variety in the souls one eats. But you
all have fears; you all have weaknesses; you all have secret or suppressed long-
ings. Each one of them is a door, and through many of them I can enter."

Morlock shrugged.

"Don't make a pretense of your strength, Morlock! I see how you're
pressing your hands against the table to disguise their trembling. You want
that cup of wine so much! I can give you the pleasure of wine without the
poison of drunkenness. Or I can give you something you want more: I can
make it so that you never want to drink again."

"So can a sharp edge, or a noose," Morlock commented. He held up his
hands in midair, turned them palm up and palm down. They didn't tremble.

"You can exert control over your impulses for a moment, for an hour, for
part of a day—oh, day after day. But not forever. You can't guard your
dreams; I've often entered into people while they were dreaming. I wouldn't
tell you this if there were any chance of your doing something about it."

This last certainly wasn't true: he might hope to provoke fear, despair,
rash action. But Morlock wasn't about to say as much. He shrugged again.

"You're ungenerous, Morlock. And you haven't even asked me my name."

Morlock said carefully, "I know the answer your kind always gives."

Urdhven's mouth laughed politely, and his body turned away to address some remark to Ambrosia.

Morlock's left arm was gripped by Jordel, and Morlock turned to face him.

"What was Urdhven saying to you?" Jordel asked.

Morlock reflected. "Nothing," he said, with perfect if misleading accuracy. He gestured slightly with his right hand, hoping Jordel would take the hint to talk about it later.

Apparently Jordel did. "All right," the vocate muttered, releasing his arm. "It's not like you're my junior in the Graith anymore. Say, do you remember that time in the Grartans . . ."

The supper wound down to its conclusion. Ambrosia rose to escort the Protector and his followers out, throwing Lathmar a look that clearly menaced an unpleasant future conversation. Morlock thought he would have to intervene in that.

The King approached him presently and whispered, "You wouldn't have drunk, I suppose? I suppose it was all for nothing?"

"I'm not sure," he replied honestly. The boy deserved the truth. "I'm never sure when I'm offered a drink whether I'll drink or not. Anyway, it wasn't for nothing: I thank you, Lathmar. You were right about the others, too; their behavior was curious. I think I'll talk with Thoke before I go to bed, and perhaps Kedlidor as well."

"What is it?" the King whispered urgently. "That thing that pretends to be Urdhven?"

Morlock was surprised by this, but not very much. The boy's insight was becoming very sure indeed.

"He wants me to think he is a shathe," Morlock said thoughtfully. "So I naturally assume he is not. Apart from that, I'm not sure."

"If—" the King began. Then he saw Aloê approaching and he fled, throwing her a wounded look. His bodyguards followed hastily, their dress armor clanking as they ran.

Aloê was smiling indulgently as she reached Morlock. "He's very young to be a player in this sort of game," she said, nodding her head toward the departing King.

"Or perhaps you're too old," Morlock replied. "You hurt him badly tonight."

"You're soft, Morlock. But that won't do him any good."

"That's what Ambrosia says about me."

"That bitch."

"And that's what she says about you."

"Well, perhaps I am, in a good cause." She put her right hand on his chest, and he grew absolutely still. They stood that way for a few moments, oblivious of the others in the room. Then she dropped her hand to take his elbow. "And you've been very uncivil to me," she said, as if continuing a conversation they'd been having. "You haven't offered to show me your workshop."

"Would you like to see my workshop, Aloê?"

"The magical workshop of the master of all makers? I suppose it might have a certain tame interest. Since you insist, I'll accompany you there."

She did, and, in the event, he did not speak to Thoke or Kedlidor that night, as he had intended.

"You are lovely in the morning light," Morlock remarked to Aloê as she stood in the western window of his workshop, silhouetted by the dawn.

Aloê, who was aware of it, said, "I wish you were. Why is it I'm never done with you, I wonder?"

Morlock paused, then answered seriously, "You are never really done with anyone."

Aloê was touched for a moment that Morlock saw her as so loyal. She knew it was a quality he prized highly. Then she realized he was thinking about Naevros.

"You're right," she said flatly. "I can never finish things with someone and walk away—even when they're dead, or in exile. What should I do about it?"

"Nothing," said Morlock the exile, with a crooked smile. "I can offer you tea and hotcakes for breakfast. It's a long way down to the nearest kitchen."

"I suppose you cook them with the same spatula you use to measure out darkleaf and dogbane."

"No, these are strictly cooking utensils. I gave up alchemy after I invented the still—"

"The still what?"

"The still is a mechanism which purifies, concentrates, and refines certain essences. That of wine, for instance."

"Sounds lovely."

"Hm. Well, it seemed a good idea at the time. Of course, I was drunk more or less continuously back then."

She laughed as if this were a joke, although she suspected it was not. "Hotcakes are fine," she said. "Anything to put on them?"

"Wyrth's own fireberry jam."

"Hm. You're sure there's no dogbane around here? Because—"

"It's pretty good jam. Try it."

She licked it off his finger, and tasted it again on his lips, and they said nothing more for a while.

"Morlock, your hotcakes are burning."

"Eh. Oh, you mean literally. Er. Breakfast will be a few minutes late."

"Indeed it will."

The sun was well up before they finally had their hotcakes and jam. As they ate, they talked about the matter at hand. Aloê was amazed at how easy it was to talk to him and to listen to him. There was a soul-deep comfort in it, the easing of a long-felt icy pain.

"I've missed you, Morlock," she said impulsively.

"And I you."

"Once I thought—it seemed to me that you threw away everything for nothing. But now that I see you the master of this great state—"

"Wait. This state is not mine. You see me as a servant of the crown."

Aloê laughed. "That's just a legalism. Why, that boy would do anything you told him to. Anyway, we all know that it's Ambrosia who has really ruled the empire all these centuries, and now she's growing too old to do it. I was shocked when I saw her. Who can she leave the job to except you?"

Morlock looked as if this had really never occurred to him, and Aloê laughed again. "Anyway. If—"

Morlock held up a hand and looked at the window. Aloê followed his gaze and saw a crow standing there on the sill. Morlock got up and stood over it as it gasped out some croaking syllables. Morlock answered briefly in the same language, and the crow's response was briefer yet. He took a fistful of grain from a closed jar nearby and scattered it on the sill with a final croaking word. Turning away he headed for the stairway door.

"Morlock! What is it?" she called.

"The King is gone." Then so was he. She ran to follow him.

When they arrived at the Great Hall, the regent was already sitting at the head of her council. Kedlidor and Wyrth were there, along with Jordel and Baran and the King's bodyguards, Erl and Karn. Ambrosia lifted her haggard face to sneer at Morlock and Aloê as they entered.

"Now we know the night's events have passed their climax," she began, "since these lovebirds—"

"Shut up," Morlock said briefly. "A crow told me that the King was taken into the dead lands by two soldiers in royal surcoats early this morning, before dawn. The guards at the King's chamber say that no one entered there since Kedlidor, late last night."

Kedlidor nodded in confirmation. "And he was well, and alone, when I left him," the Rite-Master said. "And so—"

"Wait a minute, Morlock," Ambrosia said. "Are you suggesting that two Protector's Men stayed behind from the conference, disguised themselves as royal guards, and kidnapped the King? Because I saw them out myself."

"No, I think they really were Royal Legionaries. Or had been, before their insides were eaten. Like Kedlidor here."

Kedlidor screamed, "*I have not been eaten!*"

A brief silence followed, punctuated by the Rite-Master's sobs.

Ambrosia sighed. "I knew he was a traitor, but I thought he was one of the ordinary sort. That's why I kept him in charge of the Royal Legion—as long as the news was always good for us, always bad for Urdhven, it served to overawe him. And it worked: Urdhven signed the treaty on our terms."

"The Protector is gone, too, devoured by his Shadow." Morlock turned to Kedlidor. "You say you have not been eaten."

"I'm not. I'm not. I am still *myself*."

"But his voice is always in your head. When it speaks you must obey."

Kedlidor simply sobbed and shook his head.

"He told you what to do at the supper last night—to support the Protector when he offered me a drink," Morlock continued. "Answer or die."

"Yes."

"And later?"

"I . . . He told me to go to the King as if I were suing for pardon. So I did. He told me to bribe the guards to let me in. So I did. He told me to push the King down the escape shaft. So I did."

"And there were two eaten guards at the other end of the shaft? How were they to get him out of Ambrose?"

"I don't know. I don't know. Do you think he tells me things? I tell him things; I tell him all I know, but he doesn't tell me. He doesn't tell. Doesn't tell."

"That wasn't part of your deal, I suppose?" Morlock asked.

"You don't understand!" Kedlidor screamed. "You'll never die! I'm getting old; I've been so afraid. I didn't want much. I didn't want to live forever. I just didn't want to be afraid anymore, afraid of dying. . . ."

"I can cure that," Morlock Traitor's Bane said calmly, and stepping forward, he broke the old man's neck. He threw the body negligently on the floor.

Aloê was shocked, and shocked again that no one else was. Even Jordel and Baran seemed to approve the action.

"I suppose he knew nothing more that would be useful to us?" Ambrosia asked temperately.

"Almost certainly; there was little left of him. I suspected something of the sort last night. Kedlidor was behaving oddly, and the thing that dwelled within Urdhven's body knew of matters that had been discussed at the supper before he arrived."

"What are we up against, Morlock? Surely it's time for you to speak."

"I still think our enemy is an adept. I think, though, that he has bent his power to duplicate the abilities of a shathe. That is, he can seduce a will into destroying itself, and get sustenance from the event—and control the dying will."

"God Creator," Ambrosia said. "And he has Lathmar." She turned toward the wall to hide her face.

When she spoke without moving, a few moments later, her voice was deadly calm. "If we know our enemy, we can take steps against him. Morlock, you must see to that first thing. It is unfortunate that he has taken the King, but not fatal to us: the Protector is no longer a political force in the city, whatever has become of his soul. Wyrth, perhaps you can make an illusory King to serve for ceremonial occasions. If we can recover Lathmar, we will. But we must confront the fact that he is probably lost to us."

She turned her face back to the room again; they saw the tears streaking her face. "Morlock—Where is Morlock?"

"Eh, madam," said Wyrth. "He has gone to find the little King. What did you expect?"

CHAPTER TWENTY-THREE

THE DEAD CITY

East of the living city of Ontil is the Old City—the capital of the storied First Empire. A triple curse killed it, the empire it ruled slipped away, and its people fled. Millennia later, Ambrosia and Uthar diverted the river Tilion; on its new banks they built a new city and gave it the proud name of the old one.

But the Old City was always there, just beyond the gray curtain of the Dead Hills. They remembered it and honored it by making it the domain of the imperial heir, along with the New City.

A triple curse. A drought from the sky that had never ended, not even after millennia. A curse from the sea, the curse of the Old Gods. And a curse from the earth: a plague that drove men mad and then killed by rotting the bones and the flesh.

People still came here. To hide, because no writ ran in the Old City. To die or to await death: there was no more suitable place. To uncover the past: for here it lay open for the taking.

And now its king was coming to it, for the first time since the founding of the New Empire, Lathmar reflected.

"Carried like a sack of beans by someone else, as usual," he complained aloud. "Someday someone will figure out a better way to transport a king. I just hope I'm there to see it."

He didn't suppose that he would be, but he was speaking largely for his own entertainment anyway. His captors (two men he had known as Thurn and Veck, members of his Royal Legionaries) seemed to have only enough awareness to abduct him and carry him out of the castle and the city— literally in a sack, he believed, although he had been unconscious at the time. It was not even as if they were traitors, ashamed to make conversation with the king they had betrayed. Talking to them was like talking to rocks, to a wall, to oneself.

But now he said nothing as the skyline of his other city crept above the horizon. It was like a city in a dream, in a nightmare. A forest of stone towers rose up, but they were half-eaten by the wind, etched crookedly against the bitter blue sky. Nothing lived in the streets that they shadowed: the boulevards had been dead so long that even the dust of the dead trees had blown away. But as the King and his captors approached closer to the city, he did see one living thing lurking in the shadows: a vaguely human form, its head a hairless, shapeless mass, like a rotten gourd striped in fever-blue and pus-yellow. It fled, staggering and shrieking as they came near. A plague victim—man or woman, Lathmar couldn't tell.

Lathmar was obscurely ashamed. For centuries, this place had been here, and people like him had ruled it in name and not given it a thought in reality. He had not cursed it; his people had not cursed it, nor caused the curse. But perhaps their indifference was part of the curse—a fourth curse, adding the cruelty of man to the hatred of earth, air, and sea.

"It's not as if I can do anything about it," he muttered to his peevish, unreasonable conscience.

They turned up a street where, to his surprise, Lathmar saw some dead plants. They stood in a wedge of darker earth . . . no, a sort of reddish dark streambed that ran along the broken gutter of an ancient street.

Then plants could grow here, if there was water. Or some other fluid: Lathmar wondered what sort of runoff had given brief life to those seedlings.

He was soon to know. They followed the dark stain in the ancient street around a corner. The screen of half-eaten towers parted, and Lathmar saw what he guessed was their destination. A tower unruined (or rebuilt, he guessed) standing apart from the others in a field of stumpy ruined buildings.

Surrounding it was a hedge of thorns, and the thorns climbed like ivy up and all around the tower so that it bristled black against the blue dust-strewn sky.

How did the plants grow in this dead waterless place? The dark stain in the ground was deepest and darkest near the hedge. Nearby, tossed negligently among the bare foundations of the broken buildings, were bright bones grinning back at the sun. The bones of many men and women: hundreds of them, thousands, tens of thousands perhaps. Their blood had been shed to nourish the thorns. Some of the bodies were fresher: the King watched in horror as a crow landed on the head of one of these, plucked out one of its drying eyeballs, and gulped it down, neatly snipping the string of optic nerve with its bill. It looked right at him, rather quizzically, then bowed down to eat the other dead eyeball. Lathmar turned away shuddering.

The two soldiers who had been Thurn and Veck reined in by the hedge and dismounted. They cut the King's bonds and dragged him down to stand by them—rather unsteadily: the bindings had cut off the flow of blood, and his legs and hands were numb. Lathmar was fascinated by the hedge of thorns: the leaves were small and darkish green; the thorns were as long as Lathmar's hand, with points like daggers. They were dense and intertangled: no light passed through them.

Veck's hand raised a signal horn to Veck's mouth, which blew a single blast.

A creaking mechanical sound was heard, and then the hedge of thorn began to rise in the air. At least the section nearest them was rising. It lifted and the King saw this section of hedge was planted in huge vats; when they were clear he saw the vats were resting on a section of planking like the deck of a ship. It was being lifted from the ground by some vast screwlike mechanism. A team of corpse-golems—he knew them at a glance by their mismatched limbs and dead angelic faces—were working the wheel that drove the screw.

The soldiers dragged the King down the sloping blood-brown earth left clear by the lifted thorns. As they passed, the one that had been Veck lifted the horn and blew another blast. The corpse-golems stopped, turned, and began to push the wheel the other way. The section of thorn-hedge behind them slowly began to descend again.

They walked on to the tower bristling with thorns. There was no place to enter, but the soldiers stopped just below a bare patch, some fifteen feet up the wall. The soldier that had been Veck blew two blasts on the signal horn. The bare patch of wall opened on darkness, and presently a stairway began to unfold downwards to the accompaniment of unmusical clanks.

The King took special care to look at the sky as they ascended the stair; he guessed it would be the last time he would ever see it. There wasn't much to see: the dark blue bar of the sea to the south, some black birds hovering in the west over the Dead Hills. He paused at the top of the stairs, reluctant to surrender the light. But the empty-faced soldiers simply dragged him into the tower.

There were two teams of corpse-golems here, one team in each chamber on either side of the broad windowless corridor within. They were still straining mindlessly against their wheels, striving to lower a stairway that was already lowered. The one that had been Veck blew two blasts on the signal horn as they passed. (The sound was painfully loud in the echoing corridor, but only Lathmar seemed to be aware of it.) The corpse-golems stopped; they stood; they turned and began to push their wheels in the opposite direction, lifting the stairway. (The King wondered if they would continue to try and raise it after it was all the way up, straining at the wheels until someone told them to reverse directions again.)

The blank-faced soldiers took him up a long series of stairways to the top of the tower. He was out of breath by the time they reached there—if he ever fell behind they simply seized him by the arms and dragged him till he took to his feet again.

At the top of the last stairway the King found himself standing in what was obviously an antechamber. There was a monumental door flanked by two enormous particolored winged beings Lathmar took at first for remarkably ill-made gargoyles. Then one looked at him with mismatched eyes (one red and round, another narrow and slitlike, with a black iris peering through). Lathmar looked away, shuddering from fear and exhaustion.

The soldiers halted and stared at nothingness. They waited there without words. Then the huge winged beings stood, and together they lifted the huge stone slab (which the King had taken for a door) away from the doorway.

Within the empty place was a shadowy form. It gestured at the King with long, ropy fingers.

The soldiers pushed him and he staggered, almost falling. Then he pulled himself up and strode forward into the emptiness. He heard the soldiers march after him into the chamber beyond.

"Steng, I believe?" the King said to the shadowy form. He tried to keep his voice cool, but the tone wavered; he was tired and he was frightened. But he didn't let that stop him. As a king, as a ruler in the proud tradition of Vraidish conquerors, he might be a complete failure. But he'd die like a king, at least, never giving in. "I believe I had the pleasure of your company once or twice at Ambrose, though of course we were never formally introduced."

The form laughed, in a voice that was very much like Steng's . . . or was it? It was phlegmier, somehow—creakier.

"So you have, Lathmar," the other replied, "in a way, although I'm not Steng. I'm the original on which Steng was modeled. He was made in my own image. Don't you find that amusing? But perhaps you haven't heard that one. I forget which religions are current in these parts."

There was a crash as the stone slab was set back into place, sealing the room.

It was a broad open chamber, with a work desk and chair, and other furniture harder to name scattered about. There was a hole in the middle of the floor with spiral stairs leading down to a lower level. The room was well lit by a line of floor-length windows opening onto a balcony. But the other was standing with his back to these. The King stepped around him to inspect him more closely.

This certainly was not Steng. His right shoulder was hiked even higher than Morlock's; his hair was stringy and gray; the tip of his nose and the ends of his fingers seemed to have rotted away. But, in spite of that, the resemblance was striking.

The other, meanwhile, was inspecting the King equally closely, wagging his head as in disbelief.

"No, no," he said. "Incredible. Anyway, I can hardly believe it."

After several minutes of this, the King said, as sharply as his shaky voice allowed, "Well?"

"Well?" the other echoed.

"Aren't you going to tell me why you brought me here?" the King demanded, striving (and failing) to get something like the authentic Ambrosian rasp.

The other seemed surprised. "Tell you . . . ? Oh, no. I don't think so. I mean, what's in it for me? And what good would it do you, really?"

"I'd like to know."

"People make that mistake all the time. 'Better to know the worst!' they say, and then, you know, they blame you simply because they get what they think they wanted. No, I've done with that. I don't give people what they think they want, and I don't give them what they want. I give them what I want. It's easier and there's less fuss and screaming and things."

"What would you do if I started screaming?" asked the King, wondering if he could reach this oddly sensitive semicorpse through his finer feelings.

"Kill you," the other said briefly. "I'll tell you why I *didn't* bring you here. Some of me said, 'Oh, transfer into a young body this time—the little King, wouldn't that be amusing? Why, we could be Emperor after all, after everything.' But others of me, and I'm with them, they said, 'No, take someone like Morlock, or the dwarf or Ambrosia. Even if they're slightly killed they'll last better than the little King.' And these of me are clearly right. You're practically ordinary: an Ontilian man in the street, junior size."

Somewhat confused by this, the King said, "Transfer to Gr—I mean, to Ambrosia's body—"

"Don't call her Grandmother," the other said, with every appearance of jealousy. "I hate it when you do that. You've no right, you know. She's not *your* grandmother; she's *my* grandmother. Anyway," he said, cooling off slightly, "she was the grandmother of my first body. I suppose the matter is somewhat more complicated now."

"You're not . . . not in your original body, then?"

"Well, I am and I'm not. That's the interesting thing. Even if I transferred into your body, I'd soon look like this again. The mind is subject to the body in many mundane ways, but the body yields to the mind, too. My talic imprint compels any body I wear to assume this form. Why, take this very body—it was female when I took it up, very recently dead, quite fresh and comfortable. Now it's quite male. It even has a penis. Would you like to see it?"

"No."

"Hm. No, I suppose you're right. My circulation is failing rather badly in the extremities, and I don't think I could bear to look at it myself."

The adept shrugged his crooked shoulders and turned away.

"The thorns could use some fresh blood," he said thoughtfully, looking at the two soldiers.

They walked together past the table and chair by the windows out onto the balcony. Once there, the one who had been Thurn killed the one who had been Veck. Then he slit the dead body's throat and upended it, so that the blood ran down the side of the thorn-covered tower.

There was a heavy scraping sound, and the King turned to see the other walking through the open doorway.

"What am I supposed to do?" he asked, ashamed of the piteous tone in his voice.

"It doesn't matter," said the other dismissively, and the gargoyles replaced the huge stone slab.

"It doesn't matter," the King said fiercely. "Doesn't matter." Of course, it didn't—it was what Morlock and Ambrosia did that would matter. That was why he had been kidnapped—as a distraction.

Ambrosia would not be distracted, he was sure. With the removal of the Protector, there was no other center for power than the one she chose to create. He, the King, had already proved to her that he might be more of a nuisance than an asset.

But Morlock would leave everything and come to get him—would come here, now. He could hear Wyrth saying, *Blood has no price!* as he stood there. Whereas Morlock never said it, anymore than he said blood was red, or the sea was deep, or the sky was up there in that sort of direction. Loyalty was his life. He would come, and the Protector's Shadow would have him. (Lathmar suddenly remembered the crow he had seen eating eyeballs outside this tower.) Morlock might be on his way here at this moment.

So the King would have to escape. He stepped over to the balcony, but he saw without surprise that the way was blocked. Even if he could contrive a rope, the thorns would cut him to shreds. The empty-faced body of Thurn was still holding the corpse of Veck over the thorns, watering them with the drizzle of his blood; the live soldier showed no more awareness of the King's presence than the dead one. He only knew he felt easier the farther he was from them.

There was no chance he could move the stone slab blocking the entrance. It took both the gargoyles together to do that. It occurred to the King that the Protector's Shadow was afraid of something—that this whole chamber was designed to protect something important. Whatever that might be, it wasn't obviously present on the upper level, so he went down to the lower one.

There were no windows on the lower level—apparently no doorway, either, although it was too dark to be sure. There were a few tables—almost like vats on metal stands—which shone by their own faint light. Lathmar stepped toward the nearest one.

Woozy with disgust, he saw in the vat a brain, a heart, a pair of lungs— other organs he could not identify. They were not dead: the heart beat, the veins in the brain pulsed, the lungs breathed in and out. They were alive— placed here beyond the reach of danger. The Protector's own? Or . . . those of the adept, yes. That made a good deal of sense. With these kept safe he could not be killed, any more than Morlock had been able to kill the Protector on the bridge.

The King raised his fist to break the crystal covering the vat, paused, then lowered his hand without striking. The adept would not have left him here if there were any real danger that he could do harm.

There was a snuffling, whuffling sound in the shadows across the room, near another gently glowing vat. The King was suddenly frightened, and he fled back up the stairs.

He was nowhere nearer escape, he reflected, at the top of the stairs. He looked at the two soldiers. Then he thought . . .

"Stupidest idea anyone has ever had," the King muttered to himself. "Mad pigs aren't in the running." It was the only idea he could come up with, though.

Lathmar crept toward the soldier that had been Thurn, picking up the chair from the worktable as he went. The soldier that had been Thurn did not react when the King struck him on the back of the head with it; it took several more blows before he dropped Veck's dead body and began to stagger. The King went on hitting him till he fell, until the chair was in fragments.

He stripped Thurn's body. With a curtain rope he bound Thurn's legs, with the knees drawn up to the chest. Then he took off his flowing nightshirt and put it on the soldier's body; he heaved the dead or unconscious form up on a couch and turned it so that the blank face was against the wall.

"God Sustainer, what a fool I am to think anyone would be deceived by this!" he muttered, but of course he didn't think they would be. Eventually, someone would come for Veck's body. It all depended on what came through that doorway when the gargoyles opened it. If it was the Protector's Shadow or one of his minions, the Companions of Mercy, then he was doomed. If it was one of these things like Veck or Thurn had become—empty, but capable of action at some obscure prompting—then he was unsure what would happen, what they *could* notice. But if corpse-golems came through the door, he might have a chance.

Getting into the mad-pig spirit of the thing, he took the other curtain rope and the fragments of the chair he had broken and made a pair of stilts, binding them to his legs. Getting up on them, he found he could walk reasonably well. Not with perfect naturalness, but who did, in this city of the dead?

He quickly put on Thurn's tunic and armor and spent some time walking around in them. The boots and iron greaves, both carefully laced to the wood, covered the stilts, and the soldier's tunic didn't leave much of his legs bare. They weren't quite a man's legs yet, but . . . they might pass a quick inspection, even if the eyes had a living awareness behind it.

He drew the soldier's short pointed blade and tried a thrust. Immediately he lost his balance and fell on his side. Laboriously, painfully, he regained his stance, reflecting that he wouldn't fight any duels while standing on stilts, not if he could help it.

What was he forgetting? He paced across the room once or twice (for practice) while he mulled it over. Of course! The signal horn!

Lathmar heard the stone slab scraping behind him as he strode over to the balcony. He bent down over Veck's body and grabbed the horn, yanking it to break the thong that attached it to the dead soldier's uniform. He straightened and turned as forms began to walk through the empty doorway behind him.

Two corpse-golems. One for Veck and one for Thurn. The King nearly panicked, wondering if they were to kill and drain Thurn as Thurn had drained Veck. He wondered if he could fight them off while he was standing on stilts. . . .

They stood before him and paused, as if waiting for orders. Should he speak? he wondered. Clearly not; he'd heard no one but the Protector's Shadow speak since last night. He gestured at Veck's corpse, slumped over the rail of the balcony.

The two corpse-golems picked up the dead body and carried it away. It left a ribbon of red blood behind it; the King hoped this wasn't unusual. He followed in an imitation of a military stride that was stilted in every sense.

He did not dare turn to see how the two gargoyles were looking at him. Would they notice him? Could they notice him? They didn't seem to be mere automatons. But did they know or perceive enough to penetrate his disguise? He didn't know. There was little he could do but play the scene out. He followed the corpse-golems to the stairway and averted his face when he had to turn.

When they had descended several flights of stairs the King began to breathe a little easier. But he wasn't out yet. It was likely that the corpse-golems had instructions to kill him down below, to water the thorns. Clearly the adept considered Thurn and Veck mere waste matter, a fact that bothered the King on several levels, though there was no time to think about it now.

The King tried to think about nothing as he did what he had to do next. He drew his sword and beheaded the seraphic, emptily smiling corpse-golem nearest him.

The effort sent him staggering against a wall; when he recovered he saw that the headless golem had proceeded heedlessly on its way, still holding up its share of Veck's dead body.

The King had expected that, though it unnerved him. He stumbled to catch up and, when he had, reached down into the severed neck and grasped the name-scroll in the chest cavity. He pulled it out through the neck and the golem fell, shorn of its pseudolife, at his feet.

The other corpse-golem paused for a moment, then proceeded to drag Veck's body down the stairway. The King, gagging, disabled it the same way he had the other. Then he proceeded down the long stairway alone.

He came finally to the corridor where he had entered the tower. The teams of corpse-golems were leaning motionless on their wheels, as if resting. He hated to do it—hated to draw attention to himself in any way whatever. But he lifted the signal horn to his lips and gave two blasts.

The corpse-golems sprang to movement, if not to life. They turned their wheels; the wall at the end of the corridor rasped open; the iron stair began to unfold downward on its chains.

Lathmar waited until the stair was completely unfolded and the golems stopped. He descended the stairs, wobbling as he went but neither hurrying nor lingering. After he stepped off he turned and blew two blasts of the horn again. As he turned away the iron stair began to fold upward again.

The King strode stiff-legged toward the hedge gate. He stood by the wheel and blew the single blast. These golems, too, responded, turning the wheel to lift the section of hedge, the only remaining barrier between him and escape. He could see daylight on the far side.

Then, without any visible or audible command, the golems stopped. Each golem turned its sweet dead face to the King and stared at him with dead mismatched eyes.

His disguise was broken. Perhaps someone had found the golems and Veck's body on the stairs; perhaps it had been the signal to open the hedge gate. Either way, they knew him.

But the way was open and he took it, charging up the blood-brown slope of bare earth. The wheel began to turn again, dropping the hedge on top of him.

He rolled clear, and drawing his sword, he slashed the bindings of the greaves and the ropes holding his legs to the stilts. Then he shook them off (greaves, stilts, and boots) and jumped to his feet. He ran barefoot into the dead city, shedding armor behind him as he ran.

Would he escape from an army controlled by the demonic presence who ruled the tower of thorns, in a city they knew and he didn't? It seemed extremely unlikely. The only thing that heartened him, that helped him run faster and longer than he ever had before, was the fact that the odds had been even longer that he wouldn't ever escape the tower, and he had.

Think I'll make a mad pig my heraldic banner, he thought as he dashed up a crooked alley half blocked by ruins. He threw himself to the ground between two piles of rubble so that he could rest, and breathe, and listen.

He heard some groups of marching feet, or thought he did, but they didn't seem especially near, or headed toward him, so he stayed put and thought.

What would they do? What would *he* do, if he had all that manpower (to use the term loosely) at his disposal?

The answer was clear: flood the streets of the city and cordon off the Dead Hills westward. The direction they would be least concerned with would be southward, toward the harbor of the Old City. Those streets were supposedly haunted by the curse of the Old Gods, the curse that came from the sea. But he would have to risk it. The sea might provide some protection from the magic of the Protector's Shadow. Besides, no one believed in the Old Gods of Ontil anymore. Did they?

Well, he had his wind back; he should move south before the streets were all blocked. He rose to his feet, and a black-cloaked figure dropped down on him from a window above.

Desperately, the King stabbed at it with his sword (Thurn's sword, really), landing a serious but not immediately fatal wound where his assailant's neck joined its body.

The dark figure, whose hands were incredibly quick and strong, snatched the sword from his hand and hissed, "Well struck! But I'm on your side."

"Morlock! God Avenger, forgive me!"

"More to the point, perhaps, I do. I am amazed to see you alive, much less free, my friend."

"Well, I sort of blundered into it. Or out of it."

"Tell me later." Morlock was tearing a strip from his cloak, and the King took it to bind across his neck to the opposite armpit as a makeshift bandage. "You looked as if you were headed somewhere," Morlock commented, while he was doing this.

"I thought I'd go south—follow the seacoast back to the living city."

Morlock nodded slowly. "A good plan," he said. "But you'd have been killed by the curse of the Old Gods."

Now it was Lathmar's turn to hesitate. "Do you believe in the Old Gods of Ontil?" he asked.

"Of course not."

The King nodded, relieved.

"I just believe in their curse," said the Crooked Man. "But that's the way we'll go: I've brought along some cloaks of invisibility."

"Wonderful!" said the King.

"Oh, no. Quite ordinary. It occurred to me the last time I saw it." He paused. "I'm fairly sure they'll work."

The sudden burst of confidence the King had felt was oozing away almost as rapidly. Saw what? Only "fairly sure" they'd work?

"Let's go, then." Morlock stood, a little unsteadily.

"The streets—" Lathmar began.

"No: we go up. I suspect I can get us to the old harbor across rooftops—or, at any rate, above ground."

And he did. Four years ago the King might have been incapable of following Morlock's lead, but he had grown a good deal since then, and his fencing teachers had worked him hard. Leaping from roof to roof (or, on occasion, window to window) was not so very difficult. But navigating within the ruinous buildings was tricky indeed. There was rarely anything like a floor left, and those that remained were almost never to be trusted. They followed the lines of supporting walls and inner buttresses, walking like tightrope artists. It was rare that Morlock could not find a path over even the most treacherous surface, and when he could not he found a way around. His wisdom in avoiding the streets was amply shown before they had gone more than a block: the streets were full of marching corpse-golems, captained by red-cloaked Companions of Mercy.

But the King couldn't help notice that Morlock was growing weaker. The wound in his neck continued to bleed, and whenever Lathmar suggested they stop to tend to it, Morlock shook his head, winced, and said, "No time."

Finally they reached an open area where there were no buildings. By then it was getting dark.

"We've made good time," Morlock said, sitting down—or perching, rather—at the juncture of a wall and a support beam. "We should wait here until full dark."

"Then we have time to tend to your wound," the King said, relieved. Every time the Crooked Man had paused or winced, he had felt pangs of guilt.

"Time, yes. But I don't have anything with me for wounds."

"Oh."

They waited. Finally, it was dark enough to satisfy Morlock. He reached into the wallet at his belt and drew forth a faintly glowing, slimy piece of webwork. "Stand still," he said as the King flinched.

"What is it?"

"Your cloak of invisibility. Although it's more of a shawl, I suppose."

The King stood still while Morlock tossed it over his shoulders.

"When does it start working?" the King asked anxiously. He heard many shuffling feet not so very far away; it seemed to him they would want the invisibility in short order.

Morlock eyed him critically. "It is working," he said authoritatively.

"But you can still see me?"

"Of course."

Lathmar repressed a sigh. If Morlock didn't know what he was doing they were dead anyway.

Morlock took a second piece of greenish glowing webwork from his wallet and tossed the slimy thing across his own shoulders. The King noticed that it glowed more strongly at one place than at any other, and that the greenish luminescence was carried not only by the webwork but (more faintly) all over Morlock.

Morlock met the King's eye and nodded. They dropped to the ground and ran for the edge of the harbor.

The King saw a company of corpse-golems stumble into the strangely open harbor area from the north. And there was another to the east—Death and Justice, there were crowds of them, even some coming from the west. They were surrounded. The sea was heaving strongly—surprisingly so, given how quiet the wind was. The King didn't think it would be safe to swim in it. And, anyway, maybe corpse-golems could swim.

Perhaps the cloaks of invisibility would get them out of this, but they seemed strangely ineffective. The several groups of corpse-golems, with their red-garbed captains, were heading directly for them.

"Morlock," he said, "I think they can see us."

"Of course they can," Morlock said, somewhat surprised. "We're glowing in the dark, you know."

"Then—"

The sea was raging as if there were a storm, though the sky was still as death, as clear as melting ice, lit by the clashing light of the three moons. But there was a light in the water that did not come from the sky—a greenish light, many greenish lights, rising from the heart of the sea.

The lights broke through the troubled surface of the water. They were eyes—great, filmy, glowing eyes, belonging to the heads of huge snakelike beings rising in anger from the waves.

The heads were shaped like great mallets: below each eye was a great flat snout like the striking surface of a hammer. There was no mouth that the King, staring at the beasts with his own mouth hanging open, could see.

They reared up high, staring with their glowing green eyes at the ground below, and then they fell. They fell like hammers, striking again and again at the intruders in the harbor. They smashed the corpse-golems; they smashed the Companions that led them; the great mallet-heads made the ground shake and opened up great cracks in the earth.

But they left Morlock and the King alone. The cloaks, Lathmar realized—the cloaks covering them with dim green luminescence, pulsing at the same rate as the serpents' own eyes (and *they* all pulsed at the same rate, he noticed, like many limbs fed by a single heart). For these eyes, they were cloaks of invisibility.

The King's pursuers by now had all been destroyed or fled. The serpents continued to pummel the ground in frustrated, unsated rage and finally, one by one, slipped back into the troubled sea, which slowly grew dark and calm again.

"What was it?" the King gasped.

Morlock nodded approval at his use of the singular. "It," he said, "was the curse of the Old Gods."

"I guessed as much, but what was it really?"

Morlock shrugged, winced, "That would really be a guess. Mine is: it's a security device."

"A security device!"

"A failed one," Morlock added. "The Old Ontilians had a reputation as grandiose but inept makers."

"Against who?"

"Pirates. The Anhikhs. The children of Kaen. The old Ontilian Empire didn't control the coast of the entire Sea of Stones, so their capital was subject to dangers that yours isn't."

"They made it to protect them," the King muttered to himself. "And it killed their city."

"The drought," Morlock observed.

"The river ran through the city then. The dead land could have been irrigated."

"The plague."

The King nodded and spread his hands concessively. But even as he did so he was wondering if the Old Ontilians, those *grandiose but inept makers*, had somehow unintentionally wrought the plague and the drought. The drought, after all, could have been an attempt to bring perpetual fair weather to the capital city and its environs. And the plague?

"Were there armies threatening Old Ontil by land?" the King asked.

Morlock smiled wryly, his face weirdly lit by greenish light. "Astute," he observed. "Not armies, exactly. But there was the perpetual threat of raids by barbarian tribes from the north."

"Then the plague was meant as a protection against land invasion—meant to strike only outsiders?" the King asked eagerly, then something Morlock had said struck him in a different way. "Barbarians from the north?

Including my ancestors, the Vraidish tribes? *We* are responsible for the plague?"

"Guilt is not inheritable," Morlock said firmly. "I learned that the hard way, Lathmar. Anyway, if your guess (and mine) is correct, the Old Ontilians did this to themselves and died for their folly. That's the end of it."

"Except this place is still here. Death and Justice, someday I'm going to come back here and break the curses—rebuild the city, or bury it."

"If you live through the night."

The King fell silent. Morlock led the way westward along the edge of the water, past the greasy squashed remains of several bands of corpse-golems. Past the smashed, cracked plain of the harbor region, they discarded their cloaks but did not take to the buildings again. Indeed, there were few to take refuge in: they had come to the edge of the Old City, where the Dead Hills ran down to the sea.

Presently, at some cue the King could not perceive, Morlock turned right and took a northwest course into the Dead Hills. They came, finally, to the mouth of a cave in the western face of a hill.

"Velox," Morlock said. "Trann."

Two horses came out of the darkness, saddled and ready for riding: Morlock's black, silver-eyed Velox and another—a chestnut gelding with white markings.

"From your stables," Morlock said. "Lathmar, this is Trann. He's not as friendly as poor old Ibann, but he's a sturdy, obedient beast, and we have a hard ride ahead of us."

Riding was one part of the royal education that had been skimped in recent years. Lathmar's parents had still been alive, he reflected grimly, the last time he was astride even a pony. But he shrugged, in a self-consciously Ambrosian gesture. He could do it if he had to, he guessed—and he guessed he had to. After a couple of false tries, he managed to get up in Trann's saddle.

Meanwhile, Morlock carefully put his head back and spoke three croaking syllables into the moonslit sky. A black bird came and sat on his outstretched hand. Morlock tied what appeared to be a tiny scroll on the crow's left leg. After a few croaking syllables were exchanged between the dark man and the dark bird, the crow flew off westward in the night.

Morlock turned and gestured to his horse, which approached him. He bowed his head to speak. The King heard only, ". . . nearly done . . ." and ". . . must get us there . . ." Morlock straightened slowly and, with an effort that clearly cost him pain, leaped into the saddle.

Velox, without prompting, trotted westward into the Dead Hills. The King shook his reins and persuaded Trann to follow.

It was late, but the living city was alive with light. The long war between the King and the Protector was over, and the people were celebrating the victory of the side they had secretly favored. Earlier in the day a disturbing rumor had passed through the city: that in a last attempt to gain the victory, the Protector's forces had kidnapped the young King and taken him to the dead city. Nearly spontaneous riots burst out against anyone showing the Protector's colors or known to be a supporter of the Protector.

Then word came that the King had been rescued by his terrible minister, the Crooked Man, who had gone to the dead city and slain the Protector in single combat, just as he had slain the Red Knight years ago. The regent dispatched a body of troops to bring the King and the other one, the dark man, safely home.

Now there was feasting and merrymaking throughout the city, but especially on Castle Street, the broad way that led from the Great Market to the City Gate of Ambrose. Here the King would surely pass on his way back to Ambrose, and the people of the city crowded along it to see him.

The regent, Ambrosia Viviana, watched the royal progress from the wall above the portcullis of Ambrose's outer City Gate. There were soldiers along either side of the road, but the truth was that they didn't have enough soldiers to line the street. Citizens thronged the road in front of the King. But they gave way before him.

"Have they got a couple of soldiers pushing people out of the way?" she asked Wyrth, who was standing beside her. "I hope not. This is Lathmar's chance to make a good impression on the people; it's worth a little delay."

"Eh, madam, I see none of that," the dwarf answered. "The people seem to be falling back of their own will."

They waited, Ambrosia wearing a face of ceremonial calm, Wyrth fidgeting.

Then the dwarf laughed. "Do you see it, madam?"

"Not very clearly," admitted the terrible old lady.

"The crowd surges forward; they want to see the King, to touch him perhaps. Do the people still believe that the King's touch will cure illness?"

"Some people will believe anything."

"Anyhow, they surge forward; they stop; they give way. Here: one is almost to the King; she looks beyond him and steps back. Morlock is there, with Tyrfing drawn, glaring at all who come near. God Sustainer—he's hurt."

"Who? Lathmar?"

"No, no—he seems well. You might think he'd be tired of cheers by now, but he's waving his hand and drinking it all in. It's Morlock—he's pale as a ghost, and there's a dark place on his shoulder—bloodstain, I think."

"Neck wound, maybe. They can be ugly. You brought the healing gear?"

"It's below in the guardhouse; the vocates are there. They all know leechcraft—better than I do, anyway."

They didn't speak. The heart of the cheering crowd grew nearer. Ambrosia could see Lathmar clearly now. He wore nothing but a torn brown soldier's tunic, but he had a kind of majesty about him. She was surprised at how grown-up he looked. There were tears in his eyes, tears running down his face, but he held his head like a man. Perhaps he could indeed rule, and not just reign, but she doubted it.

Wyrth was clearly right about Morlock. It was fear of the Crooked Man that kept the crowd at bay, but Ambrosia didn't see as they did. She looked at his pale face and dark-ringed staring eyes and thought, *"Blood loss."* She saw the sword wavering in his hands, his unsteadiness in the saddle, and she knew he was not far from collapse. Her brother was wounded, and this silly parade had delayed his healing.

The King finally reached the City Gate of Ambrose.

"Friend or foe?" she cried, giving the formal challenge.

"Your King returns. Open the gate!" cried Lathmar, obviously enjoying himself. The crowd thought it a good line as well, roaring its approval.

The soldiers on the gate began to raise the portcullis without waiting for Ambrosia's signal. The King rode forward and the crowd would gladly have followed, but Morlock wheeled his horse around and extended the cursed blade Tyrfing. Chastened, they fell back. Without evident command, Velox backed, step by step, over the threshold of the gate.

"Drop the portcullis when he's through," Ambrosia told the gate captain, and plunged down the stairwell.

She met Lathmar on the stairs. "Well met, Lathmar," she said, kissing his forehead. "I didn't hope to see you again. You'd better talk to the crowd."

"What should I say?" asked Lathmar, becoming less kinglike in the regent's presence, as usual.

"Tell them a bedtime story. Tell them to get home. Get out of my damn way." She hurried past him.

The King's horse (old Trann, it looked like) was standing nervously in the stairwell entrance. As Ambrosia pushed him out of the way, Morlock half dismounted, half fell from Velox's saddle. Wyrth dragged him toward the guardhouse, and Ambrosia ran up to assist him, careful not to touch Morlock's wounded shoulder.

"You stupid son of a bitch," she hissed in his face. "I'm getting sick of this. You go off to dance on the edge of chaos and we get to pick up the pieces as usual. Next time you'll listen to me or you can fucking rot. God Avenger destroy you, I hate your fucking guts!"

He kissed her tearstained cheek, and his eyes closed. The Guardians took him then and laid him on a table. Baran took shears and cut his blood-stiffened clothes away; Aloê took needle and thread and sewed up the tear in his flesh. Jordel anointed him with drugs to help him sleep, to heal his flesh, to restore his blood.

From outside they sometimes heard the King speaking to the crowd, sometimes heard the crowd roaring in response.

"I think he'll be all right, madam," Wyrth said finally to Ambrosia, who had sat silently weeping as the Guardians worked on Morlock.

"Who cares if he is?" Ambrosia said harshly. "We'd all be better off if he died now. Less to worry about."

"He'll outlive us all, madam."

"I hope so," she said dully. "I mean, I suppose so." After a pause, she continued in the same lifeless voice, "It's just that he's all I have left. Uthar is dead, and my mother is probably dead, and my father is lost to me—worse than if he were dead. People are born and grow old and die, century after century, and the new faces can never mean to me what the old ones did. And Morlock is the last, and maybe he was always the most important. Even more important than Uthar. Don't tell anyone, will you?" she said with a shaky smile.

"Your secret is safe with me, madam," the dwarf assured her solemnly.

The Guardians had taken Morlock to his room, and Wyrth had gone with them to watch over his master while he slept. Ambrosia was waiting at the bottom of the stairs with her arms crossed.

"Well," she asked, "what did you tell them?"

Lathmar looked her in the eye. "The truth."

Ambrosia grunted. "Be more specific."

"I told them the Protector was an agent of a sorcerer in the dead city. I told them the battle was not over yet. I told them how to recognize a corpse-golem and some things to do about them. I told them to beware of Companions of Mercy. I told them to burn their dead."

Ambrosia sighed. "All well said. If it had been said around the time you were born it might have done some good."

The King shrugged. "I was wondering," he said after a moment, "if he might not have a better claim than I do."

"Why?"

"He says he's your grandson."

"So are—Wait, you mean my *actual* grandson, the son of my son or daughter?"

"As I understood him, yes. He seems to be horribly old, rotting away. I mean—" he said, suddenly worried she might be offended.

She held up her hand. "You'd better tell me the whole story. Have you eaten or drunk?"

Lathmar suddenly felt faint. "Not since last night—it was—you wouldn't—"

"Never mind. Let's hit the kitchens; you can tell your tale between bites."

That was what they did. But early on in the tale she called for Erl and sent him off in search of Steng. It was clear he could tell them more if he would.

Erl looked for Steng most of that night. The poisoner had fled from the Markethall Barracks that morning during the general uprising against the Protector's people. Toward morning, Wyrth joined Erl with a drawing of the poisoner and they searched together through the slums of the city.

It was nearing dawn when they found a landlady who said she had rented a room yesterday afternoon to someone who looked like the man in Wyrth's picture.

"And now I've a question for you," she screamed after them as they ran up the stairs of her house. "Do you know what time it is?"

They went to the room the woman had described and kicked in the door. It was too late: Steng was dead.

Extremely dead.

The battle-scarred Erl hissed and drew back, his throat clenching with disgust. But Wyrth moved forward, drawn by technical interest. Steng had apparently hung some sort of weighted device from the ceiling. It was a pair of knives that rotated laterally. He had released it and stood in its path. Wyrth recognized the nose, a few ropy fingers, the hair. But Steng was now a bloody ruin.

"Why?" Erl gasped.

Wyrth thought he knew but said nothing. Time enough to ruin Erl's day later on—to tell him that there was indeed a fate worse than the death Steng had chosen.

There was a note.

He says he's done with me—that I'm no use to him now. He'll eat me or cut me up and make me a golem. I won't let him. There was no address or signature.

"What does it mean?" Erl asked.

"Nothing good," said Wyrth. "We'd better get this back to Ambrose." They ran back down the stairs, pausing only to drop some gold in the outstretched palms of Steng's screaming landlady.

"Did you say something?" Erl called to Wyrth as they were riding through the Great Market.

Wyrth, too occupied in staying atop his horse to attempt a witticism, replied briefly, "No."

"I thought I heard somebody saying something."

Wyrth thought the same, but he didn't say so.

Later they learned it had started even then.

Chapter Twenty-Four

The Dying City

"B e quiet, can't you?" Morlock muttered. "Trying to sleep."

"You've been sleeping for three days. Aren't you hungry? Aren't you thirsty?"

"Not for *that*."

"What are you referring to?"

"If—" Morlock sat up in bed and looked around. Wyrth was sitting at the right side of his bed in a circle of lamplight, a book open in his lap.

"I dreamed the adept was talking to me," muttered Morlock.

"It wasn't just a dream," Wyrth replied. "Anyway, we've all been hearing voices, awake or asleep."

"Thousands of them. But somehow all the same voice."

"Yes. Inglonor and the ones he has eaten."

"Inglonor. How did you learn his name?"

"It's a guess. He told Lathmar that he was Ambrosia's grandson, and of course that narrowed it down a bit."

"Hm. It wasn't like a dream, though—it was as if he was actually here, speaking to me."

"Well—where?"

Morlock gestured to the other side of the bed. Wyrth held up the lamp.

And there was somebody there, crouched down in the shadows. Wyrth put down the lamp and jumped across the bed, catching the other as it tried to flee.

The other laughed as Wyrth caught it by the shoulders. "I'll come for you all, soon," it said, and reaching up to grab its own throat, neatly broke its own neck. Wyrth let it go and it fell to the floor.

"Another for the corpse-fire in the gardens," he remarked.

Morlock was getting out of bed.

"Hey," said Wyrth.

"As it happens, I am hungry, and thirsty too. And it looks as if you have much to tell me."

"That's true enough," Wyrth conceded. He rang for the hall attendant while Morlock dressed.

"Treb," he said, when the attendant appeared, "it's another one of those." He gestured at the dead body.

"Sure it's dead?" said Treb.

"It broke its own neck."

"I've seen that trick before. Pretends to kill itself, and when you're not looking its sneaking off." Treb drew a long knife and passed it through the corpse's heart and neck. "*Now* it's dead." He deftly wrapped a cloth around the wounded neck to absorb the trickle of blood.

Wyrth nodded solemnly. "Better safe than sorry."

"Nice. Witty. One of your own?"

"Take the meat and go," said Wyrth, slapping him on the shoulders. (Treb was not too tall, so he could just manage it.) Treb, grinning, hauled the body away.

"That man," Morlock said, when Treb had gone, "has never before spoken in my presence."

"And tonight you were half-naked, and so especially terrifying."

"Wrong half for that," Morlock observed mildly, pulling on a tunic.

Wyrth waved his hands. "Fine. Tonight everyone makes game of Wyrth. Just so I'm forewarned. And forewarned is foreskinned—no, enough of that."

"Yes."

"It could be he's not scared of you because you are now a national hero, having rescued the young King."

"Hm. I think he might have made it back by himself. He's a resourceful young man."

Wyrth rolled his eyes. "Ambrosia considers him a bad-tempered and useless overgrown boy."

"That almost clinches it, I'd say."

"The other reason Treb isn't frightened of you . . . Well, it's been a long three days, Morlock. . . ."

It had begun for Genjandro three nights before. He had been settling his secret accounts with Vora, who kept his house and both sets of books—the ones for the merchant "Alkhendron" (his public face) and those for the spymaster Genjandro. She had been one of his agents, and a good one, too, but she had started to get nervous in the field and was making mistakes. So he had brought her in to work under his wing, and both of his businesses had prospered because of it.

"And something extra for Taan and Olis," he said. "They did far more than asked on this last job."

"Ugh," said Vora sadly. "You'll never put the spying business on a paying basis, Master Alkhendron."

"That's the treasury's problem," he observed, smiling. "If they want something, they have to pay for it. And you can call me Genjandro, now," he reminded her.

"Eh? Oh, that's right—it's your real name, isn't it? I can't get used to it. Are you going to go on being a spy, now that the war against the Protector is over?"

"Maybe," Genjandro said meditatively. "But not in the city. If Ambrosia and the King want to spy on their citizens, that's their business, but I won't be a part of it. On the other hand, I don't see why I can't import information as well as rugs and whatnot from Anhi."

Vora nodded, and they returned to their sums, working in silence.

"What?" Vora asked presently.

"I beg your pardon, my dear?"

"Did you say something? I thought you said something."

"No."

Vora nodded slowly. "Then you didn't hear anything?"

"No," Genjandro said firmly. This wasn't quite true. It was almost as if someone were whispering at his ear, but whenever he turned to look there was no one there. It had started earlier that evening, and Genjandro was very much worried it had something to do with the adept Morlock had told him of. But it seemed safer to deny the whispering, to keep it out of his acknowledged reality.

Safer for him—but for Vora? She was nervous—not a coward (she'd proved that!) but a worrier. It was why he'd taken her out of the field. Would she be safer knowing about the adept, or less safe? Would it make her worry more, or less?

"I hear him all the time, now," Vora said quietly.

"Who, my dear?"

"The adept. The evil presence in the Old City. The King told us about him."

"Did he?"

"Yes." Vora was weeping quietly, her sums put aside. "I didn't know he was evil when I first heard him. I didn't know. How could I know? He didn't tell me."

"Don't worry about it, my dear."

"Oh, it's past worrying. He's eaten me nearly entirely now; there's so little left."

"Oh. Is there?" Genjandro said, somewhat stupidly.

"I heard him first more than a year ago, Vora continued. "I was still working in the field then, cleaning in Markethall Barracks—you remember?"

"I do indeed."

"I was frightened nearly all the time. I never let you know that, but it's true."

"I never guessed it, dear girl," Genjandro assured her.

"Well, I was. And I heard his voice in a dream. He said so many things that sounded so wise. He said he could cure me of fear. He said I would never be afraid again. And so when I awoke I—I—I—I did something that let him in. He's been there ever since, eating away at me in the dark."

"My poor girl," he whispered. "We'll take you to Ambrose. You've seen Morlock—you know all those old stories are lies. There may be something that he, or those wise people from the Wardlands, can do."

Her weeping grew louder and more hysterical. "No. There's no time. There's so little of me left. But . . . he says . . . he says he'll spare me if you let him in."

Genjandro said nothing to this.

"It's easy," she said quietly, "it doesn't hurt. And he gives you things— pays for what he takes. Only, I've nothing left to take—nothing left. Please. Help me."

Genjandro didn't speak for a long time, and then he said, "She's completely gone, isn't she?"

A sigh escaped Vora's pale lips. "Yes," her voice conceded. "I finished her earlier tonight, while she was listening to little Lathmar tell the crowd about me. It was most amusing when she realized who I was and what I'd done to her."

"You shouldn't have begged. She'd never have done that."

"You'd be surprised what people will do, right at the end, when they're breaking up. In any case, I know that it's by compassion that you will come to me. You give of yourself rather easily, and someday I'll be there to take that first bite."

Genjandro laughed—not in defiance, but in simple amusement. "You don't know me, thing. I've spent my life buying low and selling high. You can't offer me anything worth what you'd take from me."

Vora's shoulders shrugged, an odd humping gesture. "Then I've misread you, and you're in no danger from me."

Genjandro stood and turned away.

"You can't get to Ambrose now, or leave the city," Vora's voice told him as he walked away. "Apart from that, go where you will and see what you like. You'll find it interesting. It's my city now."

Genjandro did find it interesting, and it was true that he could not reach Ambrose. He spent the night and much of the next day circumnavigating the walls of the city. But all of the gates were held by guards who would not acknowledge him or let him out—soldiers eaten by the adept.

The next night he slept—he could not do without it anymore—in an empty shed not far from the city's Water Wheel.

He woke the next morning to the sound of the wheel turning. He had, for a moment, the pleasant sense that everything had been a dream—that life in the city was going on as it always had.

But then, he realized, he would not have fallen asleep in this shed. He stepped out into the light, bracing himself for what he would see.

The Water Wheel was turning, the great man-powered wheel that drew water from underground rivers and aqueducts to supply the fountains of the city. It was being turned by men, not, as Genjandro had feared, by corpse-golems.

Genjandro went down to the gate where the workers entered. A great many men were waiting there—the Water Wheel was one place in the city where a strong man could always find work for wages. But with many of the men there were weeping children of various ages. And blocking the way to the wheel were several Companions of Mercy who either let a man pass or refused him at the behest of a smaller figure. As Genjandro approached he realized that the smaller figure was the dead baby Morlock had seen, still astride its monstrous dog-steed with mismatched human feet.

"No, no, no," the baby was saying impatiently to one importunate would-be worker, who held a small severed hand in his larger ones. "No exceptions. I'm not looking for souvenirs. You must bring the child here: that's all."

The man dropped the grisly object in the street and went away weeping. The dead baby turned toward Genjandro. Its eyes were wholly ruined—he could see maggots nestling there in the sockets—but it still seemed to see with them somehow, for it nodded and welcomed him by name.

"I'm surprised you remember me," Genjandro said. "You must have a great deal to think about."

The baby laughed. (Genjandro flinched, but didn't turn away: he was becoming hardened.) "But then, I have a great many minds to think with," it pointed out. "Would you be surprised to find I've thought a good deal about you in the past day or so?"

"Nothing surprises me anymore."

"A healthy attitude. A new world is being born, and I want to give you a chance to be a part of it."

"Drop dead."

"Too late!" the baby caroled cheerfully. "No, seriously, Genjandro: I hadn't realized how badly you want to get to Ambrose. I can let you pass, if you let me—"

"Drop dead," Genjandro repeated.

"You could tell them what you've seen—give them the intelligence you've gathered. And perhaps you were correct in what you told Vora. Perhaps the Ambrosii could cure you of me."

"You wouldn't suggest it if it were so."

"Not at all. I don't know, candidly—my sources inside the castle are rather limited at the moment, though I hope to have better ones soon."

Genjandro considered the offer carefully. "It's your best attempt yet," he admitted.

"And your answer?"

"Drop dead."

"You're a hard bargainer, Genjandro—I'll give you that."

"I mean to sell my life dear, if that's what you mean."

"Nonsense, nonsense," the dead baby said peevishly. "When the time comes you'll give it away. I just hope to be the beneficiary of your self-destruction, that's all."

"It's nice to have a dream."

"Oh, drop dead," the dead baby said, and laughed. "I suppose you're hungry."

Genjandro was unwilling to admit this, but found he could not deny it. Even in the nauseating presence of his moldering interlocutor his stomach was growling.

"Have one of these," the dead baby said, and one of the Companions silently handed him a wooden ticket. Engraved on it was a complicated seal with many figures around a single capital *I*.

"What is it?"

"It's a day's work-credit," the dead baby said. "The new currency of the city. Nothing else will be accepted for any commercial exchange, under pain of my extreme displeasure (which can be pretty extreme). It's what these men are working for, here." Its tiny gray hand (several fingers were bare bone) gestured vaguely at the Water Wheel.

Genjandro opened his fingers and let the thing fall to the ground. "I'd rather steal," he said.

"Oh, don't do that! All property rights will be respected, because ultimately, you know, it all belongs to me. You really won't take it?" Insofar as the sagging little face could express emotion, it seemed to be surprised. "Why, these are valuable indeed."

"I can see that. That's why I refused it. I take nothing from you: that's how it starts."

"You're taking life from me," the dead baby argued. "I could have these Companions kill you right now, but I refrain."

"Then do it," Genjandro said with genuine indifference. "I owe you nothing."

"You could owe me gratitude for eternal life!" the dead baby said earnestly. "Consider, Genjandro! You're an old man; you haven't many years of life before you. But there's no reason for me, or anyone who becomes part of me, to ever die. You could live forever! And there's nothing that people won't do for more life, even if it's only a single day. Consider this line of men!"

"And children," Genjandro observed.

"The children are tangential. It's the men I ask you to consider. I have sent out word that only those who bring one of their children to me and kill it in front of me will be allowed to work today at the wheel. Men say they love their children; they say that their children are their future, their hope of life after death in this world, but look how many have obeyed—for a single day's wages, for a day's worth of food and lodging, of life in the present, they sell their future!"

"How do you know they're bringing their own children?"

"Well, I don't, really, but do you doubt it?"

Genjandro looked gloomily up the line of hard-faced men and weeping, pleading children. "No," he said finally.

"They've picked the younger ones, the feeble or sickly ones, the crippled ones, the ones they never really cared for," the dead baby continued. "Tomorrow or the next day they will work their way up to the ones they really care about. That's when it will become really amusing; you should stop back."

"Why do you hate children so much?" Genjandro wondered.

"I don't. I don't hate anyone. I can hardly afford to, since someday I will become everyone. But the souls of children, I've found, are a little like unripe fruit: they take a great deal of effort to eat, and the result isn't worth it. Meanwhile they eat, and that's a problem, as the city's food supply is not what it was. The fewer children there are, the less strain on the food supply. Also, the dead bodies can be taken to the butcher's shops and used for food by those whom I allow to survive. It's a temporary solution until I begin to expand in the countryside, but I think it will work quite well."

"Not in the long run. If you keep on killing children—" Genjandro paused.

"I'll have to keep on expanding," the dead baby said eagerly. "Yes, of course, you're right about that. But why not? Genjandro, did you know that at one time I longed to be the Emperor?"

"No," Genjandro admitted.

"Silly, isn't it? But it's true. My father was Lathmar the Second—the son of Uthar the Great and the Lady Ambrosia. It seemed to me that I deserved the imperial throne after my father died—instead they let some little girl have it."

"Were you—was your mother—"

"Oh, she was no one important. Just an Ontilian girl my father met while traveling. That little accident cut me off from imperial power, and I was very bitter about it, even after I poisoned her. I studied magic; I laid my plans for seizing power; I worked and waited. Then, one day, it happened."

Genjandro waited.

"You don't mind getting information from me, I see," the dead baby commented archly. "Well, why not? What happened was, one of my shathes got loose in my workroom. I had a number of them prisoner, trying to domesticate them. It seemed to me that they would be fearsome weapons if they could be controlled somehow."

Genjandro nodded unwillingly. He understood that he was accepting something from the enemy, but it was too important to refuse.

"It was trying to seduce my will—to eat me. The vistas it opened up were so remarkable I almost fell. Then I realized something—something extraordinary. If it could eat me, if it could be nourished and sustained by my tal, then I could eat it. So I seduced it with the prospect of devouring me, and in the end I consumed it."

The dead baby smacked its lips appreciatively. "A hard-won meal, but a very satisfying one. In the end, I ate most of the rest of the shathes in my workshop. The others became tame, since the alternative was to be eaten. From the shathes I learned how to eat people, how to assume control of their bodies, how to use the traits and abilities of devoured entities to inhabit a legion of bodies. That was when my ambitions changed, you see. Why become the King of the Two Cities when I could become the cities themselves? Why be the Emperor when I could be the empire? To see through many eyes, to be a multitude of beings simultaneously while remaining myself, to remake the world into my own image! Would you rather rule the world or eat it?"

"Neither," Genjandro said.

"You'll find out," the baby said simply, and turned away. A hard-faced man stepped toward it, almost shyly, dragging a weeping girl with a crooked leg.

Genjandro walked off, but he did not truly walk away. As he left the wheel behind him, he heard the dead baby's voice in his head, whispering, *Was it worth it, Genjandro? I offered you the chance to go to Ambrose with what you knew, but then you knew nothing worth telling. Now you know something worth telling, but I won't let you go. I've got you now.*

Genjandro knew it was true, but he walked on. There might be a way, in spite of the voice eating him from within, to make his sacrifice worthwhile.

He went home and had breakfast (although it was more like lunch by the time he got there). Vora's body was still there, and had opened the shop for business. He said to it, "Get out, or I'll kill myself before you can eat me." His sincerity must have been sufficiently clear to the whispering presence within him; Vora's body walked out the door and he never saw it again.

He wrote what he knew and guessed in a letter to Morlock, then burned it. It was too long. He wrote three more versions, each one shorter than the one before. The last was less than half a page, summarizing what he knew (without adding how he knew it or his guesses about what it implied). He trimmed off any part of the paper that didn't have writing on it, then, on the reverse, wrote Morlock's name and sketched the heraldic crest of the Ambrosii, the hawk and thorns. It looked more like a seagull over some rocks—Genjandro didn't claim to be a great artist—but it was the best he could do. Then he put a fistful of unground grain in one of his pockets, stuffed the letter in after it, and went out to find a crow.

He saw a number of them, all dead, their heads removed. Then, on a street corner, he saw a crowd of men and women in ragged clothes, like beggars, surrounding a Companion of Mercy. One of the beggars gave it a double handful of dark bloody objects—crow heads. The Companion dropped them one by one into a bag: ten in all. He handed the beggar a work credit.

Useful employment for the city idlers, whispered the voice in Genjandro's head.

Despair crashed down on Genjandro then: the thing within him had won. It was eating him; it would eat the city; it would eat the world. If someone could stand in its way, harm it somehow, Genjandro was not that person. If it would ever be defeated, it would be too late for Genjandro and his city.

His city. It *was* his city. Not some Vraidish king's; not some Ambrosian witch's. His. Not because he ruled here, but because he had lived here and would die here. Because he belonged to the place, the place belonged to him, by some mystic law that transcended any human rules of property or ownership.

Had he bought and sold, lied and cheated on occasion, lived and grown rich, amassed what power he could, solely for himself, all for his own benefit? He had thought so. But that man, if he'd ever lived, was already dead. He had thrown away fortunes, destroyed his own property and that of others, spent magic gold that came from nowhere. As the King's spymaster in the occupied city he had killed and ordered others to kill to protect his organization. He had lived in danger every day. For himself? So that he could settle down in the peace after the civil war and sell rugs and die—old, childless, and rich, regretted by none?

It had all been for the city, of which he was a part and which, he had thought, would survive him after his death. Now he knew it would not, or at least not for long, that it was already dying of the same insinuating voice, the same withering Shadow that was destroying him. His death was meaningless if his life had been meaningless; he grieved for neither but rather for the city that, till now, had given a meaning to both.

He walked vaguely toward the river Tilion. To the extent that he was thinking of anything, he was hoping that he would be able to drown himself in the river. But he never got there.

He was wandering down a street running westward when he looked up and realized where he was. There was a burned-out building not far off, its blackened brick walls supported by wooden struts. It was his warehouse, the one he had burned as part of the dragon ploy. He stared up at it, trying to recover the feelings of reckless amusement and triumph he had felt on that day. As he was standing there, a young boy ran into him from behind and they both fell.

"Don't let them catch me!" the boy cried.

"Them?" Genjandro said stupidly.

"They're not my parents!"

"No," Genjandro said dully. "I suppose not."

The boy looked him in the face and said, "Death and Justice! You've been eaten! You're one of them!" He desperately kicked at the old man until they were disentangled from each other, scrambled to his feet, and ran off. Genjandro croaked, "Don't go in there!"

Behind him on the street came a pair of figures, a man and a woman. Genjandro did not know them at first, but then some mark on their face, perhaps the same one the boy had seen on his, gave them away.

"Oh. It's you."

"Genjandro," said the man, in a voice reminiscent of Vora's, the dead baby's, the whisper in Genjandro's own mind.

"You're going fast," the woman said, in a voice which was different, but somehow the same. "A little too ripe, perhaps—but all the better for quick eating."

"What are you doing?" he asked.

"It's most amusing," said the man's mouth.

"Isn't everything?"

"Not like this," said the woman's mouth, acknowledging Genjandro's feeble gibe with a smirk. "I've eaten the child's parents, and now I'm hunting him through the streets in their persons. The parents' awarenesses live within me and try to resist, but there's nothing they can do about it. It sets up the most delicious pattern of emotional contrasts; I wish you could experience it. But you will, soon, of course. I shall do this sort of thing citywide once I get really organized."

"Genjandro," said the man's mouth, almost excited, "there's no way out of that building, is there? The windows were all on the upper floors, and the flooring and stairs are all burned away, so there's no way the child can reach them."

"As far as I know," Genjandro agreed heavily. He supposed the enemy had read it from his own mind—if he could even call it *his* mind anymore. "There may be damage . . . holes in the walls," he continued. "The boy may be gone already."

"Just walk around and see, won't you?" the woman's mouth said.

Genjandro did as he was told, simply because he had nothing else to do, because nothing mattered anyway. There was a good deal of damage to the west side—there were more support beams on that side. The ground sloped downward there, toward the river.

"Etkondel," cried the woman's voice through the open door. "Don't go to your father. He killed your puppy. I saw him do it. Then he made me say it ran away."

"I did it for your own good," barked the man's voice. "Don't let your mother have you, boy. She'll cut your balls off, if she can. You may hate me, but at least I'll let you be a man."

Genjandro leaned wearily on one of the supports, remembering what the builder had said—the one he had consulted after the fire.

"Etkondel, Etkondel," the woman's voice sobbed. "Help! He's going to hurt me again, I know he will! If you don't help me, I just don't know what I'll do."

"She's lying. She's always tried to poison you against me, and me against you. She's good at that. If you come out now, why, I'll let you help me with her."

Master Alkhendron, the builder had told him, *we can't rebuild. At most we can keep the thing from falling down, and that's hard enough. The solution is to level it and build again.*

"Etkondel, I'm afraid! Please help me!"

"Enough of this nonsense! Come out here now, boy. Don't make me come in there!"

I understand, Alkhendron/Genjandro had said to his builder. But he felt that only now did he really understand. The city was dead, ruined, a shell propped up with great and useless effort. But if he leveled it, then the boy would be able to build again. The city was dead, but need not die.

"Etkondel!" the woman's dead voice wailed. "I know you want to do what's right, what's in your heart! You won't leave me out here to be hurt by this horrible man!"

The dead father's voice shouted, "I say what's right and what's wrong—the Strange Gods damn your heart and whatever's in it!"

"Lathmar!" Genjandro screamed abruptly. "Level it, and I'll build again! The city isn't dead, it's just dead!" That was wrong, somehow, but there was no time to change it—he could feel the will of the other trying to work within him. He pushed the support beam in front of him and it fell. He pushed the next one, and it fell. He went down the line of supports, crashing into them, falling from one to the next, struggling to keep his feet so that he could knock them all down, level it all.

Blackened bricks were falling about him like rain now. He lurched and fell and struggled to get up, but his legs were trapped by the slumping wall. A curtain of brick dropped down on him as he tried to wrench free.

The collapse of the rest of the building killed the bodies of the woman and the man. The boy escaped through a tear in the tottering wall and ran away into the twisting streets.

But Genjandro saw none of this; the collapse of the west wall had killed him also. He had been merchant, then conspirator and spy; now he was just another dead soldier, half buried by the city he had struggled to save and to destroy.

A crow who knew his voice heard him shout and heard the building fall. The crow was wise enough to know that the city was unfriendly to crows and that this might be a trick. But one of the words that the voice had shouted was important; Morlock and his dwarf often used it (though the crow did not pretend, even to himself, to know what a *lathmar* was).

So the crow risked descending into the cloud of mortar and ash rising from the fallen building. There was some meat among the ruins, but it was too fresh to be interesting, and two of the clumps had a dangerous smell about them.

It was the third pile of meat that had cried out, the crow guessed. It was mostly covered with brick, so the crow couldn't tell if it had been Genjandro. The midsection was burst open, and some of that smelled most tempting, if it were not for the falling cloud of mortar dust. The fellow's clothes were torn, also, spilling the contents of his pockets. Apparently he had been carrying some mixed seed and grain in one, a practice of which the crow wholly approved. The crow was sorting through this when he found the sheet with Morlock's name on it.

The crow squawked wearily. Why did these things always happen to him? Now he'd have to fly all the way to Ambrose—a long way to travel with night coming on. The paper looked rather large and heavy, too, a real winddrag. He was perfectly willing to play with entities he considered his equals, and he could understand playing games with pebbles and so on, but why Morlock and others insisted on playing games with paper, across such horribly long distances and tediously regular patterns, he could not understand.

Still, the crow was fond of Morlock. And it was a chance to get out of the city and get some clean food, without this dust and ash all over it. And there was the treaty. The crow irritably plucked the half-sheet of paper up, shook the dust of the city from his wings, and flew away from the wreckage of Genjandro and his dreams, north and west, straight as an arrow to Ambrose.

CHAPTER TWENTY-FIVE

THE LAST COUNCIL

"When I call this session of the Regency Council to order," Ambrosia said in dry businesslike tones. "I've asked the vocates from the Wardlands to sit with us, and Commander Erl, not just as the King's chief bodyguard but as a man of resource and courage. If any of you can think of someone else who ought to be here, feel free to name him or her."

"Wish Genjandro were here," Wyrth muttered.

"So do I," Ambrosia said clearly. She put her hand to a wrinkled, blood-stained half-sheet of paper that lay on the table before her. "But courtesy of Morlock and his feathered friends, we have Genjandro's last report. It doesn't tell us much, but what's there might be enough."

Morlock stirred at this, and Ambrosia turned toward him with a fierce unhappy smile. "Oh, are you awake there, brother? I thought you might have gone to sleep again."

The Crooked Man looked her in the eye until she looked away, a little embarrassed. "I was going to say that Genjandro's message, with the King's story, tells us what we need to know."

"How fast to run?" Jordel inquired. "I was just thanking God Sustainer for the Wards around the Wardlands."

"They're no defense," Aloê said. "Every wall, material or immaterial, is worthless unless it's guarded by soldiers. And the soldiers are the weak points, against this enemy: they have wills that can be seduced."

"I'll run if I have to," said the King in a low voice. "I'd rather defeat this thing somehow. It's eating the heart of our empire. I don't see that we'll have better luck against it in Sarkunden than we're having here."

Jordel cleared his throat, and said, somewhat nervously, "Well, you touch on a delicate point, Your Majesty. *Our* realm is a different one, and we need to look to its interests."

"Here it comes," Wyrth said.

Jordel turned to him in surprise. "It?" he said.

"*It*, sir. Now that the danger is greatest and we most need aid, you discover that you have an urgent appointment in some other part of the world. We are not your allies; you have no unbreakable ties with us either of blood or"—he glanced aside at Aloê—"other fluids. Why should you not go? If—"

"Wyrth," said Morlock, "enough."

"Master Morlock, I am your apprentice. But I am also an independent member of this council. I admit it is an anomalous situation, but I believe it allows me to have my say."

"You aren't," Morlock said bluntly. "You're having Jordel's, and damning him because you put words in his mouth. We've no time for that. We may have hours; we may have less. Shut up and let the Wardlanders speak."

There was a brief silence, and Jordel said, with unusual flatness, "We have sent messages by certain means to our peers in the Graith. We have reason to suppose that they have been intercepted. The Graith must be warned. We flipped coins and Baran lost."

"Or won," Baran differed. "I will carry word to the Graith and return as quickly as I may."

"You'd better take Velox," Morlock said.

"Thanks," Baran rumbled. "Heard about him."

Wyrth was pressing his clenched fists against his forehead. The King looked at him and then at Morlock. Morlock knew that Wyrth was still tormented by the memory of his fear in the grave lands, and he guessed that the King realized it, too. He nodded, shrugged, and waited.

"Vocates," Wyrth blurted.

"It's all right, Wyrtheorn," Aloê said quietly.

Wyrth winced at this use of the intimate form of his name and laughed raggedly. "I hardly think so. You have all deserved better from me. You'll get it another time, God Avenger bear witness."

"Morlock," said Ambrosia impatiently, "this is your hour. It's time for you to speak."

"I intend to go to the Old City and kill the Protector's Shadow."

"See how easy," muttered Wyrth.

"Kill him?" Jordel cried, amazed at the crudity of Morlock's proposal. "Which one of him? Which of the thousands he inhabits? Have we learned nothing about this enemy?"

"On the contrary," Morlock said flatly. "We have learned everything."

"If you mean his name, Morlock," Aloê interposed, "I don't see that it is so very helpful. It's true that he may have been called Inglonor—and even you, madam, can't be sure of that, I believe?"

Ambrosia grunted. "I never met him. I don't believe so. My oldest boy was an insolent little prick, in some ways, but he didn't honor me so far as to introduce his bastards."

"But," Aloê continued, "the nature changes the name. To effect a binding spell upon he-who-was-Inglonor we would need to know more than we do—perhaps the names of every consciousness he has ever consumed and made part of himself."

"His name is nothing," Morlock said. "I intend to kill him, not bind him. Look, Jordel," he said, choking off the verbose vocate's protests, "take a piece of string."

"Why, I don't happen to have any string at the moment," Jordel cried.

"He means you to consider an imaginary piece of string," Wyrth explained.

"He might have said so."

"You take the piece of string," Morlock continued, "and you tie one end to your index finger and the other to Baran's index finger. Then, when you choose, you can move Baran's finger."

"Unless he resists, you know. He's awfully strong."

"We will say he is asleep. Or dead."

"Oh, dead, by all means, if you don't mind. That way I shall inherit the family estate."

"This represents the Protector's Shadow and his relationship with the body of someone whose awareness he has consumed. The string is the talic connection between the Protector's awareness and his subject's body. For it to be effective, it must have two ends—the one in the subject and the one in the tal-body nexus of the controlling awareness."

"I assume that, enjoying this experience as I do," Jordel continued calmly, "I kill the rest of the members of this council and attach their fingers to mine with bits of string."

"Plainly."

"Well, this is a gory little thought experiment, I must say. Is it getting anywhere?"

"Jordel: your hand is tired."

"I don't think so, old fellow—I'm quite comfortable."

"The hand with the strings," Morlock prompted.

"Oh! Well, I'll move them to my other hand."

"Do that, won't you? But remember that at any moment, while your hands are tangled up with string, someone might come through the door and lop off your head."

Jordel's eyes crossed and uncrossed. "I begin to see," he said slowly. "You think it would be that difficult to transfer his awareness, along with his control of the bodies whose minds he has eaten, to a new body."

"Even more difficult, Jordel. Your awareness already has a talic connection with your other hand; the Protector's Shadow would have to establish one with his new body. He would have to put the two bodies in talic *stranj* and transfer his strands of control gradually from the old to the new. He will not do this while there is any danger that his enemies will come upon him while he is preoccupied."

"'In talic *stranj*,' urk. I wish Noreê were here—this isn't my sort of problem."

"Morlock," Aloê said intently, "surely your string-finger example isn't the only possible way the Protector's Shadow could maintain control over his subjects."

"In theory, no. I ran up several multidimensional models in my workshop after I read Genjandro's note. For instance, the central awareness could have been shared among several bodies, some of whom could have served as fall-back positions if others failed. Or each body could have been truly intercon-scious with all of the others, with talic strands extending from each of the members to all of the others. There's true immortality, if you want it."

"God Avenger, make him stop!"

"Shut up, Jordel," Aloê said curtly. "Morlock, if these other models are less vulnerable to attack . . . Are they?"

"Yes."

"Then why do you assume that the Protector's Shadow chose the most vulnerable model?"

"Bad tactics," said Ambrosia curtly, and Wyrth, with a remembering look, smiled briefly.

"I don't assume he did," Morlock said flatly. "It's what he must have done. There may be practical considerations I am unaware of—this isn't my sort of magic. It may be that sharing awareness among several physical forms would require sharing of identity. The Shadow would not eat these beings; together they would become a true group mind. This would not appeal to him."

"No," the King said firmly. "It wouldn't."

"Or perhaps he simply made a tactical error in his first improvised, er, meal, and has stuck to the model ever since. It doesn't matter. This is the method he has chosen."

"You keep saying that," Aloê said. "But—"

"He defends his body," the King said distantly.

"He—what do you mean?" Aloê asked, focusing on Lathmar.

The King shifted uneasily in his seat. He looked at Morlock, but Mor-lock simply gestured for him to continue.

"He grows these hedges of thorn around the tower. He hides the door. The only window is hundreds of feet above the ground. He blocks the door to his workroom like a tomb." The King waved his hands. "Don't you see?"

"Even more," Morlock continued. "He gutted his body of its vital organs, sealing them away to protect his body's life. If it were not vulnerable, if it were not important to defend it, he would not hedge it around with these elaborate defenses. He would not suffer the inconvenience of a rotting body. It is his weak point. We must strike it."

"Or," Jordel said triumphantly (he had been waiting centuries to say it), *"he wants it to seem that way*. Isn't that possible? That the whole tower setup is an elaborate feint to draw an opponent (you, Morlock, or Ambrosia) to death or captivity?"

Morlock nodded slowly. "I considered the possibility. I broached it to the King. He thinks it unlikely. I trust his intuition."

"He was there, you know," Wyrth pointed out.

"Yes, but, begging Your Majesty's pardon and all that," Jordel said, "suppose he's wrong?"

"Then you fight on without me. Next most likely is that there is a small core group of mind-bodies who consume together the infected minds and share control of the subject bodies. The task would be to identify and kill a significant number of these."

"'A significant number . . .'?" Aloê wondered.

Morlock shrugged. "More than one. Less than the total number of mind-bodies in the core group."

"And if it is the third model?" Baran asked. "Total interconsciousness, or whatever you said?"

"You'd have to kill them all."

"Easy for you to say," Jordel said. "You'll be dead yourself."

Morlock shrugged. "That's not how it is. If I fail, one or more of you should set out to do what I tried to do."

"Suppose we're all dead by then?" Jordel wondered.

Morlock gestured at Baran.

"Then it's up to us in the Wardlands, you mean," Baran said.

"Yes. You should contact Merlin as well. He's no friend to the Graith or the Second Empire, but I suspect that the Protector's Shadow will interfere with his plans, and he could be a useful ally. He has made a special study of necromancy."

"His plans," said Jordel musingly. "What are his plans, do you suppose?"

"He always has some plot or other afoot," Ambrosia said dismissively. "They never come to anything, always being somewhat overcomplicated. But it's nice to know one's father has something to amuse himself with in his extreme old age."

"Eh," said Jordel. His father, of whom he had been very fond, had died young.

"I take it," Ambrosia resumed, in a more official tone, "that the sentiment of the council is unanimous: Baran shall go to warn our neighbors in the Wardlands of the present danger, while Morlock shall go to the Old City to combat the Protector's Shadow. The rest of us shall man, woman, and dwarf the barricades here until some new strategy presents itself."

Nods around the table.

"I'm pleased to adjourn this last meeting of the Regency Council on a note of ringing unanimity," she said with a crooked smile. "We all have work to do, though the hour is late. Still, I ask you to wait and witness."

Morlock, who alone had heard this ritual formula before, looked up with interest. Ambrosia had stood and was walking, with a wooden box in her hands, over to where the King had seated himself, rather informally, farther down the council table. "Your Majesty," she said as she walked, "I had hoped to make this gesture with the high ceremony it deserves. But it may be that we will not all meet again. So" . . . She opened the box, took out what was in it, and cast it aside. In her hands she held an iron circlet with no gem. Lathmar twisted around in his chair to look at it.

"This is the iron crown of Vraid," she said. "With it I crowned your ancestor, my beloved husband, Uthar the First, Emperor of Ontil on the field of battle. In that dark hour without hope we won through to victory. Will you accept now the heritage of your ancestors and be our sign of hope in this dark hour?"

Lathmar squawked, "You want to crown me Emperor, now, before breakfast?"

"Certainly. Unless you would rather someone else do it." She didn't look at Morlock.

"No!" the King said instantly, to Morlock's relief. "No, Grandmother: you do it." He stood, kicking his chair to the floor, and kneeled before her.

She placed the iron circlet among his disordered brown locks, saying, "I crown you Lathmar the Seventh, Emperor of Ontil."

Then he rose and she kneeled, taking off her chain of office and handing it to him. "Your commands, my liege?" she said softly.

He gripped the chain like a lifeline, but his voice was steady as he spoke. "I affirm the acts of my late regent, my well-beloved ancestress Lady

Ambrosia Viviana. Let's leave the rest of the ceremonies for another time; we have a war to fight. And, frankly, I want breakfast."

"Hail Lathmar the Seventh, called the Wise!" cried Jordel enthusiastically. "Breakfast in droves, by all means. Maybe we should get an emperor in the Wardlands."

Baran pushed his chair over for this blasphemy, and thus ended the imperial coronation of Lathmar VII.

"Morlock," Aloê said in the Crooked Man's ear as the others were standing around the table talking. "You've other good-byes to say, so I won't keep you. But come back to me, Morlock: I say it to you like some stupid fisherman's stupid wife. Come back to me."

Morlock stood, took her by the elbow, and walked her out in the hall. "The time is come for an understanding between us," he said firmly.

She looked at him with her golden eyes and waited.

"I am no longer your husband," he said harshly. "You are not my wife. I am an exile, and you are a member of the Graith of Guardians. You could be exiled simply for saying what you have said to me. Don't throw away everything you are because of something which is nothing to you."

"Do you really believe you are nothing to me?" she said, surprised.

"You would wander with me, from place to place, without a home, because I can never come to the place that is my home?"

She laughed, dismissing this fantasy with a wave of her hand. "I can see the future better than that, Morlock."

"Prophesy for me."

"You will be in the future what Ambrosia has been in the past: the true ruler of this empire. It took a long time, but *now* you have a place to call your own. You cast a long shadow—"

"An ill-chosen metaphor indeed," he hissed.

"Choose your own metaphor, beloved. The job is yours to do. I've never known you to shirk a job that was yours. I think I understand you now, at last, and I am willing to be a partner in your destiny, wherever it leads."

He bowed his head, clenching his teeth. He thought he understood her, and rather better than she knew him. It was strange to love someone, to look into her eyes, and to see oneself mirrored there as a nothingness cloaked with power. It was the cloak of power she loved, not the man who wore it. He could not say these things; they blocked his throat, too great, too terrible to be spoken. *It is Morlock who loves her*, he said to himself. *But the man she loves is Merlin's son.* She had never realized that they were not the same man, that they would never be, that he could not let them be.

He heard a sound behind him and turned to see Lathmar standing behind them, the boy's eyes twin pools of grief and shame. The young Emperor fled up the hallway, his bodyguards following at a practiced run. Ambrosia came out of the council chamber, looked up the hall, looked at Morlock, and shrugged.

He turned back to his ex-wife. "You've hurt him," he said fiercely. "I won't forget this."

"Save your anger for our enemy," she said, smiling. "I'll be here when you get back." Then she kissed him, and he found he could not resist her. She turned away and walked up the hall after Lathmar, her red cloak swirling behind her. Perhaps he would not be able to resist her, either, Morlock reflected gloomily.

"Did you know Merlin sent me off to school one year?" Ambrosia said as he turned back to her.

"No," said Morlock, genuinely surprised.

"It was such a disaster. I'll tell you about it, sometime. Anyway, this is a little like the end of the school year—fast farewells, so much to say that nothing gets said."

So he held her hand, kissed her forehead, and said nothing at all.

She kissed him on the lips, hesitated, then kissed him again. "From Hope," she whispered, and walked away almost as quickly as Lathmar had done.

"Nothing disgusts me as much as schmaltz," said Jordel disagreeably, stepping forward, "so I won't say good-bye. No point to it! You'll be a pest and a botheration to the Wardlands until the mountains wear away and the Guard fails."

"A pest, maybe," Morlock conceded. "But a botheration?"

"Don't try to bandy wits with me at this late date; you're not equipped for it. You don't even know what a bandy is—deny it if you can! See you, Baran."

"Good-bye. Good-bye to you, Morlock," the big man added. "Thanks for the horse. Think he'll carry me?"

"He carried Ambrosia, Wyrth, and me," Morlock said. "I'm fairly sure it was him. Let him run free in Westhold when he's carried you there, eh?"

Baran said he would, clapped Morlock on the shoulder, and was gone.

"You're not even going to say good-bye to Velox?" Wyrth said querulously.

"No," said Morlock, who badly wanted to. "He might cry, and I couldn't bear that."

"Ach, you're a cold and pitiless man. I suppose you're only waiting for me because you want help with your spider."

"That, and one other thing."

Wyrth became solemn, even grim. "I know. We never talked about how I failed you in the gravelands."

"That's nothing."

"Not to me," Wyrth replied, stung.

"Then it's your business," Morlock said coldly, if not pitilessly. "I should have warned you what was in the offing or forbidden you to come. Your suffering falls to my blame. Frankly, I have worse things on my conscience."

"And I'm the one who knows," Wyrth replied. He hesitated and asked, "What's the other thing, then?"

"I call you master, Wyrth."

"What?" the dwarf said irritably. "You can't do that. I'm just an apprentice."

"I can, and you know it. I should have done it a half century ago. You know that, too."

"You're doing this as a going-away present," said Wyrth angrily. "But when you come back, we won't be able to travel together anymore. Or maybe you're thinking of giving up traveling."

"Master Wyrth, you need to sit at your own bench, work in your own shop, dream your own dreams, and do your own deeds. If you do, you may become the greatest of all the masters of Making. I say so."

Wyrth bowed his head and raised it again. "All right, ex-boss. I guess I'll see you at the craft meetings. Let's get this spider of yours on the road."

He was weeping as he walked, but he took no notice of this so neither did Morlock.

CHAPTER TWENTY-SIX

THE CROOKED MEN

yrth was glumly sorting through the accumulations of stuff in Morlock's workshop. In truth there was not so very much— no more than forty or fifty donkeys might have carried. Since, in the event, it would have to be carried by one old man with crooked shoulders and one dwarf (headed in different directions, he kept reminding himself incredulously), some sorting needed to be done.

He was tempted to carry nothing. To walk back to Thrymhaiam with nothing in his hands, stand on the Rokhfell Hill, and shout, "I am a master of Making! The greatest maker in the worlds has said so!" On reflection, this didn't seem practical—he would need food and water on the way; there were some notebooks with useful things in them; he didn't like to go anywhere without a few tools. . . . The items mounted up.

There was a folded slip of paper not far from the choir of flames. Wyrth opened it and read it to see if it was worth preserving or if, as he thought, it had been put here to become fuel for the ever-hungry choir.

The note read:

Morlock—
     I am alive.
          Hope.

"Odd," he said. Was the last word a signature or an injunction? He had heard of someone who might have addressed Morlock in this way—Morlock's other sister, Hope. But she was supposed to have died before he (Wyrth) had been born. Of course, that might have been the purpose of the note . . . to let him know it wasn't the case. Wyrth tapped the note against his nose reflectively three or four times, refolded it, and put it back where he had found it.

The Emperor entered the room quietly, as if he didn't want to be heard. The clash of his bodyguards' boots and armor outside the door made that more or less impossible, so Wyrth looked up and said, "Yes, Your Majesty?"

"Is Morlock away?" Lathmar asked.

"He has been away some hours," Wyrth said.

"Oh," said the Emperor emptily. "I thought . . . I thought he might need this." He held up the signal horn with which he had escaped the adept's tower.

Morlock and Wyrth had discussed the horn and agreed it would be useless to him—the corpse-golems would be instructed to disregard it. But, Wyrth thought, as a pretext to say good-bye, the horn would have been pretty useful. Too bad Lathmar hadn't thought of it sooner, that's all. In lieu of saying all this, he grunted.

"You're getting as bad as Morlock," Lathmar said, laughing. He grew more solemn. "When do you suppose we'll know . . . one way or the other?"

"If he succeeds or dies, you mean?" the dwarf said querulously. "I don't suppose it's occurred to you that he could succeed *and* die—or that you might be better off if he didn't come back?"

"No," said the young Emperor so defiantly that Wyrth knew he was lying. Normally he disapproved of untruths, especially unsuccessful ones, but he had to give the boy credit for trying. If Morlock fell on his sword for this young twerp, the young twerp had better prove to be worth the sacrifice.

"Well," he said, in lieu of saying all that, "what news from the walls? I guess you've come from there."

"We are besieged again," Lathmar said solemnly. "There are bands of corpse-golems led by Companions of Mercy at every outer gate."

"Where's Ambrosia? I take it she's still leading the troops."

"Yes, she's at Thorngate. She was wondering if you have something that might—might—"

"Put a bug down their hoods?" Wyrth thought it over. "We can try a few things. Give me a hand, won't you?"

The current of the river carried Morlock down to the sea. He dozed a bit, barely troubling to guide his spider craft. There would be work to tire him soon enough.

When he reached the sea, he took up the controls and directed the spider eastward along the shore. Once he was past the city he took his craft to land and began a long, oblique walk toward his goal. He went north through the grave lands, then finally turned east again when he was north of Gravesend Field. He sped across the plain between the grave lands and the old riverbed on the Tilion. Then he took the dry riverbed into the heart of the Old City.

This occupied a good deal of time; it was dark before his spider crawled out of the empty river course at what was once a riverside quay. The sky looked cloudy, too—as if it might rain for the first time in at least two thousand years over the Old City. Morlock hoped not, for various reasons, but the most he could do about it was hurry, which he had planned to do anyway.

He scanned the streets on all sides with the spider's external eye, but he never glanced at the sky. So he didn't see the dark cloud that had formed behind him, following him from the grave lands.

He approached the adept's tower from the east, the last direction he would be expected from, or so he hoped. But in the event it seemed not to matter. There were not, as he expected, companies of corpse-golems and Companions patrolling near the adept's tower.

Morlock didn't like it. True, the adept, even after centuries, could only have a limited number of undead servants. (They could not remain usable forever for very long.) Also true, he had many uses for these relatively few soldiers: he had to secure a large city and assault a well-defended castle.

But if Morlock's theory was correct, the adept's principal need was to protect his central mind-body nexus at all costs. If the tower was as unprotected as it seemed, either Morlock's theory was wrong or the adept was somewhere else—possibly hidden in the city.

"Didn't think of that, did you?" Morlock said to himself, in the jeering tone he used to no one else. "Well," he continued, more reasonably (you have to live with yourself), "I can always hope the defenses are better than they seem."

The hedge of dagger thorns was high, but the legs of Morlock's spider were longer when fully extended. He simply walked the spider-craft over the hedge.

There were no corpse-golems on the far side, either. Morlock saw the work-wheel Lathmar had described; it was abandoned. The bare patch in the ivy-thorn covering the tower could be seen, as well: the iron stairs were drawn up and the stone door closed.

Morlock considered. This, as a matter of fact, looked rather promising, as if the adept had drawn up his bridge, so to speak, and trusted to his moat and wall to defend him. If so, the wall would have defenders: the tower stair inside would be lined with the undead waiting to kill him. Morlock hoped so, as he had no intention of going that way.

He walked his spider over to the wall of the tower, away from the shut entrance.

There was a screeching sound; Morlock turned to see that a number of dagger thorns had pierced the steel hide of his spider.

"Ugh," he commented briefly, and went to the weapons locker. He was already wearing a mail shirt under his tunic; from the locker he took a helmet and put it on. He also took up Tyrfing, in a shoulder sheath that he duly strapped to his crooked shoulders. Then, of course, the jars. He strung them separately across his shoulders, as he would need his hands free for climbing.

He released the hatch and crawled out on top of the spider's body.

He found his hands were trembling as he stood there. In fact, he found to his surprise that he was frightened. It was not the height nor the fight he faced that frightened him. He had grown up in the Whitethorn Mountains and free-climbed many a rock face more treacherous than this. And he had fought and killed so many times that the prospect of doing so again, merely to protect his own life, rather sickened him.

But that was just it. This wasn't for his life. It would be better, in some ways, if he didn't live through this. But if he didn't succeed in destroying the adept, far more would be ruined than his own life. He thought of Wyrth facing the second death, of his sisters facing the mind-torments the adept would inflict, little Lathmar. . . . The boy would never break, that Morlock knew, but what horrors he might have to face before he died!

We should have fled. We should have waited for the wise ones from the Wardlands. Together, Illion, Noreê, and I could have killed this thing. I wish I had a drink.

He put his trembling hands over his face and stood there until he grew still. Then, the voices in his head grown quiet, he took the first jar in his hands and stepped toward the thorns.

The jar was made of aethrium; inside it was phlogiston. In the hours before the last council, Morlock had dephlogistonated everything he could lay his hands on, while Wyrth frantically worked every piece of aethrium Morlock had in his workshop into suitable containers. In the throat of each jar was a piece of flint that scraped against a metal wheel when the cap of the jar was flipped open. The resultant spark ignited the upward-rushing phlogiston, resulting in a sheet, a rising cloud of flame.

Morlock flipped open the first jar, holding it among the dagger thorns. A river of flame crept uphill through the dark ivy-thorn, spreading out in many branches across the face of the adept's tower.

Morlock tested the tip of a burning thorn with his bare thumb. The point was gone. The point of a thorn is its most flammable part, and a thorn without a point is just a branch. And the flame, of course, could not harm him, by virtue of the blood of Ambrose the Old. Morlock nodded grimly and climbed into the rising river of flame.

His greatest danger was that a burning branch would fail to support his weight, so he moved as quickly as he could up the side of the tower. When the fire began to give out (the thorns were green with the blood they had drunk) he uncapped another jar and the way of flame opened upward again.

He was intent on climbing when he heard the whisper of wings on the air, a hiss audible even above the crackle of burning thorns. He kept climbing with his feet and left hand, but with his right he reached back and drew Tyrfing.

As the hiss grew nearer he let his feet swing free and, hanging from his left hand, spun around so that his back was to the wall.

Silhouetted against the night sky, lit by the major moons, a winged but vaguely manlike figure was approaching, a great hammer in its hand. It must be one of the door gargoyles whom the King had seen outside the adept's chamber, Morlock guessed.

Once, when he was a young man, only just made vocate in the Graith of Guardians, his tutor in the arts of swordsmanship had made him dangle from a rope. Then Naevros had swung at him on another rope and battered him with a wooden sword as he passed. After several days of this, Morlock had gotten a wooden sword of his own to defend himself with.

I needed these skills once, fighting pirates in the Sea of Worlds, Naevros had told him, when he objected to the uselessness of the exercise. *You'll learn them because I've sworn you can learn whatever I know, despite your crooked shoulders and your damned stubbornness.*

The memory of Naevros's cool, tense, angry voice calmed him, as it had in many another fight, including the duel in which he killed Naevros himself. He braced his feet against the tower and lashed out with his sword, stretching out as far as his protesting left arm would permit. Tyrfing's edge crossed the gargoyle's hammer-bearing arm at the wrist and it screamed. Tumbling in the air, it recovered and flew away eastward. Morlock caught a glimpse of the thing's back in the moons' light as it flew off.

In a single motion, he sheathed Tyrfing and swung around to face the tower again. The thorns were burning in his hand; he had to move or fall. The gargoyle would be back in a few moments, but he had to make progress while he could. So he did, shouldering burning branches aside as he struggled upward.

The gargoyle. What was it, anyway? Morlock could swear he had seen scars like seams crisscrossing the thing's back. Its body was made of many pieces, but what sort of soul inhabited it? Perhaps the thing was a harthrang, a demon possessing a dead body—one specially made for it by the adept. But harthrangs were not so closely bound to the bodies they inhabited that they could feel pain.

So the adept himself must be controlling the gargoyle body. But that hardly made sense either. The adept's consciousness had expanded to occupy many bodies. Even if he could feel anything like pain any longer it would only be one sensation in a forest of others—nothing to make him scream.

Morlock thought of ascending to the visionary state: if he was to defeat the gargoyle he needed to know what it was. But he would need all his physical ability to ward off the gargoyle's next attack; he could not risk ascending to rapture now.

It was coming; he could hear it. He glanced over his shoulders and saw it stall in the air. Why would it do that, unless . . .

He let his left hand open and swung to the right; unburnt thorns scraped against his mail shirt, and one pierced it and him. But the hammer struck the wall where he had been. Stone shattered, and mortar-dust clung to a patch of blood on the hammer's grip. The gargoyle's blood. It occurred to Morlock there had been blood on Tyrfing when he had sheathed it.

The hammer fell and was caught in the thorns below. It left a hole in the wall, through which dead gray arms reached for Morlock. He drew Tyrfing with his left hand, snarling as it caught for a moment in its sheath (the blood had made it sticky). Then he lopped off the arms reaching for him through the gap in the tower wall.

The gargoyle was returning below for its hammer.

Morlock took a moment for cold calculation. The gargoyle had a method of attack that could hardly fail, which he could not counter. But it bled; it could be wounded; it could feel pain. There was only one thing to do.

He did it, opening his right hand and falling, like the hammer, down the wall. He landed on the gargoyle's gray winged back.

"No!" it screamed. "He'll eat me if you—"

Morlock severed the screaming head from its neck, and then abandoned the gargoyle body as it suddenly relaxed in death. He was pierced by several unburnt thorns in the patch he leapt into, but not seriously. His blood caused them to flicker with sluggish flames that soon guttered out. He clung to the dark branches, listening to the dead body hit the earth below them, recovering his breath. "All hands, abandon gargoyle," he muttered when he could, then breathed some more.

Finally he took a jar of phlogiston and opened it, burning a new pathway upward. He ascended the bright ladder of burning branches, remembering that there was another, at least one other gargoyle; wondering about the enemy who awaited him above; hoping that those he loved back in Ambrose were still safe.

They weren't. The second siege of Ambrose had been shorter than the first, and more disastrous. Before Morlock reached the tower, the sack of Ambrose had begun.

The Royal Legion had fought bravely against their eerie attackers. Wyrth had set up a smaller version of the Siegebreaker on the inner Thorngate, and it seemed as if things were going well.

Then half of the defenders began attacking the others. There were eaten soldiers among the royal ranks. No one could be sure that the soldier beside him would not turn. Some fought and died; others fled; the battle was lost. Wyrth barely had time to tumble the Siegebreaker into the river before he fled with the others.

Ambrosia led the vocates from the Wardlands, Wyrth, the Emperor, and his two bodyguards through the screaming chaos of the sack to the High Hall of the North.

"It's as good a place for a last stand as any," she explained grimly. They had ascended the narrow stairway and stood around it; the doorway at the other end of the hall was shut, bolted, and barricaded. "I can keep us safe from the whispering of the Shadow in this relatively small space—"

"But Grandmother," Lathmar broke in urgently. (He supposed he could call her Grandmother again, now that he was Emperor.) "Won't you have to ascend into the visionary state to guard us? Shouldn't you stand away from the stairwell so that we can guard your body?"

She reached under her armor and pulled out a pendant. It was luminous with power. Lathmar gaped at it for a moment, then lifted his eyes to meet Ambrosia's amused gaze.

"I am in the visionary state, Your Imperial Majesty," she replied calmly. "I have been since the enemy stormed Ambrose."

"But—" But she was walking and talking normally. But the pendant, clearly her focus of power, parallel to Morlock's Tyrfing, attested that she was acting powerfully in the talic realm. "But Morlock can't do that!" he blurted foolishly.

"Morlock, despite your touching faith in his abilities, cannot do everything," Ambrosia replied.

"Shut your mouth, Your Imperial Majesty," Wyrth muttered. "What Morlock is to makers, Ambrosia is to seers."

"Unquestionably I am," Ambrosia conceded. "Unfortunately, I'm getting a little old for this sort of thing. Still, I can shield you from the Shadow's whispering, here. If he detects me and sends his minions, and he will, they'll have to come at us one by one up the stairs. Also, there's an escape chute in the hall beyond. Erl and Karn: if the enemy's forces break in, I expect you to put the Emperor down that chute and follow him. Get him safely away."

"No!" said Lathmar, loudly if not firmly. "I'm staying here!"

"Erl, Karn: you heard me."

Karn looked gloomy, but Erl said firmly, if not loudly, "Lady Ambrosia, with respect, we serve the Emperor."

"That's what I'm counting on, Erl. If the Emperor gets away, the empire is still alive. If he doesn't, then it's just food waiting around for the Protector's Shadow to eat it."

Erl didn't answer this one way or the other, and Lathmar saw he was in doubt. Now wasn't the time to press the man, but Lathmar was damned if he was going to go along with Ambrosia's plan. His days of being carried around like a sack of beans were over.

"Maybe we should all go down the chute," Jordel said calmly, "without waiting."

"You're at liberty to do so, vocate," Ambrosia said evenly, "if you can find it. But there's some chance that Morlock may succeed in what he is about. If so, we should be together, not running about like chickens with their heads chopped off."

"Because that's what the adept's former bodies may be doing?" Aloê guessed.

Ambrosia shrugged. "It's not like anyone knows what's going to happen."

It didn't take long for the enemy's forces to find them. Lathmar anxiously wondered if that meant one of them was being eaten, or had been eaten, by the enemy. Looking around the room, he thought he saw the same doubt on other faces and decided not to voice it.

They heard the enemy's forces breaking down the door in the chamber below. They all drew their weapons and stood around the stairwell.

"Truce!" called an oddly familiar voice, coming up the stairwell. "I don't want to kill you, you know."

Ambrosia glanced at Lathmar and rolled her left hand repeatedly in a circle. She was indicating, he guessed, there was no reason not to spend time talking. He nodded his agreement.

"You can come up," she said. "But only one of you."

"There is only one of me down here."

"I mean one body, Inglonor," Ambrosia said flatly.

"It's been a long time since I've heard that name," said the familiar voice, growing nearer. "I didn't even know that you ever knew it—isn't that amusing?" The speaker appeared at the head of the stairwell.

"Genjandro," whispered Ambrosia, sagging slightly. "I . . . I hoped you had escaped, my friend. That was what the crow told us: that you were dead."

"A little bird told you?" remarked Genjandro's mouth. "You can't even trust birds these days, I guess. No, I found it possible to eat Genjandro in the end, just as I shall eat each one of you. Isn't that an amusing thought?"

Lathmar could see from Ambrosia's face that she didn't find it amusing—but that she feared it might be true.

Morlock clambered as rapidly as possible over the railing onto the balcony of the adept's tower chamber. If he had been the adept, he would have been waiting there with a blunt object to solve his Morlock problem once and for all. But there was no one present that he could see.

Near the window entrance was a sorcerer's worktable, and standing upright atop it was a strip of some translucent, irregularly glowing substance. As Morlock glanced at it he saw faces rising from the base of the strip, twisting and changing color as they passed up its length, then contracting and darkening at the top and sinking to the bottom again. Perhaps it was meant to be a lamp—there was no other light source than the window in the dim room—but it was very dim and irregular. On the other hand, it radiated power; most likely it was some sort of experiment or spell left here by the adept to run its course.

His fear that the adept was not present at all recurred to him. But, Morlock reminded himself, the adept didn't have to be here for Morlock to kill him. He saw the stairway leading to the lower chamber and leapt down it.

The lower chamber was darker; there was no window to light it. The air was thick down there, too; the whole place was redolent of rotting flesh. But the vats the King had described were there, glowing faintly by their own light.

Morlock heard a snuffling sound in the far end of the chamber. He drew Tyrfing and stepped toward it. He had not gone far when he saw its source. It was like an unfinished sketch for a body—no head, no hands or feet. From the way it flopped when it moved it seemed to have no bones. It snuffled and crept in a mindless circle around a vat containing human innards that breathed and pulsed and twitched with life.

Staring at it (the striations on its dark red surface were oddly like muscle tissue), Morlock thought suddenly of Urdhven. Was this formless form some fraction of his body, not superficial enough to be included in his walking self, not vital enough to be placed in the vat? And here it was, whuffling about in the hopeless hunger of being restored to its organs?

Morlock summoned the rapture of vision. It partly confirmed his guess: there were dim tal-lines connecting the misshapen shape with the organs within the vat. Other tal-lines stretched across the floor and up the stairs, out of sight. Going to carry life and sustenance from the vitals to Urdhven's walking shell?

He turned away. There were only two vats with organs in them; he guessed the other contained the organs of the adept's central body nexus.

These, too, were rippling with life. But no tal-lines extended from them that Morlock could see. Were they mere illusions? Morlock's insight said they weren't. He gazed at them, with his inner and outer vision, as they pulsed flaccidly on a surface that looked like the bare rock of the tower. He felt he was missing something.

He lifted his sword to strike. Like Lathmar, he felt that he would not have been allowed to come here if there was any chance of his breaking through the vat. But unlike Lathmar, he was armed with Tyrfing: it was worth attempting. The accursed blade, blazing with the black-and-white pattern of his tal, fell upon the unreflective transparent surface covering the vat . . . and bounced. He struck another time, and a third, with even greater force and less hope. The effect was the same.

Morlock shrugged his crooked shoulders. No tree falls at the first chop. Perhaps, he thought, the inner surface of the vat was what it appeared to be— the bare rock of the tower. He decided he would try to turn the thing over when he heard a soft, shuffling footstep behind him.

He turned to find Steng stabbing at him with a dagger in his long, ropy fingers. No—not Steng: the adept. He avoided the dagger and punched the other in the face with his hand that held Tyrfing; the quarters were too close to use the blade itself. The adept's rotten nose squelched and tore under the impact of his fist.

Morlock contained his reflexive utterance of disgust, but when he saw the other stagger back to the stairway and stand there, he switched the sword to his left hand and wiped the fluid and fragments from his right hand onto his cloak.

"Well, I thought I'd try," the adept said apologetically, what was left of his nose dangling from his gray face. "Your vital organs are still conveniently located in your body, you know."

Morlock didn't answer this, but focused his inner and his outer vision on the adept. A dense cloud of spider-thin talic strands extended from the adept's body up the stairwell, as if the body were a marionette controlled by thousands of invisible strings. But the strings were woven into the talic imprint that rested on the body, and every time the adept spoke they sang in dissonant harmony, a soft cacophony of other voices calling out in pain. These were the strings controlling puppets, perhaps, but here was the puppeteer.

Why did the talic emanations of control go up the stairwell? The stones of the tower, as mere matter, should have been transparent to them.

"You're very rude," the adept said coldly. "Speak when you're spoken to—that's what my dear damned mother always used to say."

Morlock shrugged. He had come here with a single purpose, to commit the ultimate incivility. Besides, he didn't believe the adept was making civil conversation.

One of the talic emanations of control did not go up the stairwell, but toward the far vat.

The adept, who must have been in something like the visionary state continuously, noticed that Morlock noticed it. His gray mouth smiled, and the talic thread twitched, whispering in Urdhven's voice.

"Yes, you must have guessed—those are the living remains of the late Protector, the fellow whose shadow you so unflatteringly called me. He was so grateful to me when I cored him! It burned bright within him. He never understood, even at the end as I consumed him, that *that* was when I first began to devour his soul. Now he knows, of course. I keep that shred of him nearby as a sort of pet: I look at it sometimes, and think of what I did to him, and he reacts, and it's terribly amusing. Terrible for him, amusing for me. And that thing, the shred of him, it wants nothing but to be reunited with its innards, and of course it can't be—they're forever inaccessible. But it would take others, if it could get them. If there were other, unprotected organs in the room . . ."

Morlock turned and spitted at the headless, boneless shape as it leapt upon him. The adept laughed, and the laugh sounded closer, as if he might be approaching with the dagger while Morlock was occupied.

Morlock reached out with his talic awareness and snapped the talic threads emanating toward the blanket of muscle and nerve, the shreds of the soul-dead Protector. They quivered and went limp. Morlock shook them off and spun around, his sword at the guard.

The adept shuffled backward to the stone stairs. "Damn it, you sicken me," he hissed.

"I frighten you, evidently," the Crooked Man replied.

"It would take more than you to frighten me," the adept sneered, his gray lips twisting behind his dangling nose. "Your sister is more formidable than you are, and I'm eating her even as we speak."

"Then she frightens you."

"Nothing frightens me."

"You should look up 'formidable' in a lexicon some time."

"I—" The adept paused. "You're trying to get at me!"

Morlock was buying time, in fact. There was something here that didn't make sense, something he might be able to sort out if he could think about it for a moment or two. He shrugged.

The adept started to say something, paused, then fled up the stairway, his robe trailing along the stairs with an odd sucking sound.

Morlock followed him up the stairs with cautious speed. It was promising that the adept was retreating, but of course there was some reason he felt safer upstairs.

The upper chamber was nearly as dark as the lower one. This was partly because the sky outside had gotten darker and cloudier since he descended. But it was largely because on the balcony was standing a gigantic gargoyle with outspread wings, a hammer in its left hand.

"Kill him!" the adept's voice sounded, from the darker end of the room. "Kill him and I'll release you; I swear it by the terms of our contract."

Morlock turned toward the gargoyle. With his inner vision he saw that it was a harthrang, a demon united to a body. But not a dead one: pretalic potential surged through the body like spicules of light interwoven with the darker flame of the demon's self.

Why did the adept want a demon who could feel pain? So that he could punish it, Morlock guessed: harthrangs could be stubborn and willful servants.

The gargoyle's body—stitched together from many different forms, human and animal, while still alive—was itself a horrific wonder of making. But Morlock could not hesitate to destroy it: he was caught between two enemies.

He leapt toward the gargoyle, knowing what he must do, hoping he had the time to do it. Beyond its gray wings, in the gray sky, lightning blinked its bright silver eyes and muttered.

Lathmar didn't like the bemused expression on Grandmother's face. It looked almost as if she were sinking into despair, and there was no point in that, no matter how desperate the situation was.

"Grandmother, he's lying!" shouted the Emperor, and he threw his dagger at Genjandro's face. The knife glanced off; the gray cheek opened, and dark blood seeped out. The cold features twisted in annoyance.

"That body is dead," Jordel said firmly. "If I understand how this thing works, he's lying about having eaten Alkhendron."

Ambrosia was nodding. But her expression didn't change, and Genjandro's dead voice continued to speak to her. "They don't understand," it said insinuatingly, "but I understand. They don't know what it's like to be lost in yourself—to be ruled by the will of another—of the horrible darkness you dwell in when your sister governs your body. If you explained to them, if you told them in so many words, they still wouldn't understand. But I understand, without you saying a word. You know what I'm offering to you, and you know that I can give it to you, and you know that you are going to accept it. While there's life, there's Hope. No life, no hope. No Hope, no life. I can free you from her, if you let me in."

"What the chaos is he talking about?" Jordel asked with mild interest.

"Hope is dead," Aloê said tensely. "I saw her die, centuries ago."

"I never knew her, madam," said Wyrth glumly. "But I think she's alive."

Ambrosia was wavering. Lathmar could see it. He started to go to her when iron-hard hands gripped his shoulders. "Erl!" he shouted. "Let me help her!"

"Majesty, I'm sorry," said Erl's flat voice. "But no one can help her. I think this was the hour she spoke of."

"No!" shouted the Emperor as they dragged him away.

"Hope," said Ambrosia thickly, as if drugged. "Hope." The light in her pendant seemed to be fading.

"While there's life, there's hope," whispered Genjandro's mouth. "There's always Hope. There's no escape from Hope. But I can give you escape. What else have you ever wanted? You've never really wanted anything else but to be free—free of her—yourself at least, at last, without Hope—"

"Hope!" shrieked Ambrosia. "Help! Hope! Help!" The pendant on her chest went dark, and she fell to the floor as if she'd been clubbed. The whispering in their minds crested in a wave that threatened to drown their thoughts.

Genjandro's body stepped out of the stairwell. "The strongest of you is gone," his dead voice said. "If—"

Ambrosia rose again behind him. Except: it wasn't her. It was a shorter woman, fairer, stockier, with blue eyes. She grabbed Genjandro's shoulders and pulled him backward. She threw her leg out behind the undead body and tumbled it down the stairs.

Wincing, she loosened the fastenings on Ambrosia's armor and looked around the room. "Aloê. Lathmar. Deor. I'm sorry I don't know you other gentlemen."

"You don't know me either, madam," Wyrth said respectfully. "But I'm honored to be taken for my father."

"Oh, you're Wyrth, of course—stupid of me. Ambrosia thinks of you often."

Genjandro's dead body came charging up the stairs, and there were corpse-golems shuffling behind it. Hope drew Ambrosia's sword and blocked the way. "I can stop him this way," she called over her shoulder, looking directly at Lathmar. "But I can't stop the whispering. I don't have the skills."

Was it an accident that she looked at him? the Emperor wondered stupidly. If Ambrosia failed, how could he succeed?

Then fail like she failed, he told himself. *Do half as well!*

"Erl," he said to his senior bodyguard (for Karn was wild-eyed with terror), "I must pass into the vision state. I will have to surrender volitional action in the world of the senses. Do you understand, Erl? You will need to stand guard over me."

Aloê turned her dark face, fierce with hope, toward him. "Champion Lathmar!" she shouted. "Jordel, you're for me."

"Always, my dear, if I understand you properly."

Lathmar was already ascending into the vision state. The cloak of matter and energy fell away. He found himself standing over his body.

Emerging from the shadowy hole of the stairway was the adept's avatar, a dark tower pierced through with myriad whispering shadows.

Lathmar leapt toward the enemy—willing himself against the other. He stretched out his hands (like nets of radiant silver wire) against the screaming shadows of the enemy. He entered the mind of the destroyer.

Of course it was too strong for him. He knew the other would break him down in the end—it began almost immediately. But he fought, as fiercely as he could, pouring out rejection for the other, and he felt the relief of the others behind him.

Aloê was beside him then, a bright danger like the edge of a bronze sword. She too struck at the enemy with her talic presence, and it eased Lathmar's burden somewhat. He felt he could fight longer now.

If there was a way to tell the passing of time in the vision state Lathmar didn't know it. After a timeless moment he sensed that the bodies in the room had moved, like chess pieces. Only in the end of a chess game there were fewer pieces on the board; now there were more, many more. Bodies without the talic imprint of souls, the empty presence of corpse-golems.

Perhaps now was the end. But how long was now? He fought on.

They were deep within the labyrinthine corridors of the enemy's mind, striking at whatever they saw. They looked out through thousands of eyes, a bewildering cacophoty of images.

Look! The command passed directly from Aloê's awareness to Lathmar's. He looked.

He saw Morlock fighting in the adept's chamber, Tyrfing in his hand alive with talic light.

The sky outside was full of bright darkness. There was a mind in the sky, preparing to think bright deadly thoughts. . . .

Lightning! Lathmar cried. *He's going to use lightning against him!*

From Aloê, a sad agreement.

Her sadness puzzled Lathmar. He would never forget how Morlock had used lightning against the Companions on the bridge. Surely it would work as well against the Companions' master?

Then he realized: they weren't in rapport with Morlock's vision. They were in rapport with the adept. It was Morlock who would suffer the blast of the lightning this time.

They struck out as fiercely as they could, to distract the adept, to disrupt his spell. But it was no use. As they fought on, the lightning fell, dazzling the adept's delighted eyes.

Morlock, as he ran, raised Tyrfing against the gigantic war hammer of the gargoyle. With his left hand he grabbed the last jar of phlogiston, snapping with his thumb and forefinger the string that held it across his shoulder.

"Leave and I won't hurt you," he said to the gargoyle.

The gargoyle stared at him with lightless black eyes and said nothing. Morlock sensed that it feared the adept more than it feared him. But it held the hammer at guard and thrust with it: clearly the gargoyle didn't want to leave itself open to attack by swinging the hammer over its shoulder for a killing blow.

Morlock parried the shaft of the hammer as if it were a blade and dodged within arm-reach of the gargoyle. It was risky, but he had no choice. The thing was reaching for him with its empty right hand. Morlock didn't doubt it could kill him with that alone. He cracked open the jar of phlogiston and held the sheet of flame under the gargoyle's left wing.

The gargoyle shrieked and struck him down. He hit the floor rolling and sprang to his feet. The adept, who had shuffled nearer, lifting the dagger hopefully, shuffled away, a cheated expression on his gray rotting features.

The burning gargoyle was dancing and shrieking with pain on the balcony. Morlock dropped the empty jar and picked up a nearby table, throwing it at the gargoyle. It saw the table coming and raised its hands quickly to protect its unlovely face. It overbalanced and fell over the edge, its fading shriek stopping short with the meaty thump of impact.

"Any more gargoyles?" Morlock said coolly.

"No—that was the last," the adept said. "It was useless to me anyway—it takes two of them to open the door, here, so we're both trapped. Isn't that amusing? I didn't anticipate you would or could climb the outer wall, and I was sure my first gargoyle would take care of you when I saw you creeping along out there."

Morlock reflected that the halls and stairwell of the tower must be packed with the adept's undead soldiery, and that enough hands and a few levers would move a stone far heavier than the one blocking the door of the chamber. But he saw no reason to tutor the adept in the principles of mechanics.

"The things were well made," he conceded. "But you should have made them impervious to pain."

"I would have, too," the adept agreed ruefully, "if I had anticipated today's events. But it made them so terribly amenable. Demons, you know, quite enjoy inflicting pain, but they never have to experience it themselves, and the effect was most amusing. They were broken to harness in record time—it was almost easier than eating them."

Morlock grunted.

"And there I thought we were going to have a civil conversation," the adept complained, tossing his head in irritation so that his dangling nose waggled back and forth. "I am a kind of maker, you know, using the substances of life. You can call it necromancy, but it's life, not death, which interests me."

Morlock glanced toward the window. His eyes told him that the play of lightning was becoming more frequent. His inner vision told him that a lightning stroke was imminent . . . and that an intention was drawing it toward this room.

He looked back toward the adept, who was smiling.

"Yes," he said quietly, "I was wondering when you'd catch on. Aether, the substance of lightning, is semi-intelligent in its ultraheated state—semi-alive. So it comes within my sphere of manipulations."

Morlock knew something about lightning, too. He knew that spicules of lightning-stuff were woven though the fabric of the universe. In deep vision he could weave a cloak of lightning particles to ward off the fire from the sky. He could assemble cells of antilightning particles as well, drawing down thunderbolts.

But he could not do so without surrendering volitional action in the world of the senses. The adept would simply step forward and kill him with its dagger.

"Unbelievably difficult to create a lightning storm over the Old City," the adept was saying cheerfully. "And it's always a dry storm—never rain."

Morlock ran across the room, standing so that the adept was between him and the window. Startled, the adept moved away; Morlock moved so that the adept was always between the window and himself.

"Oh!" said the adept, laughing. "Oh! You think—"

The lightning fell. Both Morlock and the adept were thrown to the floor. But the bolt did not hit either one. It struck the glowing strip on the worktable near the window.

The worktable itself burst into flying red ash, but the strip was not destroyed. As Morlock scrambled to his feet, the adept shuffled toward the strip of glowing faces, now shrieking silently, dark tormented lines dissolving slowly in a lightning-bright surface.

The adept picked it up and turned toward Morlock, his gray face agleam with new confidence.

"Bound souls!" he bragged. (Morlock was, after all, the master of all makers; the adept seemed to be childishly intent on impressing him.) "They hold an aetheric charge wonderfully."

"But not for long," Morlock guessed. His vision sensed the screaming of the dying souls, the agony of their bright brief damnation. "They must disorganize fairly rapidly."

"Right," the adept acknowledged, and whirled forward to strike Morlock with the sword of burning souls.

Morlock gripped Tyrfing with both hands and met the blazing sword of his enemy in a glancing parry. The shock nearly sent him to his knees, but he managed to keep his feet. The next stroke did not come swiftly—his opponent had a deadlier weapon, but he was no swordsman—and he was set for it. He even managed a glancing riposte, and the adept shuffled back.

Then the room was filled with flying black forms. The adept was laughing, swinging his bright sword, sending heaps of black feathers burning to the floor.

Crows—more than a murder, a rampage, a slaughter of crows. They must have followed him from the grave lands. God Creator, they were trying to help him.

"Get out!" he screamed. "This isn't in the treaty! You can't help me! Save yourselves!" He charged the adept, lashing out at him with Tyrfing in great double-handed blows, but the adept laughed as he saw the tears running down Morlock's face and kept shuffling away, striking clouds of black birds from the air, bright with fire, dark with departing tal.

In the end, they did flee, but countless crows (bright with fire to his weeping eyes, dark and lifeless to his inner vision) lay dead about the adept's chamber. The adept laughed at Morlock as he wept, his eyes stinging from the stench of burning feathers.

"You should never get too attached to your pets," the adept remarked.

Morlock dashed past the blazing sword, knocking it aside with a one-handed stroke of Tyrfing, and grabbed the adept's dangling nose, tearing it and a large portion of the attached flesh from the gray rubbery cheek. "For the crows!" he shouted in the adept's astonished partial face and, plunging back out of range, tossed the trophy off the balcony.

As he stood there on the balcony, staring in at the laughing noseless adept, like a spider at the center of a web of whispering talic threads, he wondered that it was so dark, so confined in the adept's chamber. How had he not seen the crows coming? Their tal should have stood out like a signal fire against the dead city. The stones of the tower should have been transparent to it. They were only dead matter . . .

But they weren't, Morlock realized. They couldn't be. Otherwise the adept would send his webwork of talic control through them. Instead, those lines of immaterial force must pass through the great window opening on the balcony.

Everything is opaque to itself, Morlock knew. Matter blocks matter; even light blocks light, under certain conditions. Only tal could block tal. Morlock looked on the talic imprint of the adept, like a tower pierced by myriads of whispering thorns, and he knew at last. Somehow, through the adept's magic, the tower itself was an extension of himself. It was through the substance of the tower that life passed from his disembodied organs to the shell of his body. He had not seen the source of the adept's life because it was all around him.

He dashed forward again, feinting left, then right, then high, finally striking low, slashing away part of the sorcerer's robe.

The adept's legs were exposed. Each had five calflike stalks descending from the knee. Each ended not in a foot, but in a broad, gray-lipped mouth pressed hungrily against the gray stone breast of the chamber floor.

"So that's how you do it," he remarked calmly, and lunged, balestra, so that Tyrfing slashed the front of the sorcerer's robe and the gray flesh beneath it.

The adept snickered, his breath whistling oddly through the bones of his torn cheek and nose. "That's how."

Morlock thought he could see scars of surgery on the exposed bones of the other's face. So what he had told Lathmar was untrue: this body had not naturally assumed this form, in response to the adept's talic imprint; it had been crafted as deliberately and as cunningly as the winged gargoyles themselves. But less vulnerably; Morlock doubted his enemy could feel pain in any usual sense of the word.

"Where's the speech?" the adept sneered. "'Now, alas, too late, I realize . . .'"

Morlock dropped from the visionary state entirely. He wove a net of blades around his enemy, dancing aside from the deadly soul-blade, now the color of white-hot gold.

"You're hoping to wear me down," the adept said. "But you can't do that. You're working ten times as hard as I am, and I'm drawing new strength through the stones every moment."

Morlock feinted left and again thrust, slashing deep into the adept's belly. He did the same a moment later. A great flap of the robe and the dry skin underneath now hung open.

"Ow, that stung," the adept said drily. "Maybe you're hoping to outlast the soul-sword? You won't. The lightning will burn bright enough to kill until dawn. By then you'll be dead."

An orange-black spider, its body the size of a human fist, crawled out of the hole in the adept's belly, clung to the shifting surface of the robe, and stared at Morlock with its eight eyes. A green, faintly luminescent cord went from its body back into the hole in the adept. A moment later, it was joined by another spider.

"Pets?" Morlock asked.

The adept laughed. "I said 'Don't get attached to them.' I never said not to let them attach themselves to you."

Morlock's next two attacks slashed the green cords, killing the spiders. He guessed, from shadows he could see within the gap, that there were more where these came from. But he could afford to wait no longer: what the adept had said was true; he was wearing out.

He closed with the adept and brought the lightning sword into a bind. Then he plunged his left hand into the open belly of the adept.

The adept screamed and stabbed him in the face and neck with the dagger. He felt several lancing pains in his left hand: spider bites, laced with burning poison. He let none of this distract him. He closed his hand on the spine of the adept and, gripping it, lifted him from the floor.

The ten mouth-feet resisted, each leaving the floor with a separate sucking plop. The adept stabbed him with the dagger again, yet again, but the strokes were weaker. Holding the body aloft, Morlock walked to the balcony of the chamber and held the adept's writhing body as far as he could from any surface of the tower.

The dagger (dark with Morlock's blood) and the soul-bright sword both fell from the adept's nerveless fingers. Morlock thought he could hear screaming, the screaming of many voices (in triumph, in hate, in fear, in shame, in death), but the adept's gray mouth was slack and motionless. Perhaps the sound came from the tower. Maybe he was hearing some echo from the talic realm, as the souls of those the adept had consumed over the centuries tore loose from the dying hulk that had eaten them. Perhaps he was dreaming the sounds, for he was very close to unconsciousness as he stood there and stood there and stood there until the sounds receded like a tide of darkness and left him there, alone in the dark.

"You're telling me you're dead," he whispered to the dead face when the whispers died. "But why should I believe you? How would I know when a thing like you is dead?"

But, in the end, he could stand there no longer. He clenched his fist till the spine within his grip shattered. He cast the lifeless body as far from the tower as he could. Falling back, he lay still and stared at the dry stormy sky.

Lathmar's spirit leapt up like a silver candle; he felt Aloê's bronze glory singing beside him.

He was far past the state where words are possible, but he shared his sense of personal triumph with the spirit who had fought so bravely and so hopelessly beside him.

She responded with a gesture that unmistakably recalled a hawk in flight over a branch of flowering thorns.

Lathmar looked down a dark corridor that was shutting like a mouth and saw through it Morlock killing the adept.

The shock of the myriadic death drove Lathmar back from his vision. His soul flew home to his body, hungry for the knowledge that he was still alive.

And he was. He opened his eyes to find Hope kneeling over him.

"Something happened," she was saying urgently. "What was it?"

"The Protector's Shadow is dead," the Emperor said. "Morlock killed him in the Old City."

"But these things, these corpse-golems, are still alive," said Jordel, who was standing nearby. "A half dozen of them just tried to charge up the stairway."

"No, they're not," the Emperor said sleepily. "Wyrth. Tell him."

The dwarf looked puzzled for a moment, then nodded. "I get it. If they're like golems, they're not alive. They're just carrying out the instructions on their life-scrolls."

Lathmar sat up. He was desperately tired. But the Emperor had work to do. "Right," he said wearily. "There will be thousands of these things—here and in the Two Cities. They'll be dangerous to us, but they can't really think. We'll first need to regroup the Royal Legion. No." He looked around the room. "Erl, congratulations. You're the new commander of the Imperial Legion."

"Um."

"The correct response is, 'Thank you for this high honor, Your Imperial Majesty; I will endeavor to justify your trust in me.'"

"He was speechless with delight, Your Imperial Highnitude," Jordel suggested.

"Um. What does Your Majesty direct me to do?" Erl said, ignoring the opportunity to banter. (Something told Lathmar he always would.)

"Take Karn—where's Karn?"

"Dead, Your Majesty. He died bravely."

So? his Majesty nearly replied. *Dead is dead.* But it did matter. When he had looked around for Karn and missed him, he had been afraid the man had run away. Karn had chosen his job, or allowed it to choose him, and died at it. Lathmar hoped he himself would have an epitaph that good.

"Take Wyrth, then," the Emperor said aloud. "The stairway is still blocked by corpse-golems? Go down the escape chute. Collect a body—I mean, collect a group of soldiers and put them under discipline. Draft anyone you come across, now that I think of it: this is everyone's fight. Come back here, clearing the corridors as you go and suiting your tactics to the occasion. That's your short-term goal. When that's done, we'll clear the castle of these things. By then we should have enough troops to enter the city. That's the long-term goal: to cleanse the living city."

Wyrth solemnly saluted the Emperor, and Lathmar suddenly realized that Wyrth was not his subject anymore. His oath had been to the King of the Two Cities; he was not a citizen of the Ontilian Empire. But if he would go along with the gag as long as was necessary, Lathmar reflected, it wouldn't matter.

"As long as everyone else does likewise," he muttered to himself.

"A true Ambrose," Hope observed to Aloê, who was smiling sadly. "Always muttering!"

The dry storm receded, and the dark sky grew silent. In a moment, Morlock thought, he would get up. He would go back to the city. He would retake Aloê to be his wife and replace Ambrosia as the power behind the imperial throne. He would again be the defender of a realm that needed him; his life would have a meaning and a purpose once more. He had succeeded, and the rest would be easy. He could now have back everything he'd thought he'd lost forever. All he had to do was betray the trust of someone who loved him.

In the dead tower of the dead Protector's dead Shadow, Morlock lay among the silent black bodies of the crows—and among silent thoughts that were blacker than crows.

Chapter Twenty-Seven
Lèse Majesté

erlin Ambrosius walked into a cave deep in the Blackthorn Mountains. His tall body was bowed with weariness, not age. He'd had a long trip. He'd had a disappointment or two. He would be right as rain with a little rest. (He loathed rain.)

He sat down next to part of an elderly woman who was lying inside what appeared to be a block of ice. But when you put your hand upon it, as Merlin did, you found it warm as human blood. Nonetheless, it was ice, of a rather special type; it was slowly melting. There were a few drops on the ground underneath its shelf in the wall of the cave; if Merlin stayed for several days, as he planned, he guessed he might see another drop added to the tiny pool.

Merlin, the woman spoke directly into his mind, *where have you been?*

"Oh," said Merlin airily, "going to and fro in the earth, and walking up and down in it."

Very funny, the woman responded. *I suppose that means you have been trying to destroy our children again.*

"Nimue, my dear, I have merely engaged in a little experiment. I set a rock spinning down a slope, a couple of centuries ago, and it has turned into a great landslide, engulfing kingdoms."

That means you failed, I suppose.

"It was just a ranging shot," Merlin replied. "I'll do better next time. At least I know where they all are, now."

Why do you hate them so?

Merlin took a while answering. But he told her the truth, since she knew it anyhow. "You should not have loved them better than me. When you betrayed me and I lost everything, I forgave you. I will always forgive you, I suppose. I can even forgive you for loving them. But I don't have to forgive *them*. I earned your love and they stole it. That's all."

Merlin, the old woman said, *we short-lived people are not like you, who live half as long as forever. We give our children life, and love, and then we die. It's the way of things. You should have let me die long ago.*

"Not until this is done."

It will never be done. Don't you see that if you destroy them I'll hate you, rather than love you? Even now you disgust me with your selfish greed, as if love were a treat you could hide from the other children and hoard, wolfing it down in secret until it makes you sick.

Merlin didn't answer this. For one so young (she had been hardly more than a hundred when Merlin had put her in the block of ice and took other even more extreme measures to keep her alive) she was very wise, but she didn't know about the deadly wasting power of time, or the things the mind can do to itself. Her body was frozen, but her mind was awake and unsleeping, one long single day through the centuries.

If need be, he would walk away and not come back until her mind had torn itself to shreds and re-formed anew. She would have forgotten the children; she would have forgotten everything. Then he would return to her. And then she would love him, because she loved life and he would be the only living thing in her world.

Then, and only then, he would thaw the ice and allow her to briefly live and forever die.

On a day, the Emperor Lathmar VII rode through his capital city and saw that things were well, but not well enough. He was glad to hear that the streets were completely free of the songs that claimed the young Emperor had personally defeated the villainous Protector (who was naturally, if somewhat unfairly, blamed for all the undead horror his Shadow had wrought) in single combat on the ramparts of Ambrose. In obedience with Lathmar's decree, no one sang these songs in public anymore. (Ten times as many sang them in secret, and more around the empire would do so every year, but he would never know that.)

The cleansing of the city was almost complete. Whole quarters, overrun by the corpse-golems, had been burned to the ground and would have to be rebuilt. Now they lay under a heavy layer of winter snow, strangely empty and unmarked by all the horror that had passed there—like pages waiting to be written on. It would be Lathmar's job to make something of them, at least write the first few words on those blank sheets, and he was hastily boning up on the principles of architecture and city planning. Fortunately he had (in Morlock and Ambrosia) two of the greatest authorities in the world as his tutors. Unfortunately, he didn't think he would have them much longer.

The weather was cold; times, in many ways, were hard. But the city, freed from the shadows of tyranny and living death, still carried something of a festival air. And the citizens loved it when their ruler rode or walked among them; any conversation he had with anyone was likely to be interrupted with loyal shouts of salute . . . but just as likely to be broken by cries of, "Get rid of them crooky-backs, Majesty!" The crowd would fall silent whenever he turned toward them after someone cried this; no one would say it to his face.

But it was obvious that most of them felt this way. The Protector was hated above all, but it was widely believed that things had gone worse because he had used the weapons of the Ambrosii against them. The world would be better off without the Ambrosii and their damn magic, people were muttering.

Lathmar rode moodily back to the City Gate of Ambrose. Erl met him there, and they discussed the appointment of the new viceroy of Kaen. . . . That is, Lathmar discussed it, and when he had given certain orders, Erl said, "Yes, Your Majesty," and carried them out.

Lathmar, feeling lonely, went up to Morlock's workshop. It was empty: most of the stuff had been packed up. Wyrth had been making noises about leaving almost since they had brought Morlock back on a shingle and it became clear he was not going to die.

There had been moments, while Morlock was convalescing, that Lathmar had almost hoped he would die. He was afraid that Morlock would carry out Ambrosia's plan to become the new power behind the throne. And Lathmar wasn't going to allow that. There would be no more powers behind the throne, no more damn Protectors. It was Ambrosia who had cast him in this farce, and he was going to play his part to the hilt; if she didn't like it, she . . .

Lathmar choked these thoughts off. Morlock, in sentences of one syllable or less, had made it more or less clear to all interested parties that the job of ruling a world-empire was more or less beneath him. He had spoken more frankly in private to Lathmar. "I am a master of the Two Arts—Seeing and Making," he had rasped. "It's enough. It's all that I am." Then, as if that settled the matter, he turned back to his latest feat of making, a magical book in the palindromic script of ancient Ontil.

Lathmar had called him a liar, kissed his terribly scarred face, and run from the room.

Now he heard from a hallway attendant (Thoke, in fact) that Morlock had gone down to the stables.

He found all of them there: the two vocates, Jordel and Aloê; Masters Wyrth and Morlock; and Ambrosia. They were crowded around a horse—Velox, it looked like, and Morlock was laughing his raspy crowlike laugh.

"What's the joke?" he asked as he and his bodyguards joined the group. Anything that made Morlock laugh had to be pretty funny.

Morlock, still smiling, handed him a scrap of paper. "This was on Velox's saddle when he wandered back this morning."

It was a note written in the secret speech.

Morlock—

Your horse keeps running away. Screw it and you—I'm walking from here.

Good fortune.
Baran, Vocate

"Poor old Baran was never much of a horseman," Jordel remarked. "Although *his* first job—"

"Spare us your memories of manure this once, Jordel," Aloê interrupted.

"I suppose we had better report back to the Graith—now that our patient is back on his feet again. Any messages for your former peers, Morlock Exile?"

"My love to Noreê, of course," Morlock said mildly.

Aloê shot him a golden glare; she turned and walked off without another word to any of them.

"What was that all about?" Lathmar wondered.

"Oh, Noreê never liked Morlock here much," Jordel explained. "Thought he should have been kicked out of the Wardlands before his parents were born—was always looking at him askance."

"No, I mean—" Lathmar began, and then suddenly reflected that Aloê's behavior reflected a disagreement with Morlock that was probably none of his business. "Never mind."

"I never do, but I'd better try to catch her up. I said my good-byes to you all when I thought we were going to die, so I won't cheapen them by repetition." He waved casually and walked off after Aloê. Lathmar never saw him again.

"Guards," Lathmar said without looking at them, "stand away." When they had, he broached his problem to the Ambrosii and asked their thoughts.

Ambrosia heard him through, though nothing he said seemed to surprise her. When he had finished, she said, "Well, if I were you, Lathmar, I'd find Morlock and me guilty of some dreadful but not very specific crime and give us ten days' law to leave the city."

"That's not funny," Lathmar said impatiently.

"I assure you, I find it far from funny. But I know a little something about this business of governing an empire—not one of the Two Arts, perhaps, but a useful trade all the same—and that's what I think the situation requires. It won't be the first time I was kicked out of Ontil, you know."

"What . . . what do you suggest?"

"How about *lèse majesté*—an offense against the monarch's dignity? It's convenient, hard to define, and quite serious—as you reminded me at supper one night."

Lathmar nodded slowly. "Well. May I ask when you traitorous dogs will be fleeing from my justice?"

"We're packed," Morlock said simply.

"Get the hell out then!" Lathmar shouted. "Who the hell needs you! I don't and no one else here does!" He was weeping uncontrollably. He knew it was wrong; he knew he was being stupid. Morlock took him by the shoulders, looked into his eyes, and turned away without a word. Lathmar clenched his eyes shut, and when he opened them he saw that Morlock had taken his horse and gone.

"Isn't anyone going with him?" he blurted.

"In a word, no," Wyrth said. "I've had enough of his endless yakking. Besides, I'm a master of Making, now. I've got to take my own path. Back to Thrymhaiam, I think—it's been a long time since I've seen home."

Lathmar wordlessly held out his hand. Wyrth took it, held it, and released it.

"See you," Wyrth said briefly, and left him alone with Grandmother.

"Hope had a dream about our mother," Ambrosia said, in the flat voice she always used when talking about her sister. Lathmar could not even imagine the accommodation they had made with each other (if, in fact, they had). "She says it's better if we aren't together—Morlock and, and us, I mean."

Ambrosia kissed him on the forehead and said, "Lathmar, you've done well, but you must do more—much more. Are you ready?"

"No."

But it was a lie and she knew it. She kissed him again and walked away, and he was alone at last in his kingdom, his empire. Even though it looked rather like a stable.

He dried his eyes and blew his nose. "Well, it's back to the books for me, I guess," he grumbled. "But, who knows? Maybe someday they'll call me Lathmar the Builder . . . or even Lathmar the Great?"

They were calling him those names already, but he didn't find out until long after he had earned them.

the end

The Lands of Laent in A.U. 330

 aent is a flat or shield-shaped land mass bordered by ocean to the west and south and empty space to the east; north of Laent is a region of uninhabitable cold; south of Laent is a large and largely unexplored continent, Qajqapca. Beyond that is believed to be an impassable zone of fire.

Along the western edge of Laent lies the Wardlands, a highly developed but secretive culture. It has no government, as such, but its borders are protected by a small band of Seers and warriors called the Graith of Guardians.

Dividing Laent into two unequal halves, north and south, are a pair of mountain ranges: the Whitethorn Range (running from the Western Ocean eastward) and the Blackthorn Range (running from the Eastern Edge westward). There is a pass between the two mountain ranges, the Kirach Kund. North of the Kirach Kund there are only two human cities of any note, Narkunden and Aflraun. The rest of the north is a heavily wooded and mountainous region inhabited by humans and others of a more or less fabulous nature.

The Whitethorn Range, by custom, forms the northern border of the Wardlands; the Graith of Guardians do not permit others to dwell there. The Blackthorn Range is divided between the untamed dragons and the dragon-taming Khroi, a nonhuman race of unknown origin.

South of the Whitethorn Range is the empire of Ontil, sometimes known as the Second Empire. Around 2800, in the reckoning of the Wardlands (see appendix C: "Calendar and Astronomy"), Vraidish barbarians began to pass through the Kirach Kund, not merely to raid or kill but to conquer and settle. After several generations, one of the Vraidish war-leaders, called Lathmar the Old, established a united kingdom out of the divided Vraidish duchies. He was materially aided in his rise to power by magical assistance and counsel from Ambrosia Viviana, Merlin's daughter. Ambrosia later married Lathmar's son, Uthar I (called the Great), who called his kingdom the New Empire of Ontil and settled its capital at New Ontil (not far from the ruins of Old Ontil). The title of King (later, "King of the Two Cities," i.e., the Old Ontil and the new capital) was retained for the imperial heir. At the time of *Blood of Ambrose*, the Vraidish Empire of Ontil extended from the Whitethorn Range south, to all the lands surrounding the landlocked Sea of Vendh, as far as the southern coast of Laent (including the formerly independent kingdom of Kaen). On the west it was bounded by the Narrow Sea and the Grartan Mountains. The region between the Grartan Mountains and the Whitethorns was called the Gap of Lone by inhabitants of the unguarded lands. Inhabitants of (and exiles from) the Wardlands called it "the Maze," because of the magical protections placed on it.

Immediately south of the Blackthorns is a wooded region of extremely poor repute, Tychar. Farther south is the Anhikh Kômos of Cities, Ontil's great rival. The largest Anhikh city, where the kômarkh lives, is Vakhnhal, along the southern coast of Laent. Anhi may or may not extend its domain to the Eastern Edge of the world—accounts differ.

Appendix B

The Gods of Laent

There is no universally accepted religious belief, except in Anhi, where the government enforces the worship of Torlan and Zahkaar (Fate and Chaos).

In Ontil an eclectic set of gods are worshipped or not worshipped, especially (under the influence of Coranian exiles from the Wardlands) the Strange Gods, including Death, Justice, Peace, Misery, Love, and Memory.

In the Wardlands at least three gods, or three aspects of one god, are worshipped: the Creator, the Sustainer, and the Avenger ("Creator, Keeper, and King").

The dwarves of the Wardlands evidently assent to these beliefs. (At any rate, they have been known to swear by these deities.) But they have another, perhaps an older, belief in immortal ancestor spirits who watch the world and judge it from beyond the western edge of the world. The spirits of the virtuous dead collect in the west through the day and night, and pass through at the moment of dawn, when the sun enters the world and the gate in the west is opened. Spirits of the evil dead, or spirits that have been bound in some way, may not pass through the gate in the west. Hence, dwarves each day (at sunrise, or when they awake) praise the rising of the sun and the passage of the good ghosts to Those-Who-Watch in the west.

APPENDIX C

CALENDAR AND ASTRONOMY

1. ASTRONOMICAL REMARKS

The sky of Laent has three moons: Chariot, Horseman, and Trumpeter (in descending order of size).

The year has 375 days. The months are marked by the rising or setting of the second moon, Horseman. So that (in the year *Blood of Ambrose* begins) Horseman sets on the first day of Bayring, the penultimate month. It rises again on the first of Borderer, the last month. It sets very early in the morning on the first day of Cymbals, the first month of the new year. All three moons set simultaneously on this occasion. (The number of months are uneven—fifteen—so that Horseman rises or sets on the first morning of the year in alternating years.)

The period of Chariot (the largest moon, whose rising and setting marks the seasons) is 187.5 days. (So a season is 93.75 days.)

The period of Horseman is 50 days.

The period of Trumpeter is 15 days. A half-cycle of Trumpeter is a "call." Calls are either "bright" or "dark" depending on whether Trumpeter is aloft or not. (Usage: "He doesn't expect to be back until next bright call.")

The seasons are not irregular, as on Earth. But the moons' motion is not uniform through the sky: motion is faster near the horizons, slowest at the zenith. Astronomical objects are brighter in the west, dimmer in the east.

The three moons and the sun rise in the west and set in the east. The stars have a different motion entirely, rotating NWSE around a celestial pole. The pole points at a different constellation among a group of seven (the polar constellations) each year. (Hence, a different group of nonpolar constellations is visible near the horizons each year.) This seven-year cycle (the Ring) is the basis for dating, with individual years within it named for their particular polar constellations.

The polar constellations are: the Reaper, the Ship, the Hunter, the Door, the Kneeling Man, the River, the Wolf.

There is an intrapolar constellation, the Hands, within the space inscribed by the motion of the pole.

This calendar was first developed in the Wardlands, and then spread to the unguarded lands by exiles. In the Wardlands, years are dated from the founding of New Moorhope, the center of learning. The action of *Blood of Ambrose* begins in the 464th Ring, Moorhope year 3242, the Year of the Hunter. But in the Ontilian Empire, the years are dated from the death of Uthar the Great. By that reckoning, the action of *Blood of Ambrose* begins in the 48th Ring, A.U. 330, the Year of the Hunter.

2. THE YEARS OF *BLOOD OF AMBROSE*

The novel begins on 25 Remembering, A.U. 330. It ends on 18 Cymbals, A.U. 333.

48th Ring, A.U. 330: Year of the Hunter

1. Cymbals.

New Year. Winter begins.

1st: Chariot and Trumpeter set. Horseman rises.
8th and 23rd: Trumpeter rises.

2. Jaric.

1st: Horseman sets. 13th: Trumpeter rises.

3. Brenting.

1st: Horseman rises. 3rd and 18th: Trumpeter rises.

4. Drums.

1st: Horseman sets. 8th and 23rd: Trumpeter rises.
Midnight of 94th day of the year (19 Drums):
Chariot rises. Spring begins.

5. Rain.

1st: Horseman rises. 13th: Trumpeter rises.

6. Marrying.

1st: Horseman sets. 3rd and 18th: Trumpeter rises.

7. Ambrose.

1st: Horseman rises. 8th and 23rd: Trumpeter rises.

8. Harps.

1st: Horseman sets. 13th: Trumpeter rises.
Evening of the 188th day of year (19 Harps):
Chariot sets. Midyear—Summer begins.

9. Tohrt.

1st: Horseman rises. 3rd and 18th: Trumpeter rises.

10. Remembering.

1st: Horseman sets. 8th and 23rd: Trumpeter rises.

11. Victory.

1st: Horseman rises. 13th: Trumpeter rises.

12. Harvesting.

1st: Horseman sets. 3rd and 18th: Trumpeter rises.
6th: Chariot rises, noon of 281st day of year. Fall begins.

13. Mother and Maiden.

1st: Horseman rises. 8th and 23rd: Trumpeter rises.

14. Bayring.

1st: Horseman sets. 13th: Trumpeter rises.

15. Borderer.

1st: Horseman rises. 3rd and 18th: Trumpeter rises.

48th Ring, A.U. 331: Year of the Door

1. Cymbals.

New Year. Winter begins.

1st: Chariot, Horseman, and Trumpeter all set.
8th and 23rd: Trumpeter rises.

2. Jaric.

1st: Horseman rises. 13th: Trumpeter rises.

3. Brenting.

1st: Horseman sets. 3rd and 18th: Trumpeter rises.

4. Drums.

1st: Horseman rises. 8th and 23rd: Trumpeter rises.
Midnight of 94th day of the year (19 Drums):
Chariot rises. Spring begins.

5. Rain.

1st: Horseman sets. 13th: Trumpeter rises.

6. Marrying.

1st: Horseman rises. 3rd and 18th: Trumpeter rises.

7. Ambrose.

1st: Horseman sets. 8th and 23rd: Trumpeter rises.

8. Harps.

1st: Horseman rises. 13th: Trumpeter rises.
Evening of the 188th day of year (19 Harps):
Chariot sets. Midyear—Summer begins.

9. Tohrt.

1st: Horseman sets. 3rd and 18th: Trumpeter rises.

10. Remembering.

1st: Horseman rises. 8th and 23rd: Trumpeter rises.

11. Victory.

1st: Horseman sets. 13th: Trumpeter rises.

12. Harvesting.

1st: Horseman rises. 3rd and 18th: Trumpeter rises.
6th: Chariot rises, noon of 281st day of year. Fall begins.

13. Mother and Maiden.

1st: Horseman sets. 8th and 23rd: Trumpeter rises.

14. Bayring.

1st: Horseman rises. 13th: Trumpeter rises.

15. Borderer.

1st: Horseman sets. 3rd and 18th: Trumpeter rises.

48th Ring, A.U. 332: Year of the Kneeling Man

(Repeats pattern of A.U. 330)

48th Ring, A.U. 333: Year of the River

(Repeats pattern of A.U. 331)

ABOUT THE AUTHOR

 ames Enge's fiction has appeared in *Black Gate*, *Flashing Swords*, and everydayfiction.com. He is an instructor of classical languages at a midwestern university.